ALSO BY E.E.

THE WORLD OF THE GATEWAY
The Gateway Trilogy (Series 1)
Spirit Legacy
Spirit Prophecy
Spirit Ascendancy
The Gateway Trackers (Series 2)
Whispers of the Walker
Plague of the Shattered
Awakening of the Seer
Portraits of the Forsaken
Heart of the Rebellion
Soul of the Sentinel
Gift of the Darkness
Rise of the Coven
City of the Forgotten
Shadow of the Brotherhood
Betrayal of the Sisterhood
Tales from the Gateway
The Vesper Coven (Series 3)
Daughters of Sea and Storm
Keepers of Forest and Flame

THE RIFTMAGIC SAGA
What the Lady's Maid Knew
The Rebel Beneath the Stairs
The Girl at the Heart of the Storm

BETRAYAL OF THE SISTERHOOD

BETRAYAL OF THE SISTERHOOD

THE GATEWAY TRACKERS
BOOK 11

E.E. HOLMES

Fairhaven Press

Fairhaven Press

Townsend, MA

Copyright © 2025 by E.E. Holmes

All rights reserved

www.eeholmes.com

ISBN 978-1-956656-23-7 (Paperback edition)

ISBN 978-1-956656-22-0 (Digital edition)

Publisher's note: This is a work of fiction. Names, characters, places and incidents are either the product of the author's imagination or are used fictitiously.

Cover design by James T. Egan of Bookfly Design LLC

Author photography by Cydney Scott Photography

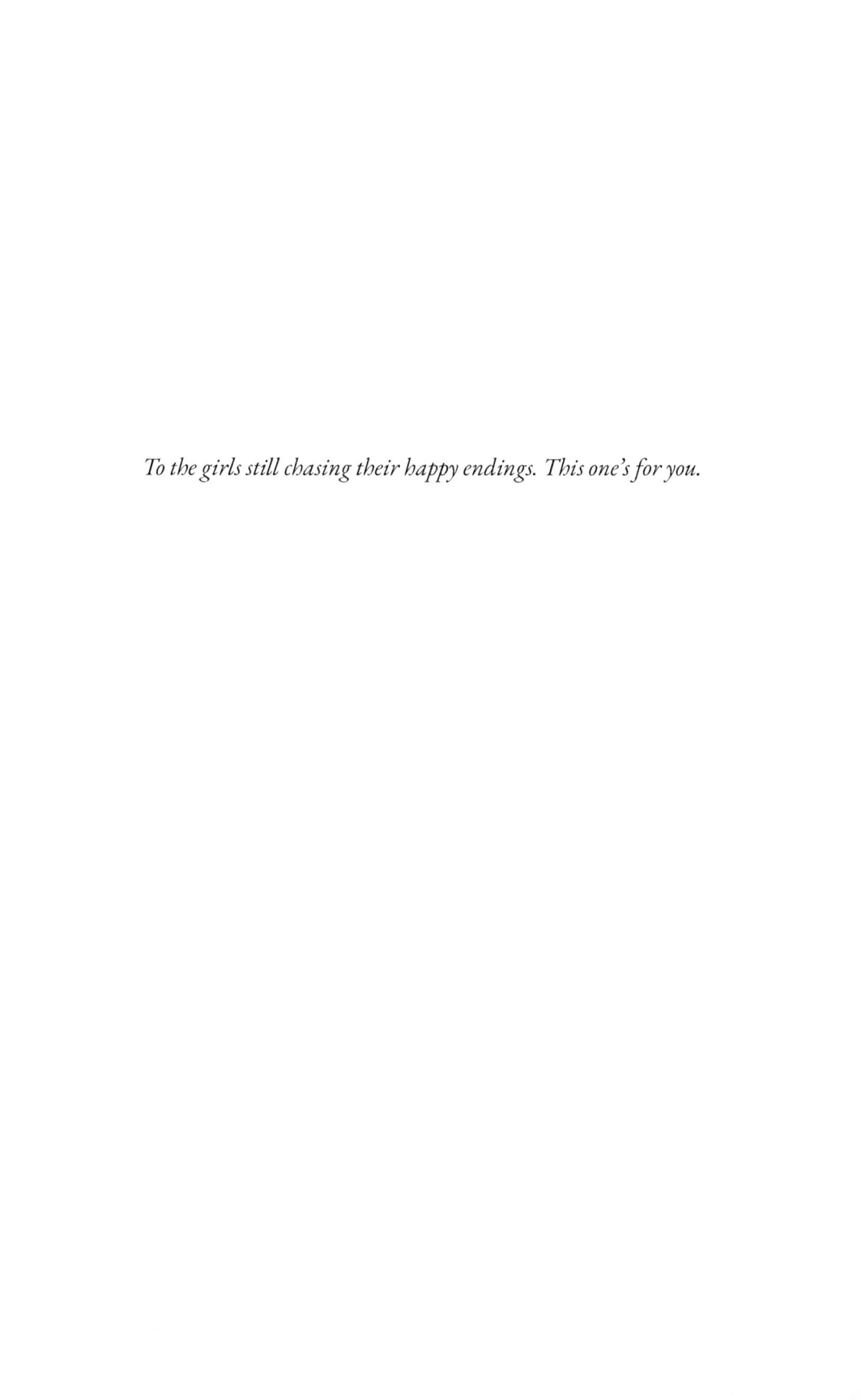

To the girls still chasing their happy endings. This one's for you.

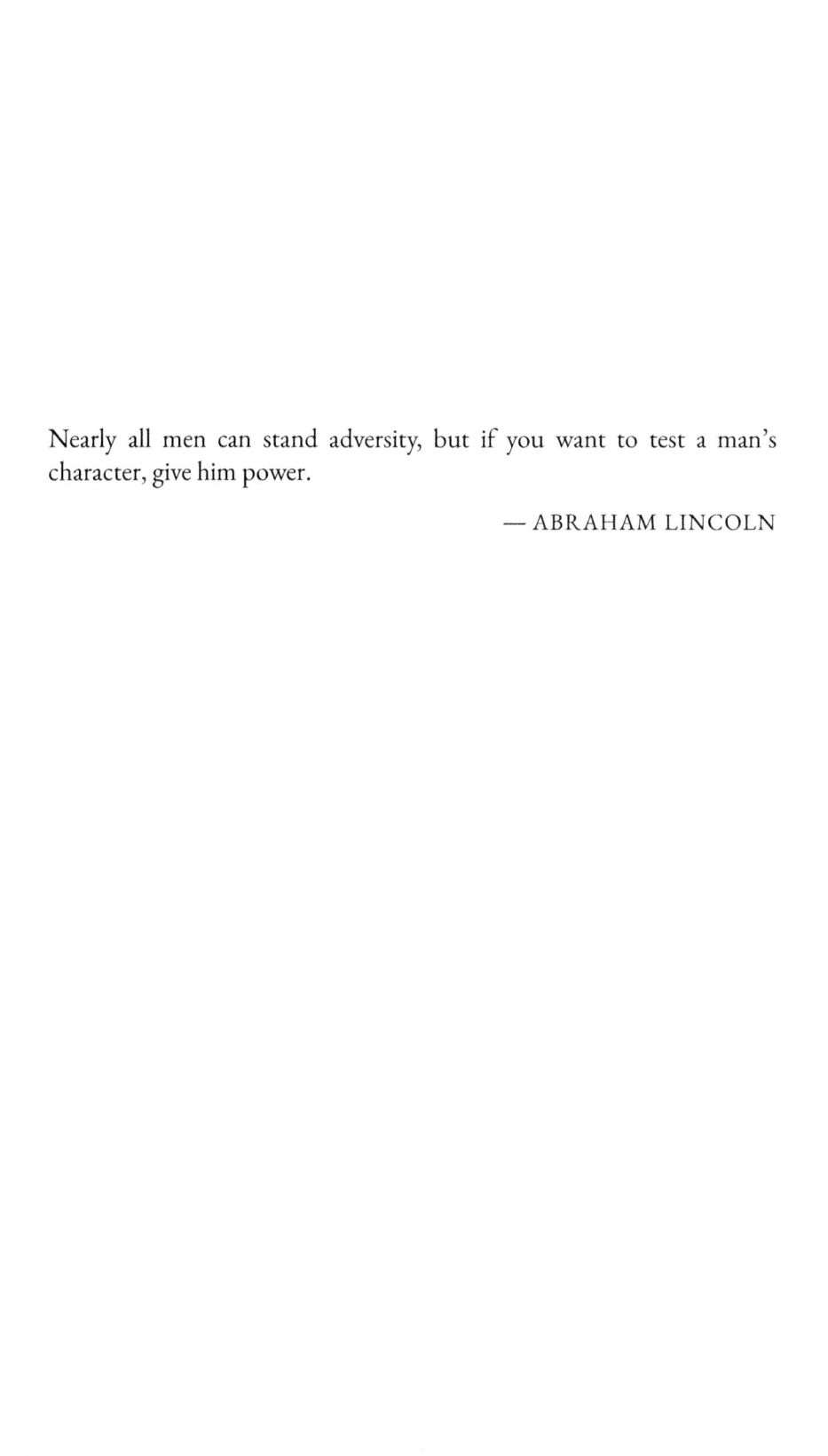

Nearly all men can stand adversity, but if you want to test a man's character, give him power.

— ABRAHAM LINCOLN

PROLOGUE

"Spirits above."

The breath whooshed from her lungs as she stared down at the book in her hands, hands that were now shaking so badly that the words she had struggled so long to find had become a blur. Afraid she would drop it or damage it, she set the book carefully onto the desk. She dropped her hands to her knees, rubbing her sweating palms vigorously on her skirt.

She'd found it. Centuries it had been hidden, a mere myth in the lore of the Durupinen, and now... now it was sitting on a desk in front of her, like it had simply been waiting patiently to be found.

She should have been thrilled. Elated. All she could manage was terror.

"What do I do?" she whispered into the silence. "What do I *do*?"

The silence didn't answer her, and the question festered like a wound. Outside, a dark cloud rolled over the moon as a gust off the sea carried in the promise of a storm.

Panic sapped the moisture from her mouth. She hastily gulped some tea and ran her hands over her face and up into her disheveled hair. She had to do something. She couldn't simply... forget about it. Hide it.

Could she?

Her head snapped up. She could. She could tuck it away again where she found it and pretend she had never located it in the first place. Who would ever know? Centuries could pass again, and there was every chance that it would be lost forever this time.

She could do that... except that the very thought of doing it filled her with such dread that she began to shake all over again. Not that it would be lost—that possibility did not frighten her in the least; and in fact, she was heartily wishing it was still lost in that very moment. No, what terrified her was that it could be found again, and she would have no control over the intentions of the person who found it. No control over the chaos that could be unleashed.

If she simply put it back, all of that would be her fault. She couldn't live with that. She wouldn't.

She looked down to find that her hands had stopped shaking. The moment the decision had formed in her head, the fear dissipated. She would not let it control her. She would act for the best. It was her duty—a duty that many of them had forgotten in their quest for power.

"But I will not forget it," she whispered to herself.

Full of determination now, she looked at the book, still sitting on the desk, with every appearance that it was simply a book, that it could not unravel the very threads of their world with what it contained. She did not reach for it. Instead, she reached past it for a piece of stationery, which she placed on the desktop in front of her. Then she reached up into her hair and extracted one of several pencils stashed there. She put the pencil to her mouth, worrying at the eraser with her lips, thinking hard.

And then, Polly Keener began to write.

1

PINS AND NEEDLES

"You look like a mythical mermaid goddess."

These words, whispered to me as I stood draped in flowing, shimmering swaths of fabric and beads, sounded so ludicrous in my ears that it was only physically possible for me to reply in one way.

I snorted. Loudly.

"I said mermaid goddess, not swine snuffling around in a trough," Milo snapped, clearly irritated.

"I'm sorry. I'm really sorry, but... mythical mermaid goddess? Be so for real right now."

"I'm going to assume that your disbelief is a reflection of your personal modesty and not a slight on my design capabilities," Milo sighed, crossing his arms over his chest.

"You assume correctly. I promise, Milo, if anyone on earth could make me look like a mythical mermaid goddess, it would absolutely be you. But even a genius like you has his limits."

With a slightly mollified expression, Milo swept around the other side of me and kept pinning.

I was standing on a small platform in Milo's new studio for what felt like my thousandth dress fitting. The fact that it *was* my thousandth fitting was absolutely my fault. I'd probably have had a lot fewer fittings if I had the patience or interest to stay still while Milo measured and tucked and pinned. Instead, I fidgeted and whined in a manner more suited to a flower girl than the maid of honor, and the result was lots of huffing and sighing and the inevitable scheduling of yet another fitting.

I could have counted on one hand the number of times I'd voluntarily put on a dress of any kind, let alone one that someone was designing and sewing from scratch. I'd have sooner burned the school down than be seen moping next to the punch bowl at a school dance, so I'd never even tried on prom dresses. But now my twin sister Hannah was getting married, and I had no choice but to submit to the machinations of our spirit guide/wedding planner.

It wasn't that I was dreading the wedding—I was genuinely happy for my sister, who had had a deeply traumatic childhood and deserved the happiest ending the universe could conjure—but the truth was that the whole wedding situation was completely out of hand. Even Hannah was at her wits' end.

It started fairly innocuously, as these things tended to do. Milo offered to make her wedding dress, and our aunt Karen offered to help secure a venue. Hannah had no idea that by agreeing to these initial demands, she would be creating a pair of dueling, wedding planning monsters. Karen soon revealed that our family had money set aside for our weddings—the kind of money that meant we could pull out all the stops. And that was exactly what Karen and Milo had been doing ever since: making sure that not a single stop was left unpulled.

It would be one thing if Hannah was excited about a big wedding—if it was actually what she wanted, I'd be bouncing off the walls with excitement on her behalf. But my sister was one of the most violently introverted people I'd ever met. She'd have been perfectly happy to sneak down to City Hall with Kiernan on a rainy Tuesday morning if she wasn't so afraid of hurting Karen and Milo's feelings. And so, because they meant more to her than any seating chart or floral arrangement, Hannah and Kiernan's wedding was shaping up to be the social event of the year in the Durupinen world and, given how much money circulated in Durupinen circles, that was really saying something.

At that very moment, Karen swept in, clipboard in hand and phone jammed between her ear and her shoulder. She was already in mid-conversation and barely looked up as she entered.

"...will need to come down and color-check that. I'm sorry, I know you sent digital swatches, and I appreciate it, but once the lighting is brought in, it's a whole different ballgame. And if the fabric has even a hint of iridescence… you see what I mean? Exactly. Right then, just check with the events coordinator for me and see when we can get back in. Okay. Right. Yes, I'll be reachable all day." She ended the call only to begin texting immediately.

"Imagine thinking we could decide on bunting fabrics without seeing them under the lighting," Karen scoffed as Milo made a noise of disgust through his nose. "Honestly, it's ridiculous. She couldn't even tell me if it was silk or satin or organza! As if anyone could make a decision with so little...oh, Jess!" Karen had finally lifted her head and got an eyeful of whatever Milo was currently doing to me. "Oh my God! You look... you look just like a... a..."

"A mythical mermaid goddess?" Milo suggested.

"Exactly! Oh, Milo, you are an utter miracle-worker!" she gushed.

I raised my eyebrows. "Excuse me, are you implying I don't usually resemble a goddess?"

"Which one, the ancient goddess of ripped denim and oversized sweats?" Milo asked, batting his lashes at me.

"Yes, that one."

"Well, let's just say you've gotten a celestial upgrade," Milo said, stepping back with a triumphant flourish of his hands. "Look!"

"I don't want to."

"You have to. I'm holding pins."

"You've already stabbed me. I'm immune."

"Look, sweetness, I can spin this out into fifteen more hour-long fittings, or we can end this today. Your choice."

Sticking my tongue out at him like the adult I was, I turned and looked into the mirror, which I'd completely ignored since the dress had been slipped over my head. I caught sight of my reflection.

"Holy shit." I gasped.

Milo's euphoric expression crumpled. "What is it? Do you hate it? You hate it, don't you?"

I couldn't speak. The woman staring back at me from the mirror was statuesque, slender, and graceful as she stood motionless and wide-eyed. Delicate, iridescent turquoise fabric clung to every curve, cascading to the floor and pooling around her feet like water. It draped in ruffles like butterfly wings off her pale shoulders and twisted into a ruched floral vine that sat on her hip, from which it split wide, revealing a gossamer layer of paler green beneath. Beading and teardrop pearls sparkled in clusters at the bodice and twinkled like scattered stars along the skirt.

"Jess?" Milo's voice was teetering on hysteria. "Say something."

"I... I'm... a mythical mermaid goddess," I whispered.

Karen burst out laughing. Milo's relief was so overwhelming that he completely abandoned his concentration. With his spirit energy diverted, his pins, measuring tape, and pincushion fell from the specters of his fingers right to the floor, with a tinkle and a thump.

"Told you so," Milo sang. "That means you're officially done. We can take it off."

It was a testament to how gorgeous the dress actually was that I felt a tiny pang of reluctance at this announcement. I got over it, though, once I'd shrugged back into my jeans and sweatshirt.

"Should I send in your next victim?" I asked, when I'd laced up my Docs.

"As long as she's not as dramatic as you," Milo replied.

The audacity of Milo to call anyone else dramatic was honestly so over-the-top that I opened my mouth to call him out on it. Luckily for him, Savvy chose that moment to barge into the room.

"Look, sorry, I'm late, mate, but you wouldn't believe what I had to—oh, hey Jess! I figured you'd still be here, so I brought you one of these." She held up a tray of iced lattes. At least that was what I thought she said, since she said all of it with a whole pain au chocolat sticking out of her mouth. She plunked the tray down and pulled the pastry from her mouth. "Had planned to bring you one of these, too, but the tube was a nightmare, and I was famished. Finn made us run ten miles this morning, the great prat. You still want the rest?"

"Hell yeah. You think I'll say no to pastry just because it's been in your mouth? Gimme," I insisted, snatching it from her outstretched fingers and immediately taking a bite.

"Ew," Milo muttered.

"Also, I brought all these pieces back from my mum, Milo. She says they're all set," Savvy added, setting a large reusable shopping bag of pressed and wrapped garments. Savvy's mother, Alice Todd, was a whiz with a sewing machine and had been working as a seamstress for Milo's fashion label since it first began to take off. Recently, he had promoted her to overseeing an entire studio full of seamstresses. This had two benefits: the first was that Alice, as the mother of a Durupinen, knew all about ghosts and could, with the help of a simple Casting, communicate with Milo while keeping the secret that the international runway's newest rising star wasn't technically... alive. The second was that Alice could finally make a decent wage and move Savvy's family out of the council flats they'd been stuck in for decades.

"Fabulous, thank her for me, Sav, and remind her she's a genius and a lifesaver," Milo said. Pinning, tucking, and draping were one thing, but the level of spirit energy control required to do things like embroidery and fine needlework was impossible to keep up with.

"I mean, if you like, mate, but it'll just go straight to her head," Savvy replied with a reluctant shrug.

"Milo, do you need anything while we're out?" Karen asked, finally looking up from her phone. "I mean, besides what we're already picking up?" She tipped him an exaggerated wink, which he returned.

"No, I'm good. Have fun!" Milo said, wiggling his fingers at us.

2

THE VAULT

"What did you mean, 'what we're already picking up?'" I asked Karen as we left the studio and got into her car. "Where are we going, anyway?"

"You'll see," Karen said, grinning. It was clear she was seriously enjoying withholding the details.

"Are you being vague because you don't want to ruin a surprise, or because you're afraid I won't come if I know where we're going?" I asked, narrowing my eyes.

"You'll see," Karen said again, with a laugh. "Now stop pouting. It makes you look like a spoiled child."

"It makes me feel like a child, being dragged around and not even told where we're going," I grumbled.

Karen didn't dignify that with a response, and instead pulled away from the curb and onto the road. I repressed the urge to shrilly ask "Are we there yet?" repeatedly, for which I thought I deserved a pat on the back.

"How goes the wedding planning?" I asked after a few minutes.

"It's chaos," Karen huffed, though I could sense the satisfaction in her voice. Karen was the kind of Type A person who adored nothing more than being tossed into a five-alarm emergency and personally putting out every trace of a fire with her bare hands. She thrived on it, which made perfect sense, given her chosen profession of corporate lawyer. "The caterers have rescheduled the final tasting twice, the hotel is having trouble getting enough valets to handle the parking, and the seating chart is still a disaster. There are just too many clans with lifelong feuds for a single ballroom. I'm going to have to start seating people in the hallway just to avoid an argument."

"Ah, come on, they're all socialites. Don't they know how to keep up appearances at events like this?" I asked.

Karen scoffed. "Of course they do, but why keep up appearances when you can make a scene? That's why the seating chart is so important. The fewer opportunities we give them to start a fight, the better."

"I still don't understand why we're even inviting all these people," I said. "Half of them hate us. Aren't we just asking for them to ruin Hannah's day?"

"Look, I know it doesn't make a lot of sense when you put it that way, but there's a long history of how things are done in the upper clan echelons. There are expectations. And before you tell me to screw the expectations," she added, raising a finger as I opened my mouth to say exactly that, "you need to realize, I'm trying to look out for Hannah here. Believe me, navigating a few sticky guest interactions will be a small price to pay for playing the game. We've got a lot of damage control to do since… well…you know."

I sure as hell did know, and the idea that we were the ones who had to do the damage control was infuriating. It wasn't our fault that generations of Durupinen had been abusing the power and control of the Gateways. It sure as hell wasn't our fault that those centuries of abuse had nearly caused the Gateways to collapse. In fact, if we hadn't defied the most powerful clans and the International High Priestess herself, and risked our lives to remove the Gateways from our bloodlines and replaced them back in the Geatgrimas where they belonged, we would have faced a cataclysmic collapse of the very links between the world of the living and the spirit world beyond. As far as I was concerned, every one of our fellow Durupinen should be down on her knees thanking us for saving them from their selfishness. Instead, we were fending off vitriol and attacks right and left. The opposing clans had tried everything from political machinations on our Council to outright witchcraft to reverse what we had done. With every new scheme they concocted, I had a harder and harder time differentiating our own sisterhood from our sworn enemy, the Necromancers.

It had been several months since we had arrived home from Scotland, where a Trackers mission had put us on the trail of a dangerous spirit, a former Caomhnóir driven half-mad with his Necromancer-inspired experimentations. It was a stark reminder of our calling—to protect the Gateways at all costs.

Ironically, Hannah and I had known nothing at all of the Gateways until we were legal adults, and now it seemed like it had fallen on our shoulders to protect them from the very families who had built their entire lives around them. Shouldn't it have been the other way around? Shouldn't they be the ones convincing us why the Gateways were worth preserving, and hard-selling us on devoting our lives to the cause? Instead, we were the ones reminding them. It was maddening—maddening enough to take that "game" Karen was babbling on about and simply refuse to play. Or even better, light the damn game board on fire and watch it burn.

We pulled up in front of a tall brick building in South Kensington and found Hannah standing outside, waiting for us. As we got out of the car, she looked up from her phone and smiled widely.

"You escaped Milo," she said, poking me in the arm. "So I guess that means you held still this time?"

"Grudgingly," I replied.

"But you liked the dress?"

"Also grudgingly," I said. "When do I get to see yours?"

Hannah hoisted an eyebrow. "Which one?"

In Milo's own words, Hannah's wedding attire was his "sartorial magnum opus," and like every great, career-defining work, it had multiple parts. At last count, Hannah had two wedding dresses, a reception dress, and a "going away" outfit, which sounded to me like something Milo invented until Karen informed me otherwise. Apparently, "going away" outfits were a time-honored tradition. Karen even pulled up her wedding photos to show me hers, a very sleek and elegant ivory pantsuit.

"How is the bride-to-be feeling?" Karen sang as she stepped up onto the pavement to hug Hannah. Then she stepped back, peering earnestly into Hannah's face. "Seriously, how are you?"

"For the millionth time, I'm fine," Hannah said, with the kind of patience I could only dream of. "I keep telling you, Karen, I'm not sweating the details. Are you ever going to take my word for it?"

Karen bit her lip. "I've just never met a bride who was so… calm. It's a little unnerving. I keep worrying that you're in denial or something, and all your nerves are going to hit you at once."

"Why, were you nervous when you were getting ready to marry Noah?" Hannah asked.

Karen rolled her eyes. "Well, sure, but that's because I should have run screaming in the other direction rather than marry him. Kiernan's different."

"Exactly. Nothing to worry about. Toasty warm feet. So what are we doing here, anyway?" Hannah asked.

"Wait, you didn't even tell *her* what we were doing?" I asked, rounding on Karen.

"No, I wanted it to be a surprise for both of you. Now, come on up."

Without another word of explanation, she marched toward the front door. Hannah and I exchanged slightly wary looks, and then hurried to follow her.

The lobby of the building was sleek and modern-looking but completely devoid of any signage that could clue us in as to what kind of building it was. Everything was shiny, and decorated in tones of cream and chrome in a vaguely mid-century modern style. A woman in a monochrome charcoal gray suit sat behind a massive silver desk with a glass top.

"Can I help you?" she asked as we approached the desk, Karen in the lead.

"Yes, thank you, I would like to enter my family's vault."

Hannah and I looked at each other. Vault?

"Your name, ma'am?"

"Karen Ballard."

"And your identification, please?"

Karen fished her ID out of her purse and handed it over. The woman then walked her through a string of security questions on an iPad, took her thumbprint and photograph, and went over her with a security wand. She then looked over her glasses at us, her expression inquisitive.

"Oh, yes. These are my nieces. They'd like to enter the vault as well," Karen said, and then turned to us and grimaced. "Security's tight, so I'm afraid you'll need to be properly checked in as well, girls. Sorry."

Hannah and I endured the indignity of the security measures, and were finally cleared to go upstairs. The woman at the desk gave us each printed badges with our pictures and names on them, which we had to attach to our shirts. The badges, she informed us, would need to be scanned to work the elevators and open the doors we were permitted to enter.

"Thank you," Karen said, leading us toward the elevators. One of them opened with a ding as she pressed her badge to the card reader.

"What the hell is in this vault anyway, nuclear secrets? A kidnapped international diplomat?" I asked as the elevator moved smoothly upward.

"I know it's a little intense, but... well, our family has always taken its security seriously, as do most of the Durupinen. It's not all about well-trained Caomhnóir… sometimes it's vaults and keypads. Ah, here we are. Our vault is down this way."

The elevator emptied us into a long hallway with beige carpets and recessed lighting. The walls were hung with paintings in elaborate gold frames, each with a gallery light affixed over it. The paintings themselves looked like they could very well be priceless works of art, and they weren't even inside the vaults. Karen walked straight down to the last door on the left-hand side, swiped her badge, and waited as the door swung inward on silent hinges.

It wasn't at all what I expected, though my expectations were based on Hollywood gangster films rather than reality. I had pictured piles of precious jewels, gold bars, and canvas bags with dollar signs spray-painted on them. Instead, we entered a room that looked something like a museum. The floors were covered in plush, cream-colored carpeting, and there were several tufted couches, leather armchairs, and polished wooden desks at which to sit. All along one wall were numbered doors, like P.O. boxes. Another wall was full of glass-covered niches, through which all kinds of artifacts were displayed. A third wall was hung with paintings, drawings, and framed documents, each with its own gallery light mounted above it, so that they could be viewed easily. And the last wall was lined with glass-fronted cabinets, in which an assortment of other items were on display on little cushions or little glass platforms. Everything was carefully labeled, and on several of the desks, I spotted a large binder stamped with two words: Clan Sassanaigh.

"Whoa," Hannah murmured from beside me.

"No shit," I replied under my breath.

Karen turned to us and smiled. "This room contains all of the most important and valuable artifacts that have been amassed by Clan Sassanaigh over the centuries. Not all of them, of course," she added quickly. "We have many items on loan to museums and historical societies, not to mention the things we have on display in Fairhaven and at the archive on Skye. These are the things that are the most personal and, in some cases, the most valuable. Everything in here will belong to you girls someday, and I thought it was high time I took you to see them. I've only ever been here twice myself."

"We own all this stuff?" I asked. Already, without taking another step into the room, I had spotted a gold statue, a tiara with a jewel in it the size of a chicken egg, and a painting I was pretty sure came from Monet's waterlily collection.

"Yes, and of course, it's all heavily insured, but not all of it is conventionally valuable. Some of it is purely historical. Take a look at this," Karen said, and beckoned us across the room.

We joined her in front of one of the glass cases. She pointed at a purple velvet cushion on which sat an extremely old book—a book we all knew very well.

"The *Book of Téigh Anonn*," I whispered.

"The very first edition our clan ever owned," Karen said, and there was a ring of reverence in her voice. "As the generations passed, we had to copy it over and preserve the original when it became too delicate to handle. But of course, we preserved it. Agnes Isherwood herself used it back in her time."

I stared down at it with a strange feeling of familiarity sounding inside me like a plucked string.

"Agnes," I whispered.

"What's that?" Hannah asked, turning to look at me.

"It was there," I said, and the memory bloomed in great detail, the fateful Rifting, when I had followed Agnes' clues and dropped through a second door to speak to her. "When I met Agnes, when I was Rifting, I saw that book. It was on her desk. I never thought about it, until now, but I'm sure it's the same one."

"And you're absolutely right. It's one of only two known relics we have of hers," Karen said.

I tore my eyes from the book. "Is the other relic here, too?" I asked.

"Yes, it's right over here," Karen said, leading us to a second case, in which a necklace sat on a purple velvet cushion, gleaming under a tiny gallery light. It comprised dozens of delicate golden wires wrapped intricately around a large green stone. Within the twists of wires themselves were hundreds of other tiny gemstones, the wires wrapping around them like fingers clutching them in place.

"Wow. It's beautiful," I murmured, watching the light dance off all the tiny gems.

"It is, isn't it?" Karen said, gazing down at it.

"It seems a shame to keep something like this locked away. Has it always been here?"

"Not in this specific building, no. Over the centuries, it has had many homes. Our ancestors passed it down and wore it, of course, but as time passed, it was deemed too valuable to wear every day. We had it at Skye, at Fairhaven, and in our family estates. It was only when your grandmother became the matriarch of the clan that she had it transferred here. She insisted it wasn't safe enough anywhere else."

"Why wouldn't it be safe?" Hannah asked. "Did she really think someone would try to steal it?"

Karen shrugged. "Your grandmother was a bit… well, obsessed with our clan history and preserving our legacy. Anything that bolstered our credentials as one of the oldest and most powerful clans. The existence of the locket was proof of our legitimacy. I need hardly tell you how wildly she clung to that proof once your mother threw our clan into scandal." Karen's head snapped up, and she grimaced. "Her words, not mine. Sorry, the second I walk into this room, it's like I can feel her glaring disapprovingly at me. It's a bit like being haunted, actually."

"We don't have to stay, if—" Hannah began tentatively, but Karen brushed her off at once.

"No, no, for goodness' sake!" she said, pulling herself together at once. "We're not gonna let a little unresolved family trauma spoil our fun!"

"Fun?" I asked, glancing around. It was fascinating for sure, but I wouldn't exactly call a trip to the family vault "fun."

"Yes, fun. Now Hannah," Karen said, turning toward her with shining eyes. "I know Milo is handling your bridal look, so to speak, but he agreed that I could contribute something by way of jewelry."

Hannah raised her eyebrows. "Are you sure? I wasn't aware Milo was capable of loosening that stylistic death grip."

Karen laughed. "Yes, I promise, I got his full permission—mostly by texting him ahead of time with photos and letting him eliminate anything that didn't fit the aesthetic. But that still leaves us with some really great heirlooms, and I thought you might like to try some on and choose something for the wedding day."

"Oh!" Hannah said, looking startled. "Oh, I… I didn't…"

Karen put both her hands up. "This is up to you, Hannah. Whatever you choose. It's your wedding day, and—"

"Wait, wait, what was that last bit?" I interrupted.

Karen frowned. "What bit?"

"Whose wedding day is it?" I asked, leaning forward and cupping my hand over my ear.

Karen rolled her eyes. "It is Hannah's wedding day."

"Okay, good, just making sure we're on the same page here," I said. Hannah widened her eyes warningly at me, but I ignored her. "Because Hannah is too polite to say it, but I'm not. She's handed everything over to you and Milo, and

I'm sure you're doing a fabulous job, but she's not going to wear some giant awful clunky old crown or something just to appease you guys. So can you please make it clear that if she looks at all the jewelry and she doesn't see anything she wants to wear, that your feelings will not be hurt and that you will not be disappointed in any way?"

"Jess, this really isn't—" Hannah began, but I held up a finger.

"Someone has to stand up for you if you're not going to stand up for yourself," I said.

Hannah opened her mouth to argue again, but Karen forestalled her with a laugh. "Hannah, she's right. Let it be known right now that I have absolutely no emotional attachment to any of this jewelry. If you decide you want to wear it, lovely. If not, I honestly couldn't care less. I just thought every bride should try on some wildly expensive jewelry before her wedding. Since we're not doing the traditional wedding dress shopping, I thought it might be fun."

Hannah looked back and forth between Karen and me, and then sighed, smiling with relief. "That does sound fun. Thanks, Karen."

"Of course. And I'm sorry if I'm micromanaging. I'm only trying to take things off your plate that would otherwise be stressful for you to have to deal with."

This apology completely ignored the fact that the things on the proverbial plate had been put there by Karen herself, but I let it go. Hannah was smiling. That was enough for the moment.

Karen went over to the wall with all the drawers in it. She waved us over to a pair of chairs in front of a little glass-topped vanity table with a mirror, and told us both to take a seat.

"Me, too?" I asked.

Karen smiled. "Since it's only for fun, why shouldn't we all try on some ridiculous jewelry? You can wear something to the wedding, too, if you like!"

I thought massive diamonds on me would probably look like petticoats on a stray dog, but I shrugged and sat. Karen pulled the first few drawers out. They turned out not to be regular drawers, but wooden display boxes with glass tops and cushions of velvet inside. She laid the first few on the table. Hannah's gasp was loud in my ear.

"Oh my goodness," she muttered.

"Holy SHIT," I yelped. "What are these, the actual crown jewels?!"

Karen grinned. "I told you this would be fun."

For the next hour, we unabashedly played dress-up like three little girls set loose in a princess's castle. We tried on necklaces dripping with emeralds, rings set with diamonds the size of quarters, hair combs and tiaras, and even a sort of headdress made of delicate golden mesh that hung over our faces like a curtain. We were having so much fun that we lost track of time, and it wasn't until my phone started buzzing in my back pocket that I realized how late it had gotten.

It was Finn.

"Hi, Finn!"

"Hello, love," Finn replied. I could hear the smile in his voice. "I'm just checking on you. I was informed that Karen has kidnapped you for wedding purposes. It sounded a bit... ominous."

"No, we're at the family vault trying on heirloom jewelry."

"Oh." He hesitated. "That... still sounds ominous, based on everything I know about you. Do you need me to come rescue you? Shall I invent an emergency? Say yes three times and I'm on my way."

I laughed. "I'm not being held hostage, I promise. We should be done soon. I'm pretty sure we've tried on everything in here."

"Well, I bumped into Catriona, and she asked if you might stop by the Tracker's office? She looked rather serious about it. She said she was about to call you, so I offered to do it. I thought my dulcet tones might be preferable to... well, let's just say she's not a ray of sunshine."

I groaned. I hadn't had a Tracker's mission since Edinburgh. I should have known it was too good to last. "I hope she realizes I can't disappear to parts unknown right now. The wedding is in four weeks."

"You know Catriona. She's not really fussed about things like social obligations."

"She should be fussed about this one, seeing as she's invited, along with every other Durupinen in existence. Have you heard the guest count is up above five hundred now?"

"Oh yes. I'm managing security, remember? I just had to bring on an additional team."

I looked over at Hannah, who was grinning into the mirror with a tiara in her chestnut curls. I wondered if she even realized how big her wedding had become. The whole thing was starting to feel somewhat like a snowball barreling down a hill, gathering size and speed until it finally crashed into us all.

"Right, well, I'll be heading over to Fairhaven after we're done here. Where are you right now?"

"On my way over to Milo's studio. I've been roped into another fitting as well."

"Ugh. I'm so sorry you have to do that."

"I imagine not half as sorry as you were to have to do it yourself," Finn replied, a smile in his voice. "And anyway, why should you be sorry? Don't you want your wedding date to look dashing?"

"I want you to look like *you*," I said. "You're always dashing."

"Well, I'll be trading in the Caomhnóir uniform for something a bit less military and a bit more... Bond. James Bond," he said.

"That's good. I think anything less than Bond would make me, as a mythical mermaid goddess, look a bit overdressed," I said dryly.

"Mythical... what, sorry?"

"Don't ask. I'll meet you at home."

Though I would rather die than admit it, a sweet little zing of contentment shot through me at the word "home." Deciding we needed to be closer to Fairhaven when I rejoined the Trackers, we'd bought a semi-detached cottage in a nearby village. The best part about it was that the other cottage was also for sale, both having been owned and rented out by the same owner, which meant Hannah and Kiernan could be right next door. It wasn't that we were co-dependent, like some twins might tend to be, but our roles as Durupinen meant we had to be close to each other. This arrangement, along with the workshop-turned-studio out in the garden for Milo, meant that we all had our own private space, and yet we were all together. Growing up, my mother and I had been nomads, never staying more than a year at a time in any one location, living out of suitcases and boxes that I eventually stopped unpacking altogether. Hannah's childhood had been, if possible, even worse—bouncing from foster home to foster home, followed by a string of group homes and even mental hospitals. Neither of us had ever really been able to put down roots anywhere. Now, finally, it felt like we might be able to say the word "home" and mean it, in every sense of the word; and for a thoroughly unsentimental person, I was annoyingly sentimental about it.

"Does this mean dress-up time is over?" Karen asked from the vanity. She still had a triple string of pink pearls around her neck.

"Yeah, we gotta go. Or at least, I do. Catriona has summoned me," I said darkly.

"Well, that's all right. We can always come back. Unless..." Karen looked over at Hannah, a question in her expression.

Hannah was looking at herself in the mirror, a delicate golden circlet in her hands. It was gorgeous, made of what looked like leaves and petals hammered from gold and linked together on a frame twisted and curled to look like a vine. The centers of the flowers were set with tiny sapphires in all shades of blue that twinkled under the gallery lights. It would look stunning against her dark hair.

"I... I think I'd like to wear this one, if you're sure it's really okay," she breathed, looking down at it with an awestruck expression.

"Of course it's okay," Karen said, smiling gently. "And very fitting."

"Fitting? Why?"

"It's exactly the one your mother chose to wear for her Initiation ceremony," Karen said, and there was a definite tremble in her voice.

Hannah's expression twisted, and it was hard to read the play of emotions there. Hannah's feelings toward my mother were far more complicated than mine, as she had never even met her. Part of our mother's plan to protect us was to separate us, and Hannah was the twin she left behind. Our mother didn't realize that her Binding, meant to block our Durupinen gifts, was not strong enough to protect Hannah from Visitations, and as a result, Hannah's entire childhood had been full of confusion, trauma, and fear. Over the years, Hannah had worked through much of her anger, her sense of abandonment, and her grief. But the feelings left over, though more forgiving toward our mother, were still quite tangled and complicated.

Karen knew all of this, and so she was quick to clear her throat and adopt a much more cheerful tone. "More importantly, though, Milo will approve. That was one of his favorites when I showed him the photos."

"And it completes the other three out of four on the bridal checklist," I added.

Hannah looked up, brow furrowed. "Bridal checklist?"

I held up four fingers, ticking them off. "Your dresses are new. That necklace is old, borrowed, and blue. Bam. Wedding achievement unlocked."

Hannah laughed, and her expression cleared. "Yes, I hadn't thought of that." She looked down at the circlet again. "Do we have to like... check it out, or something? Sign some sort of waiver?"

It was Karen's turn to laugh. "Of course not. I know the security is tight, but everything in here belongs to our clan. It can all come and go as we choose." She turned to me. "Jess? Did you see anything you wanted to—"

"I, uh..." The truth was that, though I'd looked at dozens of spectacular pieces of jewelry, my eye had kept being drawn back to one in particular—one I hadn't even dared to try on.

"Come on, don't be shy," Karen said, smiling now. "Was it that diamond one with the roses? I really thought—"

"No, it's just... would I be allowed to wear Agnes' necklace?" I asked tentatively.

"Oh!" Karen glanced over at it, like she'd forgotten it was there; an easy thing to do, honestly, amidst all the rest of the far more glamorous and expensive-looking items we'd just spent the last couple of hours draping ourselves in. "Are you sure?"

"I know it's not as fancy as some of the others," I hedged. "But... I don't know, there's just something about it. I met her, you know? I feel sort of... connected to it."

"I think it's the perfect thing to wear," Hannah piped up. "It will look beautiful with your dress."

"But if it's too delicate or expensive or whatever, it's fine," I said quickly, already regretting even asking. "I really don't need to—"

"Not at all," Karen said, shaking her head and marching over to the case. "In fact, I think it's a great idea. It will be a good chance to remind the den of vipers who they're dealing with."

"Karen, you are talking about my wedding guests," Hannah said a little weakly. "A guest list you put together, I might add."

Karen grinned a little sheepishly. "I know. I'm sorry. But you don't need to worry. They care too much about keeping up appearances to be on anything but their best behavior."

Hannah tried to look convinced, but couldn't quite manage it.

Karen took Agnes' necklace out of its case and handed it to me. I felt a strange shiver of energy run through me as it brushed against my skin. It was like I could feel the hundreds of years of history pulsing in the metal. I walked over to the mirror with it and held it up in front of my neck. Karen followed and fastened it from behind. The green gemstone—was it an emerald?—settled perfectly into the hollow of my throat, and I felt a sudden, almost inexplicable urge to cry.

"Well?" Karen urged.

"Yeah," I said. "I like it."

"What about you, Karen?" Hannah asked.

Karen looked startled. "Me?"

"Of course! They're your heirlooms, too. Aren't you going to wear one?"

Karen gaped a little, like the thought had never occurred to her. "I wasn't... I mean they're fun to try on, of course, but... well, after all, it's not my wedding."

"It's not mine either," I pointed out.

"No, it's mine, and you both should wear something beautiful!" Hannah said.

"Isn't that a bit..." Karen seemed to be searching for the right word, but Hannah cut her off.

"Karen, if you're worried about upstaging the bride, please remember who is dressing me. I assure you, it will be utterly impossible."

"Ah, go on, Karen," I coaxed, grinning. "Pick something no other hoity-toity Council Clan has. Make them go green with envy. You know, for funsies."

"Do it, do it, do it," Hannah started chanting in a whisper, and I quickly joined in.

Karen smirked rather mischievously and then picked up one of the cases still sitting on the vanity. It contained a mantle necklace encrusted with emeralds and pearls. She held it up in front of her neck, and her smirk became a grin.

"Is this hoity-toity enough?" she asked.

Hannah and I looked at each other and, in flawless twin fashion, replied in unison, "Perfect."

3

THE SCRIBE

Karen promised to keep the jewelry safe, and we left her in London to drive to Fairhaven.

"You really don't need to come with me," I said, as Hannah and I walked through the front door of Fairhaven.

"I know, but I wanted to," Hannah said. "If she's got any kind of update on Clan Rìoghalachd, I'd like to hear it."

"And it would be a really convenient way to avoid more wedding stuff, wouldn't it?" I asked, with a healthy dose of side-eye.

"Now that you mention it, yes it would," she replied.

You would think that after years of coming in and out of the place, I'd get desensitized to the grandeur of Fairhaven, but I still felt an involuntary little thrill of awe every single time. It wasn't just the architecture, which was, of course, stunning. There was something in the atmosphere of the place—something besides the ever-present spirits—which always seeped right into my bones, like a chill. It was as though history—*my* history—breathed in this place. I could feel the centuries of it like dust motes in the air that I had no choice but to inhale. The first time I'd ever come here, I knew I belonged to this place; it sang in my blood. I'd wondered, once the Gateways had been returned to their rightful place within the Geatgrimas, if that feeling would weaken, or perhaps disappear altogether, but it didn't. Something inside me still recognized my connection to this place. It wasn't precisely home—not in the warm and fuzzy sense of my new cottage, for example. After all the rejection, the trauma, the political intrigue, and the brushes with death, I'd walked away from the castle for years and had had to be quite literally dragged back. But I was tied to Fairhaven, for better or for worse, and I'd begun to make peace with all the messy parts of our shared story.

A story that was still unfolding, I reminded myself, as we made our way up the stairs to the Tracker's office.

"Jess? Hannah?"

I turned on the landing to see Celeste Morgan walking briskly toward us from the upper hallway. It had been quite a while since I'd seen the High Priestess, and I was surprised to see how altered she was. Her auburn hair was shot through with much more silver than I remembered. There were bags under her eyes, hollows under her cheekbones, and an overall sharpness to her features. I experienced a moment of panic, wondering if she was sick—we'd all watched our previous High Priestess waste away from illness—but then I remembered the political turmoil of the past year and realized it was probably just the stress of trying to hold together a crumbling sisterhood taking its toll. I certainly didn't envy her the role she had taken on. Hannah and I scaled the last few steps to meet her.

"It feels like ages since I've seen you, Jess," Celeste said, and her smile, though a bit strained, was genuine as it broke across her face. "How are you?"

"I'm okay," I told her. "Are you? No offense, but you look a bit…" I tried to settle on a word that didn't sound rude, "…stressed."

"Well, that's fitting, I suppose," Celeste said. "As Hannah can attest, life on the Council is rather fraught at the moment, but then, we knew this period would be challenging. We have faced challenging times before. It will pass."

"Anything we can do to help?" Hannah asked. Her expression mirrored my concern.

"You're already doing what you can on the Council, Hannah. Please, focus on your big day. I'm very much looking forward to attending, by the way," Celeste said, and Hannah nodded in acknowledgment. Then Celeste turned to me. "There is a favor I'd like to ask you though, Jess."

"What's up?" I asked, wary. It wasn't easy to say no to the High Priestess of the Northern Clans.

"Well, it's Fiona. I'm worried about her," Celeste said. "Not her health," she added as she watched my expression shift. "Her eyesight is no better, as far as I am aware, but she seems to be coping all right. She's always been a tough old bird in that regard. No, it's her behavior."

I snorted. "When has Fiona ever been well-behaved?"

Celeste smiled gently and shook her head. "That's not quite what I mean. She's become very... distant with everyone. She's been shutting herself away in that tower and rarely leaves it. She's missed so many Council meetings that I've had no choice but to remove her from several committees, and at this point, she's in danger of losing her seat."

I looked at Hannah. "Did you know about this?"

"I knew she missed some meetings, but then, so did I," she said, shrugging.

"Well, yes, but you were excused for Tracker business through the proper channels, and you had Karen sit in as your surrogate," Celeste said. "Fiona has just... disappeared."

"What do you want me to do?" I asked.

"Could you talk to her? Try to find out what's going on?" Celeste asked, clasping her hands in front of her. "You're one of the very few people in her inner circle. She might listen to you."

"Fiona doesn't have an inner circle," I said. "She's got a steel door with a peephole, and occasionally, she might open it a crack to yell at me before slamming it on my fingers."

Celeste smiled. "A much more apt metaphor, but still, you are one of the chosen few who could accomplish even that. Would you please try?"

"Of course," I said. "I'll head up there right after my meeting with Catriona."

"Thank you," Celeste said, her shoulders sagging with relief. "And do let me know how you get on. I don't want to have to remove her, but the other members are bringing resolutions, and I'm running out of excuses to veto them."

"I'll do my best, I promise," I said.

Celeste reached out and squeezed my arm before hurrying off again down the corridor.

"Do you think you'll be able to convince her?" Hannah asked, her tone as skeptical as my thoughts.

"I doubt it," I said. "I can't really imagine anyone convincing Fiona to do something she doesn't want to do. Frankly, I was surprised she was ever on the Council in the first place. She always treated the meetings like an inconvenience she couldn't wait to be done with, and she spent half her time disrupting them anyway. I'm sort of surprised Celeste wants her to stay on."

"I'm not," Hannah said quietly.

I stopped. There was something strange in her tone—something dark. "Explain."

Hannah sighed, looking over her shoulder to make sure no one else was approaching who might overhear us; but with classes for the Apprentices in session at the moment, the corridor was empty. "Fiona is irascible and eccentric, but she's always been on Celeste's side," she said. "With all the upheaval right now, and all the infighting, I think Celeste is afraid to lose any of the allies she's got. Some of the other clans would like nothing better than to dethrone her, and if they thought they could get the votes, they would absolutely try it."

"They can't just kick out the High Priestess," I scoffed. "That's not how it works. Finvarra did plenty of unpopular things during her tenure, and she was untouchable."

"Finvarra wasn't untouchable," Hannah argued. "She was just well-protected. And ever since we restored the Gateways, Celeste's protection has been crumbling away. Clans that used to support her have turned on her. She can't afford to lose a safe seat like Fiona's."

Anxiety curled in the pit of my stomach. Celeste and I had had our disagreements, but when push came to shove, she'd always come through for Hannah and me, from our very first fraught days as Apprentices at Fairhaven. The thought of her leadership being in question was deeply troubling to me. If she was the only person standing between us and the clans who wanted to undo everything we'd accomplished, there was no question in my mind now: I would make sure Fiona started making it to Council meetings, even if I had to drag her there kicking and screaming with my own two hands.

The Trackers office had moved since I'd first become an unwilling member of their team. Since the restoration of the Gateways, the need for Trackers on cases all over the world had exploded. Typically, Trackers handled situations in which spirits had gotten out of control in a way that threatened Durupinen secrecy. Now, Trackers were being called in to deal with the Gateways themselves, and the fact that they now existed in places they hadn't for centuries. Forgotten Geatgrimas had to be unearthed and repaired. In some instances, whole cities and towns had grown up around Geatgrimas, and now they were surrounded by people and progress that meant they needed to be hidden and protected.

All over the world, teams were working around the clock to ensure every Geatgrima was properly secured and guarded. Sometimes this meant buying up massive amounts of real estate to create a buffer. Sometimes, it meant building new barriers or reconstructing old ones. Sometimes it meant archaeological-style digs and reconstructions, where Geatgrimas had been lost for so long they'd literally been buried. I'd even heard a rumor that a government had had to be infiltrated and legislation drafted and passed to ensure that the location of one Geatgrima be declared some kind of historical landmark so it couldn't be bulldozed. It was our own fault, of course. It was our mess, and we had to clean it up. Still, that meant a lot of Trackers had to be hired and trained, and so the Trackers office was more like the Trackers department now, and had been set up in its own wing of the castle. Classrooms were shifted around, storage rooms were cleaned out and repurposed, and the whole document archive collection had been meticulously boxed up and relocated to ensure that Catriona and her newly expanded team would have the space and resources they needed to carry out their enormous caseload.

Hannah had to remind me of this recent move, and pulled me down a different corridor than usual to find Catriona waiting for us in her new digs. She was, as ever, a delight.

"Took your bloody time, didn't you?" she muttered as she looked up from her desk and saw me standing there.

"So sorry, I haven't quite mastered teleportation yet. I'll get right on that," I replied with a sarcastic smile. "Didn't Finn tell you I was in London today?"

Catriona's expression twisted. "Didn't bother to ask, actually. Have a seat." She looked past me, where Hannah was still hovering in the doorway. "You'd better stay too, Hannah. I'd just have to brief you later anyway."

Hannah nodded and came to sit in the chair beside me. "So it is about Edinburgh, then?" she asked.

Catriona raised her eyebrows in evident surprise. "No, actually. Why did you —well, yes, I suppose that would be a logical conclusion. Most recent Tracker mission and all that." She pulled a file off her desk and flipped it open. "I was just looking at the notes from the Clan Rioghalachd Caomhnóir. Kingshurst has completed its investigation. Damien Brightwell has been cleared; it has been concluded that he had no knowledge of his assistant's plans and took no part in carrying them out. Aoife O'Malley's trial date has yet to be set. I've sent your testimony, but it's possible they may call you in person. For now, she's still at Skye. It's likely she'll serve out the rest of her sentence there when she is convicted."

"I notice you say 'when,' and not 'if,'" I said.

Cat smiled grimly. "Ms. O'Malley hasn't shut up since they arrested her, despite being made aware of her rights. There's no question of 'if' after the litany of crimes she's proudly and repeatedly confessed to."

Beside me, Hannah shuddered delicately. Aoife's actions at Kingshurst College had been nearly as vile as Alasdair's. It would be a relief when we could be sure she would be locked away for good, and I'd gladly travel back to Skye to make sure that happened.

"As for Kingshurst itself, a full investigation has been ordered. It is apparent that over the years, they have been much more concerned about hushing up scandals and protecting their reputation than digging too deeply into any misdeeds committed on their campus. Clarissa MacLeod isn't too happy about it, but she's cooperating fully, at least for the moment."

"How is Clarissa?" Hannah asked. Last we had seen her, she'd been in the hospital recovering from a vicious stabbing at the hands of her own sister.

"She's fully healed and ensconced in MacLeod Manor once again. She even deigned to add her signature to these commendations for both of you, in recognition of your service to Clan Rioghalachd," Catriona said. She extracted two pieces of parchment from the folder, which she slid across the tabletop. They were written in calligraphy, with the Clan Rioghalachd seal on them, stamped in purple wax.

"Wow. That's… unexpected," I managed to say.

"Too right it is," Catriona agreed. "Not to say you don't deserve them, of course. But Clarissa knows she put herself in some hot water with Celeste after the way she treated you both. I think this might be her way of trying to smooth things over. And I hear she's coming to the wedding. Another olive branch, no doubt."

I turned to stare at Hannah. "Clarissa is invited to your wedding?" I asked, my voice rising an octave in my surprise.

Hannah shrugged. "It's tradition. All the Council Clans are invited. That's politics. And before you ask, yes, Karen gave me the option, and yes, I declined it. I don't want my wedding to make clan relations worse. If this can be a way for people to… to come together and maybe even make peace with each other, then that's what I want."

To me, this sounded like an invitation to drama, and I opened my mouth to say so, but Catriona interrupted me.

"Look, can the two of you debate the guest list later? None of this is why I asked you here in the first place," she said, a snap in her voice. "In fact, this isn't Tracker business at all, not officially. Shut that door, will you?"

Hannah looked startled but got up, shut the door to Catriona's office, and hurried back to her seat. Her face was already creased with concern.

"What's going on?" I asked.

Catriona hesitated, tapping her pencil against her desk before finally tossing it aside. "This... incident may not even be an incident. I'm not really sure what to make of it yet. But do you remember when you were at Skye looking for documentation on Alasdair MacLeod and you met a Scribe named Polly Keener?"

"Yes, of course I remember Polly," Hannah said, sitting up a little straighter in her chair.

"I... who?" I asked.

Hannah turned to me, frowning. "You don't remember?"

"Hannah, you stayed at Skye, not me," I said defensively.

"But you met Polly, too. She was the one who came out to greet us, remember?"

The memory clunked into place. The name hadn't rung any bells, but now that Hannah mentioned it, I could picture her. She was the Head Scribe at the Skye archive. She'd been a cheerful little woman, very enthusiastic about meeting us.

"Okay, yes, I remember now. What about her?" I asked.

"Well... she's missing," Catriona said.

"How can she... what do you mean, missing?" Hannah demanded.

"I mean, we can't find the woman, which is profoundly strange, because she practically never leaves the island, hasn't in years."

"Start from the beginning," I said, leaning forward now.

"Polly Keener lives on Skye, in the village of Portree. She lives alone. She has never been married and has no children, nor any close relatives that live on Skye, though she has a brother and a niece in Inverness whom she visits a few times a year for holidays and the like. But apparently, she calls them religiously every Sunday evening, and this past week, she failed to do so. Worried, her brother phoned her workplace the next day and discovered she hadn't been to work in a week."

"But surely she... I've never seen someone so dedicated to their job," Hannah said. "Do you mean to tell me she didn't show up for a whole week and no one at the archive was worried about her?"

"That was my first question as well, but as it turns out, she had sent an email explaining that she had the flu, and she would be back in when she was feeling better, along with some instructions for some of the ongoing projects she was overseeing," Catriona said. "A week wasn't an unreasonable amount of time for someone to miss work when they've contracted an illness like the flu."

"Yeah, I guess so. So what happened after the brother called?" I asked.

"Naturally, they worried her illness might have taken a turn for the worse, and so they sent a Caomhnóir over to her house to check on her. The door was locked, the windows secured, and no one answered their knocks. They forced entry and found the place to be in order, but with no sign of Polly herself."

"Is it possible she did become ill and took herself to the hospital or something?" Hannah asked. She had begun wringing her hands in her lap.

"The Caomhnóir spoke to her neighbors. Her car had not left its parking spot in front of the house, and there had been no ambulance that anyone had seen. They visited the local hospital, and she hadn't been seen or admitted. The local chemist was also questioned, and she hadn't been in for so much as some paracetamol or a cough drop."

"What the hell?" I muttered.

"Our thoughts exactly," Catriona said.

"Was anything missing from her house?" I asked.

"Yes. Her laptop, several notebooks, and all of the materials she had signed out of the archive. All of the rest of her possessions—keys, wallet, phone, clothing, everything else seemed to be accounted for, as far as anyone could tell."

"Cat, you said this isn't a Tracker matter. I've met the woman once for all of thirty seconds, and Hannah spent a few days in the same building as her. So why did you feel the need to let us know about this?"

Catriona opened her mouth to reply, but it was Hannah who answered.

"Because she was researching us."

I turned to stare at her. "What do you mean, she was researching us?"

Hannah met my gaze, eyes wide. "She was the historian for our clan, Jess. Do you remember, when she introduced herself, that she was all excited for the chance to ask us questions?"

Again, my brain grudgingly dragged up the memory. "That's right. And I told her I couldn't stay, and then you offered to speak with her."

Hannah nodded. Her expression was very troubled now, creased in places that made her look much older than she was. I turned my attention back to Catriona, who was frowning as well.

"So this Polly woman disappeared without a trace, and the only things she brought with her were a bunch of documents about us?"

Catriona pointed a finger at my face. "There it is. That's the urgency I was looking for. Are we on the same page now?"

"Yeah," I said, feeling a little dazed. "Yeah, I… do you know exactly what the project was she was working on?"

"I do," Hannah said. "It was meant to be a comprehensive history of our clan. She was excited to speak to us specifically about the Reckoning."

Anxiety twisted in the pit of my stomach. "What are we doing to find her?" I asked.

"*We* aren't doing anything," Catriona said. "As I said, this isn't strictly a Tracker case. The Caomhnóir at Skye are working to locate Polly. But given the nature of her project, I thought it right that you should know. I'll keep you posted on any developments. And it's possible someone from Skye may get in touch with you, so I wanted to give you a heads up."

Catriona nodded her head toward the door, which meant we were dismissed. Hannah and I stood up and made our way back through the maze of desks and filing cabinets in silence. It wasn't until we had left the Trackers department behind us and stood in the deserted hallway once again that Hannah spoke.

"Are you… do you feel as uneasy about this as I do?" she asked.

I looked into her eyes, clouded with worry, and knew she must be seeing the same thing in mine.

"I think so, yeah."

4

DESTROYED

"What do you think—" I began, but Hannah held up a hand.

"Let's not talk about this here," she said, glancing at her watch. "Classes are about to end, and this hallway is about to be packed. Go see Fiona. We can talk about this when we get home."

I wanted to argue, but her expression was so anxious that I didn't bother. I gave her hand a quick squeeze and we parted ways, her for the Council chambers and me to make the long walk up to Fiona's tower.

"I really need to do more cardio," I muttered to myself as I huffed and puffed my way up the endless spiral staircase. Why didn't the Trackers have some kind of physical training regimen, like the Caomhnóir did? We found ourselves running for our lives at least as often. Shouldn't we all be better prepared? And then I remembered that if Catriona had tried to implement something like that, I one hundred percent would not participate, and she'd probably have to fire me. Apparently, danger would have to continue to be my prime motivation for physical exertion. I reached the top of the stairs at last and promptly tripped over something sticking out into the doorway.

I let out a string of expletives and crashed to the hard stone floor as the thing I tripped over yelped in surprise. I twisted painfully around to find myself staring into the startled face of Gemma Dawson.

"Gemma! What the hell?"

"Jess! What are you doing here?"

Her question was more fair than mine, as mine was more curse than question, but I took a moment before answering it to assess the physical damage. I was pretty sure I'd have a massive bruise on my left knee, and I'd scraped up my elbow, but other than that, it seemed I would survive. Gemma had scrambled to her feet and extended a hand to help me up.

"Jess, I'm so sorry! I didn't—"

"It's fine. No harm done. Well, minimal harm done," I said with a rueful smile, though internally I was already thinking of Milo and his reaction when he realized I might still have a scabby elbow for the wedding day.

"I'm so sorry," she repeated.

"What are you doing, sitting out here?" I asked. I looked around the small, circular landing, but it was deserted other than Gemma's sketchpad and pencils scattered on the floor.

"I'm… well, I'm supposed to be…but…" She glanced nervously toward Fiona's door as she struggled for the words.

"Oh. I see. What did she throw?" I asked.

Gemma grimaced. "A paint can. It wasn't empty, either." She gestured to her jeans, which were covered with yellow spatter.

I sighed. I'd been the one to suggest that Gemma help Fiona with her work at Fairhaven. I'd been Gemma's mentor last year when she came to Fairhaven for her first year as an Apprentice. We'd been matched up because she was a Muse like me and… well, because Fiona was Fiona, and pairing a girl like Gemma with a woman like Fiona was akin to throwing the poor kid to the wolves. And now here I was, realizing that I'd subsequently done just that.

"What are you doing here?" Gemma asked.

"Celeste asked me to come up and talk to her. Apparently, she's concerned," I said.

Gemma's face crumpled with relief. "Would you? I'm not really sure what to do anymore. Another day or two and I probably would have called you myself."

"That bad, huh?"

"Yes, I'm afraid so."

"Before I attempt to go in there, can you give me a little more information?" I asked, starting to feel even more nervous than I usually did when attempting to interact with Fiona.

Gemma's face folded into a frown. "Well, it's all very odd. It started with a sculpture she was working on. She seemed to be getting frustrated with it, but of course, as I'm not a sculptor, there wasn't anything I could do to help. After a few days, I walked in to find she had smashed it to bits and had started on a new one."

"Oh," I said. "Is that all?"

"She's done it three times now," Gemma said in a very small voice.

"Hmmm." I considered this. Frustration was a normal part of the artistic process, and with a temper like Fiona's, it didn't seem so very strange that she'd get this way when she was working on a new project, particularly when considering the fact that she'd recently gone very nearly blind.

"Okay, thanks, Gemma," I said. "Wish me luck."

"Good luck," Gemma whispered. "Shall I—?" She gestured toward the door.

"No, stay out of the line of fire. In fact," I looked at my watch, "go take a break and get yourself a late lunch. I'm sure the dining hall is still open. Give me a little time with her."

Gemma sagged with relief. "Right. See you soon."

I watched her go, still feeling guilty. Then I took a deep breath, steeled myself, and pushed open Fiona's door.

"Holy *shit*."

Fiona's studio was always fairly disastrous, but this was next level. The place looked like it had been ransacked. The shelves I had so carefully organized and labeled for her were practically empty, their contents strewn all over the floor. The walls and floor looked like an unintentional Jackson Pollock painting. Fiona's desk was littered with old food, cigarette butts, and hunks of plaster. In fact, whole sections of the room were so heavily coated in plaster dust that it looked like spontaneous tiny snow squalls had somehow formed inside the tower.

I had about ten seconds to take all of this in before a can of spray paint whizzed past my head and clanged against the stone wall behind me.

"Oi! I told you to get out of here and let me get to work!" came a vicious bark from behind a curtained work space.

"Throw one more thing at me, Fiona, and I will throw it right back, and I promise you I will not miss!" I shouted back.

There was a three-second silence, and then a much more subdued voice said, "Jess?"

"Yes."

I waited. A moment later, Fiona poked her head through the curtain.

Her face was streaked with plaster dust and looked a decade older than the last time I'd seen her. Purple crescents sat under her eyes, which were bloodshot and drooping. Her skin seemed to sag off her bones like she'd lost weight, and her complexion was almost yellow. I suppressed a gasp at her appearance.

"What are you doing here?" she asked.

"Entering a war zone, apparently," I said. "What the hell is going on?"

Fiona pressed her lips together. "I'm working."

"Is that what you call it? Because from where I'm standing it looks like you're crashing out on some month-long rage-fueled bender and taking your whole studio with you," I said. If Hannah had been here, she would have been horrified at my tone, but I knew Fiona. Sympathy and tact bounced right off her.

She didn't answer, which I took as tacit agreement. Instead, she snorted and disappeared behind the curtain again.

"Hey! I'm still talking to you!" I called.

"No one's stopping you! So talk!" she called back.

Feeling my own temper rise, I stormed across the room, kicking debris out of my way as I went. I hesitated, though, as I approached the curtain.

"Fiona, what's going on?" I asked.

"I'm working," she repeated.

"No, I mean what's going on with you? What's wrong?"

"What's wrong?" she replied, her words sounding like she was squeezing them through tightly gritted teeth. "I have a project that needs doing, and no one will let me get on with it!"

"Fiona, Gemma is literally here to help take other things off your plate so that you can get on with it," I said. "Why are you punishing her?"

"She keeps interrupting me."

"You mean the way Celeste keeps interrupting you?" I asked. "You've stopped going to Council meetings. Why?"

"This is more important," came the terse reply.

"Look, I get it," I said. "Just when I think I might be able to get back to my actual life, Tracker shit keeps blowing up in my face. I couldn't even tell you the last time I was able to create for the sake of creating. But you know what's at stake in the Council right now. You know that Celeste is battling for her life out there, trying to keep things from descending into chaos. She needs you there."

"No. She needs me here."

I paused, confused. "What does that mean?"

"It means what I said. She needs me here."

"You're not making sense!"

"That's exactly what I'm doing! Trying to... to make sense..."

My frustration finally peaked. "Fiona, would you please just talk to me? This is ridiculous, I'm not yelling through this curtain anymore!" I reached out and grabbed the folds of tattered purple velvet, preparing to pull it back.

"LEAVE IT ALONE!"

I leaped back as Fiona barreled through the curtains, shoving against me with her shoulder so that I stumbled backward and fell hard on my backside. She turned and clawed at the curtains, seemingly desperate to ensure they remained closed. But in her panic, the curtains parted, and I caught a glimpse of what was behind them.

It was the beginning of a sculpture, only the very top of it starting to form into whatever the final shape would become. And whatever—or whoever—it would become stared right back at me before the fabric swung closed again. The face, rough though it was, looked vaguely familiar.

"Who are you—?"

"I SAID LEAVE IT ALONE!"

I stared at Fiona, my mind stunned into complete blankness as she practically gasped for breath, hands still clinging to the curtains behind her like they were the only things keeping her from collapsing on the floor right beside me. The blankness stretched on, and then suddenly, it felt like my mind was racing at a hundred miles an hour, and I could only catch at tiny fragments of the thoughts as they flashed past me. I didn't really understand what was happening, but I knew there were places in Fiona no one could reach. This—whatever it was—was buried deep in one of those places. I couldn't touch it, not unless she wanted me to. I'd seen her get obsessive over her work before, but this... this was beyond that. This wasn't inspiration or even frustration. I didn't know what it was, but I knew she was letting it consume her, and I couldn't just stand by and let that happen.

"Okay." I made my voice flat. Calm. "You don't want me in there. Fine. You don't want to show it to me. Great. But I still need to talk to you, and you are going to stand there and listen to me, or so help me God, Fiona, you will not be the only person in this room throwing things and shoving people."

She stood there silent, nostrils flaring repeatedly like gills on a fish. I waited.

"Fine."

"You have to go to the Council meetings. They're going to kick you out, and I know you don't care about that, but Celeste needs you there. I don't care if you shower, eat, sleep, or change your goddamn underwear. But you are going to go to those meetings because you know what will happen if Celeste doesn't have the support she needs in that room."

Fiona chewed the inside of her cheek furiously. Finally, she nodded once.

"Whatever this is has nothing to do with Gemma, and she is not your punching bag. You don't get to punish her for existing while you go through whatever the hell this is. So I am going to walk around this room now and make a list of things for her to do that don't require her going behind that curtain, including cleaning this place up, and you are going to let her; because if you don't, the next person who ventures up here is going to take one look around and have you carted off to a facility somewhere, and while I should probably let them, I'm going to try this first."

She bristled and snorted.

"Fiona."

A second curt nod.

I stood up, dusted myself off, and moved to the desk. "Is the desk off limits?" I asked.

She shook her head.

I dug around in the debris until I found some paper and a pencil that hadn't been chewed within an inch of its life. Then I unearthed the in-tray where I knew Fiona usually kept any files on ongoing projects around Fairhaven. For the next few minutes, I worked in silence except to ask a few questions here and there about whether certain projects had been completed or not. I kept it simple: cataloguing and organizing tasks I knew Gemma could handle without having to consult Fiona about them. I set aside anything involving restoration or deeper knowledge of gallery practices. When I finished, I read it out loud to Fiona. She listened without comment and then finally shrugged.

"That'll do," she grunted.

"Great." I folded up the list and put it in my pocket. Then I walked over to her and put a hand carefully on her shoulder. I took it as a good sign that she didn't shake it off.

"I won't pretend to know what's going on with you, but I want you to know that I'm here to help when you're ready to tell someone about it. I won't push you, because we both know there'd be no point. But I am going to check in on you, Fiona, and if I find you in a state like this again, I won't give you a choice."

Her lower lip trembled. For half a second, I thought she was going to burst into speech or, worse, tears. But she did neither. She pulled herself up and nodded again.

"Fine."

"Good. Now go take a bath or something. You smell like a goddamn locker room at a football club."

5

CORRESPONDENCE

I walked out of Fiona's office and found that my hands were shaking. I stopped on the stairs and sat down just in time, because my legs suddenly felt like they'd turned to water.

What the actual hell had just happened?

Everybody who had ever met Fiona and lived to tell the tale knew she was unpredictable, ornery, and utterly immune to social pressure. She was also a disaster—messy, disorganized, and generally scatter-brained. But she was always fully in control of herself, and she never let her quirks or temper get in the way of what was most important. Even when she was my mentor—a job she could not have wanted less—she did it. Grudgingly, erratically, but she did it. She had been there for me, in her own way, and I felt that we had forged a bond all the stronger because of the resistance she felt to forging a bond with anyone at all. Now I wondered if that bond would be enough to save her from whatever it was she was struggling with, because if I knew anything sitting there on those tower steps, it was that Fiona was struggling.

Fiona didn't confide in people. She didn't coddle them. Hell, she barely tolerated them. But in a crisis, she'd always come through for me, and I would do the same for her, even if she fought me every step of the way—and she undoubtedly would. Tough love was the only kind she knew how to give. It was also, in my experience, the only kind she knew how to accept, and so I had given it to her. I wouldn't abandon her to… whatever the hell was happening with her right now. I wouldn't let it consume her. If I had to check on her every day, I would do that, until she remembered that she could trust me, and then maybe—just maybe—she would let me in. Until then, I'd have to keep breaking down the door.

I stood up as my resolve made its way down to my feet, and I took a deep breath, feeling a little steadier. I would keep an eye on her. She would come back to Council meetings. Gemma would stay out of her way. She would work through whatever was consuming her. It would be okay. Because, as irritable and impossible as she was, I needed Fiona to be okay.

I made my way down to the nearly deserted dining room, where Gemma was eating. She stood up when she saw me, her fork clattering to the table, but I smiled at her, and her whole body seemed to relax.

"You're okay!" she said. She sounded surprised.

"What did you think she was going to do, throw me from the turret?"

"Something of that sort, yes."

I chuckled. "Well, I'm fine. And I hope Fiona will be, too. I got her to agree to a few ground rules while she works through…whatever this is—the major one being that she leaves you alone."

Gemma bit her lip. "But I'm supposed to help her."

"And that's not supposed to be a suicide mission, Gemma," I reminded her. "But you can still help her. Here." I handed her the list. "All of it needs to be done, and all of it keeps you out of her way."

"But who will—"

"She's not your responsibility. She's not really mine either, but let me worry about that."

"Thank you," Gemma said, her expression clearing. She glanced over the list and then nodded. "Oh yes, I can do all of this. And you'll be…?"

"I'll be checking in on her. Try to focus on these tasks and your school work, okay?"

"Sure, but I will. Thanks, Jess."

I decided I didn't have the energy to ascend yet another tower today, so updating Celeste would have to wait. Hannah had Council meetings later that week—she could pass my message on to Celeste then. I decided to pop down to see Savvy before I left Fairhaven for home. I found her in her office in one of the barracks buildings.

"Hey Sav."

Savvy looked up from her pile of folders and grinned at me. "What are you doing here? I thought the plan was to stay in London for the day?"

"It was," I said, "but Finn called and I was summoned to the castle."

"By who, then?"

"By Catriona. And then I ran into Celeste on the way." I sat on the corner of the desk and, after a quick look around to make sure we were definitely alone, I filled Savvy in on both situations. Her generally cheerful expression gradually dimmed, a cloud passing over the sun.

"That's right odd, innit?" she murmured to herself.

I snorted. "Not overly. Fiona has always had manic episodes. It's probably just—"

"Naw, mate, I don't mean Fiona. I mean, keep an eye on her, sure, but no. I was thinking about that Keener woman."

I blinked. "Really?"

"Disappeared without a trace, and her the Head Scribe?" Savvy said. "I don't like to think about the kind of information she must have in that head of hers."

I bit my lip. "I hadn't really... you mean, you think maybe the Necromancers are involved? They haven't exactly been particularly active lately." The Reckoning had taken down most of what remained of their power structure, after all.

"Exactly. Too quiet by half. Ain't you ever babysat before?"

"I... actually, no, not much," I admitted.

"Well, I spent half my life in charge of my younger siblings, and I can tell you, it's when they're unusually quiet that you're in real trouble," Savvy said, tapping her pencil on the desk in an agitated sort of way. "Did Catriona put you on the case, then?"

I shook my head. "She said it wasn't a Trackers matter, at least not yet. She said the Caomhnóir are handling it for right now."

"Huh. I might talk to Finn. See if I can get assigned."

"Really? All the way up to Skye?" The príosún was incredibly remote.

"Yeah. Not permanently, but I reckon if I say I've taken an interest, they might let me—"

At that moment, the door burst open and Rana came flying in. She bounded up to us, waving around a piece of paper she had clutched in her hand, and promptly threw herself into Savvy's arms.

"I just got my final qualifying marks! No more probationary period! I am a fully-fledged Caomhnóir now!" she crowed.

"Babe, that's brilliant!" Savvy shouted, picking Rana up and swinging her around several times before kissing her. "Well done, I knew you'd pass!"

"I'm glad you did, because I wasn't sure at all," Rana said, pink-cheeked and grinning from the enthusiastic PDA. "Half the instructors didn't even want to teach me, let alone pass me."

"And you gave 'em no bloody choice!" Savvy crowed, and then almost at once her face fell. "Hang on. Does that mean you know where you've been assigned, then?"

Rana's grin broadened even further. "Looks like you're stuck with me, Todd. I'm on the Fairhaven security detail."

The answering kiss was so long this time that I had to clear my throat before they broke apart.

"Sorry," Rana gasped, beet-red now.

"It's fine, I just want my turn," I laughed, and pulled her in for a hug. "Congratulations."

"Thanks. It's a relief, to be sure. I'm glad it won't be hanging over my head anymore."

"Yeah, you've been a real moper, you have," Savvy said, nudging her playfully with her elbow.

Rana narrowed her eyes at Savvy. "Yeah, because I'm sure you were a right barrel of laughs when you went through your qualifying tests."

Sav flashed her blinding smile. "A right ray of sunshine, as always," she said, crossing her heart and giving what might have been a Girl Guide salute.

"Well, I'll leave you two lovebirds to celebrate," I said, hopping down off the desk.

"Oi, don't go, I've got a bone to pick with you," Savvy said.

"Me? Why?" I asked.

Savvy crossed her arms, all traces of sunshine gone. "What's this I hear about the hen party?"

"The... huh?"

"She means the bachelorette party," Rana whispered.

"Oh right," I said. I might have lived in England now, but the turns of phrase still caught me off guard occasionally. "What bachelorette party?"

"Exactly!" Savvy shouted, throwing her hands up in frustration. "You mean to tell me your only sister—your twin, no less—is getting married and you haven't even planned her a do?"

"I asked her, she doesn't want one!" I said, taking an involuntary step back from the storm now brewing on Savvy's face.

"Of course she wants one!" she cried. "Every bride wants one! You can't get married and not have a proper send off!"

"Savvy, she literally told me she doesn't want—"

"She just doesn't want anyone going to any trouble for her. She doesn't want you to spend money and make a fuss. But blast it all, she deserves a fuss!"

"Of course she does! I'm just... Sav, I'm trying to do what she asked me to do."

Savvy stepped forward and placed a hand on each of my shoulders. "Jess, sometimes you have to accept that people don't know what they want."

"...Do I?"

"Yes."

I glanced at Rana. She raised her hands in the air as though to say, "Don't look at me, I'm just the girlfriend."

But Savvy saw my glance and dragged Rana right into it. "Rana, love, the other day, when I was on my way back from town, I rang you and asked if you wanted me to bring you food."

Rana looked startled. "Uh... yeah, you did."

"And what did you say?"

"I said I didn't need anything because I'd already eaten."

"And what did I do?"

Rana cracked a little smile. "You brought me some anyway."

"And how was it?" And before Rana could answer, Savvy held up a finger to silence her. "I'll tell you how it was, Jess. It was abso-bloody-lutely delicious, and you know why? Because she wasn't expecting it."

"I'm... failing to understand how this is the same thing."

"I didn't bring her a full-on meal, right? Just a little sweet treat. Because even though she'd already eaten, she still deserved it. And because I got it for her anyway, that made it even better than if she'd asked for it." Savvy stepped back, crossing her arms over her chest with an almost smug expression, like she'd just solved a deep mystery of the universe.

"So," I began slowly, "you're saying I should throw her a hen party, even though she specifically told me she didn't want a hen party?"

"Bingo."

I bit my lip. "Sav, you have to realize, no one is listening to her. Milo, Karen, this entire wedding has become something that is just sort of... happening to her. I don't want to add to that stress."

"No, no, I'm not talking about the kind of hen party I'd plan," Savvy said quickly. "I wouldn't let Hannah within a hundred meters of the shenanigan-fest that is a Savannah Todd hen party. Utter debauchery. Baked in misdemeanors at minimum. Not a bloody chance."

Rana cleared her throat and raised an eyebrow.

Savvy turned to her with a spectacular roll of the eyes. "Oh, come off it. Like you didn't know what you were getting into."

"Okay, so... what are you talking about then?" I asked.

"I'm talking about one of them posh ladies' nights, yeah? Brunch, fruity cocktails, spa day, that sort of thing. Just something to make her feel special. All this nonsense with the wedding is all the more reason to remind her that she's the bride and this is her time to feel special."

"Sav, that's... wow, you're right."

"And maybe just one lap dance, for a laugh."

"SAVANNAH."

"All right, all right, only joking," she said with a cheeky grin. "So?"

I sighed, recognizing defeat. "So, I guess I should start planning."

Rana and Savvy grinned at each other. "We'll help," Rana promised.

Kieran was working in the library at Fairhaven that day, and since Hannah wanted to wait for him to be finished with his shift, I took the car back to our cottage. When we'd bought it, I'd asked what the name was, and the realtor had told me it didn't have one. At first, I was disappointed about this. As an avid reader of Brit lit growing up, I'd gotten used to all my favorite locales having their own quaint and charming names. But then Finn had leaned over and whispered in my ear. "That just means we get to name it ourselves, love."

This idea sparked a frenzied hunt for the perfect name, which I had still not hit upon, much to my chagrin. I was an artist, but words were not my medium of choice. In fact, I found myself babbling and stumbling my way through basic conversations more often than I cared to admit.

"You can't rush these things," Finn told me soothingly, and he knew what he was talking about. As a poet himself, he knew the deep thought and consideration that came with crafting just the right turn of phrase. "I think the right name will strike you like lightning one day, and you'll just know." He refused to help or offer suggestions, claiming it was important, now that I'd set out to name the cottage, that I follow through.

"It is both of ours, you know," I said.

"Yes, but you've determined it must have a name. Nothing I pick will be quite right, I suspect. You're putting down roots for the first time. The naming should be yours."

The thought of jointly owning property made me feel mildly panicky, but it was the kind of panic that looked like giddiness in the right light. In other words, I knew we were doing the right thing, but I was sure I wouldn't feel totally settled until the universe sent me just the right name for the cottage.

When I got back, I stood out front for a few moments, staring at it from the chimney to the roses climbing riotously around the door.

"Damn it," I muttered, and made my way inside.

I nearly slipped on a pile of mail scattered across the doormat inside. It had been a couple of days since we'd been back, having stayed the last couple of nights at Karen's flat in London so that she could drag us around to wedding vendors, finalizing all the details. I scooped up the mail without looking at it, dropped it on the entryway table to deal with later, and went upstairs to shower and change into some comfy sweats and one of Finn's t-shirts. Then I meandered my way down to the kitchen in the back, where I rooted around through the fridge for something to eat. Living in a village was definitely going to take some getting used to—no one had ever taught me to cook properly. Like any other latchkey kid, I knew how to make eggs and boil pasta without burning the house down, but I was used to easy access to takeout. The food at the local pub was good, but I couldn't eat there every night, so I pulled out a saucepan from the cabinet and a box of penne, and a jar of sauce from the pantry and set to work. I also dug some garlic bread out of the freezer. By the time I'd finished eating, Finn was walking in the door looking a bit disgruntled.

"Any more of that?" he asked, slinging off his bag and tossing it on a chair. "I'm famished."

"Yeah, I made a whole box. Want me to warm some up for you? You look a bit—"

"Traumatized?"

I laughed as I scooped pasta into a second bowl and dumped some sauce on top. "I was going to say tired, but sure. Traumatized works. Was the fitting that bad?"

"I'm more than willing to wear a tux," Finn said, raising his hands in surrender. "But what's wrong with something off the rack and well-tailored? For Kiernan, sure, he's the man of the hour. But it's not as though I'm getting married."

Heat crept up my neck to color my cheeks. I had once stumbled upon an engagement ring among Finn's possessions, and basically imploded before finding out he'd only been holding onto it for Kiernan. The memory still made me cringe with embarrassment. I shoved the bowl of pasta into the microwave to heat up and popped another piece of garlic bread in the toaster oven as I answered.

"You know Milo. If the event's got his name on it, he has to micromanage every detail. It's kind of his thing. Besides, you're going to be standing up there beside Kiernan. You've got to look the part."

He sighed. "I suppose."

"Anyway, I'm sure you saw what I'm wearing. You're not the only one who's going to suffer."

"Actually, I haven't seen what you're going to wear," Finn corrected me.

"What? Why not? It was hanging right on the dress form in plain view when I left," I said.

Finn shrugged. "I tried. He wouldn't let me."

I whirled around, looking indignant. "What do you mean, he wouldn't let you? I'm not the bride, for godssake. It's not like there are weird superstitious rules about people seeing a bridesmaid's dress before the wedding!"

Finn shrugged. "All I know is that I asked to see it and was told, in no uncertain terms, that I was not allowed anywhere near your dress until the wedding day."

"That's ridiculous. You should have demanded to see it."

Finn smiled. "I don't mind being surprised, love. And besides, are you suggesting I pick a fight with a ghost holding pins?"

"I guess not," I grumbled, and pulled the pasta from the microwave and the bread from the toaster, plunking it all down in front of him on the kitchen island before sliding into my seat again across from him. He wasted no time devouring a forkful.

"Oh, that is gorgeous," he groaned, digging in again.

I laughed. "It's boxed pasta and jarred sauce, Finn."

"I'm a man of simple tastes."

I stole a noodle and popped it into my mouth. "Good thing, because that's the extent of my cooking skills."

I looked up to see that he was watching me closely.

"Something's off. You look troubled. Has something happened, or is it merely wedding stress?" he asked.

I sighed. "Honestly? It's been kind of a day, but I was going to let you finish eating before I dumped it all on you."

"How about we talk and eat?" he suggested. "Because now I'm curious."

So while he shoveled down his pasta, I told him about Fiona and my meeting with Catriona.

"Blimey," he said, setting his fork down. "I feel a bit of a prat now, complaining about the suit fitting."

"Don't. That's its own form of torture," I assured him.

"Let's start with Fiona. You're worried, I can see, but it doesn't sound too off the mark for her. Perhaps she's simply overwhelmed with frustration? She's an artist who's lost nearly all of her sight. I can't imagine there are many things harder than that."

I shook my head. "I've seen her frustrated. This is more than that. She seemed edgy. Almost…"

"Almost?" Finn prompted.

"Almost frightened," I finished.

Finn sat with that, mulling it over, his heavy brows pulled together over his dark eyes. "Hmm. Well, if she won't confide in you yet, I'm not sure there's much you can do but ride it out. I don't think anyone has ever managed to get as close to Fiona as you are."

I snorted. "Close" was a relative term with Fiona, but he was right. I was definitely one of the rare people who'd even had a glimpse behind her walls, and even those were hard-won and grudgingly granted.

"Now, this matter of Polly Keener," Finn went on. "What does Hannah think? She knows her better than you do."

"We haven't really had a chance to discuss it yet," I said.

"But you're concerned."

"A bit, yeah. Catriona said that not only was she missing, but all the materials she had checked out from the archive were missing as well. Materials pertaining to our clan."

"Yes, I can see why that would be worrying," Finn said, tapping his fork against his lips. "I don't like it much myself, if I'm honest. What do you say I use my Caomhnóir connections at Skye to dig around a bit, see what I can find out?"

I felt the knot in my chest loosen. "Would you?"

"Of course, love."

I leaned across the island and kissed him. "Thank you. It might be nothing—or at least, nothing we need to concern ourselves with. But I'd feel better knowing for sure."

"I could do with another one of those," he said.

"The pasta?"

"The kiss."

"In spite of our mutual garlic breath, your wish is my command," I whispered and kissed him again, longer this time.

A loud bang caused us to jump apart. We both leaped up from our seats in time to see Hannah flying through the front door and skidding to a stop in the kitchen entryway. Her face was starkly white, and her eyes were huge and dark.

"She sent me a letter!"

"Who—"

"I got home and it was just sitting there on the doormat!"

"Hannah, who are you—"

"What do we do? Do I open it? Oh God, should I even have touched it? Did I, like... contaminate it with my fingerprints? What should I—"

But I had finally made it around the kitchen island to stand in front of her. I took her face into my hands and forced her to look at me.

"Hannah, stop. Calm down. Who sent you a letter? Who was it?"

Hannah swallowed hard, her eyes bright with unshed tears.

"Polly Keener," she whispered.

6

A CRY FOR HELP

Hannah's words felt like a slap in the face. All I could do was stare at her. Luckily, Finn found his voice after only a moment.

"Hannah, have you brought it with you?" he asked, but Hannah was already holding it out toward him like it might burst into flames at any moment.

"Should we be touching it?" she asked.

"It's been through the postal service, Hannah. Fingerprints are not what we should be concerned with right now," Finn said. Regardless of this assertion, though, he took it from her carefully, handling it as little as possible, and placed it on the kitchen island. He pulled his knife from his belt clip and cleanly slit the envelope open with the blade. Then he slid the single sheet of paper inside across toward Hannah, unfolding it as he did so.

"It's not addressed to me," he said. "You read it first."

It wasn't addressed to me either, but that didn't stop me from hurrying to the island and reading it over her shoulder.

Dear Hannah,

I am sorry to reach out to you in so strange a manner, but I am afraid I don't know what else to do. Perhaps I am overreacting, and if so, we can laugh about it over a cup of tea the next time we meet, which I hope will be soon. But in case I have good cause to be cautious, I hope you will read this missive away from prying eyes, and keep its contents as secret as you see fit within even your own trusted circle.

As you are aware, I have been working on a comprehensive history of Clan

Sassanaigh for close to a decade now. It is the heart of my research career, and it has been rich and fulfilling work. I want to take the opportunity while I have it to thank you for the time you took in answering my queries and confirming certain facts with me during your most recent visit to Skye archive. Your cooperation allowed me to make tremendous progress in a very short span of time. You were very kind to me, even as you worked diligently on an unrelated matter. I will always be grateful to have spent that time with you.

In my research, I have tracked down many rare and important documents and artifacts relating to your clan. Some of them were returned to your clan, while others have been added to collections both at Skye and Fairhaven. Perhaps you have seen the tapestry of Agnes Isherwood that hangs in the gallery there? That was one of my more exciting finds, because it was a puzzle piece that helped me to complete as much of the historical picture as is possible. I have always been thrilled to make such discoveries. Until today.

I have recently stumbled upon another artifact, and now that I have found it, I cannot simply forget about it or run the risk that someone else will come upon it. I dare not give too many details in this letter, lest it go astray. But I must confess that I am wary of keeping it. I am not sure what to do next, but writing to you seemed a necessary step. I couldn't think of another way to contact you that might not be overheard or privy to discovery. Would it be too much to ask for you to come see me at Skye archive at your earliest convenience? I wouldn't ask if I didn't think it was vitally important. You needn't reply—just come as soon as you can. Nothing would make me happier than for this to be all a silly overreaction, but like many a Scribe before me, and no doubt, many a Scribe to come, I know too much history to ignore the patterns.

Come as soon as you can.

Kindest Regards,

Polly Keener

I read through the letter twice before anyone spoke. Beside me, Hannah seemed to have forgotten how to breathe.

"What does it mean?" I asked at last, breaking the very tense silence.

Hannah didn't answer. Instead, she held the letter out to Finn, whose eyes scanned over it, his expression darkening with every line.

"Hannah, when you spent time with Polly Keener, did she ever mention to you that she was looking for any kind of specific artifact or document?"

Hannah shook her head as though to clear it, and answered in a shaky voice, "No, not that I... no. She only told me that she was always searching for more information. It was one of the reasons she was so keen to speak to me. I could give her perspective on recent events that had never been recorded before."

"She didn't mention a particular event or period of Clan Sassanaigh history that she was focusing on?"

Hannah shook her head. "Her work was comprehensive. She was trying to collect whatever she could. At least, that was what she told me."

"So you have no idea what this artifact might be?" Finn pressed.

"None at all."

Finn nodded thoughtfully and then dropped his eyes to the paper again, and read it through once more in silence. Then he set the letter down and picked up the envelope.

"This was postmarked seven days ago from Portree."

"That's where she lives. Catriona told us," I said, finding my voice at last.

"How long has Polly been missing?"

"Catriona said a week. I don't know if that's exact or not. I'd have to confirm the date with her," I said.

"Well, if it is exact, then this was postmarked the very day that she was last seen."

"Do you think it's actually from her?" Hannah asked.

"I really couldn't say," Finn admitted. "What do you think?"

"The details and the tone make me think it's genuine," Hannah said. "Certainly, Kiernan was the only person who was ever privy to our discussions at Skye. I... don't know her handwriting, but it... it rings true to me."

"Hm. It would be easy enough to confirm with a simple handwriting sample," Finn said, "but even then we have no way of knowing whether she wrote it at the behest of someone else or of her own volition."

"You think someone may have forced her to write this letter?" I asked.

"As to that, I have no idea," Finn said. "I only mean that we can't rule out the possibility. But I will say this: if she sent this letter and then disappeared the next day, it seems that whatever fears she had may not have been unfounded."

"I need to sit down," Hannah said, her voice hollow. She swayed beside me, and I shot out a hand to steady her.

"Don't you go passing out on me," I said. "Over to the couch."

She stumbled her way into the living room, my hand still on her arm just in case, and sank onto the sofa, looking pale and clammy. Finn jogged over to the fridge, poured a glass of water, and brought it over to her. She took a few shaky sips and then set the glass down on the coffee table with a sigh.

"If something has happened to her, it's our fault," Hannah whispered.

"Of course it's not!" I snapped. "Hannah, we barely know that woman. Whatever she's gotten herself into, we have nothing to do with it."

"But she was researching our clan! Whatever she found, this… this artifact or whatever it is… something's happened to her because of it!"

"Now Hannah, let's not get ahead of ourselves," Finn said. "We don't have nearly enough information to jump to these kinds of conclusions. It could very well be that she's made a decision to disappear. Perhaps she thought she wasn't safe, and so took this artifact into hiding."

"But then why wouldn't she write and tell me that?" Hannah asked.

"Maybe she made the decision in haste, after she'd already written to you. Perhaps there was no time. My point is, we don't know enough, and we won't do her any good panicking before we find out more."

Finn's deep, soothing tones worked their magic on Hannah, who was now nodding slowly and attempting to get her breathing under control. When she stopped shaking, she drank some more water and ran a hand through her hair.

"I'm sorry. You're right. I'm freaking out, and it's not productive."

Finn smiled gently. "Productive, perhaps not, but certainly understandable."

"I can't just sit here waiting for the Skye Caomhnóir to investigate. I want to go to Skye and find out what's happening for myself," Hannah said, and there was now a note of steel in her voice. "Polly wrote to me. She wanted me to come. She wanted my help."

"I'll come with you," I said without hesitating. "We'll go together."

Hannah looked relieved. "Will you?"

"Of course," I said. "I'm not letting you go on your own."

"Nor am I," Finn said, chiming in just as I knew he would. "Exams and assignments are done at Fairhaven. I should have no problem getting the rest of leadership to sign off on it."

Hannah bit her lip. "What will Karen say? We're four weeks away from the wedding. Do you think she'll freak out?"

"Karen has everything under control."

"And Milo?"

"We don't have another fitting for two weeks. He has more than enough to occupy him until then," I said.

"Kiernan will want to come, too. He's going to be so upset when I tell him. He looks up to Polly Keener like a mentor."

"Where is Kiernan?" I asked. "I thought the two of you were coming home together."

"We did," Hannah said. "We were both too tired to cook, so he went to pick up a curry. I'm sure he'll be back any minute. I didn't start going through the mail until after he'd left."

"Why don't you go back next door and wait for him to get home, so you can fill him in," I suggested. "Finn and I can make the arrangements to get us to Skye."

"Okay. Oh, I don't want to break it to him," Hannah said, biting her lip.

"Would you like me to come with you?" Finn asked, taking the words right out of my mouth.

Hannah sighed. "No, it's all right. I'll do it. I'm calm now, I can handle it. It's just… it's going to be awful."

I didn't know what to say, so I just pulled my sister into a fierce hug. I felt her body relax into it, and when I finally pulled away, she had regained her usual composure.

"Eat. Talk to Kiernan. Then both of you come over, and we can go over all the arrangements," I said.

She nodded, squeezed my hand, and then made her way to the front door. It wasn't until it had shut behind her that Finn spoke again.

"You know this is quite serious, don't you?" he asked.

I felt the mask of calm and reason slip from my features at last. "Yeah. Yeah, I know."

"You met this woman too, didn't you?"

"Yes, for about thirty seconds when we dropped Hannah and Kiernan at Skye on our way to Kingshurst. Did you ever interact with her when you were at Skye?"

We didn't like to talk about that time when Durupinen law separated us, but the situation was too serious not to bring it up, however painful it was to relive.

Finn could hear the tension in my voice and reached for my hand. "No, I didn't. I heard her name, of course. I imagine I even saw her in passing. But we had no meaningful interaction. I doubt I could pick her out of a line-up, to be honest."

I hesitated. "Do you think there's any chance at all that this woman has just… gone off on holiday or something?"

"Do you?" Finn asked.

I sighed. "No."

"But just because she has vanished doesn't mean it wasn't her choice. I didn't just say that to make Hannah feel better. She may have been compelled to hide or protect this artifact—whatever it is. It's entirely possible that she simply doesn't want to be found."

"She obviously wants to talk to Hannah, though. So I guess we have to hope that we can find her," I said.

"And also that we're the only ones looking," added Finn.

We met each other's eyes, seeing our own unease reflected back to us.

"It's a bit odd," Finn said as he got up to clear his plate, "that the letter from Polly took so long to arrive. I mean, I know Skye is a bit remote, but I still would have thought—"

"We haven't been home for a couple of days, though," I reminded him. "We were staying at Karen's for wedding stuff, so the letter could have been there for... for a couple of..." My voice trailed off as I remembered the pile of mail sitting on my doormat when I'd come home.

"Jess?"

But I didn't answer. I had already turned on my heel and began running for the hallway where I'd tossed the pile of mail onto the entryway table. I started digging through, tossing bills and circulars, and catalogues left and right until...

"Finn!"

The tone of my voice was enough to send him skidding into the hall after me, tensed to fight someone. He looked confused at first to see it was only me standing there alone, until he saw what I was holding in my hands.

"She wrote to you, too." It wasn't a question.

"It's the same handwriting. The same return address," I whispered. I ripped open the envelope to find a single piece of paper inside.

Dear Jessica,

My apologies, I know we are not well acquainted, but I hope you will take the time to read this letter regardless. I have written to your sister Hannah as well, but I must admit I am anxious about the letter reaching its destination. The more I contemplate my discovery, the more anxious I become that, rather than overreacting, I may be underreacting. And so I am writing again, to you this time, as a means of ensuring this information reaches you and your sister.

In my research, I have found an artifact related to your clan that must not fall into the wrong hands. I think—I know—that it would be very dangerous, indeed, and I'm sorry to say that the number of wrong hands seems to be growing. I'm not entirely sure who I can trust, except for the two of you. Please, it is vital that you or your sister come to see me at Skye archive at your earliest convenience. I know it is a long trip, but I would not ask if I did not think it was important.

Kindest regards,
Polly Keener
Head Scribe, Skye Archive

My eyes flew so far ahead of my understanding that I had to read the letter twice before I had actually taken it in. By then, Finn had already pulled out his phone.

"Catriona?" he said, his voice heavy and dark. "We have a situation."

7

BACK TO SKYE

While Finn filled Catriona in on the letters from Polly Keener and made our travel arrangements, I took it upon myself to dive into the connection and let Milo know what was going on. The flavor of panic in my thoughts hit him before anything else, and he came barreling into my head with all the subtlety of a freight train.

"What? What is it? Is this wedding drama? My specter of a heart cannot take it, Jess." The thoughts pelted me like hailstones.

"No, the wedding is fine, this has nothing to do with the wedding."

"Thank Versace. Then what is going on? Why do you feel so—"

And like downloading a memory card, I dumped everything that had just happened into the connection, including all the wording I could remember from the letters. For a moment, my head was so empty that I thought I'd lost him.

"Milo?"

"Holy shit!" There it was, fear and anxiety and five thousand questions playing at once like a symphony of out-of-tune instruments.

"Slow it down, Milo. One question at a time."

"Right. Sorry." A moment passed while he pulled himself together, and the thoughts began to flow at a manageable pace. "So we have no idea what this artifact is?"

"No. She didn't provide any details, other than the fact that it's related to our clan and that she thinks it could be dangerous for the wrong people to get their hands on it."

"Well, that doesn't seem very—wait, what was that?"

"What was what?"

"That thought you just had? It whipped through so fast I didn't quite catch it?"

"What thought? I didn't—sorry, my mind is spinning a bit, I'm not sure—"

"You thought something about the Reckoning."

The word hit me like a two-by-four to the face, and suddenly the vague source of my anxiety, the something niggling at the corners of my thoughts came painfully into focus.

Of course. The Reckoning.

Milo listened, absorbing the rush of thought. "It has to be," he said. "Doesn't it?"

Now that he said it, I realized he was right. Why else would Polly be so worried about something from our clan falling into the wrong hands? What made our clan different from any other powerful Northern clan? We'd had High Priestesses, we'd held Council seats, we'd attained generational wealth and influence, just as so many of the others had done. As far as I knew, there were only two things that had made our clan the focus of more ridicule and outright hostility than the others: the Prophecy and the Reckoning.

The Prophecy had been no small thing, but it was over. We had ridden out that storm, and while it had been messy and bitter and frankly brutal, it was finished. I suppose there were still a few results that rankled—the changing of laws that allowed Caomhnóir and Durupinen to be in romantic relationships, for example. But that was all years ago. It didn't make sense for the Prophecy to somehow be rearing its ugly head again.

That left the Reckoning. The Reckoning had shaken up our entire world as Durupinen. It had shattered us, splintered us into factions—and those factions were still bitterly warring with each other. Wasn't Celeste worried at this very moment about being ousted? Hadn't we just had to break apart a goddamn makeshift coven because some Durupinen nepo-babies were mad that they'd have to age normally like the rest of us? For heaven's sake, the highest-ranking Durupinen of all had actually collaborated with Necromancers in order to prevent the Reckoning from coming to pass. Whatever Polly had found, whatever she was so frightened others would get their hands on, it had to be something to do with that. No other explanation made sense.

"Sorry, did you follow all that?" I asked Milo, who I'd nearly forgotten was still there.

"Yeah. And you're right. Nothing else makes sense," he replied. His anxiety was now creeping through, like a cold mist swirling in my head. "So, now this Polly person is missing? And so is whatever this artifact is?"

"Seems like it. I don't think we can leave it to the Skye Caomhnóir. Not now that we've seen these letters."

"No, sweetness, you can't. But also… you need to keep this quiet."

"What do you mean?"

"I mean don't tell anyone where you're going or what you're doing. Don't show those letters to anyone. Fly under the radar on this."

I bit my lip. "Yeah. Yeah, I think you're probably right. At least until we know more."

"You said Finn is talking to Catriona?"

"Yeah."

"Have her come up with a cover story. Have her invent something from the Tracker's end about why you're headed up there."

"Okay. Yeah, Milo, that's a good idea."

"Of course it is."

"Do me a favor and check in on Hannah? She's kind of freaking out."

"Kind of?"

"No. Absolutely unequivocally freaking out."

"I'm on it. Spirit Guide to the rescue."

I felt him pulling away, but I reached out a mental hand. "And Milo?"

"Yeah?"

"Seriously. That dress. Unfuckingbelievable."

His happiness thrummed like a song in my skull. "Thanks, sweetness. I would never let you look anything but flawless, even if you are, like, the bane of my existence generally."

"You are my favorite fake nemesis," I replied.

I hurried upstairs to find Finn, where he was still talking to Catriona on the phone. Part of me dreaded passing along Milo's warnings, mostly because I knew he was right, and Finn was always insufferable when he was feeling overprotective. But I could and would deal with that particular annoyance later. This was too important.

I found him pacing the floor in our bedroom and waved my hand to get his attention.

"Hang on, Cat," Finn said, and I launched into my explanation of Milo's suggestions.

Predictably, Finn's expression darkened, but he nodded and returned to the call. I went downstairs and tried—unsuccessfully—to distract myself with cleaning up the dishes from dinner. By the time I'd finished, Finn descended the stairs.

"Catriona is going to create a cover story—follow-up work from the Alasdair MacLeod case. She'll meet us at the helipad tomorrow morning to give us the details."

I gulped. "The helipad. Awesome."

You'd think after all the other shit I'd dealt with—possessions by maniacal ghosts, leaving my own body behind, kidnap, light torture, and facing down an Elemental—that I'd be chill about a simple helicopter ride.

You would be wrong.

However, with the help of drugs, coaxing, prodding, and a few threats, Finn, Hannah, Savvy, Kiernan, and I landed in Skye the next morning. Rana had wanted to come, but her recent assignment meant she had to stay put or risk losing her job before she even started it. Milo and Karen promised to handle the enormous wedding to-do list while we were gone for what we hoped would only be a couple of days, though Karen was not happy about it. She shifted into serious mom mode.

"Surely someone else can handle this investigation!" she'd insisted. "All of those Caomhnóir at Skye and the entire Trackers department don't have to walk down the aisle in a few short weeks!"

But Hannah and I were immovable. Polly had asked us to come, and though she was not there to receive us, we were honoring that request. In the end, Karen had no choice but to accept the situation. The fact that Milo could check in on us in real time somewhat mollified her.

Catriona's cover story for us was actually quite simple. We were to continue our investigation into Alasdair MacLeod, the same work Hannah and Kiernan were doing when they had met Polly. Our "orders" from the Trackers office meant that we had full access to the archive and all of the material in it. Kiernan's presence was particularly helpful in bolstering our position to anyone who might not have wanted us there—we'd brought our own antique documents expert, who would ensure we didn't mishandle or damage anything in our search. Personally, I was glad of his expertise. If we managed to find whatever artifact Polly had written about, we certainly wouldn't want to mess it up as a result of our ignorance. We also agreed that we would all play ignorant about Polly's disappearance.

"Vanished, you say?" Finn said to the Caomhnóir who met us at the doors and was now escorting us to the archive. "Blimey. When did that happen?"

"Last came to work a week ago," the young man replied. "She begged off sick in an email, but then the family ordered a wellness check, and she was gone."

"It's a wonder the Trackers office didn't mention that to us," Finn said, and I nodded in agreement. We'd agreed to let Finn do the talking when Polly came up, since I sucked at lying and Hannah was too emotional about the situation.

"Their office isn't handling it, at least not yet," the Caomhnóir replied. "I imagine that's why you weren't told."

It was Kiernan's turn to spin the story now. "Hmmm," he said, his brow furrowing in convincing concern. "This is going to complicate our work. Polly was the one who helped us compile our research on Alasdair. In fact, we'd asked her to keep it set aside for us."

Savvy stepped forward, throwing her hands up into the air and expelling a huff of irritation. "Well, this is a right cock-up, innit? Are you saying we came all the way here and we can't even get at the papers we need?"

Beside me, Hannah pressed her hand over her mouth to smother a smile, just as I grabbed her arm to stop myself from laughing. Savvy had begged to play a part in the initial conversation. Her bluster was impressive, if slightly overdone. I felt Finn stiffen beside me, but he managed to keep himself together. He opened his mouth to plow forward, but the Caomhnóir cut him off.

"I can talk to my superiors, see if you can get access to her office," he said, shrugging. "I don't think it should be a problem. It was already searched after Polly went missing. I think they've finished with it."

Kiernan and Finn traded a surprised look. Was this actually going to be easier than we thought?

"That'd be brilliant mate, cheers," Finn said, clapping the young Caomhnóir on the shoulder. "It'll keep us out of everyone's hair, and the quicker we can access what we need, the quicker we can head back to Fairhaven."

The young man nodded. "Just give me a minute," he said, pulling his walkie-talkie from his belt clip. He stepped a few paces away from us and began to talk to someone over the radio.

I was standing just behind Finn. He put his hand behind his back and crossed his fingers. Beside me, Hannah was trying valiantly not to hyperventilate. A few moments later, the young Caomhnóir came back, a blithe smile on his face.

"All clear," he said. "They're sending someone to unlock the office for you. Lodgings are up the stairs on the right. Here are the keys," he said, handing each of us a key on a small plastic keychain with our room number stamped on it. "Do you need me to show you up to—"

"Not necessary," Finn said with a confident wave of the hand. "I did a rotation here, so I know my way around. Thanks for your help…?" He raised his eyebrows in question.

"Enoch," the young man replied.

"Enoch. Much obliged."

Enoch smiled again, evidently glad he didn't need to escort us around the castle all day, and strode off down the corridor, whistling cheerfully.

"Well, that was easier than I expected," Finn said under his breath as Enoch disappeared around the corner.

"You can thank me later, mate," Savvy said, running a hand through her hair and looking quite pleased with herself. "I mean, we all heard that masterful line delivery, eh? I think I missed my calling. I reckon I should have been on EastEnders."

"Right well, we'll save the BAFTA award ceremony for another day, yeah?" Finn drawled.

"Seriously though, I like that bloke," Savvy said. "Did you see how he shook my hand and called me Caomhnóir Todd without a whiff of sarcasm? Class."

We let Finn take the lead and dropped our things in our rooms. Though they were not cells by any means, the rooms were stark and bare enough to serve as a constant reminder of exactly where we were.

"Let's not waste any time. Kiernan, Hannah, you know the way down?" Finn said as we all convened in the hallway again.

"Follow me," Kiernan said, and we all fell into line behind him. He walked purposefully, his characteristically open expression somewhat hardened.

I felt like I understood the meaning behind that look.

Someone had messed with the librarians, and our resident mild-mannered librarian was pissed.

8

BURNED

I'd briefly been a prisoner at Skye, and even though it was a ruse to get myself into the building under cover, I still had to suppress a shudder as we walked through the place to the archive. It wasn't only the fact that it was a prison in every sense of the word—stone walls, iron bars, desolate landscape—but also it was the knowledge of the evil this place contained. All around us as we walked calmly through hallways and down staircases were dozens, perhaps hundreds, of extraordinarily dangerous convicts who had committed atrocities against souls, both living and dead, that most people could barely conceive of, let alone perpetrate. It didn't help my overall sense of comfort and security that at least half a dozen of them had a personal grudge with me. I had to remind myself repeatedly that we weren't entering any prisoner spaces before my heart rate started behaving itself again.

In that telepathic twin way she had, Hannah knew just the moment to reach out and squeeze my hand.

"I know," she whispered. "I don't like being here either."

I wish I could say it was relief when we reached Polly's office, but the tense knot in my stomach only tightened at the sight of the brass plaque on the door bearing her name. Kiernan stepped forward and tried the door to find it had already been unlocked for us.

"Sav and I will patrol out here while you work," Finn said, glancing up and down the deserted hallway.

"You mean keep look out?" Savvy asked.

Finn frowned. "I... suppose? Means the same thing, doesn't it?"

"It just sounds better when you say it that way," Savvy said, shrugging. "Makes me feel like a spy or a baddie or something instead of just someone standing in a hallway."

"Right. I'll... bear that in mind," Finn said, taking his place by the door and doing his damnedest not to roll his eyes.

I followed Hannah and Kiernan into the office. The air felt slightly stagnant, but that was probably because of all the dusty old books and documents crammed into the space. The initial impression was that the office was a disaster, though as I looked more closely, I realized it was just very, very crowded. Every inch of wall space was covered in bookshelves, except for the far wall, which instead was covered in tiny drawers that I realized, on closer inspection, were a filing system rather like the old card catalogues libraries used to have. It didn't surprise me in the slightest that the Skye archive would be aggressively analog—after all, Durupinen were obsessed with secrecy, and computers could be hacked. In that moment, I also realized the likely reason Polly had sent us letters through the mail rather than just firing off an email. Sure, it took longer, but in some ways, it was more secure than an inbox.

On top of the card catalogue were dozens of cardboard storage boxes, meticulously labeled in what I could now recognize as Polly's handwriting. More of the boxes were stacked neatly in the corners and beside the large wooden desk, which was home to several in-trays full of folders and notebooks. Shoved up against the shelves on the opposite wall from the card catalogue was a long, narrow work table over which reading lamps arched gracefully like swans. Three rickety wooden chairs were pushed into this table, which, apart from the center of Polly's desk, was the only clear work surface in the room. The very thought of four people working in here at once made me feel claustrophobic.

"Does anything look out of place?" I asked as Hannah and Kiernan looked around.

"Not that I can tell," Hannah said slowly as she walked the perimeter of the room. She pointed to the table. "This is where Kiernan and I would work when we were here. Some of the documents we were searching were only allowed to be handled under the direct supervision of the Scribes. But it all looks the same, as far as I can see."

"Her laptop is gone, though," Kiernan said, indicating Polly's desk. "Of course, she may have just brought it home with her."

"Wait," Hannah added. "I don't see the research log."

"The what?" I asked as I pulled out one of the card catalog drawers for a look.

"The research log," Hannah said, sounding a bit nervous now. "It was this big leatherbound register where Polly recorded who used the archive and what materials they requested."

"Maybe she took that home as well?" I asked, but Kiernan shook his head.

"It wasn't her personal log. It belongs to the archive. All the Scribes use it," he said.

"Maybe the Caomhnóir took it?" I tried again. "As part of their investigation into her disappearance?"

Hannah nodded, though she was still biting nervously at her lip. "Yes. Yes, I suppose that's possible."

"Do you think it's important?" I asked.

"Well, I think it's odd that it's not here," Kiernan said. "Even Polly herself would have to keep meticulous track of the documents and artifacts she made use of, how long she had them, and when she returned them. So if she found this mysterious artifact while she was doing her research here—"

"Then she might have actually recorded it," Hannah finished.

I poked my head out into the hallway. "Hey, Finn?"

He jumped a little, looking hopeful. "Have you found something already?"

"Actually, this is about something we didn't find," I said, and quickly explained about the log.

"You want me to ask the Caomhnóir doing the investigation if they have it?" he guessed.

"Yes, but can you find a roundabout way of doing it? Say we wanted to revisit some documents that Hannah and Kiernan looked through last time? Make it sound like we need it for the Alasdair MacLeod case, okay?"

"I'm on it," he said, and then turned to Savvy. "Are you—?"

"I've got it handled, sod off with ya," Savvy said with a confident nod, and returned her attention to watching the hallway.

Just as Finn turned to go, a young woman passing in the hallway stopped in her tracks, staring at us. She was around my age, with wide, dark eyes behind gold-framed glasses and a cascade of finely braided and beaded hair draped over one shoulder. She hovered there, seemingly undecided about whether to approach us or not, and then plucked up her courage.

"Excuse me," she said. Her voice was husky with anxiety. She cleared her throat and continued. "Are you here to investigate Polly's disappearance?" She looked at all three of us in turn, but as her eyes lingered on me the longest, I was the one who answered.

"Um, no, actually. We're here to finish up some work on the Alasdair MacLeod case," I said. "But we were really sorry to hear about it. Are you one of the other Scribes here?"

The young woman nodded, wringing her hands. "My name is Abigay Campbell. I worked for Polly. And you're Jessica Ballard, aren't you? I worked a bit with your sister on compiling the MacLeod documents."

"Yeah, I am," I said, slightly surprised that she knew who I was, but thrusting out a hand to shake hers all the same. "Hannah's here, too, actually, she's—"

But Hannah had heard her name and poked her head out of the office.

"Abi! It's good to see you," she said, with a flash of a smile that faded quickly. "I'm... I was so sorry to learn about Polly. Is there still no word?"

Abi shook her head. "Not that I know of. Not that anyone has been very forthcoming. They don't want to jeopardize the investigation, I suppose, but I'm not sure why keeping all of her colleagues in the dark is helping anything. We're all terribly worried. It's not like Polly to miss even a single day of work. She hasn't missed one in the nearly ten years I've been interning and working here."

"Yes, I was impressed by her dedication even in the short time we were here," Hannah said, "but I'm sure they're doing everything they can."

An odd expression crossed Abi's face—a sort of involuntary impulse to speak which she quickly attempted to quash. For a moment, it merely looked like she had something stuck in her throat, and then she swallowed it back and nodded.

"Abi? Are you okay?" Hannah asked.

Abi darted a glance around the hallway before saying "I should probably get back to my desk. Please let me know if you need anything." Then she hurried away.

"That was... odd," I murmured.

"Yes," Hannah agreed. "But then, I'm sure she's on edge. She's one of Polly's proteges here. They work very closely together."

"I'll go see about this log, then, shall I?" Finn said, and followed Abi down the hallway.

Together, we walked back into the office. I looked down at the spot where the research log should have been, thinking. It wasn't only what we found that was important; it was also what we didn't find that might be significant, just like the log. I grabbed a pencil and a blank index card from the desk.

"Let's keep a list, all right? Anything that you notice is missing or out of place, like that log book, let's write it down."

"Good idea," Kiernan said, and then turned on the spot. "As for that artifact… good lord, where do we even start looking for something when we don't even know what that something is? If we only had a bit more to go on—even what type of object it is."

Hannah laughed, a helpless, slightly hysterical sound. "I guess we'll just have to hope that we'll know it when we see it. Somehow."

For the next two hours, Hannah and Kiernan went through Polly's office inch by inch. They pulled books from shelves, emptied drawers, checked for loose floorboards, and secret panels in the furniture. The only thing they were sure of was that the "artifact,"—whatever it was—would not be lying out in the open for anyone to stumble upon. Polly had sounded almost paranoid in her letters, which meant she would keep the artifact carefully concealed. At last, they had to conclude that she hadn't hidden it inside her office.

Kiernan looked frustrated, but Hannah only looked more determined. "Where do we go from here?" she asked.

I sighed, rubbing at my knees, which were sore from kneeling on the bare wooden floor for so long, searching through the bottom rows of books. "I don't know. Are there any other places in the archive she might have stored things?"

Hannah looked at Kiernan, who shook his head. "All the rest of the workspaces here are communal or belong to other Scribes. And as for the secured areas of the archive, Polly wasn't the only one who had access. She has two assistants who both have keys and codes. Abi is one of them."

"Do you think maybe she would have asked Abi or one of the other Scribes to keep the artifact for her, even if she didn't tell them what it was?"

"Not a chance," Hannah said. "You read those letters, Jess. She sounded paranoid. Remember the part when she said she didn't know who she could trust? I can't imagine her giving the artifact to anyone else."

"And she wouldn't have left it anywhere someone could accidentally find it," Kiernan added. "So I'm not sure even the secured areas of the archive are worth our time."

"Let's check in with Finn, then," I said. "We need to regroup and decide what our next move is."

We filed out into the hallway to find that Finn had returned from his trip down to the Caomhnóir office.

"What did you find out?" I asked at once. "About the log book?"

"They have it down in the Caomhnóir offices. It's being held as evidence for the time being, so there's no chance of getting our hands on it," Finn said, frustration etched into the creases in his brow. "How about you three? Any joy?"

"Nothing," Kiernan said, his brow equally furrowed. "She only had three items in there related to Clan Sassanaigh, and they were all commonly accessible. We've got copies of them in the Fairhaven library."

"Ah, researching the in-laws, eh?" Savvy said, grinning at Kiernan. When he didn't so much as crack a smile, she cleared her throat. "Not a joking moment, then. Right. Message received."

Finn, however, was frowning. "Seems a bit odd that she'd only have three books in there related to your clan. I mean to say, she's your official historian, isn't she? Shouldn't her office be full of books and documents on Clan Sassanaigh?"

"Actually, we've got our own small collection room. Polly's the one who curated it," Hannah said.

"We do?" I asked, startled.

"Of course," Hannah said. "And we're not the only ones. Most of the oldest, most powerful clans do. Clan MacLeod has one. We spent a lot of time in there when we worked with Polly."

"My clan has one as well," Kiernan said.

"And mine," Finn added.

I glanced over at Savvy, who was looking offended. "Oh, I see, and I'm just rubbish, I suppose."

I reached over and pinched her cheek. "No, just one of a kind, Sav."

"So then we ought to go there next, right?" Finn said. "The Clan Sassanaigh collection?"

Hannah looked doubtful. "I really don't think she would—"

"Finn's right," I said. "We've come all this way. It seems foolish not to check."

"But we'd be looking for an artifact related to your clan in... a room full of artifacts related to your clan," Kiernan said, with a bewildered sort of laugh. "How would we ever know if we located the right thing?"

"The collection must have some kind of inventory list, right?" I asked. "Maybe we would know the object by its absence?"

"Polly said she stumbled on the artifact," Hannah said. "Which makes it unlikely that it would be something that was inventoried."

"But it could have been… I don't know, hidden in something else? A document tucked in a book? Or something that had a secret compartment. It's worth a look, at least. We came all this way."

Hannah looked skeptical, but she agreed, and together we made our way down to the Clan Sassanaigh collection. It was strange—almost as strange as the vault back in London—to be surrounded by so much family history. Both Hannah and I had grown up in a virtual vacuum of information about where we came from, and to be able to see with our own eyes not only how deep and detailed and rich our family history was, but also how revered it was in the small circle of people who were allowed to know of it, was almost overwhelming. For hours, we searched and dug and opened and flipped through every item we could find, leaving dusty, exhausted, and frustrated. At last, Kiernan shut the inventory with a snap.

"That's it," he said. "Every single item is accounted for, with the exception of the five currently sitting in Polly's office. "Absolutely nothing is missing."

"Which means whatever she found wasn't inventoried at all," Hannah said, wiping a sheen of sweat from her forehead, but leaving a smudge of dust in its place.

"Well, this was a bloody waste of time," Savvy said, stretching her back and making several concerning cracking noises. "Now what?"

Even Finn was looking frustrated. "Now, I suppose we go back to our rooms and try to get some rest. Do you realize it's nearly eight o'clock and we haven't even eaten yet?"

"Oh, I promise you, I noticed," Savvy said, looking both grumpy and slightly desperate. "If we don't find some nosh soon, I'm likely to start bloody hallucinating."

Finn went off to find food while the rest of us trudged up to our rooms. Everyone looked defeated and exhausted. Savvy looked like she might actually cry from hunger. I was probably ravenous, too, but my stomach was too sick with worry and disappointment to register something as mundane as hunger. I guess I really thought that after an entire day of searching that we might have come up with something, but who was I kidding? The Caomhnóir had already gone through everything with a fine-tooth comb. If there'd been something to find, surely they'd have found it already, and we had little hope of finding out, since we were here under the pretense of an entirely different case. Before I'd stopped to consider it, my phone was out of my pocket and up to my ear.

"Jess? What's going on?" Cat's voice was sharp, though whether with anxiety or annoyance, it wasn't always easy to tell.

"Hey, Cat. We just finished searching Polly's office and the Clan Sassanaigh collection."

"And?"

"Nothing. At least, we don't think so. After all, we don't really know what we're looking for."

"I suppose. Do you need something from me?"

"I'm not sure yet. Hannah doesn't think it's worth checking any of the other archive spaces here. She's convinced Polly wouldn't stash the artifact anywhere someone could stumble on it by accident."

"And I'd wager she's right," Catriona said. "So what now?"

"I guess that's why I'm calling. What would you recommend?"

"Are you asking for my advice?"

"I guess so, yeah."

"Hang on," Cat said.

"Sorry, is there someone else there?" I asked.

"No. I just need a moment."

"For what?"

"To etch this moment into my memory. Jess Ballard, asking my advice instead of storming ahead and doing whatever she bloody well pleases. It may never happen again, and I'd like to savor it."

I rolled my eyes. "Take all the time you need."

Cat huffed out a sarcastic chuckle, but when she spoke again, her tone was sharp, and I knew she was taking me seriously. "If it were me, I'd check her house."

"What?"

"Polly's house, down in Portree. You could have a look through it, see if you turn anything up."

"Can we do that?" I asked. "Won't that look suspicious? The Caomhnóir here think we're investigating Alasdair MacLeod, not Polly's disappearance."

There was a moment's pause, and then...

"Don't tell them."

"Don't... what?"

"Get in the car. Head down to Portree for a bite to eat. Get some air. And break into a house."

A nervous bark of laughter burst from my mouth. "You're serious."

"Deadly serious."

"And if we get caught?"

"Then, surprise, you were here on a Tracker mission all along. I'll back you up."

I took a deep breath. She was right. We had to stop pretending we were just having a simple poke around.

"So?" she prompted.

"So, we're breaking and entering tomorrow."

"Excellent. Keep me posted."

The line went dead. I tossed the phone aside, somehow feeling relieved that I now had a plan to commit a crime. The irony of this was not lost on me.

There was a soft knocking on my door, and I chuckled under my breath. The psychic twin connection was very, very real sometimes. I rolled off my bed and opened the door.

"Hey Hannah, I was just gonna—"

The face staring back at me did not belong to Hannah. It belonged to Abi Campbell.

"Abi! Hey, I… what can I do for—"

But Abi didn't wait for me to finish. She slipped in through the partially open door and then spun around, her expression slightly panicked.

"Close it!" she whispered. "Please!"

Puzzled, I did as she asked, pulling the door shut behind her and then turning to face her where she stood in the middle of my room, arms crossed tightly over her chest, bouncing from foot to foot like she might take off running at any moment.

"Are you okay?" I asked her, trying to keep my voice as calm and unconcerned as I could, even as my heart thundered in my chest.

"I… I'm really sorry to just bust in like this, but I didn't want anyone to know I was up here. I didn't want anyone to see me."

"That's okay," I said. About a hundred questions were swirling around in my head, but I didn't know which was the right one to ask—she looked so skittish, like she was already half regretting walking in here in the first place. So I bit my tongue and waited for her to speak first. She paced for a moment, seeming to gather her courage, before the words tumbled out of her in a heap.

"Polly wouldn't just leave," she finally blurted out. "They keep saying not to worry, that she's probably just taken a holiday, but—"

"I know," I said. "Hannah and Kiernan said the same thing."

"I don't think they're taking it seriously," Abi said, shaking her head. "The questions they were asking me... did she have a boyfriend, was she fed up with her job, all this utter rubbish."

"Well, I would think they want to rule out all the possibilities," I said slowly, all the while wondering where she was going with this, and why she was talking to me about it. As though she could hear these silent questions, she stopped pacing and looked me dead in the face for the first time.

"I think something's happened to her."

I hesitated, unsure how to answer.

"You think so, too. That's really why you're here, isn't it?" Abi asked, the words coming out in a jumble.

I met her gaze, read the fear there, and decided in that moment to blow our cover.

"Yes, it is."

Abi dropped her face into her hands, breathing raggedly. "I knew it," she whispered. "I just knew it."

I wanted to reach out and put a hand on her shoulder or hug her—anything to comfort her, but I kept my arms locked across my chest. I didn't want to scare her off, not now. Instead, I gestured to the bed and said "Why don't you sit down, Abi. Do you want some water or something?"

Abi sank onto the edge of the bed, and I moved carefully over to sit next to her. I offered her the unopened bottle of water on my bedside table, but she waved it away.

"I'm afraid to talk to anyone here about it," she whispered. "I don't know who I can trust."

"You can trust me. And my sister. I promise," I said.

Abi drew a shuddering breath. "I think they're asking the wrong questions, the investigators. Or maybe they're just avoiding the real ones. I don't know which it is, and I don't want to sound paranoid, but... I'm not sure if they really want to find her at all."

I felt my pulse quicken, but I kept my voice even. "What makes you say that?"

"I'm not sure... it's just this awful feeling I have. Her brother was here, you know. Came down from Inverness all raging and storming that they weren't doing enough, and why hadn't they made any progress? He was furious, and he only got angrier when they tried to placate him with these ludicrous suggestions about running off with someone or taking a holiday. He was half-mad with the shouting before they could calm him down. I thought they were going to have to drag him out. I could hear it all from my office. And also..." She swallowed hard, twice, and for a moment I thought she was about to be sick.

"Go on," I said when I was sure she was okay.

"That Caomhnóir you brought with you, the male one. You trust him?"

I fought back the urge to laugh, because the thought of not trusting Finn was so ludicrous to me, but laughing in this poor girl's face was the exact opposite of helpful. "I trust him with my life, and so does my sister."

Abi scrutinized my face like a document she was studying and then nodded, apparently deciding that I was telling the truth. Then she said, "I heard him in the Caomhnóir office, talking to the investigators. He said he was looking for the archive's research log."

"Yeah, he was. We thought whatever Polly checked out of the archive might give us a clue as to what happened to her. Why do you bring it up?"

Abi bit her lip.

"Do you know something about the logbook?" I pressed.

"I saw Polly rip a page out of it," Abi whispered, "the day before she disappeared."

My heart broke into a gallop. "Could you tell me a bit more about that?"

"Well, she'd been acting odd all morning," Abi said, her hands twisting in her lap. "I know you didn't know her, or—I don't know, did you?"

"Hardly at all," I confirmed. "I only met her once, and just for a minute."

"And how would you describe her?"

"She was... friendly? Cheerful—like, maybe even overly so?"

Abi nodded along like I'd said exactly what she'd expected me to say. "That snapshot is her. She's like that all the time. I've never seen her less than absolutely chuffed. It was almost unnerving when I first met her, but I got used to it, and eventually I even began to appreciate it. It started to rub off on me. She's one of those people who always manages to help you look on the bright side of things."

Her eyes filled with tears. Impulsively, I reached out and squeezed her hand. She didn't rebuff the gesture.

"But that day when she came in, she was definitely agitated. She always comes in and greets us all first thing, but that morning she went straight to her office and shut the door. When I knocked to bring her some coffee, she opened the door only a crack, and though she tried to put on a happy face, it was strained. She took the coffee and thanked me, but then shut her door again. I decided she must be working on something important, so I let her be, but my mind kept drifting back to her all morning. When she didn't emerge for lunch, I decided to go check on her. Her door was slightly ajar, and that's when I saw her with a paper in her hand. I... I couldn't be sure, but it looked like a page right out of our logbook."

"What did she do with it?" I asked eagerly. "Did you see what she did with it?"

"She..." Abi swallowed hard. "She burned it. In her fireplace."

I felt my heart sink. We'd looked in the fireplace when we'd searched the office. We'd even stuck our arms up the chimney to see if anything had been jammed up the flue. The grate had been swept clean, and fresh logs stacked inside. No ash, no fragments of paper. Polly had been very careful indeed.

"You don't happen to know which page she burned, do you?" I asked.

Abi nodded. "I needed the logbook later that afternoon, and so I asked her for it. She looked startled, which was odd in itself, because we pass around that logbook all day in the archive. But she handed it over to me. When I first opened it, I was confused. As far as I could see, there were no dates unaccounted for. But then I looked more closely and realized that a page had been removed. If you weren't looking for it, I doubt you would notice. It was done very neatly and very close to the binding with something sharp, like a scalpel or something."

"Could you tell which day's entries were missing?" I asked.

Abi shook her head. "That was the strange thing. At first, it didn't seem as though there were any entries missing. But then I realized that she had copied them over. She removed a page and then wrote a new one in its place on the next page in the log."

"How did you know she—"

"Because all of the entries for that day were in her handwriting—but I knew for a fact that I'd personally written several entries in the log the previous day, and so had several of my colleagues."

"So the page she replaced was for the previous day?"

"That's right. And then the next day, she didn't come in, and we had that strange email saying she was sick," Abi said. She raised her eyes from her twisting hands, and I could see now that they were full of tears. "She's not sick. She's not on holiday. Something terrible has happened to her, and I don't even know who I can talk to about it, and—"

That was the breaking point for Abi. She burst into tears, and all I could do was pull her in and put my arm around her while they passed. I couldn't bring myself to tell her about the letters. It wasn't that I didn't trust her—every instinct I had was screaming at me that she was telling the truth. But I didn't want her to be even more anxious than she already was. Yes, something had happened to Polly, but there was no use in telling Abi that until we knew exactly how terrible it was. Instead, I tried to refocus her to get any more information she could give me.

"Abi, can you remember anything at all that might have been different about the log book page?" I asked, keeping my voice as gentle and encouraging as I could. "She must have destroyed it for a reason, and I think that reason was to hide the details of what documents and artifacts she had checked out that day. Nothing else makes sense."

Abi took off her glasses and swiped at her tear-filled eyes with the sleeve of her sweater. "I can't be absolutely sure—I really wasn't paying close attention, because signing the logbook is such a mundane thing, we all do it several times a day, but..." she cleared her throat, "...I think I remember spotting a difference."

"Yes?"

"There was a name on the original page that wasn't on the page Polly copied over."

"What was it? What was the name?"

Abi's voice shrank to a whisper. "Agnes Isherwood."

9

NEIGHBORHOOD WATCH

"I knew it! I knew it had something to do with the Reckoning!" Milo's voice was ringing and triumphant through the connection.

Abi had barely vanished around the corner from my room when I'd gathered the others into Hannah's room for an emergency meeting. And because I didn't want to have to explain everything Abi had told me more than once, we'd opened up the connection and patched Milo through as well. Milo's reaction was by far the only excitable one. Everyone else's expressions ranged from terrified to borderline nauseous.

Hannah flinched as Milo's reply reverberated in our collective headspace. "We don't actually know that for sure," she said. Then she turned to everyone else, ready to repeat his words out loud.

"Ugh, I can't stand this. It's like listening to everything on a delay. Hang on," Milo said. I felt him pull out of our heads like a plug being pulled from a sink.

"What's he doing?" Hannah asked.

"Coming here, I think," I said.

"What, now?"

"Yes, now!" Milo replied, and with a grunt of effort, he materialized through the wall and into our room.

"How the hell did you do that so fast?" Savvy asked.

"Piece of cake," Milo replied, though he sounded winded, which was odd for someone who didn't need to breathe. His form was also pale and fuzzy, like he was having trouble holding on to it. "Whoa. Should have taken a bit more time with that."

"Just conserve your energy and listen," I said.

Milo pouted. "But I came to gloat."

I ignored that, turning to Finn instead. "What do you think?"

Finn was standing motionless, his stress rendering him as still as a statue. Only the slight movement of his eyes as his mind worked rapidly gave away that he wasn't, in fact, carved of stone. Finally, he sighed with frustration. "I don't know. But... it seems likely."

Agnes Isherwood. Everything always seemed to come back to our High Priestess ancestor. She'd been the one who had discovered how to put the Gateways into our bloodlines to begin with. She had warned her fellow Durupinen of the dangers—warned that it could only be a temporary solution to the imminent threat of the Necromancers, but over time, her warnings were lost, her pleas ignored. By the time Hannah and I were inheriting our gifts, the fact that the Gateways weren't meant to be in our blood was almost completely lost.

And some very powerful people wanted it to be lost again.

"What could she have found?" Hannah asked into the silence that followed Finn's words.

I shook my head. "I just don't know. But whatever it was, Polly wanted to cover her tracks."

"Or someone else wanted to cover them for her," Savvy said. "Look, I know no one wants to hear this, but there's a good chance Polly's already a goner."

Kiernan made a strange sound, rather like a groan. "You're right. No one wants to hear that," he muttered.

"But if someone wanted this artifact badly enough—" Savvy said stubbornly.

"Then they could easily have taken it without killing Polly," I interrupted. "And since we have no proof that she's dead, let's not jump to conclusions." I said it with as much force as I could muster, even as a little voice in the back of my head agreed that Savvy had a point.

"They may have needed to keep Polly alive," Hannah said, an edge of desperation to her voice, "if they needed her knowledge. A lot of the old artifacts and documents need to be translated and interpreted."

"Or Polly could simply be in hiding," Kiernan said, meeting Hannah's mounting hysteria with equal calmness. He reached out and took her hand gently as he went on. "If she thought someone was closing in, if she thought they'd discovered what she had, she might have taken it and run."

"Speculating is getting us nowhere," Finn said, his tone a bit sharp in his distress. "We have a plan, and everything that Abi has told us only further convinces me that it's the right plan. Tomorrow morning, we search Polly's house. And we keep a low profile about it."

"You don't think they'll have it guarded?" Savvy asked. "The Caomhnóir, I mean?"

"They might," Finn admitted. "And if that's the case, we'll just have to admit why we're here. But if we can have a good look around without giving ourselves away, I'd prefer it. We don't know who we can trust."

"Do you think we can trust that Abi woman?" Savvy asked.

"I think so," I said. "She seemed genuine."

"Yeah, plenty of good liars seem genuine," Savvy countered.

"I talked with her a bit when we were here last," Kiernan said. "She's only second generation. In fact, she chose to train as a Scribe because she wanted to learn about a history she never knew existed. She's not from a rich or powerful clan. I can't think what kind of stake she'd have in all of this."

This seemed to satisfy Savvy. As a first-generation Durupinen, the centuries-deep political intrigues and inter-clan clashes meant little to her, except in moments like this, when they affected all of us.

"So we're decided, then," Finn said, looking at each of us in turn. "Tomorrow morning, we head into Portree. Let's see if we can find any clues the others overlooked."

The following morning dawned foggy and brisk, with a fierce wind whipping in off the cliffs, and a thick mist scudding low over the landscape, like fallen clouds. The sky above us was iron gray as we piled into the van, and cold, needling rain began to lash at the windshield as we pulled away from the príosún.

No one had questioned our request to sign out a van and head into town. The food at the príosún was terrible, and guards and Scribes alike frequently went back and forth to avail themselves of the local pubs and shops and escape the gloom of the fortress in which they worked. Most of the Scribes maintained a residence outside of the castle, like Polly did, though many lived far enough from the remote location that they took advantage of the dorms during the week, and only returned home on the weekends. Portree wasn't far, though, and we had learned that Polly commuted daily back to one of the candy-colored row houses that Portree was famous for. Catriona provided us with her address, along with instructions to tread carefully.

"The more you tell me about this situation, the less I like it," she said, when I called her the previous night. "I should have sent you with more back-up."

"Speaking of leaving people without proper back-up, do you know how Gemma's getting on with Fiona?" I asked.

"Well, she hasn't killed the poor girl, if that's what you mean," Cat replied dryly. "And she showed up at our Committee meeting yesterday. She looked like she'd been in a wrestling match with a feral cat, but she was there."

Well, at least one thing was moving in the right direction, I thought, as I ended the call. I couldn't concentrate on the task ahead of us if I was worried about Fiona.

Ideally, we would have liked to search Polly's house at night, when the neighbors weren't out and about. The area of Portree where she lived was right along the bustling waterfront, a popular area for tourists, especially in the summertime. But we all decided that it would be much more suspicious if we snuck out of the príosún in the middle of the night than if we made an excuse to pop down to Portree in the middle of the day. But since we were going to do this in broad daylight, we had to be careful and make sure not to draw too much attention to ourselves.

Finn parked the van around the corner from Polly's house to keep it out of sight. There was a cafe only a few doors down in one direction with a little arrangement of outdoor seating under colorful umbrellas. We agreed that Savvy should order a coffee and nurse it outside the cafe to keep eyes on the street, and make sure we weren't being followed or watched. She was reluctant at first, but then she noticed the sandwich board by the entrance advertising the Scottish equivalent of a full English.

"Challenge accepted," she said, and set off down the pavement whistling.

Once Savvy was set up at a table outside the cafe, Finn turned to Milo.

"Ready?" he asked.

Milo gave a flourish-y sort of twirl and disappeared from the inside of the van. We waited in tense silence until he popped into our heads through the connection.

"There's no one here. The place looks spotless. You're good."

"The lock?" Hannah asked.

"Oh yeah," Milo said. "I'm on it."

Hannah turned to Finn and gave a thumbs up.

"All right, then," he said. I'll find a spot across the street. Be thorough, but also don't waste any time."

I nodded and exited the car along with Hannah and Kiernan. We had a cover story in case we needed it. It was time to search the place and see if we could find anything the Caomhnóir had not.

Kiernan didn't follow us to the front, but cut around to the other side of the block where a narrow alley ran behind the houses. The plan was to let him in the back door after we had gotten in through the front, which Milo would unlock for us from the inside. Kiernan gave Hannah's hand a quick squeeze as he turned away from us, walking at an easy pace, hands in pockets.

Hannah and I strolled up the row of houses, doing our best to look like we knew exactly where we were going. There were definitely people around, but most of them looked like tourists, which meant they were paying more attention to their phones and the surrounding sights than they were to us. But as we approached the house we knew to be Polly's, painted a shocking shade of bubblegum pink, we noticed someone with a broom out in front of the neighboring blue house.

"What… is she doing?" I whispered.

"She appears to be… sweeping her section of the sidewalk?" Hannah whispered back, sounding totally bemused.

Sure enough, as we surreptitiously observed her, the woman was pottering back and forth on the pavement in front of her house, sweeping furiously and muttering to herself. Her hands were gnarled like knotty branches around the broom handle, and she wore a bright yellow linen apron over a housecoat and a red checkered kerchief tied over a head full of pink plastic curlers. We were so distracted by what she was doing that we were only a few feet away from her before we realized what was happening.

"Oh!" Hannah gasped, just in time for the woman to look up and meet her eye.

"Well, now," the woman said, staring beadily at us both. "You're just like her, then, are ye?"

"Just like wh—oh!" Classic Jess, a few seconds behind everyone else, but I got there eventually.

"She's a ghost," I muttered to Hannah.

"She sure is," Hannah muttered back.

"She can hear ye as well," the woman snapped.

"Sorry," we both said at once.

I glanced anxiously around us, but no one seemed to have a glance to spare for us.

"Um, you said we were just like someone else, is that right?"

"Och, aye," the old woman confirmed, still sweeping vigorously.

"Who are you talking about?" I asked.

"That woman there, what lives in that house. Polly, her name is," the old woman said. She hacked out a cough and spat squelchily onto the sidewalk. Or at least, she would have if she'd been alive. The sidewalk remained clean of her phlegm.

Hannah hoisted on a friendly smile, which only made the woman look more suspicious. "So you know Polly, then?"

"No."

"No?"

"No one knows the woman. Secretive, like. Keeps herself to herself. Doesn't like to mix," the old woman said, shaking her head.

"What's your name?" I asked, also endeavoring to keep a friendly tone.

"And why would I be telling the likes of you?" the woman snapped.

"Who else are you going to tell?" I snapped back, annoyed. "Talk to many other people around here these days?"

The woman narrowed her eyes and raked them over me from top to bottom, like she was assessing me. Finally, she snorted. "Suppose you've got a point, lass. The name's Bridie. Bridie MacNulty."

"Well, Bridie MacNulty, can you tell us anything else about the woman who lives here?" I asked, pointing to Polly's house.

Bridie looked at Polly's front door, considering her words. "A strange one, she is. Pleasant enough when you speak to her, but distant. Never invites you in for a cuppa, even when you bring her your prize-winning cranachan in welcome. Rude, some would call it."

I couldn't muster enough curiosity to ask what the hell a cranachan was. It didn't surprise me that Polly kept to herself, though. Many Durupinen did, just out of caution. It wouldn't do for the neighbors to suspect you could see ghosts wherever you went.

Bridie was already sweeping again, muttering angrily to herself. "Dinnae know why I even bother. They'll only muck it up again the minute I turn my back. No respect for the locals." Even as she said it a man walking past us flicked a cigarette butt onto the pavement. Bridie glared after him, and a moment later, he stumbled forward as though someone had shoved him hard in the small of his back. Bridie cackled. The man turned and looked at the sidewalk behind him, as though expecting to see a crack or an uneven bit of pavement that had caused him to stumble. I smothered a laugh. This woman was a menace. I kind of loved it. Hannah, however, was impatient.

"Do you know that Polly hasn't been here in a week or so?" Hannah asked.

Bridie turned a beady eye on her, leaning her hands on the top of her broom. "Aye, I noticed."

"Do you happen to know anything about where she went?" Hannah asked, though there was little hope in her voice.

"Now, why would I know something like that?" Bridie asked irritably. "The woman barely spoke two words to anyone."

"Maybe you saw her leave?" I suggested. "Maybe you saw her get into a car with someone, or maybe call a taxi?"

"I saw no such thing," Bridie said. "But then, I suppose she left in the middle of the night, as criminals do."

Hannah and I traded a startled look. "Criminal?" Hannah repeated.

"What other conclusion can a law-abiding neighbor come to? The house is empty for a couple of days, and suddenly, the authorities descend by the dozens. Vanloads of them, searching the place from top to bottom in the middle of the night, with torches and gloves and all. Drugs, you mark my words."

She touched the side of her nose with one arthritic finger, and nodded wisely.

"That must have made a real mess of the sidewalk," I said gravely. Hannah smacked my arm, but didn't dare look at me.

"Och, aye, but it did!" Bridie confirmed, fuming. She pointed a crooked finger right in my face and started wagging it ferociously. "But if she's been dealin' in drugs then she got as much as she deserved. Either that or she took her money and ran before the authorities could catch up to her. Good riddance, I say."

I took a step back for my own safety. "Right. Well, thanks for your help," I said, and turned with Hannah to Polly's door.

"Wait a minute, now!" I felt a force exerted on the back of my shirt, like this woman was actually tugging me backward. I turned, aggravated.

"What?"

"Ye cannae just walk into someone else's house! What's your business here? Where's your credentials?" She crossed her arms, broom in hand, and waited, a truculent expression twisting her wrinkled features.

"Why do you care? I thought you said she was a criminal who got what was coming to her?" I asked.

"That may be true, but that doesnae give you the right to pilfer her things! Next thing you know, you'll be helping yourself to whatever you please from every house on the block when we've nipped out to do the shopping!"

I shot a glance at Hannah, who was just staring at Bridie now, open-mouthed, as the little woman glared back with all the ferocity of a feral animal.

"What the hell is taking so long?" Milo's irritated voice twanged along the web of our connection.

"You wouldn't believe me if I told you," I thought back, transmitting as I did the entirety of what was happening outside.

"You've got to be kidding me! Are we really being held up by an old lady with a broom?" he asked.

"Trust me when I tell you, this broom might as well be an automatic weapon," I shot back. "Just give us a minute."

"Well, I've already let Kiernan in through the back. He'll start searching until you can shake her off."

I took a deep breath and turned to Bridie. I did not have the time or patience for pretense, not today.

"Look, Bridie, I realize you didn't know Polly very well, but we did. Not personally; we didn't spend a lot of time together. But we shared some things in common—things like being able to see you the way you are right now. When you first met Polly, you were alive. Now, well… you know that, don't you? You know that you're… well…"

Bridie narrowed one beady eye at me, considering. Then she said, almost grudgingly, "I'm not a fool, lass. I know it. I know I'm not for this world any longer, though I cannae seem to quit it."

I nodded, acknowledging that it probably wasn't an easy thing to admit.

I went on. "The thing is, that kind of thing can put a girl in complicated situations. Even dangerous situations. Polly didn't want to draw attention to it. That's why she wasn't a regular at the neighborhood potluck. You understand what I'm saying?"

I could tell she didn't want to cede the ground of her dislike for Polly, but again, Bridie capitulated. She gave me one, curt nod.

"Well, we think that ability she had might have landed Polly in some trouble. We need a look around to prove whether that's true. We're not going to steal anything, and we won't bring any trouble on the place that wasn't already here. So, how about you step aside and let us help your neighbor?"

Bridie went very still. It was difficult for her, I knew, to cast aside her role as neighborhood protector. It seemed that not even death could keep her and her eagle eye from watching over the place she so fiercely loved, and while she was thoroughly annoying me in the moment, I could respect her for it. Finally, with a reluctant shuffle and a grudging snort, she stepped aside and cleared the path to Polly's front door.

"I still say it's drugs," she grumbled.

"Well, if it is, we'll make sure she gets her comeuppance, all right?" I said. "Thanks, Bridie. Now, back to it. Give 'em hell." I gave her a cheeky salute that very nearly drew a shadow of a smile from her, and we turned to the door at last. The knob turned easily under my hand, which meant Milo had had no problem with the lock.

We stepped inside Polly Keener's deserted house.

10

A CLUE

"I thought we might run into some obstacles, but that was not what I had in mind," Hannah said, once the door had closed behind us.

"Right? Who would have thought our biggest worry of the day was how to get past the ghost of the Portree Neighborhood Watch?"

"Do you think we should stay with her out there? Do you think she'll interfere?" Hannah asked.

"I don't know," I hedged. Honestly, I wouldn't have put it past Bridie to float right through the wall to spy on us; though, as a Durupinen, Polly probably had the place Warded. I certainly would have, if I lived next door to a ghost like that. But then...

"Hey Milo?"

"Yeah?"

"You were able to get in here?"

Milo stared at me, then glanced at Hannah. "Jess, you do see me standing right here in front of you, don't you, sweetness?"

I rolled my eyes. "Yes, it's just... wouldn't it be standard practice to have this place Warded? A Durupinen lives here."

Understanding lit Milo's features. "Oh! I sort of didn't think of that. But I felt... hang on..."

He zipped away from us in a blur toward the back of the house and then returned again within seconds. "That's weird. I can see the markings around the windows and doors, but I was able to get in."

Hannah frowned. "That doesn't make any sense."

But I was barely listening. An idea had just occurred to me. "Huh. I wonder," I muttered.

"You wonder what?" Hannah and Milo asked together.

"You two start searching. I'll be right back," I said, and went right back out the front door again.

I pulled out my phone and held it to my ear, just in case anyone heard me talking.

"Hey Bridie?"

Bridie looked up from her sweeping again, looking thoroughly annoyed to be interrupted, despite the fact that her spectral broom had no discernible effect on the state of the sidewalk.

"What is it now? Find the stash already?"

"No, not yet. I was just wondering, can you get into Polly's house? Have you ever tried?"

Bridie's shriveled face colored pink, so that she looked for a moment like a sentient crab apple. "Of course I haven't! What impertinence!"

I smirked. "Ah, come on, Bridie. You know what goes on around here. You're telling me you never peeked through a wall? Inspected a strange sound? For neighborhood safety, of course," I added, sobering my expression.

Bridie shifted uneasily from foot to foot for a moment. Then she lifted her chin defiantly instead. "I may have done. For safety."

"Have you ever tried to get into Polly's house?" I asked.

Bridie's expression soured. "Och aye, I tried. Couldnae get through the walls. Too solid. She's got some kind of strange security on them that keeps even the likes of me out."

"How recently have you tried to get in?" I asked.

Again, she seemed reluctant to answer but finally admitted, "Just t'other day. When all them vans and men were here. Hoped I might be able to get a peek at what they found, now that she was gone, but those walls were as impenetrable as ever."

"We'll keep that in mind," I said, already opening the door again. "Thanks again, Bridie."

She only snorted in reply as I closed the door again.

"The place is Warded," I called from the entryway. "The deceased neighborhood busybody can't get in. Which means—"

Hannah appeared in the entryway, eyes wide. "Which means she altered those Wards to make sure we could."

"Wait, what? Can she do that?" Milo asked, appearing over her shoulder.

"Yes, Wards are entirely customizable," Hannah said, looking frankly shocked that Milo did not already possess this information. "You can Ward a place against a specific ghost, allowing all others to enter, or you can Ward against all ghosts except for those you choose to grant access."

"So, couldn't Polly have just Warded the place to keep that neighbor out?" Milo asked. "I mean, full offense, but she seems like an absolute nightmare."

But Hannah was already examining the runes carved over the front door. "She could have, but the runes would be different. These ones are the standard ones, meant to keep all spirits out, but this one here?"

She pointed to another rune, one that had been inked onto the doorframe beside the carved ones. It looked sort of like an old-fashioned keyhole. I knew I'd seen it before, but I'd always been garbage at remembering runes.

"This was added more recently," Hannah said. She looked at me, her expression almost shocked. "She changed it. She changed her Wards so that Clan Sassanaigh—or any ghost associated with us, at least—could enter unimpeded."

"Wait, so that's like... a Milo specific rune?" Milo asked, looking between us with wide, incredulous eyes. "Like, she thought you might send me?"

"Maybe, but it also includes any spirit tied to our bloodline—past, present, or future," Hannah clarified.

We all looked at each other. The letters from Polly had been an invitation, certainly, but this? This was proof of preparations she had taken to ensure we could enter her home, even if something happened to us and only our spirits remained.

"Whatever it is, it's here," I whispered. "She hid it here, and she only wanted us to find it."

"Hannah?" Kiernan's voice called out from another room, and we hurried to meet him.

He was standing in a part of the house that seemed to be part living room, part library. While Hannah explained to Kiernan about the runes, I was momentarily distracted from everything else by what seemed to be a general explosion of yarn. I remembered that when I met Polly, she'd been wearing a crocheted granny square cardigan. I wondered at the time if she had made it herself. Now I saw that it was only one of many, many things she had made. Nearly every surface of the room was draped or covered, or accented by something made of yarn. Pillow covers, blankets, a tea cozy, wall hangings, everything was wrapped in Polly's artistry, like the room had been padded for our protection. There was a wall of shelves to the right of her stone fireplace that was devoted entirely to a rainbow collection of skeins of yarn, as well as dozens of crochet hooks hung from the fronts of the shelves in long rows.

"Jess?"

I tore my eyes from the granny-square explosion.

"How should we do this? Where do we start?" Hannah asked.

I took a deep breath and tried to really see the room this time, past all the unexpected yarn work to the actual contents. My eyes fell on a long wooden desk, a filing cabinet, and the rest of the shelves in the room, which were crowded with the kind of old, musty books I would fully expect the Durupinen equivalent of a librarian to possess. "Let's split up. Hannah, you and Kiernan should check this room. It probably has the most books and documents and stuff, and I think Kiernan would be the most likely out of all of us to spot this artifact if we came across it."

Kiernan nodded and, wasting no time, headed straight for Polly's desk in the corner and began easing open drawers.

"I'll take the upstairs," I said. "The bedroom seems another likely place someone might stash something."

"What about me?" Milo asked.

"How about some general reconnaissance? Just keep sweeping the perimeter, keep an eye on the doors and windows, so we're not interrupted."

"On it," Milo said, and vanished.

And so we scattered to the four corners of Polly's house, searching for a mysterious something we only prayed we would recognize when we found it. When I reached the top of the stairs I made a quick inventory of the rooms, which comprised two snug bedrooms, a linen closet, a bathroom, and a third little room without a door on it that might have once been a closet or an undersized office, but was now a hoarding place for more crochet projects. Somehow, this room felt like a sacred little space, unlikely to be the hiding place for anything that didn't bring her crafting joy; but I started there, opening each bin and bag and box, but finding only crochet supplies and projects in various stages of completion.

The linen closet yielded nothing but towels, spare sheets, and interestingly, a squirreled away box of chocolates. The bathroom, with its cheery yellow bath mats and matching shower curtain, was so small that it took only minutes to search it. It felt sleazy, going through a stranger's medicine cabinet, so I tried not to look at the labels on her prescriptions as I turned them over to make sure they actually contained medications. Aside from learning that this woman bought antacids by the truckload, I came up empty again. The secondary bedroom was barely big enough to contain the narrow brass bedstead, tiny bedside table, and, crammed next to the window, a high-backed wingchair. I pulled back the colorful crocheted bedspread, pulled up the mattress, checked for slits and hidden compartments, even unscrewed the heavy brass knobs from the ends of the bedposts and peered inside. Nothing. As I felt along the underneath of the bedside table and lampshade, I noticed a framed photograph. The frame looked like it had been made by a child—there were sparkly plastic jewels and little seashells stuck to it with glitter glue. In the photo, Polly and a young girl with two missing front teeth grinned at the camera, their arms around each other. I wondered if it was her niece in Inverness, and then felt a lump come into my throat. Surely this was the room the girl slept in when she came to visit. I had a momentary vision of Polly bustling around in anticipation, smoothing out the homemade blanket and maybe sneaking a chocolate under the pillow for a surprise. I blinked back tears for this girl I'd never met, for this woman I barely knew.

I redoubled my efforts in Polly's bedroom, which was only slightly larger than the guest bedroom: pulling at floorboards, feeling into corners, emptying every drawer, and feeling into every pocket of every clothing item hanging in the cramped closet. Reluctantly, I had to conclude that there was nothing here or, if there had been something here, someone else had already found it. The thought slipped like an ice cube into my insides, making me shiver. I headed back down the stairs, feeling defeated, to find Milo hovering at the bottom. Whether he read my face or my mind, I couldn't quite be sure.

"Nothing?"

"Nothing."

Hannah and Kiernan were still working their way through the living room, and so I searched the kitchen, emptying every cabinet and drawer, even the refrigerator, to no avail. Every muscle in my body was starting to ache, but I was also aching with disappointment and growing dread. Finally, I heard Hannah's voice, heavy and slow, from the living room.

"Jess?"

I peered around the doorframe. Kiernan and Hannah sat on the floor, surrounded by neat piles of books and papers. I recognized the disappointment mirrored in their faces. I didn't even ask. I simply watched Hannah shake her head as Kiernan pulled off his glasses and rubbed at his eyes.

"It's not here," Hannah said, her voice little more than a hoarse whisper. "Whatever it is, she's taken it with her."

"Or someone else has," Kiernan added. His face looked about ten years older than usual as he arranged his glasses back onto the bridge of his nose.

"What do we do now?" Hannah asked. "We're at a dead end. If it's not at Skye, and it's not here…"

"Then we're too late," Kiernan said. The words were hollow. Heavy.

I sank down onto the edge of the couch. If only we hadn't stayed in London that extra night. If only we'd gotten home a day earlier, found her letters sooner. Would it even have made a difference? Or was it all over before we even knew we ought to be searching for something?

The arm of the sofa on which I perched myself was covered in a crocheted cover which shifted beneath me so that I slid halfway off onto the side table, knocking a picture frame to the floor.

"Shit! Sorry!" I said to no one in particular as I bent awkwardly to pick it up. I turned it over to find another photo of Polly and, beside her, a face I knew better than almost any other in the world.

"Hannah!" I cried. "This picture. It's of you and Polly together. Did you see this?"

"Huh?" Hannah looked utterly bewildered as she got up from among the piles of books, and came over to stand beside me. She looked down at the picture and then gave a little laugh. "Oh, I remember taking this. It was on our first day at the archive during the MacLeod case. She asked if we could take a selfie together. She was all embarrassed, like she was asking to take a picture with a celebrity or something."

"Well, you are something of a celebrity to her," Kiernan pointed out, coming over to look as well. "She has devoted most of her career to documenting your clan, after all, and you're arguably the most famous member ever."

I cleared my throat pointedly.

Kiernan laughed. "I beg your pardon. How rude of me. One of the *two* most famous members ever."

"That's better," I said, giving what I hoped was an imperious nod of forgiveness.

"I can't believe she has it framed in her house," Hannah said, and her voice sounded shaky. "I... had no idea it would mean so much to her."

As Hannah took the frame from me and adjusted it so that she could examine the picture more closely, something on the back of the frame caught my eye.

"What is that?" I asked.

"What's what?"

But I was already taking the frame out of her hands and flipping it over. On the back of the frame, sticking out from the gap between the matting and the backing, was something white, like the corner of a piece of paper.

"What is it?" Hannah repeated.

"I'm... not sure," I said. I felt the telltale drop in temperature that told me Milo had floated over behind me to come take a look as well. My heart was suddenly hammering. I pressed my fingers against the little metal tabs that held the backing on the picture frame, and they bent easily away. Then, using my fingernail to wedge into the gap, I lifted the backing carefully off the frame. There, pressed in tightly against the back of the photo, was a torn piece of paper, folded in half.

I could feel the excitement rolling off Milo in waves that almost made me dizzy.

"Can you, like, take the ghostly equivalent of a deep breath, Milo? I feel like I'm going to pass out by proxy here."

"Oh! Sorry, sweetness," Milo murmured. A moment later, I could still feel the nerves, but at least they weren't being channeled directly into my body anymore.

I took the paper carefully from the frame and set the frame back on the table. I unfolded it to find two words scrawled in pencil across it: *tanacetum vulgare.*

I stared at the words, feeling confusion begin to course through me. What was this? What was I looking at?

"I don't understand," I finally said out loud.

"Neither do I," Hannah said, taking the paper from me.

"Tanacetum vulgare. Hmm. I don't know what it means, but I'm nearly certain it's Latin," Kiernan said.

I gave a yelp that made everyone jump as my phone began to buzz in my pocket. I pulled it out to see Finn's name on the screen.

"Finn? What's up?"

"I'm checking in. What's your status? Have you found anything?"

"We're... not really sure. Maybe? Hang on, I'll be right out."

I hung up and held out my hand. "Here, give me that, I'll show it to Finn. Do we think we've looked everywhere we can?"

Hannah sighed. "I think so. I really don't think there's anything here to find."

"Okay, well, get those last few piles of books back on the shelves and let's get out of here. We've pushed our luck long enough. We should get back to the príosún before people start wondering where we are."

Hannah and Kiernan set to work, and Milo followed me out the front door onto the pavement. I could see Finn making his way across the street to meet us, and further down the road Savvy was rising from her seat at the cafe. She'd obviously spotted us.

"Oi, how does he get in and out, then?" came a harsh bark of a voice. Bridie was still standing on the pavement, glaring at Milo with one beady eye squeezed shut.

Milo leaped back in alarm, muttering, "What in the weird sisters—"

"It's okay, Bridie. He was invited," I said.

"Oh, so that's how it works, then. Imagine that, not inviting your own neighbor. Unfriendly, I told ye, and this only proves it, didn't want any locals poking or prodding around in her..." she went on, much more to herself and her broomstick than to us.

Milo opened his mouth, but Savvy sauntered up to us at that moment, just as Finn managed to reach the pavement.

"Oi, all right then? Any joy?" she asked.

I threw one cautious glance over my shoulder at Bridie to make sure she wasn't listening, but she was contentedly grumbling away. I unfurled the paper clutched in my hand and quickly explained, in a whisper, about how we had found it.

"Well, it's not the missing artifact, that's for sure," Finn said. His brow was so tightly furrowed it looked like it had been knitted together into one long eyebrow. "That's Latin, isn't it?"

"Kiernan thought so."

"But that's got to be a clue of some kind, doesn't it?" Savvy asked. "I mean, she hid it behind Hannah's picture. Surely she meant for Hannah to find it."

"Sure seems like it," I agreed. "So, now what?"

"Now we head back to the príosún and see if we can figure out what this clue means, if that's even what it is," Finn said. "Are Hannah and Kiernan—?"

"They'll be right out. They were just straightening up. We didn't want it to look like we'd been here, just in case the other Caomhnóir come back," I said.

"Good thinking," Finn said. "Wait here, I'll get the van."

"I think I've figured you out!" Bridie's crackled old voice rang out sharply from behind us.

Savvy turned. "What's that then, Ghost of Busybodies Past?"

"You can spin a good yarn, but you can't fool me!" Bridie chided, wagging a knobbly finger at us. "You're just more police, aren't ye? That man what just left, he's dressed just like the others."

"You mean the ones that were here before?" I asked. "I already told you, Bridie, we're not—"

"No, the ones that are here now! The ones parked outside the back garden!"

It took half a second for her words to penetrate my irritation. Then I whipped my head around to look at Savvy and Milo. Both of their faces reflected first my shock and then my fear.

"The police you saw before are here now?" I asked Bridie.

"Och, aye. I saw them arrive not ten minutes ago. Here to pick up the drugs you've found, I have no doubt." Bridie said with the triumphant air of someone coming to an unassailable conclusion.

For one more second, I just stared at her in horror. Then I turned and started sprinting toward Polly's house. The front door loomed twenty, fifteen, ten feet in front of me.

Then it exploded.

11

PERIL

Everything seemed to happen in a slow, crawling silence. I was sailing backward through the air with the force of the blast, the heat searing my face, shards of glass and debris flying with me, pelting off my skin. Everything went black as I slammed into the ground and all the breath whooshed from my body in one violent motion. For a moment, the world was dark, muffled nothingness, reality reduced to fog-clouded vision and the sound of my own blood pounding in my ears. Distant sounds echoed off this strange bubble I landed in, ghosts of screams and specters of shouts and dull echoes of footsteps.

Then the bubble popped.

Pain hit from every side, making me gasp, but even the gasp hurt as the smoky air burned its way down my lungs. I coughed and gagged, rolling onto my side. I tried to open my eyes, to blink away the tears that clouded them so that I could see again, and when the world around me finally started to come into focus, the first thing I saw was Savvy on the ground beside me.

"Sav?" I choked out, but she was moving, struggling into a sitting position and taking frantic stock of her body, as though checking to see if all of it was still there. She was bleeding rather badly from a gash on the side of her head, but otherwise she seemed okay.

"Jess!"

Finn dropped to his knees beside me, his face frantic with worry. He seemed almost afraid to touch me, his hands hovering an inch from me as he seemed to take the same kind of inventory Savvy had just made of herself.

"I'm okay," I said, not even sure if it was true. "I'm... I'm okay..."

But even as the words fell from my mouth, an automatic response without any real meaning, my eyes focused for the first time on Polly's house... or rather, what was left of Polly's house.

I know I saw the flames. The smoke. The rubble. The hole that obliterated the front hallway so that we were staring directly into the wreckage of the crochet-covered living room. I saw it, but my brain registered none of it. From the moment reality clicked into place in my head, I had only one thought, and it detonated in my brain like a secondary explosion.

Hannah.

"Hannah!" The name tore up my throat and burst from my mouth. Finn was speaking, trying to restrain me. Savvy was shouting. I heard nothing, felt nothing but the yawning, gaping hole inside me that screamed for my sister. I was on my feet. I was shoving Finn violently away from me, ripping Savvy's restraining hands from my clothing. Nothing mattered. Nothing mattered if I couldn't get to her. If I couldn't be with her.

Every part of my body was numb with fear and shock, but I ran, ran as hard as I could, stumbling, tripping, falling, running again, until I reached the void where the front door had been. Suddenly, as the connection broke open, my head was full of not only my own fear, but Milo's as well, swirling together in a whirlpool of terror that threatened to pull us both down, down, down into nothingness. I didn't know which thoughts were mine and which were his, but it didn't matter. They were all full of the same horror, the same unspeakable dread.

Before I could heave myself over the threshold of broken, smoking rubble, Finn was there, his arms locked tightly around my midsection, pulling me back.

"Let go of me! Let go, I need to find her! I need to—"

"Jess, no! It might happen again! There might be a secondary—"

"I don't care! I DON'T CARE!" A tiny detached part of me wondered, whose voice was that, keening like a wounded animal? Whose words were those, screeching into the empty sky? Surely they couldn't be mine. Surely I wasn't capable of making a sound like that.

"Jess, I can't find her!" Milo's voice was in my head now, filling it with frantic terror. "I don't see her here, I don't know where she—"

"Let me go! I have to help, I have to find her!" I was shouting at Finn even as

Milo's words reverberated off my skull, each one feeling like its own explosion, every second that ticked by feeling like an eternity I couldn't survive.

And then...

"Jess!"

I wasn't sure if it was the connection, or my ears, or some denial-ridden hallucination born of desperate desire to hear her, but I heard it. Hannah's voice, inside my head.

"Jess, I'm here, I'm... I'm okay, I... Kiernan's here, he's okay, we're..."

Milo's relief felt like a tidal wave, flooding the connection. "Hannah! Oh, my God! Thank... thank God!"

"Hannah, where are you?" I hadn't meant to say it out loud, but I obviously had, because Finn stiffened behind me. He grabbed me by the shoulders and spun me around to face him, his expression wild with hope.

"You can hear her? Is she... did she...?" He couldn't even string the words together.

I nodded, even as I reached into the connection and felt her there, her fear and her pain and her shock all like the breath of life to me; because it meant she was still with me, she was *alive*.

And then Savvy was there, slamming into us in her haste to reach the place where we stood.

Finn was still bombarding me with questions. "Where is she? Is she hurt? Can you tell what she—"

"Hannah? Is she okay? What about Kiernan?" Savvy's voice was ragged with tears as she struggled to catch up, to share in our relief.

"I've got them!" It was Milo, and though his voice clanged like a gong inside my head, I'd never heard anything so welcome, so wonderful in my entire life. "They're round the back of the house, they're... I think they're okay!"

"The back," I managed to gasp, and then took off at a run around the side of the house, past the growing crowd of panicking people now spilling out into the street from the surrounding buildings, past the ghost of Bridie, who was shrieking like a banshee about drug lords and contract killings and foreigners and whatever else her paranoid mind had concocted to explain why her meticulously clean sidewalk now looked like a war zone.

The explosion had blown out all the windows in the house, so that we were skidding on broken glass and other debris all the way around to the back of the block of houses. And there, at the very back of the tiny garden, lying against the low stone wall looking shell-shocked but mostly unharmed, were Hannah and Kiernan.

I knew there was a continuous barrage of curse words streaming from my mouth, but I was completely unable to stop them as I clambered awkwardly over the stone wall, stumbled across the wreck of the garden, and flung myself on top of my sister. I was probably crushing her, but she didn't seem to mind. All she seemed able to do was dig her fingers into my back and pull me tighter to her, like she was trying to absorb me into her body. I would have let her if I could.

"Jess. Oh my God, Jess, I thought you were... I thought we were... I thought..."

"I know. I know, I did too. It's okay, it's okay, it's okay..."

Milo was blubbering against us as well, and then Savvy added her weight, muttering what sounded like a prayer over and over again.

"It's okay," I kept saying, as much to myself as to reassure anyone else. "It's okay, it's okay..."

But even as I was saying it, a tiny voice in the back of my head was screaming that it wasn't okay. We were in danger—we were probably still in danger. Finn knew it, and so did Kiernan. Finn had helped Kiernan to his feet and, swiftly assessing that he wasn't gravely injured, ran out into the narrow street that ran along the back of the gardens, Kiernan right on his heels. I pried my face far enough off of Hannah's shoulder to watch what he was doing.

"Finn?"

"They took off this way," he said, pointing to a fresh set of tire marks on the pavement. The scent of the burned rubber was still in the air.

"We saw them take off," Kiernan said, still breathing heavily. "Or rather, I should say, we heard them—the tires squealing, I mean. We couldn't see much of anything, there was too much smoke and dust and—"

"Did you see anyone?" Finn asked.

"Only a figure—a sort of shadow taking off through the garden," Kiernan said. "We didn't see the vehicle either, I'm sorry, it was all so—"

"Don't apologize, mate, I'm just glad you're all right," Finn said. "But we've got to get out of here before the police—I've got to make a phone call, we've got to—bloody hell!" Finn pulled out his phone, hit a few buttons, and held it to his ear. "We need to get to the van."

"Give me the keys, I can—" Kiernan began, but Finn cut him off, laying a hand on his shoulder.

"I appreciate it, mate, but you've just been nearly blown to smithereens, and the shock is bound to set in. I don't think you should be behind the wheel when it does. Sav, here!" He pulled his keys from his pocket and tossed them through the air. Sav caught them deftly in one hand. "Go get the van and bring it round to the end of the lane there. You see, where the lamppost is?"

"On it," Savvy said and, with one last squeeze of Hannah's hand, she took off at a sprint back the way we'd come.

Whoever Finn had called had picked up. He spoke in a low, urgent voice for a few seconds, then hung up.

"Hannah, do you think you can walk?"

"I... yes, I think I..." But as Hannah tried to get to her feet, she swayed alarmingly and clutched at my shoulder.

"Maybe I can—" I began, but Kiernan was there, scooping her up into the cradle of his arms as though she weighed nothing.

"Kiernan, are you—"

"I've got her," he said, and his voice was so quietly fierce that I didn't dare try to argue with him.

"Right, we need to get away from here, before anyone else spots us."

"Or tries to kill us," I added. It was a hysterical joke, but Finn only nodded in agreement.

"Come on," he said, and we all followed.

The adrenaline was still pumping through my veins, or I don't think my legs would have held me, but we pushed on at a jog. We'd just about reached the van when Savvy came peeling around the corner. She reached over and threw the passenger side door open, while Milo used his energy to fling the back door of the van wide. We all piled in, slammed the doors, and Savvy took off, tires screeching.

We didn't return to the príosún, not right away. Finn drove in the opposite direction out of Portree and onto a narrow and entirely deserted road that wound off through the wild and untamed landscape of Skye, until he pulled over at the top of a hill where we could see for miles in every direction.

"If anyone is following us, we'll be able to spot them from here," he explained as he killed the engine. "Let's get out and get some air."

No one spoke at first, piling out of the car and into the weak sunshine. Kiernan helped Hannah to a large rock onto which she melted, still pale and shaking like a leaf. Kiernan sat beside her on one side, and Milo tucked his pale form against her on the other. He was shimmering in and out of view in his stress, unable to focus completely on his manifestation. Savvy hopped up onto the hood of the van and sat there, staring back down the road we had traveled like a hyper-focused watchdog.

I felt like my body was vibrating with energy, but what that energy was, I had no idea. Adrenaline? Fear? I finally settled on unadulterated rage. Someone had almost killed my sister, and my nervous system was melting down because of it. I leaned over into a tall patch of heather and threw up. No one so much as reacted.

When I'd recovered myself, I found Finn in full-on Caomhnóir mode. He was quietly and calmly checking Hannah and Kiernan over to assess the nature of their injuries. I just stood numbly watching him do it, until at last he straightened up and let out a sigh of relief.

"Well, miraculously, I don't think we have to go to the hospital. Aside from a few minor cuts, abrasions, and bruises, you both appear to be okay."

Hannah didn't react, except to lay her head on Kiernan's shoulder. Kiernan's grip on her hand tightened, the knuckles whitening.

"Okay, let's start with what we know," Finn said. "Hannah, Kiernan, can you tell us what happened in there? Did you see anyone?"

Kiernan looked at Hannah, and she picked up her head. "We were cleaning up," she said, her voice hoarse and shaking. "And I thought I heard something from the back of the house, but I… I didn't pay much attention to it. It's a busy area. I thought it was just noise from outside. It was Kiernan who…" She looked at him, as though hoping he would take up the thread, and he did.

"It was the window," he said. "The one beside the back door that leads from the kitchen into the back garden. I heard it squeak. Hannah had heard it the first time, I think that was when it was opened. I stood up and went to check, and that's when I saw it on the floor."

"Saw what?" Finn asked.

"The explosive," Kiernan said. Hannah shuddered beside him. "Hannah had followed me to the kitchen door to see what was going on. We were closer to the back door than we were to the front at that point, so I just grabbed her hand and we ran for it. We barely made it down the back garden steps before it went off. The blast propelled us out into the garden."

Milo shot up, his form flickering violently as he struggled with his anger. "This is my fault. I was supposed to be watching the windows and doors, but I followed Jess out instead. I was just… I was so excited that we'd found something, I didn't…" He looked around at all of us with a desperate expression, almost pleading.

"Don't be a prat, mate, it's not your fault," Savvy barked. "We all got distracted by that bit of paper. I left my post, and if I hadn't, I might have seen the van coming or going. That's what the old bat said, wasn't it? There was a van just like ours out back?"

"I didn't see it, but I heard it peeling away just before the explosive went off," Kiernan said. "I couldn't tell you if it was a van or a car, but there was certainly something back there, and they tore off right after the explosion."

"I… I think I saw that it was a dark color," Hannah said. "But it all happened so fast, I… I couldn't swear to it."

"Well, regardless, I think we have to take Bridie's word on this," Finn said. "She clearly prides herself on getting into everyone else's business. If she says it was the same van as the ones the police brought—and we know 'the police' were actually the Skye Caomhnóir—then we have to assume that's who it was again."

"Which means the Caomhnóir just tried to kill us," Kiernan said.

"Bloody hell," Savvy whispered.

We all sat in a stunned silence for a few moments, letting the reality of this wash over us.

"I just don't see it," Finn said, shaking his head, and I could tell from his expression that he really didn't want to believe it of the brotherhood he had dedicated his entire life to. "If this really is about the Reckoning, then there are some very powerful clans involved, right? Those are the ones who are angry that the Gateways were restored."

"Yeah, there are Caomhnóir who are part of those clans, too," I pointed out. "So they'd be just as angry, wouldn't they?"

But Finn was shaking his head. "Not here. Not at Skye. Look, a post at Skye Príosún is basically a punishment. It's where they sent me when I was seduced by an evil Durupinen temptress," he said, quirking the merest suggestion of a smirk at me. "It was like being sent to Siberia. No one with actual clout or power gets sent here. They've all got cushy jobs guarding their own families or else important strongholds like Fairhaven. What motivation would a Skye Caomhnóir have to do something like this?"

"Reprieve," Kiernan said. I was stroking Hannah's hair, her head once more on his shoulder. "It would be easy to bribe someone who resented his post here, and that's most of them. Pay him off, promise him a better post when it's all over, and I bet you'd find the place would be full to brimming with would-be assassins."

Hannah shuddered again. Finn swore under his breath, which meant he knew Kiernan was right.

"Well, I think we know one thing for sure," I said, and everyone turned to look at me. "Whatever artifact Polly found, they must be one hundred percent certain that it's not in her house, or they never would have risked destroying it like that. There was nothing there to find, except maybe that clue, and we found it first."

Finn nodded. No one else spoke. A brisk wind blew over the hill, whipping the landscape into a series of waves, undulating like the sea.

"What I don't understand," Milo said, "is why they didn't try to kill you at the príosún. Why make such a public spectacle and risk collateral damage with that explosion when they could have smothered you in your beds last night? They had you within their own walls."

"Further proof that this is a small group of rogue agents," Kiernan said. "They couldn't risk doing it right under the noses of the other Caomhnóir, especially the leadership."

"So, what do we do now?" I asked. "We can't go back to the príosún. It's clearly not safe. Whoever tried to kill us is probably already back there plotting another attempt, and if they're desperate enough, they might even try it there."

"I think we have to go back."

It was Hannah who spoke. We all turned to look at her.

"Hannah, you can't be serious," Milo said.

"I am serious. We have no choice."

"Hannah, I think Jess is right about this," Kiernan said. "I want to keep searching as well, but we can't risk it now. We'll have to call in the Trackers and—"

"We have to go back. That message was meant for me to find," she insisted.

I groaned. "Hannah, you—"

"And more than that," she pressed on, raising her voice, "I know what it means."

I blinked. "You know what *what* means?"

"The message. Those two words. The last thing I did before we ran for our lives was Google them."

"And?" I asked. Everyone seemed to be holding their breath.

"Tanacetum vulgare is the Latin name for tansy."

She looked directly at me, and I felt the realization click into place like a puzzle piece.

"Oh, my God."

"What?" Savvy asked, looking back and forth between us with increasing frustration. "What the bollocks does that mean?"

"The Tansy Hag," I whispered.

12

CAVALRY

Of all the experiences I never wanted to have again, interacting with the Tansy Hag was solidly in the top five.

It wasn't just that she was something out of a very dark children's tale come to life; I'd come face to face with several beings that would have made the Brothers Grimm wet themselves in terror and never pick up a pen again. It was one of the hallmarks of my life, at this point—it was almost mundane, to live through what to any rational person would be a nightmare. And when all was said and done for all the lore and children's rhymes, the Tansy Hag had only ever been a woman—a woman who became a ghost, who held a secret too terrible to ever reveal, and so we turned her into a monster that no one would dare to approach.

No, it was the fact that the Tansy Hag had been part of one of the most terrifying journeys of my life—an experience that had taken everything I'd ever accepted at face value and turned it on its head. She was part of the most twisted of stories—the story of how the heroes became the villains. It was the story that turned our family's shining golden legacy into something tarnished and rotten.

Over the centuries, The Tansy Hag had been reduced to something akin to a nursery rhyme monster—the witch in the woods, luring Hansel and Gretel to her house. There had even been a children's rhyme that clan children all sang, like "Ring Around the Rosy."

> "For boys and girls who will not mind,
> Who trouble court and mischief find,
> The Tansy Hag, she lies in wait
> To leave her mark upon your gate."

In reality, the Tansy Hag had simply been a Traveler Durupinen who worked with Agnes Isherwood to create the Casting that removed the Gateways from the Geatgrimas, and sealed them into the bloodlines of the Durupinen. Lore and history had vilified her and reduced her to a dreadful stereotype. But I had seen her. I had spoken with her. She had been terrifying, yes, but only because she had been locked away for centuries in the deepest bowels of the príosún, held under Castings so powerful that the cells required no guards to ensure the captivity of the inhabitants.

And now, Polly had led us right to her. A clue that could mean nothing else.

"Jess?"

Hannah's voice pulled me back out of my jumble of thoughts.

"Huh? Yeah, sorry, what's up?"

"I said, what do you think?"

"About? Sorry, I sort of mentally rabbit-holed for a second there."

Milo raised an eyebrow. "A spot of príosún PTSD, perhaps?"

I considered this. "Actually, yeah, probably. Anyway, what were you saying, Hannah?"

"I was saying that we need to get down into the old spirit block," Hannah said.

"And I was saying that it's not safe because whoever tried to kill us is probably back at the *príosún* and is not going to stop at one attempt," Finn said, sounding very much like he was struggling to keep calm. He and Hannah were practically glaring at each other.

"Finn, I'm not trying to downplay the situation. It's dangerous, and we should get out of here as soon as we can," I said. "But we cannot ignore this clue. It's too important."

"So, then what do you propose?" Finn asked.

I hesitated. "I… haven't gotten that far yet."

"Well, if you ask me, what we need is a good distraction," Savvy said.

We all turned to look at her. "What do you mean?" I asked.

"A distraction. You know. A classic 'they all look left and we go right' type scenario."

I rolled my eyes. "Sav, I know what the word distraction means. I meant what type of distraction did you have in mind?"

Savvy grinned. "We call in the big guns."

I shook my head. "Sorry, I'm not following. I need the non-metaphor version, please."

Savvy hopped down off the hood of the car and came to sit next to Hannah, slinging her arm over Hannah's shoulder as she did so. "Look, Hannah's right. We need to get down into that spirit block, and there's no way to get down there without everyone knowing what we're up to. It's too obscure. You probably need special permission or something, right?"

I tried to remember my last trip down into the old spirit block. "There were guards, yeah. And we were questioned before we went down."

"So we need to create the kind of distraction that will not only draw guards away from the area, but also keep them all on their best behavior," Savvy said.

"Okay, makes sense, but I still don't see how—"

"Celeste," Savvy said, flinging the name down between us like a winning hand in a high-stakes poker game.

We all looked at her. Everyone else looked as bemused as I felt.

"What about Celeste?" Hannah asked.

"What do you think would happen if it was suddenly announced that the High Priestess of the Northern Clans herself was on her way here?" Savvy asked. "What do you think the Caomhnóir would do if they heard that?"

Still completely bewildered, I turned to Finn, expecting him to share in my confusion; but to my surprise, I saw a slow smile spreading over his face. "You really are a bloody genius sometimes, Savannah Todd."

Savvy grinned back. "I have my moments, sure."

"Okay, can someone catch me up here, because I'm still confused," Hannah said.

"That makes two of us," Kiernan murmured.

"Right, so we already thought this had something to do with the Reckoning," Savvy said, pacing now. "And now that Polly's pointed us toward the Tansy Hag, that all but seals it. We're in a race against God-knows-who to find this artifact, wherever it is, and so we need to act fast. We need to tell

Celeste. We tell her everything we know so far, and we tell her we need her help. She'll want to do what she can, won't she?"

Hannah's eyes lit up, and I realized she had finally caught on. "She's been thwarting clans right and left that are trying to remove her and reverse the Reckoning. If she thinks this is a real threat, she'll be here in a heartbeat."

"And her presence serves two purposes," Finn said. "A visit from the High Priestess will mean all hands on deck. With her and all her security on the premises, they wouldn't dare try to—"

"—kill a Council member and her sister right under her nose?" Hannah finished for him.

"Exactly," Finn said. "But even more than that, it's really a warning. A sudden visit from the High Priestess might spook whoever's behind all of this. If they think there's a chance she knows what they're up to, they'll back off, at least for long enough for us to search that spirit block."

"Bang on!" Savvy said, clapping her hands together. "You see? It's like bringing the headmistress into the classroom when the kids are acting up. They lose all their nerve because they know they're being watched."

"Except in this case, we're talking about probable kidnapping and attempted murder, not throwing spitballs," I said dryly.

Savvy scoffed. "Ah, come off it. With the stakes this high, it's bound to work even better."

She looked around at all of us hopefully. Everyone was considering, nodding. Finally, Finn turned to Hannah.

"You're closest to Celeste. Do you think she'll come?" he asked her.

Hannah nodded. "I don't know what's going on back at Fairhaven right now, but I can't imagine it's more dire than this."

"Only one way to find out," I said. "But how do we get in touch with—"

I yelped as my phone started vibrating in my back pocket. I pulled it out and stared down at the screen.

"It's Cat," I said, and picked up at once.

"Cat?"

"Jess! Oh thank God! I thought you were—where's Hannah? Finn?"

"We're all here, we're fine," I said. "But how did you know what happened?"

"It's fairly standard operating procedure to alert the department head when you think one of their Trackers has been blown to kingdom come," Cat snapped, though I could tell the snap in her voice was more stress than sarcasm.

"My God, what the hell happened? The Skye Caomhnóir office called to say you'd been at Polly's house and there was an explosion!"

"Did they mention that one of them probably set it off for the express purpose of murdering us?" I asked.

"WHAT?!"

With Catriona sputtering and cursing throughout, I explained as quickly as I could what had happened and about Savvy's idea.

"What do you think?" I asked. "Do you think Celeste would come?"

"I… I don't… I'll have to go find her and explain, but… yes. Yes, I think she'll come. I know she will."

"And would you—"

"I was coming anyway," Catriona said, and I was surprised to hear that her voice was shaky. "I was halfway through getting my things together, and I'd already ordered the chopper."

"Thank you."

There was a pause, heavy with unspoken tension.

"Jess, if this is true, if this was basically an ordered hit… whatever Polly found must be truly monumental. You have to be careful."

"You seriously think I don't know that?" I asked, aggravated that I could hear the note of hysteria in my voice. We were mere feet away from being flambeed, Cat. I promise I am fully aware of the seriousness of the situation. It's the whole reason I was about to call you."

"Right. Well, hang tight, and don't go back to the *príosún* until we arrive, do you understand?" Catriona ordered. The fact that I could hear the stress in her voice when it was usually dripping with ennui only heightened my stress. If Cat sounded like that, we were undoubtedly in very deep shit.

"Fine."

"I'll be in touch."

The line went dead. I stuck the phone back in my pocket and returned to the van to bring the others up to speed. The cavalry was coming. Now all we had to do was wait.

The anticipation made the hours drag. Finn paced so much that I thought he was going to create an actual rut in the road. Hannah and Kiernan sat huddled together, their hands intertwined. Anticipating that there would be no chance for rest once we went back to the *príosún*, Savvy had stretched herself out in the back of the van and was snoring softly. Milo had gone statue-still in his stress, so that he looked like a pale painting of himself standing in the rippling heather. I knew he was still blaming himself for taking his attention off the windows and doors; the errant thoughts, heaving with self-loathing, occasionally drifted through the connection like noxious fumes under a door. I was angry at myself as well. We'd let our guard down, and someone had taken full advantage of our momentary distraction. We couldn't let that happen again. We had to follow what clues Polly had left us to ensure we discovered what she had found that had left us, once again, in the crosshairs.

Finn made periodic check-ins with Celeste's security, so that we knew of any changes in the timeline, however small. Between these, he thrust bottles of water and protein bars at everyone, demanding we stay hydrated and keep our strength up. Finally, he received a text on his phone that alerted us to the imminent arrival of Celeste's helicopter, at which signal we piled back into the van and began the drive back to the *príosún*. He drove carefully, trying to align our arrival with that of the chopper. Sure enough, as we rounded the final bend around a rocky crag that brought the *príosún* into sight, the distant whirring of the helicopter could be heard on approach.

We pulled onto the grounds, but parked on the outskirts of the helipad instead of closer to the *príosún*, and stood clustered together as the chopper whipped the air into a frenzy around us on its final descent. A contingent of Caomhnóir marched out to greet the High Priestess. I scanned their faces, trying to make a mental note of anyone who might look startled or displeased to see us, but from what I could tell, they were an unbroken wall of stoic, emotionless faces. I could feel Finn's entire body stiffen beside me as they marched closer. I knew he was fighting every impulse he had to tuck me under one arm, Hannah under the other, and put as much distance between us and that *príosún* as he possibly could.

Instead, he took my hand and we stepped forward together as the doors to the chopper began to open. It was a much larger chopper than the one we'd taken, with a much longer body. A door opened toward the back, and two Caomhnóir stepped out smartly. Then they lifted down a set of stairs and rolled a long purple carpet out toward the front doors of the *príosún*.

"Oh, she's pulling out all the stops," Finn murmured, and I saw he was smiling slightly.

"What do you mean?" I asked.

"The carpet? The full guard in dress uniform? She's making sure they know she means business," he replied.

I realized he was right. This was all much more formal than Celeste would typically arrange things when she traveled. And the Caomhnóir were wearing the sashes with her clan crest on them, another overt show of power. As I took this in, four more Caomhnóir stepped out and lined up on either side of the door—her full protective guard, then. Celeste stepped out next, dressed in a plum velvet pantsuit, and looking as regal as I'd ever seen her. She wore her clan sash, her circlet, and the mark of the High Priestess on her chest in the form of an ornate gold necklace set with amethyst and diamonds. But all of this was mere ornament—she would have still looked like a queen if she'd arrived covered in dirt and dressed in rags.

Finn nodded, and our party stepped forward to meet Celeste. As we approached, two more people stepped out of the helicopter. The first, predictably, was Catriona. But behind her was a figure the sight of whom made my jaw drop.

Fiona.

"What the hell?" I muttered under my breath. I shot a sideways glance at Finn, who looked as perplexed as I felt. But there was no chance to discuss it. We were almost level with Celeste.

"Jess. Hannah," Celeste said each of our names like a sigh of relief, as though she hadn't really been sure we were okay until she'd seen us with her own eyes. She folded us both into an embrace that nearly made me lose my already shaky grasp on my composure. "Thank goodness you're all right. You're not injured?"

"Aside from a few scrapes and a mild ringing in the ears, we're just swell," I said.

Celeste narrowed her eyes skeptically, so Finn hastened to add, "I assessed them thoroughly. No signs of concussion or any other traumatic injury. We were extremely fortunate."

"I'm not sure that's the word I'd use," Celeste said rather darkly. "But I am very grateful you are alive, all of you."

Catriona appeared at Celeste's shoulder. "Are we ready to proceed?"

Celeste turned to us. "I intend to address all the Caomhnóir here in the trial hall."

"The trial hall?"

"It's the largest gathering space they have, and the only place I can possibly gather them all."

"How long will we have?" I asked.

"No more than an hour, I expect, once we are all assembled. I have prepared remarks, but I also intend to make inquiries that will require the testimony of several of the Caomhnóir in leadership. I will draw it out for as long as possible, but you should still move swiftly. Where is it, exactly, that you need to go?"

"To the old spirit block, to see the Tansy Hag," I said.

Celeste frowned. "The Tansy Hag? But she's gone."

13

REFLECTION

I felt my heart stutter. "Gone? What do you mean, gone?"

"I mean, she was released. Crossed over, after the Reckoning came to pass," Celeste said. "She hadn't committed a crime that we could find a record of. It is my belief that she was locked up merely for the knowledge she possessed. I didn't think it was safe for her to linger, and in any case, the Necromancers had promised her freedom in exchange for her cooperation. I didn't feel it was right to keep her there, after she'd been promised a release we owed her. I oversaw her Crossing myself. I'm so sorry. I thought you knew."

My mind was spiraling. The Tansy Hag was gone. She was gone, the one being I thought might have information about what to do next. I felt nauseous, on the verge of tears.

"When?"

"Excuse me?"

I cleared my throat, trying to sound like all hope hadn't just been extinguished inside of me. "When did she Cross?"

"Oh, many months ago now."

"And Polly would have known this?"

"I imagine so, yes. She works in the *priostín*, and by all accounts, she followed everything related to your clan very closely. I would frankly have been astonished if she hadn't known."

I looked at Hannah. To my surprise, she didn't appear to be spiraling, like I was. She looked thoughtful, but far from despair.

"We'll still need to check," Hannah said. "Thank you for telling us this."

"Of course," Celeste drew herself up to her fullest height and assumed an air of authority. "Use every minute I can give you." She threw a sharp look at Finn and Savvy. "Don't let them out of your sight."

"Wouldn't dream of it, High Priestess," Savvy said, clicking her heels together and giving a bow, though she ruined the effect of it by winking cheekily.

Celeste's lips twitched rather like she was smothering a smile. Then she lifted her chin and began to walk toward the waiting Caomhnóir, Catriona just behind her.

I caught Cat's elbow as she passed. "What the hell is Fiona doing here?" I asked.

She shrugged and answered out of the corner of her mouth. "I have no bloody idea. Absolutely refused to let us come without her. Be careful down there." And she swept past us to keep up with Celeste.

As I stood and watched them pass, Fiona stumped along behind them, using the walking stick she'd carved and repurposed as an assistive device. I stepped toward her as she passed, laying a gentle hand on her arm.

"Fiona."

She pulled her arm away as though I had burned her.

"Let me go."

"Fiona, what are you doing here?"

"What does it look like I'm doing here? I am assisting my High Priestess."

"Bullshit," I hissed. "We can barely get you out of your tower to a Council meeting, and somehow you've gotten onto a helicopter to Skye? What's really going on?"

"I said let me go!" she growled, yanking her arm out of my grip, and increasing her pace so that she closed the distance between herself and Catriona, who shortened her stride to allow Fiona to walk alongside her.

"Jess?"

Hannah was beside me. I turned to see her gazing inquisitively at me.

"Huh?"

"We really need to follow them. We can't afford to waste any time."

"Yeah," I said, my eyes still on Fiona's retreating form. "Yeah, let's go."

I have to admit it was satisfying, watching the Skye Caomhnóir contingent bowing and scraping in their efforts to flatter the High Priestess. Celeste wasn't the kind of person to demand that sort of behavior, but on this occasion, she let them carry on. After all, she was here to make a show of power, to remind them who they were meant to be loyal to; if that meant tolerating some groveling and sucking up, then so be it.

We followed behind the Fairhaven contingent, close enough to remind the Skye Caomhnóir that we were, in fact, under their protection. I tried not to look too hard at the Caomhnóir as they marched past us, but it was hard not to wonder who was involved and whether they'd been bribed enough to try again. I found myself scanning their faces again as I had, searching their features for signs of animosity or incredulity; but I should have known better—the ability to keep a stoic, unreadable expression was a hallmark of Caomhnóir training.

As Celeste led the procession to the trial hall, we broke away toward the prisoner blocks. As we had hoped, we met no guards on the way, and the door that led down to the old spirit block was completely unmanned. Here, though, Kiernan turned to us, his expression thoughtful.

"I think perhaps we should split up," he said.

"What? No!" Hannah gasped, looking at him like he'd lost his mind. "Why would we—?"

"Of course, the old spirit block is the most obvious place to look, and we should check it out. But I also don't think we should stay any longer in this place than we need to, and there is one other place we should check."

"Where?" Hannah and I asked together.

"The archive," Kiernan said.

Hannah scoffed and opened her mouth to argue, but I had suddenly remembered something.

"He's right," I said, and now Hannah turned her incredulity on me.

"What are you talking about?" she demanded.

"Don't you remember how we discovered the Tansy Hag was down in the old spirit block to begin with?" I asked Hannah.

She squirmed a little. "Lucida," she said quietly.

"That's right," I said. "She was the one who told us about the mark of the Tansy Hag. But we didn't want to take her word for it, so Flavia and I looked it up."

"But I thought the Tansy Hag wasn't in our history books," Finn said, frowning. "Which meant that, hundreds of years later, she had been reduced to little more than a fairy tale."

"Exactly," I said. "And Flavia knew it. That's why we found her in children's books. Is that what you were getting at, Kiernan?"

I looked at Kiernan, and he was nodding along. "We should leave no stone unturned," he said. "Polly was the Head Scribe. She knew about those books. We should check them, just in case."

Finn nodded, convinced. "Very good. Savvy?"

"I've got him, mate. Won't let him out of my sight," Savvy assured him. Then she turned to Hannah. "You get that? I promise. No one will get near him."

"I'll go with them, too," Milo said at once. "That way we can all stay connected in real time."

Hannah hesitated only a moment, then her expression cleared. "Okay."

"Where should we meet?" I asked.

Finn considered this. "Right outside the trial hall. Celeste only gave us an hour, so keep an eye on the time."

Kiernan checked his watch. Then, after a swift peck on Hannah's cheek, he jogged off in the direction of the archive, Savvy hot on his heels.

Finn turned back to Hannah and me. "After you, ladies."

I rolled my eyes. "How chivalrous of you."

I had ventured into the old spirit block once before. I hadn't been alone—Flavia had come with me, which turned out to be an absolutely brilliant coincidence, because we didn't know that the Tansy Hag was actually a Traveler; and it wasn't until Flavia accidentally blurted out an exclamation in Romany that she was comfortable enough to manifest.

Today we would need no translator. It seemed we wouldn't be communicating with the Tansy Hag at all. But that didn't make a stroll down the old spirit block any less dangerous.

Skye Príosún was home to the absolute most dangerous criminals in the Durupinen world. Every Necromancer we had had the misfortune to encounter—Charlie Parker among them—was housed here, serving out an existence that was, in my opinion, the definition of cruel and unusual. Then again, the Necromancers who had landed themselves here were, themselves, cruel and unusual, and so it seemed that the punishment fit the criminals.

But we weren't interacting with Necromancers this time around—or, at least, no Necromancers who were still alive. The old spirit block did not house living prisoners. Instead, it housed ghosts who were too dangerous to set free—ghosts whose spirit forms had presented no impediment to committing the most heinous of crimes. No bars were necessary to keep these prisoners in their cells—a powerfully magic array of Castings and runes did that. I explained this to Hannah and Finn as we continued the long descent down the stairs. Finn grunted in reply, but Hannah didn't make a peep. I turned to see that her face had gone milk-white. She looked like she was fighting an impulse to run right back up the stairs.

"You okay?" I asked her.

She twisted her hands together. "I... yes. Sorry. Is it crazy that, in spite of knowing that they'd be of no help whatsoever, I really wish there were bars?"

I laughed nervously. "I thought the same thing. A visual representation of the barrier would tend to calm the nerves. But they can't get out, I promise. The Castings have held for centuries."

"You sound like you're trying to convince yourself of that, too, love," Finn said, one corner of his mouth pulled up into a cheeky smirk.

"You've never been down here, have you?" I asked him.

The smirk disappeared. "No."

"Yeah, well, I don't think you'll begrudge me the little pep talk after you've seen it," I muttered darkly.

The closer we got to the entrance to the spirit block, the colder the air around us became, so that by the time we reached the door at the base of the stairs, I could see my breath clouding up in front of me. Normal, I reminded myself. Utterly ordinary, when there was a high concentration of spirits or spirit energy. Nothing to worry about. My pulse, ignoring my reminder completely, sped up into a gallop. Beside me, I could hear Hannah's breathing quicken.

The enormous metal door was unlocked, but it took Finn's help to push it open. The old spirit block unfurled before us, stretching out like a long, dark tunnel, lit only by a row of bare bulbs that dangled from the ceiling. The floor might have been stone, but it was covered with such a thick layer of dust and grime that it felt like dirt beneath our feet. On either side, cells like caves had been dug out of the walls, their insides dark and filthy and barely visible in the half-light.

"Bugger me," Finn muttered, and pulled a flashlight from his belt clip. Its narrow beam revealed the vast collection of runes and Castings etched, painted, and carved into every visible surface. The whole room felt electrified with the power of it. I could taste a metallic tang on my tongue.

"Oh my goodness," Hannah whispered. She reached for my hand just as I reached for hers, and our fingers tangled up as we scrabbled for the safety of each other's grasp.

"Where do we go?" she asked, once she had gotten her breathing under control.

"All the way down to the very end," I said.

"Obviously," she said weakly.

We began the long, frigid walk to the end of the block. We all knew it would be better not to interact with the spirits on either side of us, knew it would be best to keep our eyes locked straight ahead and ignore everything else; but never had we traversed a place full of more disturbing apparitions, and it was impossible not to look.

We passed a cell that I'd remembered from my last foray down into this place —a cell covered ceiling to floor in mirrors. Mirrors hung from hooks, mirrors leaned against the corners, mirror shards were cemented into the walls on all sides, so that it seemed the spirit within floated inside a giant mirror ball. Reflections of her skeletally thin form moved in perfect synchronicity on all sides as she gazed at herself, clawing at her face, at her arms, at her hair. I'd barely chanced a glance at her the last time I'd been here—now I had a hard time tearing my eyes away from her. And so, it seemed, did Hannah.

"Who is she?" Hannah whispered. "What's wrong with her?"

"I don't know," I said. I had a sudden vision of a circus sideshow, a ringmaster in a red tailcoat twisting his waxed mustache as he drew our attention to each terrifying specimen in turn. *Step right up if you dare and gaze upon the Mirror Lady! A thousand reflections, one tortured soul. Mirror, mirror on the wall, is she the fairest of them all?*

Hannah took a step closer to the cell, seemingly as entranced by the spirit as the spirit seemed to be by her own reflection.

I swallowed an urge to call out to her not to get too close. It was unnecessary, I reminded myself. The spirits were secure. They couldn't hurt us, as long as we stayed out of their cells.

The spirit in the cell froze as Hannah approached. She had caught sight of Hannah's reflection behind her own in her mirrors. It was almost as though she had no concept that we were there, unless she could see us in the mirrors, and suddenly we were real. Her eyes, glazed and dreamy, were suddenly sharp and predatory.

"Lovely," she whispered. "So lovely." She reached out a hand and stroked the mirror where Hannah's awestruck face gazed out at her. It was then, watching her watch my sister, that I really looked closely at her for the first time, and noticed the scars.

Now that I saw them, they were all I could see. The spirit was covered in terrible scars, covering her hands and her arms, snaking up her neck and down her legs, and marring the features on her face, so that all of her looked blurred and twisted.

"What happened to her?" I wondered aloud, the words a faint whisper that the ghost nonetheless seemed to hear. She turned sharply, twisting her head unnaturally on her long, slender neck to glare at me with a sudden and ferocious fury.

"I don't think she likes that question," Finn murmured from beside me. His body was vibrating with tension, and I knew he also hated the sight of Hannah so close to that cell. I pressed my lips together, cursing myself for speaking and wishing the ghost would look at anyone, anything, but me with those flaming eyes.

As though the spirit had heard my plea, her attention snapped back onto Hannah. She turned the rest of her body smoothly, sinuously, until she was facing Hannah, then drifted toward her by a foot or two, an unbearable longing in her expression.

"So lovely," she whispered again. "Won't you let me feel that again? Oh, to be lovely!"

Her voice was a rasp, a papery thin flutter of breath, but the words made Hannah stumble backward as though the spirit had screamed them. The spirit's expression twisted with fury as Hannah put this additional distance between them.

"Come here," the spirit rasped again. "Come closer. I only want to be lovely. We could be lovely together, young one. You and I, lovely forever." She reached out a badly scarred arm, extending it toward Hannah, a deadly invitation.

"Hannah."

My voice was thick and choked with terror. This ghost was dangerous—I knew it without knowing how I knew. My mind raced ahead, envisioning what would happen to any living person who dared take her hand, who foolishly accepted her invitation. The spirit's eyes were locked on Hannah with a greedy intensity—a gaze that could swallow you whole, if you let it.

It was Finn who had the sense to reach out and pull Hannah back, and even as he did, the spirit's face twisted and she let out a wild shriek of frustration.

"She's not why we're here," Finn reminded Hannah, who was still staring at the spirit with a mixture of revulsion and pity on her face. "We need to focus on the task at hand before we run out of time. We can't do anything for her."

His words jolted me back into the full scope of the moment. I glanced at my watch and received a shock—fifteen minutes of the hour Celeste had promised us had already slipped away.

"Right," I said. "Let's keep going. Hannah?"

With difficulty, Hannah tore her eyes from the spirit and turned her back on its siren call. "Yes. Of course. I'm sorry, I… I don't know why I was so—"

"She's down here for a reason," I reminded my sister. "Let's not give her any more chances to prove how dangerous she is."

We continued down the spirit block. This time, I didn't allow my gaze to slide to the cells on either side of us. I kept them firmly fixed on the very end of the block. I reached behind me and waited until I had felt Hannah's small, cold hand slide into mine. I focused my senses on her hand—the smoothness of her skin, the fragility of her slender fingers, the porcelain chill of her palm against mine, the faint thud of a pulse against the pressure of my grasp. Though the connection was not wide open, I could feel her energy, the way it thrummed with tension, and tried to imagine that tension unwinding slowly. Whatever spirits lurked on either side of us, we had to push forward.

At last, we reached the very end of the spirit block, and before us, like the dark, dank lair of some feral animal…

"This is it. The Tansy Hag's cell."

It looked just like I remembered it: the rounded opening that looked like it had been gouged out of the earth, the mysterious rune, known as the mark of the Tansy Hag, cut and drawn onto nearly every inch of the floor and the walls. Finn shone his flashlight so that it illuminated even the furthest corners of the cell. It didn't just appear empty, like some of the other cells; it *was* empty—no trace of spirit energy, no lingering presence to send a chill up my spine.

"Do you really think Polly hid something here?" I asked. Even in the absence of its former inhabitant, the cell itself seemed to repel the very idea that someone might enter it voluntarily. I certainly couldn't imagine cheerful little Polly strolling into that hellhole.

"We'll have to search it," Finn said.

"I'll do it," Hannah said at once. I turned to look at her in surprise, but she was already pushing past me.

"Are you sure you want to—"

She turned and looked at me, the steel in her gaze reminding me that my fragile-looking sister was, in fact, as tough as nails, and that I would do well to remember it. Then she dropped to her hands and knees and crawled toward the entrance.

She hesitated for a moment right at the edge of the cell, her head twisting around so that she could take full stock of all the runes and Castings that had been carved right into the stones that marked the edges.

"Fascinating," she murmured. "Not a single Casting that would prevent someone from entering. No effort to keep people out. A person could simply walk into any of these cells if they chose to."

"Yeah, well, if you'd seen what I did the last time I was here, you wouldn't wonder about that," I muttered in reply. "No one was entering that space with her voluntarily."

Hannah reached a hand forward, testing the magic that had held the Tansy Hag at bay the way someone might test the intensity of an electrified barrier. She reached further and further, until she was apparently satisfied that she could cross the boundary fully. Then she crawled forward.

"Take this, Hannah," Finn said, holding out his flashlight. "I realize there's no ghost in there anymore, but that doesn't mean there couldn't be... other things of the creepy crawly variety that you might rather avoid."

Hannah actually managed a smile. "Thanks, Finn."

Finn and I moved toward the entrance and squatted down so we could watch Hannah's progress. She set the flashlight in the center of the cell and then carefully worked her way around the perimeter, starting in the front left corner. She used her hands, probing with the tips of her fingers, pressing and prodding, digging and poking, looking for any sign of a hiding place in the dank darkness. She'd only been searching for a few minutes when she gasped.

"What is it? Spider? Cockroach? A second, long-forgotten spirit bent on our destruction?" I asked in a hiss.

"No! It's... I'm not sure what it is, but I think it might be... maybe..."

Hannah's voice trailed off. It was much too dark to see what she was doing, crouched in the very back of the cell, hunched over something.

"Hannah, I realize you're distracted, but the anticipation is killing me. Can you throw us a bone here?" I snapped.

"Huh? Oh, sorry. Here, let me…" She began moving awkwardly toward the mouth of the cavern, scooting in a half-crouch while she cradled whatever she had found against her chest. She scooped up the flashlight and tucked it under her arm, momentarily blinding both Finn and me. Finally, she slid out of the cavern and dropped onto the floor with an "oof!"

Finn and I dropped at once to our knees and Finn grabbed the flashlight so we could examine the object now clutched in Hannah's hands.

Whatever it was, it was about the size of a shoebox and wrapped in a small, crocheted blanket, the sight of which brought a lump to my throat. If I'd had any doubt Polly had been here, it vanished at the sight of those pink and purple granny squares. Heart pounding, my patience entirely expended, I reached eagerly for the corner of the blanket, preparing to pull it off and reveal the object Polly had risked so much to conceal.

The lights in the spirit block went instantly, blindingly dark.

"What the hell!" Finn exclaimed. He swung around, the flashlight in his hand swinging wildly as he attempted to train it back on the entrance to the spirit block. No sooner had the words escaped his lips, though, than pounding footsteps thundered toward us. We had only a glimpse of a hulking figure barreling in our direction before the flashlight was knocked from Finn's hands and a scuffle began.

For the next few frantic moments, I operated entirely on fear and adrenaline. The figure, whoever they were, had launched himself at the three of us. All I knew was a desperate flailing tangle of limbs, of fists, of grunts and curses and struggle. Something—maybe an elbow?—collided with the side of my head, making lights pop in front of my eyes and sending me sprawling to the ground. I heard Hannah shriek and Finn roar with anger. There was scraping and gasping and another loud bang as something or someone crashed into the wall. Then there was a shout and footsteps stumbled away, pounding up the spirit block. Those footsteps were instantly echoed by a second set of footsteps, another deep yell, and then a scuffling, scraping sound.

"Finn!" I shouted hoarsely, knowing he must be fighting with our attacker. I began to feel around frantically with my hands, desperate to find something that would help. My hands found Hannah first. She screamed as I clutched at her clothes, but then broke off into a sob when she realized it was only me. My fingers scrabbled like frantic spiders over the ground until—

"Yes!"

I found the flashlight, fumbling it up into my shaking hands and finally managing to turn it on. I swung it around, pointing the beam of light wildly around the room, searching. The light caught a sudden, violent motion, and I steadied it just in time to see a figure reeling backward into the wall, and then disappearing from sight.

"Finn!" I called again.

"Here! I'm here!" that blessedly familiar voice shouted back, and at last the light found him, crouched on the ground, chest heaving, one arm wrapped around his ribcage. "I'm okay... I'm... oh bugger *everything* that hurts!"

A dry sob behind me helped me find Hannah next. I spun around, training the flashlight on her now.

"Hannah? Are you okay? Did he hurt you, or—?"

Her voice was shaking badly. "No, I'm... I'm okay, but he got the artifact. I had it in my hands and then—"

"I've got it!" Finn called. "The artifact, I wrestled it away from him, but I don't know where he—"

At that moment, a terrified shriek shattered the room, and we all yelped and shouted as we searched for the source of the sound. I grabbed Hannah's hand, yanked her up onto her feet, and ran with her to Finn's side. When we reached him, he snatched the flashlight out of my fingers and trained it on the cell right in front of him.

Our attacker was slumped in the corner of the mirror cell, and the ghost within was bearing down on him, a ravenous look on her face.

There's a hundred Castings keeping them in, but not a single one to keep anyone out...

"Get out of there!" Finn shouted. "For God's sake, get out of there before she—"

But the man seemed to have been stunned when he fell, or else he was paralyzed with fear at the spirit's approach. His heels scuffed the ground as he struggled to get himself up into a seated position, his hand thrust out in front of him protectively. He was muttering something that didn't sound like English, but I couldn't understand the words over the rising voice of the spirit.

"At last," she cooed. "At last... so young..."

And before the man could do anything more than moan out a plea, before Hannah could turn away or Finn could shout another warning, the spirit flew at the man, clawed fingers outstretched and began, with feral snarls and cries, to tear into him. It was as though she was trying to burrow into his very flesh, to slide underneath it. The man's screams rent the air, their echoes rebounding, amplifying the terror and pain. Finn was shouting, fumbling for his Casting bag, and Hannah was screaming for the spirit to stop; but I could do nothing but stand there, frozen, locked in the grip of a memory.

A darkened library...

A desperate spirit...

An unendurable agony...

I was watching, from the outside, an experience I had once barely lived through—a spirit forcing its way into a living person. This wasn't Habitation... this was invasion and destruction—the rapid and all-consuming insatiability of a parasite.

"Do something!" Hannah cried, lunging forward toward the cell, but Finn grabbed the back of her shirt and pulled her backward.

"You can't! If you enter that cell, Hannah, she'll destroy you too! I just have to—" Finn finally found what he needed and attempted to Banish the spirit as she continued her ravaging, but the Casting had no effect at all. Finn cursed loudly and tried again, but the words did nothing. The Castings on the cell itself were too powerful, interfering with his attempts to break through them. The man's screams rose and peaked, mingled with the spirit's desperate cries...

There was nothing we could do, and I couldn't bear to watch anymore. I closed my eyes and waited for it to end. A few seconds later, it did, as a heavy silence fell, broken only by Finn's panting and Hannah's hitched and broken sobs. The man was still, his body twisted into a strange knot of crooked limbs. Every part of him looked like it had been bent at the wrong angle. His face was contorted, his mouth stretched wide, his eyes bulging from his skull, the muscles of his face rigidly frozen into an endless, silent scream.

I didn't need to get any closer to know that he was dead.

Then he moved.

It was wrong, the movement. Stilted. Clumsy, like someone had attached hooks to his body and was now jerking them sharply so that he now sat upright, arms dangling, face still stretched in that agonizing, silent scream. Another jerk, a dragging thump, and he was upright, his leg tucked under him, his ankles bent, his feet dragging along. The body turned, swayed, and dragged itself toward the nearest mirror. One of the lifeless hands flopped up onto the cheek, and we could hear the spirit again, this time staring at the reflection she had stolen.

"So young... unblemished..."

"She killed him," Hannah whispered. "She killed him and now she's… wearing him."

"Who is he?" I asked, even as a voice in my head corrected me. *Who was he?*

"He's a prisoner," Finn said, and for the first time, I registered what the man was wearing in the harsh light of the flashlight beam. His clothing was a uniform, the same dull gray scrubs worn by all the living prisoners within these walls.

"But how did he get out?" Hannah asked, her voice rising now as the shock wore off and the hysteria began to set in. "How is there a prisoner just… just running around in here? And why did he attack us?"

"I only know the answer to the last question," Finn said, holding up the artifact, which was still wrapped in the crocheted blanket. "He knew we were down here. He knew what we were looking for."

"But how?" I asked.

"He's in no state to tell us now, is he?" Finn said darkly. "But I can tell you this—in the last hundred years, not a single prisoner in this place has managed a break-out without inside help, which means we still need to get out of here as quickly as possible." He handed the artifact back to Hannah, who clutched it protectively to her chest.

"But what do we do about him?" Hannah asked, barely able to pull her eyes from the stolen man trapped in the mirrors.

"There's nothing we can do for him," Finn said. "He was lost the moment he breached that cell. We can alert the other Caomhnóir once we're safely on our way out of here. Now, let's go."

And we raced out of the spirit block, leaving the ghost alone to toy with her newly acquired plaything.

14

LOCK AND KEY

Emerging from the old spirit block was like surfacing from an icy lake; we took in greedy lungfuls of fresh air, and felt the relative warmth seep slowly into our bones, gradually thawing us after the stagnant, frigid atmosphere below.

When we reached the doors to the trial hall, Kiernan, Milo, and Savvy were already there waiting for us, and looking immensely relieved to see us coming around the corner.

"Thank goodness," Hannah murmured.

"Please tell me that's what I hope it is," Savvy said, her eyes widening as they fell on the object still carefully wrapped in Hannah's arms.

"We think so," Hannah said.

"And somebody else sure as hell thought so, too," Finn said, and without delay he lowered his voice and explained about the attack down in the spirit block.

Kiernan's expression was stony with anger. "They're attacking even with the High Priestess here? They really are desperate, aren't they?"

"I don't think we should linger even long enough to examine it. Best take it where it's safe," Finn said.

"We've found something, too," Kiernan said in a whisper. "At least, I think we did."

"You can tell us all about it on the trip back," Finn said, and I could tell from the sharp edge in his tone that he was ready to be the hell out of there. "Hannah, Kiernan, get yourselves safely onto Celeste's chopper."

"Celeste's chopper?" Kiernan asked. "What about the one we took?"

Finn shook his head. "Too risky. It's been sitting around unguarded since we got here. If someone wanted to disable or rig it somehow, they'd have had ample opportunity by this point. Celeste's chopper has been guarded since it landed. Catriona made sure of that, so we're hitching a ride."

At this point, Hannah's complexion was chalky white, but her expression was fierce as she nodded her agreement with the plan.

"Savvy? Milo?" Finn said, turning toward them.

"We won't let them out of our sight," Milo said, and the four of them took off toward the front doors. I watched them go, feeling the tiniest bit of my stress leave with them. I couldn't wait to be away from this place, even if it meant more flying. Finn and I stood together outside the doors to the trial hall, the air between us buzzing with tension. Any minute now...

There was a round of applause from inside the trial hall, followed by the shifting and shuffling of hundreds of feet. Finn and I stepped back from the doors just in time for them to burst open, and the rows of Caomhnóir began filing out. I thought I noticed a few nasty side-eye glances thrown our way, but that was probably just my hypervigilance rearing its ugly head. I was looking at every person who passed us as a potential enemy at this point.

The line of Caomhnóir splintered into many lines in the entrance hall, as the guards returned to their shifts in the various wings of the prison, or back to their barracks for their leisure time. We watched them, like ants in an ant farm, march in formation until the entrance hall was empty once again. A moment later, Celeste emerged, her guard surrounding her, and Fiona and Catriona brought up the rear.

Celeste gave me a significant look, and I nodded. We all knew that discussing the reason for this whole charade was dangerous. Her face relaxed, and she turned to Catriona.

"Can we return to the chopper now, or is there any other—"

"Chopper is waiting. The sooner we take it, the happier I'll be," Catriona said.

Fiona snorted from just behind Catriona, but everyone ignored her.

We followed Celeste and the others out through the entrance hall and across the front lawns to the chopper. I felt exposed, turning my back on the *príosún* and everyone in it, my walk turning to an impatient jog as we approached the open door of the helicopter. As I buckled myself in and felt the blades whir to life over our heads, I felt something I had never before felt when leaving solid ground: relief.

"Okay, but for real, what the hell is going on with Fiona?" I asked.

When we landed at Fairhaven, I had tried, once again, to talk to my former mentor; but she brushed me off again and stumped off to her tower, claiming she did not want to be disturbed. When everyone else was out of earshot, I proposed my question to Catriona.

Cat pressed her lips together, and for a moment, I thought she wasn't going to reply. But then she seemed to deflate, letting the air hiss out between her teeth. "Blast if I know, but I'll tell you this, I'm really worried about her."

"So am I. I've been worried about her ever since Celeste asked me to check in on her. Do you have any idea what's going on with her? Has she mentioned anything?"

Cat snorted. "Oh sure. Because Fiona is such a trusting and open soul. We've had a real heart-to-heart about it all."

"So, nothing, then."

"Not a bloody word. If she hasn't confided in you, I don't know who she would talk to."

"Really? None of her friends on the Council?"

Catriona raised an eyebrow. "Friends? Fiona doesn't have friends. You know that."

"Okay, fine, 'friend' was the wrong word. Colleagues? I mean, come on, you've all been through some shit together. You must have earned a bit of trust."

But Cat shook her head. "Not enough to get over this wall she's built up, not this time. She's always been a loner, sure, but that was much more about ambivalence than animosity. It wasn't that she didn't like people, she just sort of… couldn't be bothered with them. But this… I've never seen her closed off to this degree. She's outright hostile."

"So then, how did this happen? If she's so closed off and hostile, how did she wind up on the helicopter in the first place?"

"She was standing there in Celeste's office when I went to inform Celeste about what had happened to you," Catriona explained. "It wasn't as though I was going to filter myself in front of Fiona—I know how much you trust her, and anyway, there was no time. Fiona didn't say a word, just listened along with Celeste. But when I asked Celeste to come here to Skye, Fiona went absolutely mental. Started shouting about the risks, and we had to send someone else."

"She tried to stop Celeste from coming?" I asked.

"You should have heard her shouting. I was gobsmacked. Of course, Celeste told her that a real show of power was the only way to get you all out of there safely, and that she was going to the *príosún*, end of. Fiona must have realized it was pointless to try to argue, and so she announced that she was coming, too. You know how she gets. I didn't fancy another round of argument, so we just let her come."

"I don't get it," I said, shaking my head in bewilderment. "I could barely get her to speak two words to me when she got off the helicopter."

"She's hardly spoken two words to anyone," Catriona said. "I couldn't get any sense out of her on the ride over here. She kept pretending she couldn't hear me over the sounds of the blades, but I knew that was absolute bollocks. Her hearing is sharper than ever it has been, now that she's lost most of her vision. She usually only ignores people like this when she's in the throes of a creative project."

"She's definitely working on something," I confessed. "When I was up in her tower a few days ago, she was working on a new sculpture. She has it set up behind a curtain, and she nearly scalped me when I tried to take a peek. But it seems to me that if she was so invested in it, she wouldn't have left it behind to come to Skye."

"Yeah. Yeah, it doesn't make much sense. Not that Fiona ever has, really. Mad as a hatter, that one."

I couldn't help but feel a little frustrated as we walked the rest of the way to Celeste's office. Yes, Fiona was as mad as a hatter, but I couldn't dismiss her present behavior as a hallmark of her usual eccentricities. I would just have to keep monitoring the situation and hope that, at some point, Fiona would let me in.

Up in the High Priestess' tower, Celeste thanked her guards for their committed service that day on her journey and then promptly dismissed them, making sure not to address the rest of us until we had all watched the door swing shut behind them. Savvy, Hannah, Kiernan, Milo, Catriona, Finn and I all stood in a semi-circle around Celeste's desk, our anticipation building until the tension was as thick as fog in the circular chamber.

"Well," Celeste said, settling into the chair behind the great carved desk and pressing the tips of her fingers together. "If Catriona has explained all of this sufficiently, then I am to understand that what you've found is some kind of artifact discovered by Polly Keener, Head Scribe at the Skye Príosún, who is currently missing?"

A few hours ago, I'd have been hesitant to tell anyone about Polly's letters, but we'd all agreed that, if this artifact was as important as we thought it was, Celeste would have to be informed. There were many people in positions of power all through the Durupinen hierarchy who I wouldn't have trusted as far as I could throw them, but Celeste was not one of them. She had fought fiercely for the rebuilding of our world post-Reckoning and had defied every attempt to bribe, persuade, or discredit her. Celeste was on our side in this situation, even if we didn't fully know what the situation was. Still, Hannah caught my eye, and I could sense the hesitation there as she placed the object, still swaddled carefully in its crocheted wrappings, in the center of Celeste's desk.

"You haven't examined it yet?" Celeste asked.

"No," Hannah said. "We didn't feel it was safe."

"We were attacked again down in the spirit block as we tried to retrieve it. Someone was very desperate indeed that we not get our hands on this," Finn added.

"You were attacked while we were there?" Catriona asked, looking flabbergasted.

"As I said, someone was desperate," Finn repeated. "With two attempts on our lives in a single day, we knew we couldn't waste another minute there."

"But who was it that—" Cat began, but I raised a hand.

"Can we deal with those details later?" I asked. "I'd kind of like to see what we're risking our lives for now that it's safe."

"I'm not entirely sure it is safe," Celeste said. "Oh, I don't mean the trustworthiness of the people in this room," she added, for she could see the wariness that had crept into all of our faces. "But I mean we do not know what kind of Casting might be on this object, and we would do well to prepare ourselves, just in case."

"Prepare ourselves how?" I asked.

Celeste was already opening the top drawer of her desk and extracting a Casting bag. "Just a few simple precautions," she said, sliding the drawstring open and pulling out a piece of chalk. As we all watched, she drew a neat circle around the object, being careful not to touch it. Then she added several runes to the perimeter of the circle, lit a small candle, and dripped the wax over the runes to seal them, muttering to herself in old Gaelic. I recognized several runes that stood for containment—used in Cagings and other protective Castings. Celeste then fitted the still-burning candle into a brass holder on her desk and sat back, looking satisfied.

"That ought to protect us from the effects of any Casting the object has been placed under, while still allowing us to examine the object. But you must make sure to keep the object within the confines of the circle, or the protection will be broken," she explained.

Again, Hannah hesitated, but then, with a steadying breath, she reached into the circle. I could feel a sort of vibration in the air, a disturbance of energy, caused by her hands penetrating the boundary of the circle. She looked up at Celeste, who nodded encouragingly.

"Go on. It can't hurt you," she promised.

Hannah gently pulled the corners of the crocheted blanket back, like peeling back the petals of a colorful flower, revealing the object nestled in its center. It was a wooden box, nearly black with age, and carved heavily all over with runes and vines. I leaned closer and got a whiff of mildew and something else—something sharp and slightly metallic, like static charging the air.

"Bugger me," Cat whispered. "Is that… what I think it is?"

"I do believe it is, yes." Celeste had gone statue-still—if she hadn't answered Cat, I'd have doubted she was even breathing.

"Would someone care to enlighten the rest of us?" Milo asked, "Because I'm pretty sure I'm not the only one who has no idea what we're looking at."

"My apologies, Milo. What we have here is a very old, very primitive example of a Casting Cage," Celeste said.

Hannah, Milo, and Savvy all looked as confused as I felt. Only Kiernan let out a soft "oh" of recognition at her words, and Finn's eyes went wide. Both of them shifted their stances closer to the desk, as though suddenly more eager to examine it.

"Yeah, we're gonna need a little more than that," Milo said. "Still don't know what's happening."

"A Casting Cage is a device that is built to contain a piece of Durupinen magic," Celeste said.

"You mean there's instructions for a Casting in there, locked up?" Savvy asked.

"Not exactly. It's not like recording an incantation in a book—which you could argue is another way to contain magic. A book can only contain the information about the Casting, not the Casting itself. No, this is a more complex device, a way that was devised to carry out a Casting and contain the resultant magic itself inside an object—an object that would stop the Casting from taking effect until the object was breeched, or else made to release the Casting."

"So it's like… putting a piece of magic in a safe, and you can't get it out unless you have the combination to the lock?" Hannah asked.

"Something like that, yes," Celeste said, her eyes still on the box.

"It sounds useful," Milo said, his eyes falling on the Casting bag that Celeste had just used to create the protective circle. "I mean, it's not always possible, in the moment, to have everything you need to perform a Casting. This would be like… Casting-on-the-go."

"Yeah, insta-Casting!" Savvy said, grinning broadly. Knowing how she had struggled with memorizing Castings during her training, it was no wonder she found the idea so appealing. I couldn't think of it in quite so positive a light. My brain was dredging up the myth of Pandora's box, releasing its swift and enduring horrors into the world when someone dared to breach it. As though she could hear the fear rattling around inside my head, Celeste spoke.

"Unfortunately, it's not quite so simple. There's a reason Durupinen aren't walking around with half a dozen Casting Cages in their handbags," Celeste said. "And the reason is not the Cage itself. It's the means by which one must open the Cage."

"Why?" I asked. "How do you open it?"

It was Catriona who spoke, and her voice shook a little. "A Casting Cage works a bit like a Gateway did, back when we carried them in our bloodstream. There were two parts to the equation: the Door and the Key. The Gateway is inside both of them, but it can only be opened when the two are brought together. Whoever created this Casting Cage also created a sort of key with which to open it."

"And the manner in which a key is created," Celeste said, gathering up the thread that Catriona had left dangling, "is death."

The word hung there, sucking all the air out of the room.

"I'm sorry, come again?" I finally said, and my voice had shot up at least an octave. I cleared my throat. "What do you mean, death?"

"I mean," Celeste said calmly, "that a person had to die in order to create the key that would open this Cage."

"And not only that," Catriona added, "but someone else has to die for the key to open the Casting Cage. It requires a sacrifice."

Silence again.

"Yeah, I can, uh… I can see why that would put a damper on using 'em, then," Savvy said, somewhat hoarsely.

No one else spoke for a moment, as we all absorbed the horror of what we'd just heard.

"So am I correct," Hannah finally ventured, and her voice, though small, felt unnaturally loud in the room, "that we only have one part of the puzzle here? I mean, we have the Casting Cage, but we don't have the… the key or whatever to open it?"

Celeste looked up at her. "Was there nothing else hidden in the cell? Nothing else here concealed in the wrappings?"

We all held our breath as Hannah searched through the folds of the blanket with shaking fingers, making an obvious effort not to touch the Casting Cage if she could help it. At last, she stepped back, shaking her head sadly.

"There's nothing else here," she said, though we all knew it.

"I wouldn't expect there to be," Catriona said. "A Casting Cage is meant to be concealed and heavily protected. Only a fool would hide the key and the Cage together, and Polly Keener is no fool. You might as well just giftwrap whatever magic is inside, if you're going to make it that easy."

"So, we've finally found the thing that Polly risked her life to pass along to us, and we can't even open it to see what's inside?" I asked, frustration welling up inside me. "And she's left no clue to where the key is, so what are we supposed to do with it?"

"Maybe Polly has the key," Finn said. "Maybe she had it with her when she was… I mean, when she disappeared." I caught his eye and knew he had been about to say, "when she was killed," but stopped himself. I, for one, thought he was probably right. Ever since the explosion, I'd been harboring less and less hope that Polly was actually still alive.

"I don't think so," Kiernan said, and we all turned to look at him. He reached into his pocket and pulled out a folded piece of paper. It was old and faded, and I could tell from the guilty look on Kiernan's face that it hadn't come into his possession by the acceptable channels. Sure enough, as he unfolded it, I recognized it as a page torn out of a book.

As though she read my mind, Savvy leaned over to me and muttered, "Poor bloke couldn't bring himself to do it. I had to rip the page out myself while he turned his head."

We all leaned forward over the page as Kiernan smoothed it out. It looked like...

"A children's book," Celeste said, sounding disappointed.

"Children's books are the only place in our literature where the Tansy Hag exists," Kiernan said. "Polly knew that, and she was aware that we knew it, too. I thought, when we discovered the clue in the picture frame, that there was a chance she had hidden a clue in the children's books that had a mention of the Tansy Hag. And I was right."

He pointed at the pen and ink illustration that took up most of the page. It was a rendering of the Tansy Hag herself, as she had come to be known in the Durupinen children's tales—little more than a wicked old witch, a crone in a dark hooded robe crooking gnarled fingers at sweet little children playing in the flowers, and trying to lure them into the shadows of the forest. If he hadn't pointed directly to it, I would never have spotted it—I suppose that was Polly's hope. There, nestled in the folds of the Tansy Hag's cloak, was a single word: *tapetum*.

"That's Latin, isn't it?" Catriona asked.

"Yes, and I've already looked it up. It's the Latin word for 'tapestry,'" Kiernan said.

"Tapestry," Savvy repeated, and then looked expectantly at each of us in turn. "Just the one word. And we're supposed to make heads or tails of that, are we?"

"Okay," Hannah said, beginning to pace. "Okay. The first clue she left us was a Latin word that led us to where she hid the Casting Cage. It also led us to a second clue, a second Latin word. So this word, tapetum, must be trying to lead us to the key."

"I mean, the logic makes sense," Milo said. "The clue, however, does not."

"Tapestry," Celeste repeated under her breath. "Tapestry. Was there a tapestry at Polly's house?"

"Not that I saw," I said, racking my brain to picture every crevice of Polly's house. "And even if there had been, it wouldn't do us much good now, as it's likely a pile of ash."

"What about at Skye?" Catriona asked. "There've got to be at least a dozen old tapestries in there. Hell, there was one on the back wall of the trial hall!"

"Yes, which makes me think it's unlikely she'd be referring to a tapestry there," Hannah said. "Remember, she's trying to leave clues specifically for us, things that only we would manage to find and interpret. If the answer to everything was hanging on the wall in plain sight at Skye Príosún, it wouldn't exactly be very well hidden, would it?"

"Things often hide in plain sight," Finn said. "The Tansy Hag is proof of that," he added, tapping his finger on the illustration of the real-life woman who had been turned into a fable to frighten misbehaving children.

"Yes, but I think Polly was trying to be more specific than that. I think we should consider that she was leaving these clues for us, therefore she must think that the word "tapestry" would mean something to us. Something specific."

Hannah looked right at me, and I stared back, feeling more lost than ever.

"Hannah, I don't—"

"Jess, the Reckoning came about because of two women," Hannah said, her voice quiet but urgent. "The first clue led us to one of them. What if this clue is meant to lead us to the other?"

"Hannah, just say what you—oh. *Oh.*"

I smacked myself in the forehead, making everyone jump, but I couldn't help it. How could I be so dense? I turned on my heel and ran right for the tower door.

"Jessica! Where are you going?" Celeste called after me.

I paused with my hand on the doorknob only long enough to reply, "Agnes Isherwood is the other piece of this puzzle. I'm going to look at her tapestry."

15

FACELESS

Everyone shifted like they were going to follow, but I held up a hand.
"No. I have to go alone," I said.
"Don't be daft, we're coming with you!" Savvy said.
"The tapestry isn't out in the gallery anymore," I reminded her. "It's in Fiona's tower, and the last few people to attempt a visit there nearly got their blocks knocked off. She'd never allow this many people in her tower on a good day, never mind when she's going through... whatever the hell it is she's going through right now."
"Oh, right," Savvy said, shuffling back toward the desk at once. "Yeah, I'd rather not get on the wrong side of Fiona. I've already had one near-death experience today."
"Well, I'm coming with you," Hannah said, stepping out from around the desk. "This is about both of us, Jess. You might need my help."
I considered arguing with her, but her expression was so determined that I knew it was useless.
"Okay, fine, but I'm going in first, and if I tell you to duck, you'd better listen."
Her expression twitched into a fleeting smile. "I promise."
"We'll wait for you right here," Finn said. "I'm sure the High Priestess still has more questions for us, and we need to finish briefing Catriona on the

explosion and the attack down in the old spirit block." Would Celeste or Catriona say anything in this conversation? Aren't they right there?

"We'll be back as quick as we can," I promised, and darted out the door.

"I'll keep the connection open, in case things go south," Milo called after us. "Let us know if we need to come rescue you."

The long journey from one tower to the other left us with barely enough breath to talk as we went.

"You think Polly knew about the tapestry of Agnes?" I asked.

"Of course she does. She was an Apprentice here, once upon a time. And as our clan historian, it's her literal job to know everything about us and our history. I have no doubt she knew about the tapestry."

It was hard to hold on to my doubts when Hannah sounded so sure of herself, and I wanted so badly to be sure of something—anything. I felt a surge of hope as we climbed Fiona's tower stairs, though that hope had slightly soured by the time we reached the top.

We did have to deal with Fiona, after all.

I hadn't spoken at all to Gemma since we'd left for Skye, so I had no idea what we might be walking into, but I also knew that, regardless of the situation, I wasn't going to wait. The clock was ticking to unravel this mystery, and every second that passed could mean more danger for Polly.

I knocked loudly on the door and listened, pressing my ear to the heavy wood panels. When I heard no reply, I knocked again. Still, nothing.

"Should we come back?" Hannah asked.

"No," I replied. "We should just let ourselves in."

"Are you sure?"

"Hannah, trust me, this will probably be easier if she's not here," I said, pulling my set of keys from my pocket and inserting the right key into the lock. This wasn't the time or place for pointless things like etiquette.

I pushed the door open and peeked around it. The studio was definitely better than when I had last seen it; Fiona had at least allowed Gemma to do some tidying. The air smelled less stale—I spotted an open window, the curtain fluttering gently—and all the old food and garbage had been cleared away. It also looked like Gemma had begun to reorganize the shelves again, though she'd only managed to finish two of them so far.

"Hello?" I called tentatively. Only my own voice, echoing around the cavernous space, answered me. Hannah started forward, but I held out an arm to stop her. There was still a good chance something would hit us from across the room. I counted to ten, and when nothing happened, I lowered my arm. "You can't be too careful in here," I told her. "Those paint cans hurt."

We crossed the room to where the tapestry hung on the wall. It had been moved to Fiona's office the previous year to be restored, a project I had been put in charge of because of Fiona's diminished eyesight. But instead of cleaning it, I'd somehow managed to trigger a hidden Casting on it that revealed a map of all the Geatgrimas around the world, a map that the Trackers were still using to ensure that the restored Gateways were functional and safe. I stared at it, my eyes raking eagerly over it, looking for something—anything that might trigger some sort of understanding.

"Jess."

I turned to see Hannah staring at the tapestry in dismay. The look on her face sent my heart into overdrive.

"What? What is it? What's wrong?"

"This tapestry is wrong," she said, gesturing up to it.

"What do you mean it's wrong? This is the tapestry of Agnes Isherwood, the only one there—"

"But it's not of Agnes Isherwood," Hannah whispered. "Not anymore."

I looked back at the tapestry and my heart, galloping a moment before, felt like it fell with a clunk right into my shoes.

"You think the clue meant the old image—the design that was hiding this one," I realized.

"I think it must. That image of Agnes was centuries old—a kind of portrait. I realize it was designed to hide this map, but we didn't know that until about a year ago, and I doubt Polly knew it at all. It's been over a decade since she last set foot in Fairhaven—she told me so when we were working together."

I looked back at the map again, and a lump rose in my throat. This was another dead end, another question without an answer. My despair must have been written on my face because Hannah grabbed my hand.

"Hey! Hey, don't look like that, don't give up! Just because the original image is gone doesn't mean there's no record of it!" she said. "Come on, you've been working with Fiona for years, you know that."

"What do you—oh!" It had taken my brain a moment to catch up to my disappointment, but of course, the tapestry was documented. I knew there was an archive room with a whole file on it, including sketches and photographs. "Right. No, it's okay. We can still see what it looked like. I'll just need to check Fiona's filing system to figure out where to find the documents."

"Fiona has a filing system?" Hannah asked, her tone incredulous as she glanced around the general chaos of the space.

"Shockingly enough, yes," I confirmed. "I actually helped her update it a couple of years ago."

From excitement to crushing disappointment to excitement again in about two minutes, I was starting to feel like an emotional yo-yo. I crossed the room at a jog, which, based on the amount of junk I had to dodge, swerve, and jump over, was really more like parkour than anything else. The filing cabinets were located on the far side of the room near the area Fiona used as sleeping quarters. I gave the spot a wary glance out of the corner of my eye, but apart from a couple more liquor bottles than I'd have liked to see, it seemed to be mostly in order, by Fiona's general standards. Her fireplace caught my eye, and I took a step closer to examine the odd-looking contents of the grate.

There was plenty of ash, but there was also debris, including several twisted metal things that turned out to be the spiral wire used to hold together the pages of spiral-bound notebooks. I picked up the poker and shifted the ash around, finding charred clumps of paper still clinging to the wire bindings, and a few partial pages that hadn't quite been destroyed. I couldn't make out much of what was on the pages, only enough to realize that they were charcoal sketches, and a few of them had human forms on them—an outstretched hand, a foot sticking out from the bottom of a long garment. Why was Fiona burning sketches? I mean, she showed my work no mercy when we were working together, but she usually stopped short of actually burning it; and anyway, she had no students now, not since her accident. Was she burning her own work?

I turned away from the fireplace, and passed the curtained area behind which Fiona had been working the last time I'd been here. On that occasion, she was so fierce about not letting me see what she was working on that she'd basically tackled me—it was a truly feral reaction. Now I stood outside that same curtain, with no Fiona here to assault me. Did I dare look behind it?

I hesitated. I knew how protective I could be about my own work, but this wasn't about simple respect for the creative process. This was about Fiona and whether or not she was cracking up right in front of our eyes. I'd seen her deal with the regular throes of creativity—classic tortured artist shit—but this wasn't that, and I'd known her long enough to spot the difference. I decided I'd feel less guilty about spying on her than I would feel if I ignored the signs and let her crumble.

I stepped forward to pull the curtain and noticed a lot of broken plaster on the floor—like she'd recently taken a hammer to yet another of her creations. It only strengthened my resolve to take a closer look. I yanked the curtain back.

The space was dominated by a sculpture, but it was hard to tell if it was the same sculpture I'd seen when I'd last been in this room. In the first place, this sculpture had no face—it had been hacked into jagged obscurity by Fiona, hence the plaster all over the floor. The only real glimpse I'd gotten of the previous statue was a face, and so I couldn't tell, from the rest of the work, if it was the same sculpture or not.

What I did know, though, was that it was disturbing as hell.

The statue was that of a woman—a now faceless woman—who had dropped to her knees, the skirt of her long dress pooling around her like rippling water. One hand was stretched out in front of her like she was reaching for something, fingers splayed. The other hand was pressed to her chest, fingers caressing the handle of the knife protruding from her breast.

I froze, my eyes on the knife, plunged to the very hilt into this faceless woman as she reached for—help? Mercy? Revenge? Without an expression on her face to read, I couldn't be sure; but I knew that the longer I stared at it, the more details I took in, the more horrified I became. I stumbled backward, dragging the curtain closed again to hide the view.

"Jess?"

"Gah! What?"

I spun on the spot—I'd been so engrossed in the statue that I hadn't even been aware that she was walking up behind me. I was filled with a panic I couldn't explain, trying already to blot what I'd seen from my memory, trying to intentionally blur the details, soften the reality.

"Are you okay? You look like you've seen... well, you know," Hannah said, in a hesitant attempt at humor.

"Oh yeah, I just... got distracted."

Hannah's face asked the question, but for some reason, I couldn't bring myself to answer it. Why didn't I just show her? Just pull back the curtain and let her see what I'd seen? I couldn't entirely explain it to myself, except that a part of me wanted to spare her the awful feeling that flooded me when I'd looked on that statue. Of course, that feeling was also a very good reason to show it to her—in most ways, she was more rational than I was, and less likely to be sent spiraling by a gut feeling. And yet, looking at her face, I couldn't do it.

"The filing cabinets are over here," I told her, and walked over to them.

I felt Hannah's eyes on me, probing me curiously as I searched through the catalogue of Fairhaven's artwork, but she didn't ask any more questions. I dug through until I found the section on the Gallery of High Priestesses and then the file on Agnes' tapestry.

I could still remember the feeling that ran through me the first time I saw her face gazing serenely down at me. My friend Mackie—who I hadn't seen in ages but who Karen informed me had RSVP'd that she would be attending the wedding—had been escorting me right here, to Fiona's tower, for the very first time. She took me through the Gallery of High Priestesses, where artwork of all the previous High Priestesses hung. And in a moment when I was feeling that I didn't belong, she pointed up to Agnes Isherwood, at the obvious resemblance between us, and reminded me that I did, in fact, belong. From that moment on, whenever I questioned my connection to the Durupinen, to my own legacy, Agnes' face was there in my memory, reminding me to hold my head up high and claim my own place in our sisterhood. There had been many moments in the years since that I had wished that connection severed or forgotten. But in the end, it had anchored me in my own life and pointed me to a truth that had nearly been lost to time.

I carried the file folder over to Fiona's desk, Hannah shadowing my every step. I opened it and began to sift through the papers inside. It only took a few seconds to find the visuals.

There was a pencil sketch of the tapestry, complete with measurements and notes about the fibers used, the plant dyes detected, the method of weaving, the size of the loom—a bunch of useless details, as far as we were concerned. The image of the tapestry itself was not detailed enough for us to study it much further, so I set it aside and shuffled a few more papers until I found the photographs.

Several 8×10 photos were taken of the tapestry in its entirety, as well as several photos of smaller sections of the tapestry, in which the detail was more apparent. We stood staring at them in silence for what felt like quite a long time before either of us spoke.

"Any idea what we should be looking for?" Hannah asked in a small voice.

"Nope." I was trying not to let my disappointment color my voice, but even I could hear it. What had I expected, that I'd take one look at the tapestry and somehow innately know what part of it was relevant to our search? I should have realized it wouldn't be that easy.

The tapestry had been beautiful before it had all unraveled to reveal its inner imagery. Agnes Isherwood stood at its center in a flowing green gown, her long waves of reddish hair billowing out on all sides of her like she was caught in some kind of supernatural storm. Her feet were bare, planted in the green of the earth, so that she looked physically rooted to the ground. One hand rested on the hilt of a dagger that was holstered in the golden belt around her waist. The other hand held a lantern aloft, in which a candle had been lit. Her expression was determined, her shoulders squared, her chin raised almost defiantly. She looked like the kind of woman who could appear out of nowhere before you, demand, "Come with me. Now," and you would not hesitate for a moment to follow her. She looked like an ancient queen or a Celtic goddess on the eve of battle.

The background of the tapestry revealed a Geatgrima in the distance, perched on a rocky precipice, bathed in an unearthly glow that seemed to emanate from the stone archway itself. Above her head, birds wheeled in the sky, casting their shadows over the round belly of a full moon.

"It's beautiful," Hannah whispered, "but I... I don't know what Polly wants us to find. I don't know what we're looking for."

"Neither do I," I admitted finally, gathering up the photos and closing the rest of the file. "Let's take these with us and get out of here. I wouldn't put it past Fiona to wring our necks if she finds us in here without her permission."

"Hurry," Hannah said, her eyes growing wide at the very thought.

I replaced the file folder carefully in its rightful place in the filing cabinet, keeping my eyes intentionally averted from the curtain and what lay behind it. I didn't want to think about the sculpture. Something about it made the hairs on the back of my neck stand up. It was as though I could feel the featureless face staring at me from behind the heavy folds of velvet. I tucked the photographs of the tapestry under my arm and nodded for Hannah to follow me. I felt the eyeless gaze of the dying woman on my retreating back long after I closed the door behind us.

16

A TASTE OF DANGER

After days of what felt like a high-stakes chase for clues, our investigation ground to a halt.

Though we all studied the photographs, we had no idea where to go next. Polly's clues had seemed to lead us to a dead end, and we still had no idea where she was or what had happened to her. Hannah had frantically searched the mail when we returned home, but no more cryptic letters had arrived.

"Not that we'd be able to trust any correspondence from her now," Finn pointed out. "For all we know, she's being held by the very people she was trying to hide all of this from, which means any letter she sends you is more likely to be a trap than a clue."

Catriona was back on a chopper the next day with an elite team of Trackers determined to blow the case wide open. As we now knew, there was a good chance that someone among the Caomhnóir was involved. We could no longer trust them to investigate, nor could Hannah and I risk openly continuing to investigate ourselves.

"You would be a danger magnet at every turn," Cat said curtly when I argued. "Is that what you want? To endanger our entire team just by your proximity?"

I ground my teeth together before I could retort. She was right. There was a better chance of her finding Polly if we weren't involved, and that fact made me want to spit fire. Catriona updated us almost daily, though, which meant that she'd only been at Skye a few hours when she called us to let us know that they'd identified our attacker.

"His name was Gabriel Durand," she said. "He used to be a Caomhnóir at Havre des Gardiennes, but was arrested for his complicity with the Necromancers."

"So, is that who we think is behind this? The Necromancers?" I asked, my heart beginning to race. Just when we thought we were rid of them, they reared their ugly heads again.

"It's entirely too soon to tell. I still think the most likely scenario is that one of the Caomhnóir here used him—struck some kind of bargain: his freedom in exchange for attacking you and retrieving the artifact. But whether that Caomhnóir was in league with Necromancers or Durupinen, I have no idea, and that's a sentence I never thought I'd say in my lifetime."

"Yeah," I agreed. When I'd entered the Durupinen world, the lines in the sand were clear; the Durupinen were the good guys, protectors of the spirit world, and the Necromancers were the villains. The Reckoning had revealed that to be a fallacy, and the black-and-white reality had faded and muddied into shades of gray. "So what's next?"

"We are in the midst of questioning not only the Caomhnóir, but also the other prisoners on Durand's cell block. If we can identify who let Durand out of his cell, we'll be one step closer to unraveling this whole conspiracy."

I wished her luck. Cat was more than capable of looking out for herself, but there was no doubt she was charging right into a lion's den.

For a solid week, we pored over the photos for hours with magnifying glasses, while Kiernan dug up every reference he could find in Durupinen art to birds, moons, knives, and lanterns—all the hallmark details of the tapestry's design. He even found an article about the tapestry itself, in which its construction and design were discussed at length.

"...differs from the official portraits of the other High Priestesses in both its informality and its dynamism. It was traditional for High Priestesses to have their images captured in formal settings, usually with all the traditional ceremonial trappings of their position. Agnes Isherwood's portrait flies in the face of this tradition: barefoot, hair wild, holding nothing more regal than a lantern as she traverses the night. One must ask, as we look: is it an invitation to follow her, and where will she lead us?"

"I wish she would lead us somewhere—anywhere," I grumbled.

"We'll just have to keep looking," Hannah said, with maddening patience.

"The clue has to mean something. That tapestry has an answer in it. We just need to find—oh."

"What?" I asked.

"It's just... this article," Hannah replied, swallowing hard. "I just realized. It was written by Polly."

I felt a surge of excitement. "Do you think—?"

But Hannah was already shaking her head. "No. It's over twenty years old. Whatever it is she's trying to tell us now, she didn't know it when she wrote this article."

After a week of fruitless investigation, I ventured into Fiona's tower again to retrieve the rest of the tapestry's file while she was in a Council meeting. But though I scoured the pages within, reading every word, examining every piece of documentation, I couldn't find anything else we hadn't already considered. By the time I shuffled down the stairs and into the entrance hall to meet Hannah, I was feeling incredibly frustrated. At least, I thought I was, until I caught sight of Hannah as she stalked out of the Grand Council Room doors, her face a veritable storm cloud.

"Tough meeting?" I asked.

"I have literally never been so insulted in my entire life!" Hannah ground out.

"Really?" I asked, thinking back to all the shit people had said about us just in this castle. It was a very extensive and offensive list.

"Do you know what that... that... that *woman* said to me?" Hannah hissed, spitting out the word "woman" like it was the most vile of curse words.

"Sorry, what woman?" I asked.

"Clarissa MacLeod! Do you know what she *said*?!"

"No, I... wait, is Clarissa well enough to be attending Council meetings already?"

"Probably not, but why would that stop her?"

"Fair point. Well, I wasn't in the meeting, so... no, I don't know what she said."

"She suggested in front of everyone that the reason I'm marrying Kiernan is not because I am in love with him, but because I'm trying to consolidate power!" Her nostrils flared repeatedly like the gills on a fish, and her cheeks flamed with angry color. It would have been amusing if she didn't look like she was about to rip someone's head off.

"What does that mean, consolidate power?" I asked. "That doesn't even make sense."

"She likened it to two royal families joining forces," Hannah fumed. "That somehow, by our clans coming together, we are planning some sort of power grab. It's so insulting! So... so..." Hannah just stood there, vibrating with rage as she tried and failed to find the right word.

"They could argue Finn and I are doing the same thing," I said, shrugging.

"It's different. You're not getting married, and you're not on the Council."

"They're just pissed that their own stupid rules prevented them from doing the same thing first," I said. "In fact, they're probably doubly mad about it because the Prophecy that made them enact the rule was about us to begin with, and now we're sidestepping it."

"It doesn't matter why they're mad! How can they even say such a thing! It's... it's slander!"

"They're just jealous, Hannah. Ignore it."

"How am I supposed to ignore an accusation like that?" she gasped.

"The same way we ignored every other awful thing they've said about our clan since we arrived here the first time," I said. "You were always better at it than I was. In fact, I remember several conversations when you had to physically restrain me from fisticuffs with snot-nosed little Apprentices who thought they could Mean Girls us out of here. Oh my God!" I added on sudden inspiration.

"What?"

"Did it finally happen?"

"Did what finally happen?"

"Did I become the responsible, level-headed twin?"

Hannah glared at me and stalked away, hands still balled into fists at her sides.

"Well, you didn't smack me, so I guess probably not," I muttered, as I hurried to catch up with her retreating form.

"I can't talk about this anymore, or I'm going to storm back in there and start tearing people to shreds."

"Ooh, verbally or physically?" I asked, waggling my eyebrows.

"I haven't decided yet," Hannah said, "so we'd better leave before I give it too much more consideration."

"Yeah, good call," I said, nodding sagely. "Karen wouldn't be too happy if you showed up to the Grand Dutchess Hotel looking like you'd just been in a bar fight, and I'm assuming Clarissa plays dirty. Probably carries a shank in her purse."

Hannah finally cracked a smile, and I knew we would make it out of the building without violence.

The Grand Dutchess Hotel was the crown jewel of posh hotels, a stately stone edifice in the heart of the swankiest part of London, and known for its five-star accommodations frequented by celebrities and even royalty; so naturally, when it came time to plan Hannah's wedding, it was at the very top of Karen's list. Within days of the engagement, Karen had created an entire PowerPoint presentation about The Grand Dutchess, with in-depth detail about the food, the luxury services, and, most importantly, the grand ballroom, which looked like something out of a Jane Austen Regency novel: the kind of room where a girl could find her happily ever after with a stately if standoffish gentleman who had, by general report, approximately £10,000 a year.

If Hannah hadn't been hyper aware of how much such a venue must cost, I have no doubt she would have been delighted to be married there, but there was no escaping the looming shadow of the price tag. No matter how much Karen explained that the money had been set aside in a family trust specifically for our weddings, and no matter how much I insisted that I would never be using my share of that money, Hannah remained unconvinced that we should spend so much on her wedding. It was only when Karen made an appointment with the general manager of the hotel, and assured Hannah that our many Durupinen connections meant a reduction in price, that she would even consider it. In the end, it was Milo, a star-struck reality TV junkie, who convinced her to give in.

"Just imagine, Hannah. My designs on the dance floor of The Grand Dutchess. It's untoppable. I'll basically be able to retire at that point," he'd gasped.

Hannah didn't bother pointing out that ghosts never needed to retire. She'd just sighed and given in.

On the plus side, though, once the deal had been struck and the deposit paid, Hannah and I had been frequenting The Grand Dutchess for one wedding planning meeting after another, which always resulted in free champagne and free food. The woman in charge of the weddings at The Grand Dutchess was named Evangeline Blythe, and event planning was her entire personality. It was also highly convenient that she was a Durupinen cousin, and knew enough about our world that Karen didn't have to tiptoe around her.

"Ladies! Hannah, our stunning bride-to-be, and Jess, our illustrious maid of honor, welcome back to The Grand Dutchess Hotel," Evangeline said every single time we walked in the door. I could only tolerate the greeting because I knew snacks would be forthcoming.

That day, Evangeline greeted us in a perfectly tailored green silk suit and matching four-inch pumps. Her blonde hair had been set in finger waves and garnished with a bejeweled hair comb, like she was trying to evoke a flighty Fitzgerald heroine. Her complexion had an almost airbrushed quality, and I shuddered to think how many products she had slathered onto the unsuspecting skin of her face to achieve such an effect.

"You're both looking lovely, as always," Evangeline gushed, not quite planting kisses on both cheeks.

Hannah nudged me before I could reply sarcastically. I was well aware that I looked like absolute garbage due to a full week of hardly any sleep, and a lack of even the barest of makeup.

"Nice to see you, Evangeline," Hannah replied, smiling diplomatically. "Has my aunt arrived yet?"

"Yes, she's waiting for you in the dining room," Evangeline said. "She's never been less than fifteen minutes early for any appointment we've had, bless her."

I couldn't tell if this was a compliment or a dig, but I decided I didn't care. I could already smell the delectable aromas wafting to us from the dining room that Evangeline was now leading us to.

Traditionally speaking, the bride and groom would have a tasting to choose the various culinary offerings at their wedding. In this case, though, Kiernan had panicked so much at the prospect of having to make such a decision that Hannah had let him out of the obligation, and brought me instead to spare him the anxiety. As for me, this was one wedding task I did not mind volunteering for, seeing as The Grand Dutchess had one of the most celebrated kitchens in all of London. I had only one reservation.

"Is this going to be good food, or posh food, do you think?" I whispered to Hannah as we followed Evangeline's willowy figure to the dining room.

"Is there a difference?" Hannah hissed back. "I thought posh food was meant to be synonymous with good food."

"Oh, I'm sure it's *meant* to be, but it's not really," I said, wrinkling my nose. "If this place is known for classic or traditional cuisine, then we might be okay. But if their chef has been described in any food publication as 'adventurous' or 'avant-garde' then I'm pretty sure we're screwed, tastebud-wise."

"I don't remember Karen saying anything like that," Hannah said, but she looked nervous now. "She wouldn't pick a hotel that didn't have good food."

"Again, that depends on whose definition of 'good' we're working with here," I said. "Look, all I'm saying is that if someone puts a tiny plate in front of us and tells us the food is topped with any type of foam, we should immediately run to the nearest chippie and not look back."

"Agreed," Hannah said, shuddering delicately, and then putting on a brave face again just as Evangeline pushed open the dining room doors.

It was a gorgeous room, a smaller version of the ballroom located on the opposite side of the lobby. Towering pillars propped up a chandelier-strewn ceiling high above our heads, and all around us, neat round tables draped in white tablecloths sprouted from the marble floor like toadstools. Karen was sitting at one of these tables in the far corner of the room. Her face lit up as she watched us enter and approach her.

"I'm so glad you made it," she said, embracing us each in turn. "I was worried you might be delayed with—"

"Of course we made it," Hannah said, smiling a little too broadly. "We wouldn't have missed the chance to pick the menu."

Karen took the hint, turning to Evangeline and smiling indulgently. "We made sure to bring our appetites."

Evangeline smiled. "Well, our executive chef will be delighted to hear that. Shall I tell him you're ready to begin the tasting?"

"Yes, please do," Karen replied.

We all waited while Evangeline floated across the room and through the swinging doors to the kitchen. As soon as she disappeared, Karen's entire demeanor changed. Her unruffled manner became, quite instantly, very ruffled.

"Any updates?" she asked, her voice low and urgent.

"Not since we spoke to you last," I said, feeling the pang of frustration at the words.

"I just can't believe Catriona and the Trackers haven't found Polly yet," Karen said, flexing her hands against the tablecloth so that her knuckles went white. "What in the world could have happened to her?"

"Have you ever met her?" Hannah asked, sounding like she was eager to steer the conversation away from Polly's disappearance.

"Oh, yes," Karen said. "She was... well, a bit of a pest, actually."

"What do you mean?"

"Well, for a while there, after your mother disappeared, it was a bit like having a one-woman paparazzi hounding us," Karen said. "Polly called, wrote, and showed up on our doorstep nearly every week. Your grandmother actually tried to have her formally reprimanded by the Council. Of course, we were in such disgrace by then that the Council chose to do nothing at all."

"Why did she want to talk to you so much?" I asked.

"Well, it makes sense if you think about her career. She watched us crumble from the very height of power to the very dregs of Durupinen society. It seemed almost as important to her as it was to our mother that we regain that lost status."

"But why?" I asked. "Why would anyone care so much about the reputation of a clan that wasn't her own?"

"Polly Keener's work was—is—her life," Karen said, flushing a little as she slipped into the past tense. "And we were her work. In a strange way, when we fell from grace, so did she."

We had to stop talking at that point, as two waiters followed Evangeline back to our table.

"Ladies, here are your choices for the passed hors d'oeuvres. You'll find the descriptions on the menu cards in front of you. Please savor them at your leisure, and we'll bring you the options for the plated courses when you've finished," Evangeline said, waving her arm over the table like she was casting a magic spell over the plates.

"Thank you," Karen said, smiling indulgently. "Everything looks absolutely wonderful."

This time, Evangeline didn't disappear back into the kitchen, but took a position across the dining room where she could observe our table without hovering over us. We had no choice but to start eating while we talked, which was fine by me, because I was starving.

"Here. These are gruyere and caramelized onion tartlets," Karen said, referencing her menu card before passing the little platter around so that we could each put one on our plates.

"Holy shit, this is delicious," I said, having popped the whole tartlet into my mouth. Karen and Hannah stared at me, a fork and knife in each of their hands. "What?" I asked, feeling suddenly defensive. "They're passed hors d'oeuvres. It's finger food. No one's going to hand you utensils on the dance floor."

Hannah considered this for a moment, then put down her knife and fork and popped the tartlet into her mouth. She chewed for a moment and then whispered, "Oh my God."

"Right? You definitely have to pick these," I said. There was still one left on the platter, and so I swiped it before anyone else could.

"Anyway," Karen said, cutting her tartlet into pieces to sample it, "It felt like Polly wanted to find your mother even more than we did. She even went so far as to conduct her own search; though of course, Lizzie was always two steps ahead of her, just as she stayed ahead of everyone else who was looking for her."

Karen's knife froze mid-bite, as though she had suddenly remembered something. Based on the slightly flustered expression on her face, and the way she kept shooting covert glances at Hannah, I thought it might be the fact that we so rarely spoke about our mother. Hannah had no memories of her, and having been abandoned to deal with her gift entirely on her own, her feelings toward our mother were much more complicated than mine. But if Hannah was upset about the mention of our mother, she didn't show it. She was studiously reviewing her menu card as she finished chewing her tartlet, and when she spoke again, her voice was even.

"These are the broiled oysters with parmigiano and 'nduja,'" she announced, passing the plate around. We each took one. I looked down at the oyster and felt my stomach squirm. "I don't know if I'm brave enough to try this," I admitted.

"You've never had oysters before?" Karen asked, eyebrows raised.

"Nope."

Hannah also shook her head.

Karen closed her eyes. "Girls, I am sorry. I have failed you. I should have my Boston card revoked."

I laughed. "What are you talking about?"

"I am your bougie Boston-bred aunt. Oysters were absolutely one of my solemn duties. I will do better from now on."

"I'm not convinced this is an experience I need to have," I said, looking down at the oyster again. "Seriously, I think I'm good. And what is 'nduja,' anyway?"

"It says here it's a spicy Calabrian sausage," Hannah said, consulting the card again.

"I just… it looks so… boogery," I whispered.

Hannah clapped her hand over her face to muffle snorting laughter that burst out of her mouth. Even Karen was working hard to keep her face straight.

"Jess, this one's not even raw. It will be delicious, just give it a try."

I decided I couldn't eat it if I had to look at it, so, taking up the previously discarded fork, I cut off a tiny piece, closed my eyes, and popped it into my mouth. My eyes flew open.

"OH."

I looked over at Hannah, who had likewise tried the oyster. Her expression was rapturous.

"So... boogers on the menu?" I said.

"Oh, most definitely," she agreed, scarfing the rest of her oyster and beating me to the extra one on the plate.

"Okay, scallops wrapped in bacon next," Karen said, passing them around. And speaking of what's next, where do we go from here?" Karen asked. "With the investigation, I mean?"

"Well, Catriona won't let us be involved anymore, not formally anyway. She says it's too dangerous to the other Tracker members for us to be out investigating with them," Hannah said.

Karen raised an eyebrow. "Yes, so of course, you've completely walked away from it and stopped looking for clues?"

"Obviously," I said, deadpan. "We would never even dream of continuing to investigate a case that has so clearly put us in its crosshairs. Why would you ever suppose such a thing?"

Karen smiled a little, but it slipped off her face quickly.

"You want us to stop looking into it?" Hannah said, reading the shift in expression.

Karen sighed. "I want you to be safe. That's what I want—it's what I always want. But it sounds to me like you won't be safe as long as Polly is missing and this mystery remains unsolved. So how can I say I want you to stop looking for answers, when the answers are likely to keep you out of danger?"

I narrowed my eyes at her. "This sounds strangely like you're starting to accept the fact that we're adults who can make our own decisions."

"Does it?" Karen asked innocently. "Huh. That doesn't sound like me at all. Must be the champagne."

I glanced at her untouched flute, which she picked up and took a pointed sip from.

"I just want you to be careful. And listen to Catriona, whatever you do," Karen said, as she set the flute down and picked up her menu card again. "Now, what's next? Ooh, truffled mushroom puffs!"

We worked our way through the rest of the passed hors d'oeuvres without much talking, since Evangeline had taken it upon herself to check back in with us as we sampled the mushroom puffs, which were just as delicious as everything else we'd tried thus far. In fact, it seemed impossible that we would be able to eliminate any of the options from the menu at all, until we tried the beluga caviar and crème fraîche on blinis, which we both agreed was not nearly worth the hype. Sometimes, something is a delicacy because it's delicious. Sometimes, it's merely something expensive that's much more status symbol than anything else.

If Evangeline was disappointed that she hadn't upsold us on the caviar, she soon rallied her spirits when Karen informed her that we would, in fact, like to have the champagne fountain and that the options for the main course would include the two most expensive from the tasting menu: the filet mignon and the stuffed lobster tail.

"Positively divine choices," Evangeline gushed, as she recorded them on her clipboard. "Let's move on to dessert, shall we?"

By this point, I was seriously regretting the fact that I'd worn pants with an inflexible waistband. I also considered texting Kiernan to tell him he'd missed out on the culinary fever dream that was this tasting. I'd never been a person who thought "expensive" was synonymous with "delicious:" I'd had many a takeout meal at tiny hole-in-the-wall dives on both sides of the Atlantic by now, and I knew that, generally speaking, the best food you could acquire was cheap and cooked by someone else's grandmother in massive portions in a restaurant no one knew about unless someone told you where it was. That said, despite the price tag, this hotel knew how to produce delicious food. The closer we got to the wedding, the more I realized that Karen really did know what she was doing.

Finally, after we had tasted (or, in my case, devoured in their entirety) the choices of cake accompaniments, Hannah had settled on a finalized menu. Karen treated us to a glass of champagne and, after ensuring us that we could stay as long as we liked, Evangeline whisked herself away to help another set of clients.

"Jess, what's wrong? You look... concerned," Hannah said, frowning at me. "Do you think I should have picked something else? It's not too late to change things, Evangeline only just wrote it down."

"No, no, it's not that, it's just..." I sighed. "I don't think I'm going to be able to eat all of this again on the day of the wedding."

"Why not?" Karen asked.

"Because I don't think that damn dress had any room in it," I practically wailed. "Like, it's skin-tight around the mid-section—how's a girl supposed to chow down without popping a zipper?"

Hannah giggled. "I hadn't thought of that," she admitted.

"Well, neither did I, until this moment, and now I'm thinking I might need to ask Milo for a second dress for the dinner portion of the evening."

Karen laughed. "Something with an elastic waistband, you think?"

"Yeah, and a matching bib, because seriously, you cannot take me anywhere, look at this!" I cried, noticing for the first time that I'd dribbled truffle butter on my shirt.

"If it makes you feel any better, most of the pictures will be taken before we eat," Hannah said. "And besides, there's always Photoshop."

This did, in fact, make me feel slightly better.

"Look, girls," Karen said, draining the last of her champagne. "I know it's hard to focus on these kinds of things when there's this mystery hanging over your heads. I know it's frightening. But you're back now, and you're safe. I have no doubt that Catriona and her Trackers will find Polly. For the present, I hope you can find a way to enjoy these last few weeks leading up to the wedding. It's meant to be an exciting time, and after all, you only get married once. Well, maybe twice," she added, smirking at the allusion to her own divorce.

"Once," Hannah said, reaching across to the last of the chocolate-covered strawberries and popping it in her mouth. "I'm only doing this once."

17

SLEEPLESS

The dreams started that night, when we got home from the tasting.

The first was strange and bright—a somewhat psychedelic Alice in Wonderland type of dreamscape. Somewhere in the back of my brain, the part that knew I was dreaming, I decided it was just too much rich food wreaking havoc on my system. I wasn't used to eating like a Rockefeller.

It's the oysters, I told myself. Oysters are like the mushrooms of the sea. It's no wonder my dreams are trippy.

But then, I settled into the dream and things got real. Very, very real.

Was a dream supposed to be such a vivid sensory experience? I felt like I could taste the air, smell the sour, mildewy scent, and feel the uncomfortable dampness on my skin. I had to squint into the darkness of my surroundings to make them out. Slowly, my eyes identified objects—a bench bolted to the floor, a metal bucket from which an appalling smell was emanating, and a small square window crisscrossed with a grid of metal bars.

What was this place? Had I been there before? It felt somehow familiar and unfamiliar at once, a sensation that shivered in an unsettling way up my spine and into the roots of my hair. Something scuttled in the darkness, and there was a steady sound of water dripping against something metal and hollow, like a pipe, maybe. I wanted to call out, but I didn't seem to have control over my voice in this dream. I tried to move, but I found I had no control over my body, either. Was I dreaming I was in this place, or was I simply observing someone else's time there?

For what felt like a long time, nothing happened—aside from the occasional squeaking of a rat, and the flicker of the sickly yellow light that bled underneath the door. It felt like I'd spent hours there, just waiting, instead of the way dreams usually felt, when time slid past in strange, slippery clumps. I could hear a steady breathing, in and out, unlabored but ragged somehow, like a person badly in need of a drink.

Finally, just when I thought this was the most boring dream I'd ever had, a shadow passed under the door and stopped there: a pair of legs. Then there followed a clanking sound, and the breathing cut off with a grunt, and then a whimper.

"Please," came a cracked and desperate voice from the dark beside me. "Please, I've already told you. I don't know anything!"

My heart leapt into overdrive. Did I know that voice? I couldn't place it, especially full as it was of fear. The door began to creak open, a slow, unbearable creaking that made goosebumps erupt over my arms as the fear in the voice began to infect me, too. Even as I told myself it was only a dream, that primal fear continued to mount, turning my blood to ice, my limbs to water.

"Please! Please, not again! I'm begging you, I don't know anything! Please!"

The door continued to open, the woman beside me let out a keening cry, and my eyes flew open.

A minute later, I was standing in the bathroom, trying to keep myself on my feet while splashing cold water on my face. Finn appeared in the doorway, his hair wild with sleep.

"Nightmare?" he asked.

"Not sure," I said. My legs were shaking, but I tried not to lock my knees.

"Spirit-induced dream?" he tried again.

"Also not sure," I said.

Shall I make some tea, and you can tell me about it, or do you want to go back to sleep?"

"Sleep isn't happening any time soon," I said. "So I'll take the tea, thanks."

We curled up on the couch together, steaming mugs in hand. I fit so perfectly against him, two puzzle pieces slipping together with a soft, satisfying click. He leaned his chin on top of my head, stroking my hair with his free hand. My eyes began to close—maybe I was wrong about the sleep thing. I fended it off to tell him all about the dream.

"And you're afraid it's Polly." It wasn't a question.

I nodded. "I definitely couldn't be sure, because I barely know her, but it could have been. It was definitely a woman's voice."

"You couldn't see her?"

"I could hardly see anything. I was straining my eyes against the dark. All I really got were the basic outlines of things, and nothing was very noteworthy or unusual."

"You said the door opened at the end. Could you see the person who opened it?"

"No. It was just a big black shadow, silhouetted in the light from the hall. I think it was male, but it could have been a really broad-shouldered woman, I suppose."

"And you're sure you didn't recognize the place? Not even when the light came in from the hallway?" he asked.

"No. I've experienced a frankly alarming number of dark, dank cells, and it was impossible to tell if this was somewhere I'd been before. It could have been Fairhaven, it could have been Skye, it could have... oh my God!"

"What?" he asked, his hand going motionless mid-hair stroke.

"What if it was Skye? What if they had Polly locked up there the whole time? We should have gone through all the prisoner blocks, made sure she wasn't—"

"Jess, I'm sure it wasn't Skye. No, listen," he said, because I had opened my mouth to argue. "Just think about it. The risk is too great. Even if a handful of the Caomhnóir from Skye were involved in her disappearance, it would be entirely too risky to keep her at the *príosún*. She knows too many people there, and too many of them know her. She'd be discovered, no question, so put that out of your mind."

"But—"

"Look, Catriona is there. If it makes you feel better, I can ask her to send a Tracker through the prisoner blocks to confirm, but I'd be surprised if she hadn't already done it. Okay?"

I nodded, settling back against him again. "Sorry. I'm just... the guilt is getting to me."

"I know."

"There is one other thing..."

"Hmm?"

"I heard a couple of voices from the corridor, and I... I can't be sure, because they were muffled, but I don't think they were speaking English."

"Is that so?"

"Yeah. It... I couldn't swear to what language it was... French, maybe? It sounded sort of... liquid."

"Hmm," he said again, and I could almost feel his brow furrow behind me.

"What do you think I should do?" I asked. "Should I tell Catriona?"

"Well, it certainly can't hurt. And if you were seeing Polly, then any clue could be the one to crack the case."

"But why am I seeing her, if that's what's happening?" I asked. "This wasn't spirit-induced—I could hear her breathing."

"A Seer vision, perhaps?"

"I don't know, it didn't feel like the future. It felt very real, very... immediate. I felt like I just dropped right down next to her in her reality. Sorry, it's hard to explain."

"I think you're explaining it admirably. I say we head back to bed and call Catriona at a more human hour. You can tell her what you saw, and we can get another update on her investigation. How does that suit?"

I bit my lip. It felt wrong, going back to bed when somewhere right now, Polly might be facing something terrible—maybe even torture—at the hands of whoever had opened that door. But, I reminded myself, I wasn't even sure she was the person I'd seen, and even if she was, what could I do from here in the middle of the night? Finn was right. We could tell Catriona in the morning.

We finished our tea and shuffled back to bed. When I eventually nodded off, my sleep was punctured by faceless cries for help that repeatedly startled me into consciousness.

***

I decided not to tell Hannah about the dream. What was the point? She would only torture herself even more, wondering where Polly was and what was happening to her. As Finn suggested, I called Catriona first thing in the morning and told her what I'd seen. She didn't scoff at me or ask me why I was wasting her time babbling about dreams, both of which seemed like distinct possibilities as I waited for her to pick up. Instead, she probed me for every detail I could drag from my sleep-deprived brain, and took careful note of all of them.

"One thing I can promise you is that she isn't here at Skye. I had all the prisoner blocks searched when we first arrived with the team. I thought it was a long shot that they might try to keep her here, hidden in plain sight, right under our noses. She's definitely not here."

"Is there anything you can tell us? Any progress at all?"

Cat made a sound somewhere between a snarl and a growl. "They've closed ranks, I think. They clammed right up about Gabriel Durand. The records of who was on patrol that afternoon have mysteriously vanished, and not a single prisoner can seem to remember who might have been on guard. There's also no record of anyone taking a van out on the morning Polly's house blew up, all of which should be impossible, because Caomhnóir records are, by definition, meticulous and thorough. Which means, either the van was stolen and returned without anyone noticing, or someone was able to cover for it, either by doctoring records or flat out destroying them."

I tried to feel disappointment, but all I could muster was a grim kind of acceptance. Of course, they had covered their tracks. I expected nothing less.

"We're conducting interviews, going straight through the ranks here, but I'm not hopeful anyone will crack," Catriona went on. "And without evidence, we don't know where to apply the pressure. The truth is, there's no mastermind here. Whichever Caomhnóir are involved, they're doing it at the behest of someone very powerful, which means they're in danger whether they talk or not."

"So you're giving up?" I asked, trying to swallow back my despair.

"I beg your finest pardon? Who said anything about giving up?" Catriona snapped. "Don't you dare put such defeatist words in my mouth, Jessica Ballard. Do you really think I got where I am by throwing the towel in every time I met a little obstacle? I was sent here to find Polly Keener, and I will bloody well find her. It's just taking a bit longer than I'd like."

I knew better than to question Cat when her voice had that much steel in it, so I thanked her for the update and ended the call. She probably wouldn't answer the next time I tried to call her; I'd committed the cardinal sin of reminding her that she hadn't yet accomplished what she'd set out to do, and that was frankly unforgivable.

My body was telling me to spend the day in alternating states of frantic panic and paralyzed indecision about Polly and what we could possibly do to help her. My brain seemed to be totally onboard with this plan, until my calendar reminded me that I had actual shit I had to get done. As frivolous as it felt, my sister's wedding was less than three weeks away, and I, as her maid of honor, had responsibilities that I could not shirk. Even if our wider world was in shambles, Hannah still deserved to have all the beautiful and memorable moments that every bride should have and, as Savvy had so convincingly reminded me, that meant a proper bachelorette party or, as it was better known in our new home, a hen party. Hannah's was scheduled for the weekend, and I still had a to-do list long enough to successfully distract me from Catriona's investigation.

Because they disliked spending more time away from each other than was absolutely necessary, we enlisted Finn's help and planned both Hannah's hen party and Kiernan's stag night for the same evening, in the hopes that they would be able to fully enjoy themselves without wondering what the other was doing at home without them. This turned out to be a very good plan, because both of them had tried, at one point or another, to get out of their own party, and it was only by reminding them that their significant other would be out enjoying their own special night that we convinced both of them to stick it out.

True to her word, Savvy had been not only helpful but indispensable in the planning process. Though this hen party would be vastly different from anything like the debaucherous free-for-all she would plan for herself, she still managed to present me with pages of suggestions for how to tailor the night to Hannah's more refined tastes. Between the two of us, and with some additional help from Rana, we were sure the twenty-four hours we had planned would be memorable for all the right reasons, rather than a blurry memory that someone else has to explain with the aid of their smartphone camera.

On Saturday morning, I said goodbye to Finn, who was, of course, going to be at the stag night. I started to notice him dragging his feet as the time for his scheduled departure drew closer.

"I know that look," I said to him, narrowing my eyes. "You've got that party pooper look."

"I have not got—what does that even mean?" he asked.

"It means you're worried about something. So, spit it out. What's the problem?"

He sighed. "All right, fine. I would feel better about you all going into the city if you had more protection with you."

"*More* protection?" I repeated with an incredulous laugh. "Finn, we've got two Caomhnóir among the guests, for goodness sake. Savvy and Rana are more than capable of—"

"I'm not doubting their capabilities, believe me," Finn said. "They are both excellent guardians. But they won't be on duty, and I highly doubt they'll be sober. It is a hen party, after all."

"We've also got a Caomhnóir driving our limo for the night," I reminded him. "A Caomhnóir you hand picked, I might add."

"Yes, yes, but he won't be with you the whole—"

"Finn." I waited for him to look me in the eye. "We will be perfectly safe. We're not going anywhere sketchy, much to Savvy's chagrin, and we won't be walking anywhere in the dark. But if it makes you feel better, there's pepper spray on my keychain. Now, how are you going to enjoy yourself if you're worried about us the whole time?"

"I didn't—"

"Hannah isn't the only one who deserves a fabulous night on the town. Kiernan does too, and he's not going to get it if his best man is moping and distracted the whole time."

Finn looked indignant now. "I'm not moping!"

"You're damn right, you're not! You're going to put us out of your head, and you're going to focus all your energy on making sure that Kiernan has a great time tonight, okay? And not for nothing, but you also deserve to have a great time. I can't remember the last time you let yourself have a fun night out."

"Fun nights out aren't really my thing," he said a little stiffly.

"Well, that doesn't mean you can't enjoy one. You work too hard. In fact, when all this is over—the wedding, all this mystery with Polly—we should plan our own getaway. A real vacation, where you can completely forget about work for a week or two."

"A vacation? Together? I like the sound of that," Finn said, lips curling up into a smile.

I snaked my arms around his waist and pulled him closer to me, so that our bodies were pressed together. "Somewhere quiet and secluded. Sandy beach? No one else for miles?"

"Better and better," he admitted. "Shall we ditch the nights out and go now?"

I kissed him and then gave him a playful shove away. "Not a chance. Go have a raucous night with the lads. Have a drink too many. Have fun. You know how to do that, don't you? Have fun?"

"I am vaguely acquainted with the concept, yes," he said. "I'll do my best. But could you just—"

"Leave my phone on. Yes. I know."

"Thank you. And you enjoy your night, too," he said, stealing one last kiss. "What time will everyone be here?"

"In just about an hour. I need to hop in the shower."

He raised his eyebrows. "And you expect me to leave now that you've just told me that?"

"Yes, I do!" I said, and shoved him toward the door again.

I sighed as I heard the door close behind him. I couldn't start worrying about the night, not when I still had to sell Hannah on it. And it would be a hard sell.

18

ON THE TOWN

"Look, it's been a really long week," Hannah said, as she opened the door to us an hour later, looking both disheveled and mildly terrified. "Are we sure we don't just want to stay in, sleep a bit, maybe watch a movie or two on the couch?"

"Hannah, at the risk of sounding like a two-bit gangster out of one of your American shoot-em-up films, we can do this the easy way, or we can do this the hard way," Savvy said with a sigh. "Our friendship will not prevent me from picking you up and carrying you out of here over my shoulder. So, what's it going to be, voluntary surrender, or abduction?"

Hannah looked at Milo, who snorted. "Don't look at me for help, sweetness. I will be aiding and abetting this kidnapping if you try to back out now." Like Savvy, Milo had been looking forward to this night nearly as much as the actual wedding.

"I... I still have to pack," Hannah hedged, licking her lips nervously.

"No, you don't, because I snuck in here yesterday when you were out and packed your overnight bag for you," I said, holding up the bag that I, until that moment, had slung over my shoulder. "It has everything you need for every part of the day and night."

Hannah opened her mouth, and closed it again.

"Look, you're overthinking this," Rana said, her tone calm and so very rational. "You're letting your imagination run ahead of you. Right now, all you need to do is throw some slippers on and come over to your sister's place for mimosas and pastries."

Hannah twisted the hem of her t-shirt. "What kind of pastries?" she asked in a tiny voice.

I grinned. "All the kinds. It's a pastry buffet, and the bride gets first pick."

"And that's how we'll manage it, all right?" Rana said. "One thing at a time. So can you handle pastries in your pjs?"

Hannah cracked the tiniest of smiles. "Yeah, I can handle that."

Back in my living room, we lulled Hannah into a false sense of security with carbs and brunch cocktails. As she started to loosen up just slightly, the doorbell rang, and I encouraged her to answer it.

"I heard there was a bachelorette party happening, and I couldn't miss that!" said the young woman standing on the doorstep.

"Tia!" Hannah exclaimed, leaping forward to hug my former roommate. "This is wonderful, I didn't know you were coming!"

"I was told to keep it a surprise," Tia said, returning the hug with gusto. "And don't worry, as a fellow non-partier, I'm also here to support you in being a party pooper, should you so choose."

Hannah laughed even as I shouted, "Hey! That is NOT why we invited you!"

"Oh, I'm well aware, but I know my value-add, and I want the bride to know it too," Tia said, laughing. "That said, I'm on my first academic break in a very long time, and I promise, we are going to have so much fun—within reason, and while making safe choices, obviously."

Savvy looked at me with a frankly devastated expression, but I just patted her shoulder and handed her another mimosa. "It was always going to be an uphill battle, Todd," I told her. "We soldier on and hope for the best."

"Safe choices? Bugger everything," she muttered, and then drained her mimosa in a single go.

"You were the one who told me we needed to tailor this night to Hannah and her personality," I reminded her.

"Ah, that was just a load of bollocks to get you to agree to throw her a hen party in the first place," she grumbled. "We all know the night needs to devolve into some jolly good chaos at some point, or it doesn't count."

"Well, the night is young, as they say," I told her. "In fact, it's barely 10 AM. Don't give up hope yet!"

But as Savvy watched Tia show Hannah her purse-sized first aid kit, I could see the hope draining from her eyes, and had to smother a laugh in my champagne flute.

My only experience with bachelorette parties was what I saw in popular culture, so I had to rely on the internet and Savvy to give me a clearer understanding of what was standard. Right off the bat, we knew certain activities—strippers and body shots, for example—would be off the table. And so, when we gathered around to give Hannah gifts to start off the day, they were not the type of gifts Savvy might have encouraged. Still, Hannah looked understandably wary when we told her it was time for presents.

"Just some stuff to help you get your marriage off on the right foot," I told her.

Her expression changed from wariness to outright terror as she plucked the first gift bag from my fingers.

"Should I... can I open it later?" she asked.

"Oh my God, it's not a vibrator, Hannah, just open it," I yelled.

"More's the pity," Savvy mumbled.

Everyone laughed, even Hannah, and she yanked the tissue paper out of the bag with a bit more confidence.

"Oh! These are beautiful! So cozy!" she exclaimed, pulling my gift from the bag. It was a pair of Turkish bathrobes monogrammed with "Mr." and "Mrs." on the chest pockets.

Clearly more confident that the contents would not be mortifying, Hannah opened the rest of the gifts. Rana gave her a pair of cut crystal wine glasses with the words "His" and "Hers" etched into them, along with a bottle of champagne. "For whenever you decide you want to celebrate together," she explained. Tia gave her a book called "The First Year of Marriage: A Couple's Workbook."

"Tia, did you give the bride *homework* as a gift?" I asked, incredulous.

"No, don't be ridiculous, it's not homework, for goodness sake!" Tia said. "It's a place to write down all their firsts—see there are spots for photos and a calendar to record important dates, and writing prompts, and—"

"Sounds like homework to me," Savvy said, grinning.

"Oh no, this is great!" said Hannah, who was flipping through the book now. "It's cute, there are questions we can ask each other and lists of favorite things: favorite date night spot, favorite take-out for a night in, favorite use of a wedding gift... thanks, Tia!"

"There's some other stuff in there, too," Tia said, smiling, and Hannah pulled out a Polaroid camera and a book of scrapbooking accessories, "to help you fill it all in. Then, when you're old and gray, sitting in your rocking chairs on your front porch, you can read through it and remember your first year together!"

It sounded cheesy to me, but I knew that meant Hannah would love it. Sure enough, her expression was delighted as she gave Tia a hug and thanked her again.

Savvy was up next.

"Don't worry, Jess and I agreed, nothing naughty. So I've opted for naughty-adjacent," Savvy said, with a trademark roguish wink.

Hannah threw me a slightly panicked look, but all I could do was shrug. Other than making her promise she wouldn't give Hannah a bag of sex toys, I hadn't discussed the gifts with Savvy. I had no idea what "naughty adjacent" meant. After all, Savvy had once worked in an X-rated shop, so she didn't exactly have a layman's concept of what qualified as "naughty."

A few moments and a rustling of tissue paper later, I heaved a sigh of relief. Savvy had opted for a set of massage oils, some scented candles, and a gift card for a couple's massage from a swanky spa in Soho. Even Hannah seemed relieved, though she turned cherry red when Savvy informed her that the oils were, in fact, edible.

"Yeah, you can just lick them right off," she informed Hannah cheerfully. "Taste pretty good, too… I mean, uh… according to the reviews, because I certainly have never had the opportunity to try them myself," she added hastily, as Rana narrowed her eyes in suspicion.

"My turn, my turn!" Milo sang, and his gift—well, gifts, because there were no less than five gift bags—slid across the table toward Hannah.

"Milo, this looks excessive," Hannah said.

"Thanks, that's what I was going for," Milo said, bringing his hands up under his chin in a demure gesture.

Inside the bags turned out to be a set of handmade bathing suits and cover-ups, each with a matching hat and a matching pair of sunglasses.

"For the honeymoon, obviously," he said. "And since you rejected my idea of a honeymoon photographer, I demand an absolute avalanche of beach selfies. And now you have no excuse because you have the perfect outfit for every single day."

Hannah looked a little askance at one of the bathing suits, which seemed to involve a lot of strings and not much fabric. "Do these come with instructions?" she asked, "or like... a diagram?"

"I'll give you a tutorial before you go," Milo promised.

"Where are you going on your honeymoon?" Tia asked.

"Greece," Hannah said. "We're going to visit Santorini, Mykonos, and Crete."

"Ooh, I've always wanted to go there, ever since I saw that Mamma Mia movie!" Rana said. "It looks like paradise!"

Savvy did a double-take. "You've seen the Mamma Mia movie?"

"Only about a hundred times," Rana said. "The music's so catchy, I can sing the whole soundtrack!"

Savvy shook her head and rubbed her temples. "Bloody hell, am I in for a lifetime of movie musicals? Just break it to me now."

"A lifetime? You really think I won't dump your arse long before that? A bit presumptuous, there, aren't you, Todd?" Rana said, grinning and then planting a kiss on Savvy before she could retort.

"How long will you be in Greece?" Tia asked.

"Two weeks. I've never been, but Kiernan has, so I let him plan everything," Hannah said. "He said it's the most beautiful place he's ever been, and that the food is wonderful, especially the seafood. I told him, as long as I can curl up on a beach and read, I'll be happy."

"That sounds wonderful," Tia sighed.

"The whole Mediterranean set out in front of you, and all you can think of is keeping your nose in a book," I said, grinning.

"I'd enjoy the view between pages," Tia said, a bit defensively.

"I will for sure look up every chapter or so," Hannah added, smirking.

"Well, here's my other gift then, speaking of your honeymoon, and making sure you don't just read the entire time," I said, pushing the little gift bag forward.

"You already got me a gift!" Hannah protested.

"Yeah, yeah, you're my twin, let me spoil you a little," I said.

Her expression intrigued, Hannah yanked the tissue paper out of the bag and pulled out the paper inside. She frowned at it for a minute while her eyes raced over the fine print, then her face broke into a smile.

"Jess! This is too much!" she gasped.

"Really? I think it's just enough," I countered.

"What is it?" Rana asked eagerly.

"She's rented us a sailboat for the day," Hannah said, referring to the paper again, "that includes a sunset cruise off the coast of Santorini, a snorkeling lesson, and a private candlelit dinner on deck. Oh, Jess!"

"Surprise! Well, actually, it's only a surprise to you," I admitted. "I had to tell Kiernan so that he didn't plan something else for you to do on the same day."

"This is wonderful, Jess, thank you!" Hannah cried, and launched herself at me in a hug that came impressively close to knocking me over given how tiny she was.

"Yikes! You're welcome!" I chuckled.

"By the way, because I know you're wondering, yes, I knew about it, and yes, I did manage to keep it a secret for a totally unreasonable amount of time. Also, I've researched the location and color scheme of the boat itself, and determined which of your honeymoon beach ensembles you need to wear that day, and it's the white one," Milo said in a stage whisper.

"Of course you did," came Hannah's muffled voice, still buried in my shoulder.

Having come through the gift-giving portion of the day relatively unscathed, Hannah seemed to relax a little more after that. We lounged around for a bit with one of her favorite rom-coms on the TV, and then the doorbell rang.

"Are we expecting anyone else?" Hannah asked, and her gaze snapped to Savvy. "This better not be some 'police officer' who's here to arrest me for being a bad girl."

"Nah, Officer Tightbuns was already booked for this weekend," Savvy said, rising to answer the door. "Only joking, only joking! There will be a man in a uniform on the other side of this door, but don't get your knickers in a twist, it's only our chauffeur."

"Chauffeur?" Hannah asked.

"Yup," I confirmed. "Come check out your ride for the day."

We all followed Savvy to the front door. She opened it, and a man in a gray suit and matching cap gave a neat little bow. "Ladies," he said. Beyond him, parked in the driveway, was a black stretch limo.

"Oh, my," Hannah whispered.

"How'd you get him to wear that uniform?" I whispered to Savvy.

"I challenged him to a game of poker," Savvy hissed back. "As you can see from his jaunty little cap, he lost. Don't ask me what I would have had to do if I'd lost. It's not suitable for polite company."

What followed was a day of pampering in London. We started with mani-pedis and facials at a spa, where they served us cucumber water and canapes while we were filed, plucked, and moisturized. Hannah seemed embarrassed by the attention at first, but relaxed more and more the longer we stayed. Then we arrived at a gorgeous bistro for lunch, where we had the rooftop patio all to ourselves. The views of London were stunning, and the food was delicious.

"All right, I take it back, some of these posh places do know how to do food properly," Savvy admitted, patting her stomach and leaning back in her chair. "Don't suppose this is the kind of place I can undo this top button on my jeans, is it?" she asked.

"No," replied everyone else in unison.

We treated ourselves to a round of drinks in the limo, and then pulled along the Marylebone High Street and stopped in front of Daunt Books. Both Milo and Savvy had grumbled at me when I said a bookstore ramble was on the schedule. However, Milo brightened up when I showed him photos of the place —he was now planning to scout it as a photo shoot location for his next collection, which, according to him, was going to "redefine tweed." Primarily a travel bookshop, Daunt Books was known for its stunning interior, with a conservatory-style glass ceiling, green glass lamps, and a full second-floor gallery that arced elegantly around the shop, making it look like a private library in a stately home rather than a shop. I had arranged a private appointment with one of the booksellers to show Hannah a handpicked selection of books about Greece, since she would be traveling there in just two weeks. When I explained this to her, her face lit up!

"That's wonderful! I've barely had a chance to read up at all!"

The plan was to browse while Hannah met with a soft-spoken young woman who had arranged a whole display of books on a table for her; but Tia and Rana wound up listening to most of the presentation the bookseller had prepared. Tia actually took notes on her phone. Milo, meanwhile, swooped through the upper gallery like a well-dressed bat, gauging the light and muttering about "draping" and "angles" while Savvy and I wandered the fiction section.

We all climbed back into the limo, Hannah, Rana, and Tia all carrying bags of books, and headed off to Karen's flat. Desperate to do something to help, Karen had offered us her flat for the afternoon so we could hang out and change our clothes between activities. When we let ourselves in, we found that Karen had also surprised us by decorating the place, and making sure it was well stocked with treats, including chocolate-covered strawberries, a massive charcuterie board, and plenty of champagne.

"This is too much!" Hannah mumbled for about the hundredth time that day, looking around at all the balloon arches and the giant banner which read "Hannah's Last Fling Before the Ring!"

"You know Karen," Milo said with a satisfied nod. "The woman is literally incapable of underdoing anything and, frankly, I'm here for it."

"I invited her to come, but she said no," I told Hannah, as we tossed our bags onto one of the massive king-sized beds.

Hannah looked upset. 'Oh, no, really? Why? I hope she didn't think we wouldn't want her here!"

"No, no, nothing like that," I assured her. "She just laughed at me and said we didn't want any old ladies spoiling our fun."

"She's not old!" Hannah said, indignantly.

"That's what I told her, but she wouldn't budge. She said she wanted us to have our fun without any chaperones.'"

Hannah laughed. "She's overestimating my version of fun." She leaned toward me and dropped her voice. "Is this the part where we change back into pjs and hang out eating snacks in bed for the rest of the night? Because I'd be totally cool with that."

"Dinner first," I told her, "and a little after dinner entertainment."

Hannah nodded, and I giggled at the forced bravery in her face. I felt bad that she looked so nervous, but not bad enough to spoil the rest of the evening's surprises.

We lounged around at Karen's for a while, grazing on all the snacks and admiring the view from the balcony, until it was time to get ready for dinner. I made sure Hannah had several outfit options, but of course it was Milo who ultimately styled her for the evening with the help of Rana, who was surprisingly skilled with a makeup brush, for a woman who rarely wore much makeup. Not that she needed it; her skin was flawless and glowing, her lashes thick, her lips plump and moisturized. In fact, it was almost rude how beautiful Rana was with absolutely no makeup on. When I pointed this out, she laughed.

"My job is too dirty and sweaty to attempt makeup every day," she said, making a face. "So I've had to refocus on a really good skincare routine instead."

"Well, it's working," I said, watching her as she applied Hannah's eyeliner. "Seriously, you look airbrushed."

"Aw, you're too kind," she said. "Just for that, I'll do your makeup, too, if you like."

When we were all glammed up to Milo's standards (which took several rounds of approval and a few accessory adjustments), we took some photos and headed back out to our waiting limo. The driver took us up the street for dinner at a new Asian fusion restaurant that was the hottest reservation in the city, according to Karen, who made all the appropriate phone calls to make sure we got on the list.

"Look, it's not too late to add a pub crawl to the schedule," Savvy whispered to me from behind her menu. I've got a list of places where we could—"

I turned to her. "Sav, I'm gonna hold your hand as I say this: Let. It. Go."

Sav frowned and returned to her menu, grumbling something about sticks and where I might have shoved one.

Finally, it was the last stop of the night, a karaoke bar in the West End. This part had been the one aspect of the night that Savvy refused to budge on.

"There's got to be some manner of musical shenanigans. Hannah won't go to a strip club or dance on a bar at a nightclub. That only leaves karaoke. There is no other choice."

To my shock, Hannah didn't cringe back into the limo when she saw where we were. Maybe it was the two cocktails at dinner, but we didn't even have to drag her inside. She turned red and groaned, but the groan was almost a laugh, and there was a grudging resignation in her voice as she said, "Okay, okay, let's get it over with."

"That's my girl!" Savvy crowed, and went off to buy the first round of drinks.

The place was crowded, but we had a booth reserved in the corner, close to the stage where everyone was taking turns performing. The woman on the stage, as we slid into our booth, was belting out "Love is a Battlefield," mistaking her beer bottle for her microphone approximately fifty percent of the time. Despite how drunk she was, she was obviously very good.

"I've just realized, the West End is probably not the best place to do karaoke," I said into Rana's ear. "At least, not when you're terrible."

Rana laughed. "If it cheers you up at all, I don't think many of the professionals would risk blowing their voices after a show. But it is probably a more talented crowd than down the local pub, I reckon."

"Personally, I don't think good singers should be allowed to do karaoke," Savvy said as she returned with a waiter on her heels carrying a tray of drinks. "It's not fair, is it? That stage should be reserved for the plastered and the tone deaf. A sacred space to make a bloody fool of yourself, knowing everyone else who gets up there is also going to make a fool of themselves. Anyways, I've slipped the DJ a few quid to move us to the top of the list, so who's going first?"

We all looked at each other with varying degrees of horror on our faces.

"Ah, come on, let's at least see what songs they've got!" Rana said brightly, and with that, she grabbed Hannah's hand and hauled her off to the table in the corner where the DJ kept his binders of music. I reached for the drink Savvy had gotten me and took a sip. I flinched.

"Sav, what the hell is in this? It tastes like battery acid!"

"Ah, just a little something to loosen everyone up. Come on, drink up. It'll put a little hair on your chest!" Savvy boomed, knocking her own drink back. "A bit of liquid courage so you can sing your tits off up there!"

I snorted and put the drink down. Anything that tasted and smelled like that meant a painful morning, and I knew it. My phone began to buzz in my pocket as Rana and Hannah came giggling back to the table.

"Oi, no blokes tonight! Ladies only!" Savvy yelled as I pulled the phone out to check it. She made a grab for it, but I danced up out of my seat and out of her reach.

I looked pointedly at Milo, who scoffed. "Nice try, honey, but I'm no poster boy for gender norms. I am a fixture at ladies night, and we all know it."

"You know what I mean," Savvy said. "No boyfriends!"

"We only made that rule so Hannah couldn't try to bring Kiernan," I said. "And besides, what kind of bullshit rule is that, anyway? You get to bring your girlfriend with you, but I can't say hi to my boyfriend on the phone?"

Savvy grinned, pulling Rana in for a kiss. "Okay, yeah, it's a loophole, I admit it. Score one point for the sapphics."

While everyone else put their heads together, probably trying to pick a song to perform, I answered my phone.

"Finn?"

His answer was barely audible as the entire place erupted into a chorus of "Don't Stop Me Now" by Queen.

"Hang on, Finn, let me get outside where it's quiet," I said, weaving through the crowd to reach the front doors. I waved at the bouncer, so he could see I was just stepping out to take a call, and at his nod, broke free of the hot, crowded interior into the cool night air.

"Sorry about that, Finn," I said. "I should be able to hear you now."

"'S fine, Jess. Is this Jess? Have I called the right person?"

"Finn? Is that you?" He didn't sound like himself. His words were sliding together, almost like... *oh, no.*

"'S me. I'm here. Hello? Did you call me?"

I smothered a laugh. Oh my God, he was hammered. Like... spectacularly hammered. "No, you called me," I reminded him. "You sound like you're having a good time."

"Jess... Jessica... I... I messed up," Finn said in an exaggerated stage whisper.

"What do you mean, you messed up?" I asked, though I had a pretty shrewd idea already.

"I... I said I wasn't going to drink very much, but... well, Kiernan's cousins are a... they're... they're a bad influence." He dragged the last two words out, exaggerating every syllable.

I had to press my lips together and compose myself. "I see. So instead of only drinking a little...?" I let it trail off into a question.

Finn sighed. "I joined in the fun. Bit too much fun. Entirely too much fun. And now I can't drive us back."

I couldn't hold it in anymore. I started laughing.

"'S not funny," Finn slurred. "I've failed the mission."

"Finn, it's not a mission, it's a stag night. In fact, most people would say you've performed admirably. Savvy would probably give you a medal."

"I don't deserve a medal!" he practically yelled. "I've... I've... succumbed to peer pressure like a bloody schoolboy."

"It happens to the best of us," I said, still laughing. "It'll be a miracle if I escape Savvy's attempts to get me plastered. I think she just ordered a round of rubbing alcohol."

"What should I do?" Finn said. "It's not just me, it's Kiernan, too. I've got to get him home—us home—and I can't bloody drive like this!"

"Can you get an Uber?" I asked.

"In London on a Saturday night in the summer? All the way to Cambridgeshire? Not a chance."

"Okay, fine, I'm on my way," I said with a sigh. "Can you text me your location?"

There was a second or two of silence. "I'm not sure," he finally admitted.

"You know what? Don't worry about it. I can track your phone. I'm on my way."

I ducked back into the karaoke bar to find Hannah, Tia, Rana, Savvy, and Milo all up on the stage shouting and laughing their way through a raucous rendition of "Girls Just Wanna Have Fun." Savvy spotted me from the platform, gave a shout of delight, and reached right down to yank me up onto the stage. I sang along for a verse or so, and then yelled into Savvy's ear.

"I've got to go!" I said.

"Go? Go where? You can't go now, we've got three more songs!" Savvy shouted back.

"I won't be long. I have to go pick up Finn. He's taken your advice and had a bit too much fun, and now he can't drive."

"Finn's pissed? Like, properly pissed?"

"Decidedly."

Savvy threw her head back and let loose a roar of laughter that could be heard even over all the intoxicated singing.

"Ah, this is just too bloody good. Can you get a video for me? I need documentation. Can you start a live? Please, I need this."

"Oh my God, Sav, I'm not going to broadcast him on the internet!"

"Come on! Just a little bit! If he's really that blitzed, he won't even notice!"

"Savvy, NO."

"Aw, you're no fun."

"Just keep an eye on everyone. I'll be right back. If you head back to the cottage before I get back here, just text me, okay?"

"Yeah, all right. Are you sure you aren't doing this just to get out of karaoke?" she asked, narrowing her eyes at me.

"Who me? Of course not!" I gasped, clutching pearls I wasn't wearing. "Savvy, I am hurt and offended!"

"Yeah, yeah, sod off, then," Savvy said, shoving me away from the platform, but unable to keep the grin off her face.

I didn't think anyone else had noticed my departure, but as I leaned into the limo window to explain to the driver where I needed him to take me, Milo sidled up behind me.

"Sober Finn would kill me if I let you go across the city without an escort," he said.

"It's not across the city," I corrected him. "It's only about a mile from here, actually."

"Well, still. I know my role, and the Spirit Guide does not shirk his duty, even when there are drunken karaoke shenanigans at play," Milo said loftily, throwing out his chest like a soldier at attention.

"Okay, fine. But I must warn you. I am picking up a bunch of drunk men. This probably isn't going to be cute or filter-worthy," I said.

Milo rolled his eyes. "Sweetness, I know that. Why do you think I'm coming? Aside from keeping an eye on you, you might need backup."

"Okay, it's your choice. But your job is to keep an ear on the connection and update Hannah as needed on our whereabouts. Deal?"

"Deal."

We climbed (well, I climbed, Milo floated) into the limo, using the address that had come up from tracking Finn's phone. The city was bustling with nightlife, hordes of people looking for excitement and connection, an experience that would fling their lives into an entirely new and thrilling direction. Most would simply wake up the next day with a headache, but there was always that chance that an encounter could change everything. The night in the city was alive and thrumming with possibility. I could feel it, even though I wasn't looking for it.

We pulled up in front of a pub full of big-screen TVs replaying a dozen different sporting events. It smelled like stale beer, cigarettes, and regret out on the sidewalk. The bouncer took one look at me, eyed the line of men waiting to get in, and gestured me inside. Once we made it into the bar, it was obvious why I'd been allowed to cut the queue, as nearly every eye in the place turned to ogle me. I ignored them all, searching for Finn and the others. Finally, I spotted them in a red leather booth, the table absolutely littered with empty beer bottles and shot glasses. Milo took one look at the evidence and made a dry-heaving sound.

"Irish car bombs," he said with a shudder. "Oh, no wonder the poor boy is trashed. I had quite the incident with those back in my corporeal days. Thank God I can't smell it or I'd have to wait for you outside."

Several of the other lads were heavily invested in a football game on the nearest screen, shouting at the players as they pelted up the field, oblivious to our arrival. Finn and Kiernan, however, spotted us at once as I approached the table.

"Jess! What are you doing here?" Finn asked, blinking at me in an almost sleepy way.

"You called me," I reminded him. "Because you didn't think you could drive home."

Finn shook his head. "No, I can't. Can't drive home. Terrible idea. Might get myself arrested," he whispered, leaning toward me and looking warily around, like a cop was waiting to arrest him for being drunk in a pub. God, he was so adorable—so straight-laced that he didn't even know what to do with himself when he'd had one—or in this case, several—too many.

Kiernan squinted at me. "Jess! You're here! Why are you here?" he asked, bewildered.

"I'm your ride," I told him. "Finn, I need the keys."

"Right. Right," Finn muttered, fumbling around with his various pockets until he finally located them. "Here you go. Are these my keys, then?" he asked, holding them up and looking at them suspiciously.

"Looks promising," I told him, taking the keys from his outstretched hand. "Okay, who's coming? Everyone?"

Finn shook his head, then swayed. "No, that lot want to keep going. Pub crawl. But we..." He lowered his voice to what he obviously thought was a whisper, and yet was somehow louder than he'd been a moment before. "Jess, if we don't go home, I think Kiernan and I might have to literally crawl."

I tried not to laugh, even as Milo snorted with mirth behind me. "Okay, then. Let's go. Have you settled the tab?"

Finn threw a handful of bills onto the table and nudged Kiernan, who looked ready to fall asleep. Kiernan blinked, then spotted Milo for the first time.

"Oh no!" he mumbled. "Milo, you're here! Is the connection open? Can she... can she see me right now?" He looked around the pub as though Hannah might pop out from behind the nearest barstool. "Is she watching? I don't... I don't want her to see me like this. Not like me at all. Got carried away."

"No worries, sweetness, I'm no snitch," Milo said, looking at Kiernan like he was a lost puppy or something. "Let's get you to bed, though, okay? You need sleep and water." He eyed the car bombs again. "And maybe a shower."

Kiernan and Finn stumbled out of their booth without even saying goodbye to the others and followed us outside. For a moment, I thought Finn had forgotten where he'd parked, but then he set off down the block, weaving crookedly around the first corner and pointing triumphantly to the black SUV they'd borrowed from the Fairhaven fleet of vehicles.

"Ta-da!" he said. "Abracadabra!"

"Nice one, Houdini," I said, clicking the key fob so that the car rumbled to life. It took Kiernan two tries to open his door, and Finn almost fell out trying to climb into the back seat. The seatbelts alone were a five-act comedy, but eventually, we got everyone settled into the car.

"Okay, next stop, bed," I said, pulling out from the curb. "I would like to remind all our passengers that we have a 'no vomiting' policy. Your cooperation is greatly appreciated."

We began our drive, inching along in the weekend traffic. I opened the connection up and found Hannah there waiting for me.

"Savvy told me why you left. Is he okay?" she asked at once.

"Finn, or Kiernan?"

"Both, I suppose."

"They're fine. I mean, they'll be hungover for like three days, but they'll be all right."

"Remember my Irish car bomb story?" Milo added.

"Oh, no!"

"Oh, yes."

"How's the karaoke going?" I asked. "Did you bring down the house?"

"Oh, it was so embarrassing, but we had fun," Hannah said. I could feel the light and bubbly tingle of her energy in the connection, and realized I could tell she was tipsy. I could also tell she was having a ball, despite all her earlier misgivings.

"I'll check in once we get back to the house," I told her. "If you're still in the city, we can join back up with you."

"Please be careful," she said, and I felt anxiety pop a few of those effervescent little bubbles. "You sure you're okay to drive?"

"Absolutely," I said. Like a lot of kids who grew up with an alcoholic parent, I was hyperaware of myself any time I chose to drink. "We're safe. And the limo will be waiting for you if you head out before I get back."

"Okay, I...oh. Oh, for heaven's sake, I have to go. Savvy has just started the whole place on the Grease Mega mix."

"Good luck," I snorted as I felt her exit my headspace. Beside me in the passenger seat, I heard Milo chuckling softly as well.

"You're picturing her doing the choreography for Greased Lightning, aren't you?" I asked him. "God, I kind of regret leaving now."

To my surprise, Milo didn't answer me out loud, but in the connection instead.

"No, no, it's not that. I'm eavesdropping on Jack and Daniels back there."

Taking the hint, I refocused my attention on the conversation going on in the back seat.

"…knew I shouldn't have gone along with them. They've always been able to drink me under the table."

"I think those blokes could drink almost anyone under the table," Finn said.

"But I'm just so anxious. I let my nerves get the better of me."

"Ah, everyone gets anxious before they get married. That's what they say, isn't it? Haven't got the experience myself."

"No, it's not that," Kiernan said, shaking his head so hard that he overbalanced himself and bumped into the window. "Ow."

"What is it, then? Go on, you can tell me," Finn encouraged him with a slap on the back that overbalanced him again. "Oh, sorry, mate," he added, as Kiernan knocked his head on the glass again.

"It's not getting married. Knew I was gonna marry that girl from the first time I met her—no, it's only… what if I hurt her?"

I froze, listening hard.

"You won't. You love her," Finn said confidently.

Kiernan shook his head so hard that he was probably dizzy by the time he'd finished. "No, but I mean… what if I hurt her by accident? What if something I say or do makes her feel hurt? How do I live with that?"

"It's Hannah. She loves you. She'll forgive you," Finn said, sounding a little mystified now, like the conversation had drifted out of safe territory.

"No! She shouldn't have to—she's been hurt too much already. She's had to forgive so many people—people that probably don't deserve to be forgiven, but she did it anyway. She'll always do it anyway. That's who she is. What if I become one of those people who doesn't deserve it, and she's stuck with me because she made a promise that she's too noble to break?"

I snuck a glance in the rearview mirror and saw that Finn had pulled his eyebrows into a deep furrow of concentration, even as he appeared to have trouble keeping his eyes open.

"Ah, that's an easy one, mate," he said after a minute's deliberation. "She won't let that happen."

"What do you mean?" Kiernan asked, sounding close to tears.

"I mean, she's a Ballard," Finn said, and then leaned in closer to Kiernan, like he was trying to tell him a secret. "I'm not sure if you know this, but I've got a Ballard girl as a partner, too. It's true. I'm dating her sister. Did you know that? You probably know that."

Beside me, Milo was barely able to smother his laughter.

Finn went on, "And the thing is... the thing about the Ballard girls... the thing is..."

I was suddenly holding my breath. Beside me, Milo was almost wild with glee at this unfiltered moment.

"You're just loving this, aren't you?" I muttered to him.

"Oh my God, this is like my Christmas," he hissed back, and then immediately shushed me, as Finn finally got a hold of his train of thought.

"The thing about the Ballard girls is that they are so much tougher than they look," he finally said. "You want to protect them... 'course you do, they've been through so much. It's not fair, is it? But the thing is that they can protect themselves. They've always done it, see? They had to."

I could feel the smile slipping off my face, and something more tender, more vulnerable taking its place. Milo was utterly silent beside me.

"They're survivors," Finn said. "And they're not ever gonna need us like that. I keep trying to learn that lesson, but I'm rubbish at it. I'm a guardian. I'm always going to try to protect her, whether she needs it or not. And so are you. But you need to remember... they're a bit like fire, mate. At first, it seems you'll never get close without getting burned. But if you're lucky—and we're real bloody lucky—they let you in, and then... well, there's nothing better than that warmth, is there?"

I could hardly breathe. I chanced another glance into the rearview mirror. Finn was gazing out the window as a light drizzle began to fall, spangling the glass and turning all the passing lights to jagged starbursts.

"You're lucky, mate. She chose you. Let you in, past all those walls, all that hurt and protection and pain. Only a fool would go and cock that up. And you're no fool, Kiernan. So just keep loving her. Keep loving her, and I reckon you'll be all right."

"That's... that's deep, mate," Kiernan mumbled, resting his forehead against the window. "That's really... well, that's just it, isn't it?"

"I expect so," Finn said with a sigh. "Just... don't cock it up. Don't know if I'll ever get the chance to... to marry Jess... don't know if she'll choose me. But I'm choosing her, however she'll have me, for as long as she wants me. Because she's all I'll ever want. And that's... that's all there is to it, I 'spose."

"Yep. That's all there is to it," Kiernan agreed.

"Hey mate, don't... don't tell her I said that, all right?" Finn said. "If... if you see Jess..."

Within seconds, there was the sound of snoring, and Finn's head lolled back against his seat. I could feel Milo's eyes on me, burning into the side of my face. Finally, as we slowed for a light, I chanced a glance at him.

"What?" I snapped under my breath.

"Nothing," he said. "Nothing at all."

"You can't tell anyone he said that," I warned him, keeping my voice low. "It wouldn't be fair, he's had so much to drink."

"Ah yes, I know it well. That's the true danger of Irish car bombs: the truth serum effect," Milo said, shuddering a little. "Been there, done that."

"So, you won't...?"

"My lips are sealed," Milo replied solemnly, then winked at me. "I won't forget it, though. And neither should you."

I didn't reply. In truth, I felt guilty about the fact that I'd just overheard what Finn had said. It felt like eavesdropping, even though I knew it wasn't. But to hear those words come out of his mouth, so simple, so honest, and in such a vulnerable moment... it had my mind and heart racing. Suddenly, I was arguing with myself inside my head.

He wants to marry you.

I already knew that.

But you don't want to marry him.

It's not... I mean, I love him, and everything he said is exactly how I feel.

But you still don't want to marry him?

You make me sound so heartless! It's not that I don't want to, it's just complicated.

Sounds pretty simple to me.

Well, it's not. It's scary, okay? Marriage is scary.

What's so scary about it?

I don't KNOW!

A tiny growl of frustration escaped me, and Milo shot me a curious look, though, surprisingly, he didn't say anything. He also didn't work his way into the connection to see what I was thinking, another surprise. Maybe he didn't need to, I thought. Maybe he can read the whole thing playing out on my face like subtitles. I smoothed out my expression and tried to focus on driving. It was entirely too late and dark, and rainy for an existential crisis behind the wheel. I'd have to save my inner monologue battle for another time, when I could concentrate... and when I didn't have a nosy spirit guide sitting right next to me watching me like the latest episode of *Real Housewives*.

19

COMPLICATIONS

We arrived back at home, and successfully put first Kiernan, and then Finn, to bed.

"Jess! What are you—am I home?" Finn asked me, as I maneuvered him into the house.

"Yes, we're home," I grunted, as he leaned into me a little too hard. "You called me, remember? I came to pick you up."

He squinted at me. "You did?"

"Sure did," I said, as I helped him sit on the edge of the bed.

"That's so nice. You're so nice, you know that?" he asked me.

It was hard not to laugh at him, but I did my best. "Oh yeah, I'm a real peach, just ask anyone."

"You're so nice. And beautiful. I hope you don't break up with me because I got pissed. Are you going to break up with me because I got pissed?" he asked, sounding almost morose as he flopped back against the pillows, like he already knew the answer was yes, and he was just waiting for me to say it.

"Not this time," I assured him, as I unlaced and removed his boots.

"Oh good," he sighed. "That's... that's brilliant, that is..."

But by the time I came back in with a glass of water, he was snoring with his mouth hanging open. I left the trash can next to the bed, just in case, and closed the door behind me.

"Good news," Milo said, as I walked back down the stairs. "Hannah says they're on their way back."

"Oh thank God, because I was just trying to figure out an excuse for not going back into the city," I said, heaving a sigh of relief.

"No excuses needed. But just a heads up that Savvy was crowned the karaoke queen, and the subsequent number of drinks that were purchased for her means she's going to be at least as hung over as Finn and Kiernan tomorrow," Milo informed me, smirking.

"The queen of karaoke?" I repeated. "Okay, I will admit, I am lowkey sorry I missed that."

Milo grinned. "Oh don't you worry. Apparently, Rana videoed the whole thing, and it's currently going borderline viral on socials."

"Oh my God," I gasped, and without further delay, I scrambled for my phone so we could watch it together.

My sleep was a technicolor tangle of wild dreams, each vision stranger and more nonsensical than the next until at last I landed with a cold, hard thud in the same cell I'd dreamed about before. Yet again, it was entirely too real, every one of my senses tingling with the foul, dank reality of it all. In the darkness beside me, I could hear the same labored breathing, punctuated now and then with a stifled sort of cry. I was more sure than ever that it was Polly, reaching out to me somehow for help; and yet I couldn't find a way to communicate with her, to tell her that I was there, that I was listening, ready and desperate to help her. As pale light began to creep into the cell, as sounds of life began to echo in from the corridor beyond the locked door, I found my consciousness trying to pull me away.

No, I told it. *No, I have to find more clues.*

But sounds from the waking world began to break through, causing the cell to dissolve around me, and jolting me back into reality.

"What the hell is that?" I gasped, as the sound reverberated again.

I lifted my head from my pillow where I was sleeping on the loveseat. Across the room, two tousled heads were rising from a tangle of blankets on the sleeper sofa, looking bewildered and exhausted.

"Is there a fire?" Tia muttered, still half asleep.

"What is that?" Hannah gasped. She hadn't washed her face when she came home, and there were raccoonish black circles under her eyes. "Was that the door?"

"I don't know, but whoever it is, is going to wake the whole house," I grumbled, sliding out from under my blankets and shuffling out to the front entryway. Rana and Savvy were crashing in the guest room, and Finn was up in our bed; and I knew Finn and Savvy, at least, were going to need all the sleep they could get after last night.

I pressed my eye to the peephole, sighed, and yanked the front door open.

"Karen, I love you, but it's not even seven o'clock," I said, stifling a yawn behind my hand. "What are you doing here so early?"

"I just… I wanted to check in on you," Karen said, looking unaccountably nervous. "I told you I'd bring breakfast," she added, showing me the two shopping bags dangling from her hand.

"Oh, right. I almost forgot. I guess when you said breakfast, we were thinking more brunch. But anyway, we're fine. Well, some of us are going to be spectacularly hungover, but that's par for the—"

Karen bit her lip. "Have you uh… watched the news at all, or…?"

I stared at her. "The news? Karen, it's the crack of dawn. We're all still asleep and probably will be for a few more hours." My sleep-addled brain started to wake up as I clocked Karen's wringing hands and pale complexion. "Why? What's wrong? Did something happen?"

She didn't answer. Instead, she pushed past me down the hall and into the kitchen.

"Karen, seriously?" I said. "I know bachelorette parties have a reputation for being completely out of control, but this is Hannah we're talking about. We really don't need an adult intervention. We were responsible. Well, most of us," I amended, thinking of Finn and Savvy upstairs sleeping it off.

But Karen was shaking her head violently, like she was trying to dislodge a fly. "I'm not here in an attempt to chaperone or butt in. I wouldn't have come at all, except—except I thought I needed to tell you in person."

Hannah appeared in the kitchen. "Karen? What are you doing here?"

"Oh, hi, Hannah, honey. Did you have a good night?" Karen asked as she placed the bags on the kitchen island and started pulling things out of them—boxes from a local bakery, bottles of orange and cranberry juice, a whole quiche—and placed them all on the counter. She did it with a manic sort of energy, like this was the one thing she could control.

"What do you need to tell us in person?" I prompted her, when she finally stopped flitting around the kitchen.

"What?" Hannah's eyes went wide, and she looked back and forth between Karen and me, fear blooming on her face. "She needs to... what's going on? What's wrong?"

Karen bit her lip. "I didn't want you to find out from anyone else. I wanted to be the one to tell you."

Beside me, Hannah swayed on the spot, a sway that had nothing to do with the comparatively reasonable amount of alcohol she'd consumed last night. She grabbed my arm to stop herself from falling over.

"It's Polly, isn't it?" Hannah whispered. "Polly's dead, isn't she?"

"No!" Karen gasped, clapping a hand to her head and then running her fingers over her hair, attempting to smooth her entirely flawless hairstyle. "No, I didn't mean to... I'm so sorry, it's not Polly. I haven't heard anything about her —surely you would have heard before I did. No, it's about The Grand Dutchess Hotel."

Hannah's stricken expression melted into bewilderment. "What about The Grand Dutchess Hotel?"

"It's... oh, Hannah, I don't even know how to tell you this, but... it's gone."

"Gone? I don't under—"

"There was a fire. A terrible fire. The Grand Dutchess Hotel has been destroyed."

It took several seconds before my brain caught up with my ears.

"What did you say?" I asked.

"The Grand Dutchess Hotel has been destroyed in a fire. It's all over the news. I'm actually shocked you haven't seen anything about it, although I'm relieved you heard it from me instead of stumbling across some social media livestream of the whole mess. There were no casualties, but a few people had to be treated for smoke inhalation."

"We weren't supposed to be on our phones," I said. "It was one of Savvy's requirements. She said we couldn't savor the moment if we were on our phones the whole time."

"Savvy is rather brilliant, I think," Karen said with a wan half smile. "At least, in this instance, her advice allowed you to enjoy the night without discovering the truth."

"What do they know about it?" Hannah asked. "Any details on how it started or... or where?"

"My lawyer credentials don't afford me the same access to law enforcement information that I enjoyed back in the United States. However, the Durupinen still have connections everywhere, and the Trackers are looking into it."

"Do they suspect foul play?" Hannah asked.

"Don't you?" I said darkly.

"I'm not sure they've determined that yet," Karen said, but Hannah and I were looking at each other.

"You don't think…" she muttered.

"Of course I do!" I said.

"But we weren't even there," Hannah said. "We were nowhere near the place! Why would someone who wanted to hurt us try to burn down a building we weren't even in?"

"I don't know, but it seems to me like two buildings we're associated with going up in flames in the course of a few weeks is just a little too much of a coincidence."

"Well, Polly's house, sure, I mean we were there, Jess, but why—"

"I don't know!" I almost shouted. I pressed my hands to my face, taking a deep breath and running my hands back through my hair. "Sorry. I'm not… I'm not trying to yell at anyone. I'm just so on edge."

"It's okay," Hannah whispered.

"No, it's not. I can't be blowing up at you guys—that's not where this anger should be directed," I said, from beneath my hands again. I pressed them against my eyes, so that strange glowing shapes burst and swirled behind them. Thank God I wasn't hungover, or my head might have exploded right there.

"Jess, I realize it's quite the coincidence," Karen said, looking stricken, "but it just doesn't make any sense. You weren't there!"

"Maybe someone thought we were there," I said. "We've certainly been there often enough over the last few weeks, finalizing details."

Karen shook her head. "I'm sorry, but I don't buy that. Whoever is behind all of this with Polly must surely be more careful than that. If this were some kind of attempt on your lives, it's far too amateur."

"I think Karen's right," Hannah said. "I just don't think this can be connected to us in any way. The only thing they've managed to do is cheat me out of a wedding venue, and even our enemies don't burn down entire buildings out of pettiness." She looked over at Karen, suddenly wary. "Would they?"

"Definitely not," Karen said firmly.

At that exact moment, Milo came drifting through the wall, cackling. "Holy three-day hangover, you should see Savvy this morning. Not that anyone's surprised. I've never seen someone so—oh!" he stopped short at the sight of Karen. "Hey, Karen! I didn't know you were..." His voice trailed off as he looked from one stricken face to another. "Oh God. What is it? What's happened?"

Rather than making Karen explain it again, Hannah just opened the connection and info-dumped our conversation directly into his head. His eyes went wide, and he froze, his mouth hanging open. A full minute later, he was still utterly frozen with that same expression.

"Milo?" Hannah asked tentatively.

"Can ghosts go into shock?" I asked.

"I don't think so," Karen said, her expression full of pity as she looked at our spiraling spirit guide; "but I think wedding dress designers who just found out their dream venue burned down can."

Hannah pulled herself up off the couch and went over to Milo's motionless form. She reached out and placed her hand on his ghostly shoulder. He flickered feebly, like a lightbulb that hadn't been screwed in all the way.

"Milo? Are you okay?"

"I... I can't... you can't be serious," he finally managed to whisper after several unsuccessful attempts to make sound. "You absolutely *must* be fucking with me."

"Milo, we would never be that cruel, you know that," Hannah said.

"I know, but I was hoping for a minute that I was wrong, and you were just being merciless bitches. Please tell me you are being merciless bitches," he replied, still in a strangled whisper. He flickered again, and his bottom lip twitched.

"Sadly no," I said. "Not even me."

"Please?" Milo repeated.

"Look, Milo, it's going to be okay," Karen said, suddenly brisk and businesslike. It was as though she'd taken one look at Milo's face and realized she had to pull it together or no one else would.

"How?" he gasped, his form blinking in and out like a bad signal now. "How can this possibly be okay?!"

"We're just going to have to find another venue," Karen said, crossing her arms.

"A... a-another venue?" he cried, his voice shooting up an entire octave by the time he managed to squeak the word out. "It's... it's impossible! We tailored everything, every design element, to that hotel. The flowers, the lighting, the tablescapes. The food! We'll never be able to get another venue on such short notice!"

"Of course we can," Karen said.

But Milo was coming out of shock into panic now, and he snorted so loudly he sounded like a spooked horse. "Oh, of course! How silly of me. You're right, there must be a hundred five-star luxury hotels in the heart of London with a Saturday night inexplicably available at the height of wedding season. No problem. Piece of wedding cake. Oh, the cake!" he added with a little sob.

"Milo, I think you're forgetting who you're dealing with here," Karen said, a lawyerly snap in her voice now. "The Durupinen pull strings in the highest echelons of society. If we need a new venue—and I think we have to assume that we will—then I'll have us one secured by the end of the day."

We all stared at her now. "The end of the day?" I repeated, incredulous. "Come on, Karen, I know you're good, but you're not that good."

"I am exactly that good," she shot back.

"But—"

"Look, whether by machination or by random misfortune, the universe seems bent on ruining a day that I have been planning tirelessly for well over a year. Now, I don't know why this has happened, but I do know that I will not take it lying down. The fact remains that, even in a clan as embattled as ours, there are still a hell of a lot of strings I can pull, and I intend to pull them, unless..." Karen paused in her tirade, turning suddenly to face Hannah. "...unless you don't want me to."

Hannah looked startled. "Huh?"

"I said, unless you don't want me to. As much as I have taken on in planning this wedding, the one thing I've never done is make a decision without your approval. So, I need to know, do you want me to find us a new venue, or do you want to postpone the whole thing?"

For a second, I thought Hannah might jump at the chance to just cancel the entire spectacle and sneak off to City Hall, but she shook her head. "No. I want to get married."

"Then that settles it," Karen said.

"But... but... how?" Milo gasped.

Karen raised an eyebrow. "What makes the world go 'round, Milo? Money," she said dryly. Then she turned to me. "Jess? Can you walk me out, honey?"

"Sure," I said, startled. Hannah and Milo threw curious glances at us as we stepped out into the hallway. When we were out of earshot, I asked, keeping my voice low, "What's up?"

"I told you girls that your weddings were paid for, that your grandmother set aside money, earmarked specifically for that purpose. But if we're going to pull this off, it's going to be expensive. I mean… really expensive."

"Okay," I said, drawing out the word, making it a question.

"Expensive enough that I'm probably going to have to dip into your half of that money," Karen said. "And I don't want to do that without your permission."

I looked at her, blinking slowly, for about ten seconds. Then I laughed.

I laughed so loudly that Karen backed a step away from me in alarm. I laughed until I was gasping, until my sides hurt, until tears of mirth leaked from the corners of my eyes. I bent double, trying to get control of myself. Finally, I straightened up, wiping my streaming eyes and hiccupping for a deep breath.

"I'm sorry. I'm sorry, it's just… oh my God," I wheezed, breaking into a renewed fit of laughter.

Karen looked like she couldn't decide whether to be annoyed or amused. "Jess, what in the world is so funny?"

"Just… the look on your face. Like you were asking me to… to sacrifice my firstborn child or one of my internal organs," I choked, still swiping at my eyes with the sleeve of my shirt. "Holy shit. Absolutely priceless."

Karen's face twisted in confusion. "Jess, I still don't see what—"

"Take it," I said, flinging my hands up in the air. "Seriously, Karen. Take all of it."

She looked shocked. "Oh, I don't think that's going to be necessary. We will, of course, get our money back from The Grand Dutchess. I only thought I might have to dip into—"

"Karen. Look at me. I. Don't. Care," I said, making each word its own complete sentence. "You could take that wedding money, hire a plane to Atlantic City, and blow it all on blackjack and lap dances. In fact, if that sounds like something you wanna do, be my guest. Spend every penny."

"But why do you—"

"Because I don't want it. Because I literally break out in hives at the thought of marriage. Because I once thought Hannah's engagement ring was actually mine, and I had such a panic attack that Savvy nearly had to sedate me. I'm not getting married, and if Finn ever does manage to drag me down an aisle, it will be the drive-thru aisle of a Vegas chapel, and I will be wearing my comfiest jeans and a pair of very well broken-in Doc Martins. I mean, come on, can you really imagine me a blushing bride? Seriously?"

Karen looked like she was trying really hard to picture it. Like, *really* hard.

"See? I am so very serious," I said, and I composed myself so that my expression matched my words. "Blow the wedding money. Pull out all the stops. Make this the wedding they'll all remember. Fix it for Hannah, and for Milo, and for yourself. Please, please do not worry about me. I'm good. I promise."

Karen's face finally split into a smile. "Okay, fine. But I'm going to feel terrible if you ever change your mind," she said.

"Let's go ahead and roll the dice on that one, okay?" I replied. "For real. I really like those odds."

Karen gave me a swift hug, and headed out the door just as Hannah called, somewhat warily, "Jess? What's... what's so funny?"

"Nothing," I said. "I'll tell you later." Frankly, I didn't think she'd find it as funny as I had.

By now, Tia had ventured into the kitchen, and Hannah had told her about The Grand Dutchess Hotel.

"Oh, I'm just so sorry," Tia effused as she sat down at the kitchen island, face eloquent with pity. "That's so awful. What are you going to do?"

"It sounds like Karen is going to handle it," Hannah said, with an air of determined calm. "So I'm just going to let her and hope it all works out."

"Milo, are you okay?" I asked, as I spotted him in the living room. Milo had drifted down onto the sofa like a feather, hovering there, looking like the ghostly version of a Bronte heroine in the last stages of consumption.

"I just can't believe this," he muttered. "It's unfathomable. How could this happen so close to the wedding?"

"I think we should just be glad it didn't happen while we were in the building, personally," I said.

Hannah sighed. "Jess, please don't start."

"Start on what? What did I miss?" Milo asked.

And before Hannah could object any further, I dumped my theory directly into Milo's head. He sat up like my thoughts were a jolt of electricity through his form. He stole a glance at Tia, who was fully occupied cutting herself a piece of quiche, before he responded.

"Are you for real?" he hissed.

"No, she's being ridiculous," Hannah muttered. "Not to mention paranoid."

I looked at Milo, raising my eyebrows. "Yeah, paranoid, after there's already been one attempt on our lives in the last month."

"Jess, we weren't in the hotel!" Hannah said, slapping her hand down on the arm of the couch.

"Okay, well then they're intentionally trying to ruin your wedding!" I said.

"Oh sure, they couldn't kill us, so they decided to compromise by messing up the wedding photos," Hannah said, and then snorted. "Come on, Jess, it doesn't make sense."

"It's... I don't... well maybe it was someone else, then!" I said, getting defensive now.

"How many sets of mortal enemies are we supposed to have, exactly?" Hannah asked.

"Well, maybe not mortal enemies, but certainly enough people who would like to make sure Clan Sassanaigh doesn't get to have the wedding of the season!" Milo said. He flew up off the sofa and looked suddenly furious.

Hannah now turned her "you must be crazy" gaze on Milo instead of me—a welcome break.

"Has everyone lost their minds?" Hannah cried, glancing at Tia again to make sure she wasn't listening. "Milo, I know you're disappointed, I know how much you loved The Grand Dutchess Hotel, but you can't let that cloud your judgment. The other Durupinen are not petty enough to burn down a landmark London hotel just because someone they don't like is going to have a wedding there."

Milo simply folded his arms, looking smug. "You can tell yourself that all you want, but you clearly don't watch enough reality television. The Real Housewives of Fairhaven are *exactly* that petty."

Hannah tried for the next few minutes to rationalize with him, but Milo refused to change his mind. Finally, she gave up, throwing her hands in the air with a groan.

"You see what you've done?" she snapped at me, but I only shrugged. I still thought it was sabotage, whether petty political revenge or something more sinister, I didn't know.

"Ugh," Hannah grunted. "Whatever. Enjoy your conspiracy theories, you two. I'm going back over to my cottage to check on Kiernan and take a shower. Then I'm going to call Karen and see if there's anything I can do to help her." She paused in the doorway and said, in a grudging voice, "Last night was really fun. Thanks again for planning it, even if you both have gone off the deep end now."

"You're welcome," Milo said.

"We're crazy but thoughtful," I added.

Her lips were twitching as she turned to head next door.

I started to wonder, after Hannah shot down my suspicions, if I was just being paranoid; but Finn quieted those doubts. A couple of hours later, after Tia had had her breakfast, she said her goodbyes and took an Uber back to London. Hannah returned with Kiernan in tow. He was looking tired but less ill than I would have expected. Then, around ten o'clock, Finn finally peeled himself out of bed. I was waiting for him with a cup of black coffee.

"Hey, party animal," I said by way of greeting.

"Shhhhh," Finn said, his eyes still squinted shut.

"Oof. That bad, huh?" I said, dropping my voice to the approximate volume and tone I'd employ for a funeral.

"Choices were made," Finn said, lowering himself slowly onto one of the kitchen island stools. "And those choices were very, very dumb. But I think you already know that."

"Well, here. This is for you," I said, pushing the mug of coffee toward him.

He picked it up, took a long sip, and sighed. "Yeah, that might just start to make a dent in it. Cheers, love. Did I hear people up and about here early this morning? I realize not everyone is suffering like I am, but I really didn't think we'd have such early visitors, given the lateness of the, ah... festivities last night."

"I could tell from the degrading quality of your texts that you were having a good time," I said, grinning.

"Oh, yes. Brilliant. Absolutely spiffing. No regrets whatsoever." He cleared his throat, which seemed to hurt.

"Do you uh... remember how you got home?" I asked.

Finn scrunched up his face, considering. "...Safely?" he tried, with a sheepish expression.

"It was me. I drove you and Kiernan home," I said.

"Did you?" Finn asked, "Oh blast. I'm sorry."

My grin widened. "No apologies necessary. It was... very amusing, actually."

Finn lifted his head and squinted at me, looking wary. "Amusing how?"

I shrugged, stirring the spoon around in my own cup of coffee. "Oh, you know. Just the general banter of a car full of men who were well and truly sloshed."

"What did I say?" he groaned.

"Oh, a little of this, a little of that," I teased.

"You aren't going to tell me, are you?"

"Oh no, this is much more fun," I said, laughing now. "Although I will say, if I had any doubts that Kiernan loves my sister—and I didn't—they'd be long gone by now."

Finn managed a small smile. "Is that so?"

"Some men go out for their stag night to forget all about their future wives. Kiernan couldn't shut up about his. It was quite sweet."

"Yeah, I've known him a lot longer than you have, and I must agree. Your sister has chosen very wisely."

"We are, both of us, very wise in that way," I murmured, leaning toward him.

His smile widened, and he leaned toward me, accepting what I made sure was a very gentle and quiet kiss.

"I love you, but you still smell like the floor of a pub," I whispered against his lips.

"Sorry about that, love," he said. "I'll remedy that as soon as I've finished this coffee."

"Well, I've got a wedding update for you that you need to hear first," I said.

"Oh dear," Finn said, looking me in the eye and seeming, for the first time, much more awake. "That sounds ominous."

I explained about The Grand Dutchess Hotel. Finn listened with an increasingly stony expression.

"What do you think?" I asked him. "Am I overreacting?"

"I want to tell you yes, because I want it to be true," he said slowly, "but no. I don't think you're overreacting."

The validation felt good for about five seconds, and then the dread set in.

"Until we find Polly or solve the mystery she left behind for us, we aren't going to be safe, are we?" I asked.

"No. No, I fear we're not," he replied.

20

ALWAYS A BRIDESMAID

It was a quiet day. Half of us were hungover, and all of us were worried about what the destruction of The Grand Dutchess Hotel meant for the wedding. Milo took off after Karen, claiming he wanted to help her, but was actually just physically incapable of not being on the spot for any and all wedding updates. The rest of us loafed around and watched the news throughout the day, listening for updates and any new information about the hotel.

"While the fire has shocked and devastated the residents of London as well as the many visitors who stay at The Grand Dutchess every year, who want answers, the authorities are not yet willing to confirm the cause of the fire, or to speculate whether it was indeed a case of arson."

"I'll tell you this, if it was a case of arson and the Durupinen were behind it somehow, they'll never be able to prove it was arson at all," Finn said. "We are too good at covering things up. If they say it was an accidental fire, that will feel more like confirmation than a ruling of arson would."

"So if it's not arson, it's probably arson?" I asked.

"Something like that, yes," Finn said.

"He's right," Kiernan added, from the chair in which he and Hannah were curled up together under a blanket. "Historically, we've had to commit some crimes in order to protect our secrecy, or do damage control for angry spirits. I honestly think only the Trackers could spot our handiwork."

"I don't know why we're bothering with the news, then," Hannah said, feeding Kiernan a bite of scone from her plate. "We should really just wait for what Catriona has to say."

Around noon, Rana appeared from upstairs, messy-haired but seemingly unscathed from the night out.

"How are you feeling?" Hannah asked her.

"Me? Oh, I'm fine, really. Just needed a good lie in—can't remember the last time I was out so late," she said, helping herself to a bagel from the tray on the counter, and smearing it with a generous amount of cream cheese. "Don't suppose I could do up some dry toast and coffee for Sav? The karaoke queen is, uh... feeling a bit low."

Hannah helped her get a tray together and carry it upstairs. An hour later, Savvy appeared.

I couldn't help but grin. "How ya doin' there, Todd?" I asked.

"Who, me? Never better," she croaked, but the cocky toss of the head unbalanced her a little. "Just... just a bit out of practice is all. Being a full-time Caomhnóir hasn't left me much time for my traditional levels of shenanigans."

"Thank God for that," Rana muttered, but she winked affectionately at Savvy. They both came to join us around the tv—Savvy requesting that we lower the volume a bit—and we filled them in on The Grand Dutchess Hotel. While dismayed, neither launched into any conspiracy theories about what might have happened.

"Bad luck, mate," Savvy said, patting Hannah on the arm, "but it sounds like Karen will soon have it sorted. Bet she'll find you someplace even posher."

It was hard to imagine anywhere "posher" than The Grand Dutchess, but we all agreed anyway, just to keep Hannah's spirits up.

Around three o'clock in the afternoon, there was a frantic knock on the front door, followed by the sound of the door opening and then Karen's voice.

"Hello?"

"We're in here, Karen," I called to her.

Karen came bustling into the living room, and I could tell from the smug glow of triumph on her face that she had, indeed, been successful. Sure enough, Milo popped into existence beside her, looking thoroughly pleased about something.

"Well?" Hannah asked, rising from the chair, fingers still entwined with Kiernan's.

"We've done it," Karen said.

"Crisis averted, wedding back on!" Milo added triumphantly.

"How? Where?" Hannah asked.

"Well, the how was nothing more than calling in every favor and connection I could think of to everyone I know this side of the pond," Karen said. "But the where was actually a bit simpler. It was so obvious, I can't believe we didn't consider it in the first place."

"Where?!" Hannah repeated, sounding almost frantic now.

"Fairhaven," Karen replied.

No one spoke. No one even moved.

"Be serious," I finally squeaked out.

"I am serious!" Karen said, her triumphant expression falling just slightly. "It was kismet, honestly! I was in the midst of making calls back at my flat, and suddenly I got a call from Celeste. She told me she had heard about the hotel—it was all over the castle, apparently, given that nearly everyone of consequence there is invited to the wedding—and she called to see if there was anything she could do. And I, jokingly, of course, said, 'Well, if you've got a wedding venue up your sleeve that's available in two weeks, that would be helpful.' And she said, 'But that's why I've called. I want to offer up Fairhaven Castle for the wedding.'"

I looked at Hannah, who looked as utterly dumbstruck as I felt. She glanced at Kiernan, who shrugged helplessly.

"I... could we really... is Fairhaven equipped for that kind of thing?" Hannah asked.

"Of course it is!" Karen said. "You'd have no way of knowing this, but the castle has actually been the home to quite a few weddings over the centuries. I think the last one was in the 1960s, if I'm not mistaken. Anyway, if you stop thinking of it as Fairhaven and start thinking of it as a big, historical castle, you soon realize it's absolutely perfect."

"Picture it," Milo said, jumping in and throwing his hands up in front of his face, like a director setting a scene. "The guests ascend the long gravel drive, adorned with floral accents and lanterns lighting their way. The front of the castle is festooned with garlands and lights, with formally attired guards on either side of the door like royal footmen. The entrance hall with its sweeping staircase and vaulted ceilings will be decorated to the hilt and swarming with tuxedoed waiters and their trays floating among the guests, offering champagne and showing them the way to the central courtyard, which will be transformed with seating and a carpeted aisle leading to a flower-drenched cupola, where they will watch you tie the knot, whispering all the while behind their flutes that you are the most flawlessly dressed bride and groom they've ever seen."

"Milo, move it along, sweetheart," Karen muttered out of the corner of her mouth.

"What? Oh, right, sorry. Getting a little carried away," Milo said with a wink. "Anyway, then they open the doors down the little walkways to the Grand Council Room, which will be transformed into a ballroom, with tables all around the perimeter and a dance floor in the center. Imagine the chandeliers all lit up, the Council benches repurposed for the band, the main platform home to the long table where the wedding party will sit. It's literally perfect!"

In spite of myself, I found myself envisioning what he was describing. He was right. It would be magnificent... except...

"But the code of secrecy," I said. "Surely they're not going to let all these wedding guests wander the place unattended."

"There are very few non-clan guests, honey. But just in case, Caomhnóir will keep the right doors locked and guarded," Karen said, waving her hand dismissively. "We've had outsiders in Fairhaven Castle plenty of times before. It's been crucial to the cover story of it being a prestigious university—people would be suspicious if said university had never opened its doors to non-students. We've hosted charity events, art shows, historical events, and yes, even the occasional wedding."

"Surely, Celeste needs to get approval from the rest of the Council," Hannah said, a bit weakly. "I can't imagine the rest of the staff will be thrilled that we're turning their school and workplace into a function hall for the night."

"But she already has the approval," Karen said, her faltering smile beginning to widen again. "In fact, she said it wasn't even her idea to begin with!"

"Whose idea was it, then?" Hannah asked.

"What does it matter? The point is, she spoke with the primary Council members and even assembled the instructors. The decision was unanimous. They've agreed that your wedding will take place at Fairhaven. Unless, of course, you don't want it to?"

We all turned to look at Hannah, whose expression went blank with the horror of being asked to make this decision on the spot.

"I... I'd just never considered... Kiernan, what do you think?" she asked, stalling for time.

Kiernan looked almost equally panicked at being asked to form an opinion on the matter. "Oh! Well, it never occurred to me that we might be married at Fairhaven, but... it's certainly convenient. It's also where we met for the first time, so that's rather sweet, isn't it?"

"Yes, it... it's been the site of many unforgettable things," Hannah replied, and though she was trying to smile at Kiernan, I knew what she was getting at. We'd been through some of the most harrowing experiences of our lives on those grounds: battling the Elemental, the mural in the entrance hall, the near burning down of the place to make our escape, the battle against the Necromancers when the Prophecy came to pass... rather a lot to balance against the warm fuzzy memories we'd managed to make within those castle walls.

"Our same florist is coming to decorate," Karen jumped in, perhaps sensing the hesitation. "I already sent her photos, and she's confident we'll be able to use much the same scheme we had planned for the hotel. We were also able to hire the entire kitchen staff from The Grand Dutchess to cater the meal, which means your menu can stay the same. Of course, there's nothing we can do about the fact that the invitations have already gone out, but we can send updated details to the guests, and we've found a lovely hotel in Cambridge where people can stay, and we can arrange shuttles back and forth. And even better, the wedding party can all stay right at the castle and get ready there before the ceremony." Her expression, as she looked back and forth between us, was a mixture of excitement and anxiety. "So... what do we think?"

I glanced at Hannah. She and Kiernan were looking at each other, having a silent conversation. Finally, they turned to Karen.

"That sounds like a wonderful solution, Karen," Hannah said.

Karen heaved a sigh of relief that nearly deflated her. "Thank goodness, because I honestly don't think I could have pulled it together anywhere else at this point. Celeste is arranging it all for us. We have unfettered access to the castle between now and then, which means we can make up for lost planning time. She's going to move Council business to another space so that we can start transforming the Grand Council Room into a ballroom. It's going to be stunning, I promise."

"We trust you completely, Karen," Hannah said.

"Personally, I find it to be poetic justice," Milo said. "The very place they tried to brand you as outcasts, and now you're going to host the wedding of the decade there and make them all watch. I am here for it!"

"Okay!" Karen said, clapping her hands together. "It's settled. A wedding at Fairhaven!"

There was a grunting snore from the corner, and then Savvy's disheveled head peered out from under a blanket on the couch.

"Oi? Who's getting married at Fairhaven?" she mumbled.

21

CARVED IN STONE

With the bachelorette party behind us, the wedding now loomed in less than two weeks. It was a strange feeling, after so much anticipation and preparation and anxiety, that it was actually about to happen. For me, having waited so long, two whole weeks still felt interminable. For Karen and Milo, however, it was a down-to-the-buzzer emergency of epic proportions.

"I guess it's good you don't have to sleep," I told Milo when I glimpsed his to-do list.

"Sweetness, the perpetual wakefulness isn't enough. I'm going to need a time machine," Milo said, a faint note of hysteria in his voice. "I really do need to learn how to delegate, but I'm literally in the afterlife at this point, so I don't really think this diva is learning any new tricks."

As Karen and Milo ran themselves ragged getting everything ready for the big day, I was left to torture myself over the fact that we still hadn't found Polly or decoded her clue about the tapestry.

"Do you think we missed something?" I asked Hannah one night about a week before the wedding, as we were poring over all the images of the original tapestry for the thousandth time.

"Well, yeah, clearly, seeing as we haven't solved it yet," she replied, tossing a photo aside and rubbing her eyes with her hands like a sleepy child.

"No, I mean the clue. Do you think maybe there was more in that children's book, and Kiernan and Savvy just didn't find it?" I ventured.

But Hannah shook her head. "I don't think so. Polly was careful about where she left that message, and she knew it was a long shot that we would even find it. I can't imagine she would make it harder by spreading the message out on more pages of the book. She was desperate. She had to keep the clues simple."

"Yeah, simple and undecipherable," I grumbled. "If I wasn't dreaming about the woman every damn night, I might not feel so—" I froze.

Shit.

"You're dreaming about her? About Polly?" Hannah asked, suddenly alert, all trace of sleepiness gone.

"...no?"

"Jess! Don't you dare lie to me!"

I sighed. "I'm not lying to you. Technically."

"Technically?!"

There it was. The danger note in her voice. The one that meant I'd better come clean with everything or she would prove to me, yet again, why tiny was very often frightening.

"Look... I'm not a hundred percent sure, which is why I didn't say anything. I've never seen her face. I've never been able to recognize for certain that it's her voice."

"Oh, come off it. You didn't say anything because you knew I'd get upset," Hannah cried.

"And I was right, wasn't I?" I shot back. "You are upset!"

"I'm upset because you lied to me!"

"I didn't lie to you, I just... kept that piece of information to myself until the right time."

She crossed her arms. "And the right time was when it accidentally slipped out of your mouth?"

"...yes?"

Hannah growled with frustration. "Jess, I do not need to be coddled through these next few days, okay? I'm not some fragile porcelain doll. I need to be in the loop."

"It just felt like you had enough going on," I mumbled.

"Oh, I do. But that's not an excuse for keeping me in the dark. Don't do it again, I mean it," she demanded.

"Okay, okay!"

"Promise, Jess."

"I promise."

She took a deep breath and visibly calmed down. "Thank you. Now tell me about these dreams, please."

Though it was the last thing I wanted to do, I told Hannah everything, every detail I could conjure, every sound and visual I could describe. When I had finished, I could tell she was horrified, but she was also doing her best to hide that fact. She kept her face carefully composed, as though determined to prove to me that telling her was the right thing to do, but she couldn't hide the increasing alarm that was sparking in her eyes.

"And you really thought keeping this to yourself was the right decision?" she asked when I had finished. "The Trackers could use that information to—"

"Hannah, for God's sake, I'm not an idiot. I told Catriona right away, and I've been updating her every time I have another one, which has been basically every night now. The only person I kept it from was you."

"Oh," Hannah said, and she looked somewhat mollified. "Right. Well... good. And what did Catriona have to say?"

I sighed. "She was glad for the tips, but mostly she's just aggravated at me that I haven't been able to pinpoint the exact location. As though Seer visions are something a person can actually control. I mean, does she really think I'm not frustrated out of my mind? Does she really think I wouldn't kill someone to know what those dreams mean and where Polly is right now?" Suddenly, without me realizing that it was happening, there were tears running down my cheeks.

"Oh!" Hannah gasped, all trace of anger gone. "Oh, Jess! Don't cry!"

"I'm not crying!" I shouted, and promptly burst into noisy sobs. "Okay, I guess I am," I amended between stuttering breaths.

"Oh, I'm sorry I shouted at you, come here," Hannah cooed, and pulled me into her arms. I buried my face in her hair and gave myself up to the tears that I had apparently been fending off for a very long time, without realizing it. I actually scared myself with how hard I was crying, which, ironically, only made me cry harder.

"Holy shit, Jess, get a grip!" I blubbered, as I tried to get my breathing under control. Hannah said nothing, just stroked my hair and shushed me until I finally cried myself out.

"See what happens when you carry too much?" Hannah whispered, now rubbing my back. "You don't need to shoulder everything, Jess. We're all here to deal with this. It's not your burden to bear."

"I guess it just felt like everyone else already had extra burdens," I explained.

"Yeah, but that includes you," Hannah reminded me. "No one wants or expects you to martyr yourself, Jess. Besides, what if something you told me triggered a memory, and I knew where that place was?"

I yanked my face away from her shoulder and stared at her. "Wait, do you?"

"No, but I might have! That's my point!" Hannah said. "Have you tried drawing it? I feel like that has helped you understand things better in the past. You're such a visual person."

"Only about fifty times," I said, peeling myself off the sofa to snag my sketchbook from under the pile of photos of the tapestry. I'd been drawing that as well, trying to see if the act of drawing would unlock some kind of understanding; but I'd been left just as clueless as ever. I flipped past all of these to the other sketches, the ones I hadn't shown her, of the cell. She stared down at it, a spasm of something flashing across her face—it looked like grief.

"It's awful," she said. "It looks so…"

"Yeah."

"And Catriona doesn't—?"

"Not a clue. She tries to sound like they've made progress, but I don't think we're any closer to finding Polly than we were on the day we discovered she was gone."

"And no closer to solving this riddle," Hannah sighed. "I'm starting to worry that we never will."

"Well, I suppose the silver lining there is that, if we haven't solved it, maybe no one else has either—which means this artifact, whatever it may be, is at least safe."

"Yeah," Hannah said, though she didn't sound convinced. "For now."

Now that the wedding had been moved to Fairhaven, we were spending almost all of our time there. Karen had a veritable army of vendors who had to be met with and shown around the relevant spaces, so we were all put on rotation to help with that. There were surfaces to be measured, parking arrangements to sort out, and security plans to be made. In this last capacity, Finn found himself suddenly almost as stressed and busy as Karen.

"It would have been bad enough at The Grand Dutchess," he said. "But at least they have their own security staff to supplement. But at Fairhaven, it's not only the people we have to protect, it's the location! We have too many secrets, too many artifacts, too many incalculably valuable pieces of artwork and history. We'll be as worried about keeping people away from these things as we will about the safety of the people themselves!"

"Can't you delegate? You are the best man, after all," I said.

Finn gave me a withering look. "I think there's about as much sense in asking me to delegate as there is in asking Milo to do the same. Neither of us will be able to rest with the reins in someone else's hands, so we may as well just get on with it. I'll sleep when I'm dead."

"You won't actually," I teased him. "Frankly, that's Milo's whole strategy for getting everything done."

Finn's phone rang and he answered it. I watched his face crumple.

"Hmmm. I'm not sure who I can spare to... well, I'll send someone over."

"Who was that?" I asked.

"Karen," he said.

"Karen called you? Why?" I asked.

"As if she didn't have enough on her plate, there was a break-in at your vault last night."

"Our vault? What the hell?!" I replied. "What did they take?"

"That's the strange thing. It seems that nothing is missing. But of course, she still wants it investigated anyway. I'll send a couple of the lads over to check it out."

"That's so weird," I said. "Why would someone go to all the trouble of overcoming all that security and then leave all those priceless jewels and stuff untouched? It doesn't make sense."

"Who knows? Maybe they tripped an alarm and panicked. We'll find out more when I get someone down there. Karen can't possibly be expected to deal with this right now."

As Finn hurried off, his phone to his ear once again, I turned to find Celeste walking toward me.

"Everything all right?"

"Uh, yeah, just dealing with some stuff," I said, not wanting to get into it.

"It's a busy time! How's it going in there? Do you think I could take a peek?" She gestured to the closed doors of the Grand Council Room. Her eyes were shining with excitement.

"Oh! Yeah, I'm sure that's fine. You are the boss around here, after all."

Celeste leaned in and dropped her voice. "I think we can all agree Karen is the boss around here, at least for this week."

I laughed and pushed one of the double doors open so that she could sneak a glimpse.

"Oh, it's coming along just beautifully!" Celeste gasped as we slipped into the room. "I must say, it's lovely to have a gathering to look forward to within these walls. It's gotten to the point that I actually dread walking in here. At least on Saturday, I'll be able to enjoy this space again. And who knows, maybe the wedding will foster a bit of goodwill between the clans again."

"A sort of, let's get drunk and dance and make up?" I asked, laughing.

Celeste laughed too. "Yes, something like that, I suppose. Sometimes, I think we get so wrapped up in the in-fighting that we forget we're supposed to be a sisterhood. It's meant to be all of us, united together in our common calling, our common goal. It was never supposed to be about power or greed, or what we could get out of it for ourselves."

"Yeah, well. We're humans and, historically speaking, we fall into this trap a lot," I said.

Celeste gave me a sad smile. "Yes. I suppose we do. Still, we've got to keep trying."

"Yes, we definitely do," I agreed. "And speaking of 'keep trying,' I'm going to check on Fiona and see if we can't tempt her back into reality."

The smile slipped. "Yes, please do. While I do appreciate that she has made an effort to come to the Council meetings, each time I see her, I grow more and more concerned. I'm starting to think she really isn't well."

My response was only a shrug. Because I couldn't think of anything to say.

I made my way up to Fiona's tower with a pit in my stomach. Every time I'd seen Fiona over the past couple of weeks, she had literally scurried away from me. Mysteriously, she couldn't hear me when I called out. When I'd knocked on her studio door, no one came to answer it, even if I could hear movement on the other side of the door. I'd even let myself into the studio once, and still, there'd been no interaction. It was obvious at this point that Fiona was avoiding me, but I still didn't know why. Maybe today I would get an answer to that question.

As I expected, there was no answer to my persistent knocking. I called Fiona's name, but again, nothing. I pressed my ear to the door and held my breath, listening. At first, there was only silence—maybe she really wasn't there? But then I heard something—something that frightened me.

Sobbing. Raw, desperate sobbing.

No longer caring about privacy or permission, I turned the handle and pushed the door open, bursting through into the studio and staring wildly around for the source of the sound. It only took a second before my eyes found Fiona lying on the ground in a jumbled mess of broken plaster, head on her arms, crying like the broken pieces around her were her heart instead of her art.

"Fiona!"

I ran to her, dropping to my knees beside her. If she heard me, she didn't respond, just continued to weep. My hands hovered uselessly over her for a moment as I struggled to decide what to do, how to help her. For a moment, I could think of nothing, but then raw instinct kicked in over my shock, and I did the only thing my body could conceive of—I lay my body down gently on hers, wrapped my arms around her, and held her. I braced myself for the likelihood that she would reject my touch and throw me off her, but she didn't. In fact, she lifted her head off her arms, pulled herself up onto her elbows so that she could fling her arms around my neck and continue to sob into my hair like an abandoned child. Lacking context and therefore the words to comfort her, I just shushed her repeatedly like a mother trying to lull her child to sleep. In her helpless tears, I could hear all my fear and frustration of the past few weeks, felt the catharsis and the release. Just as Hannah had soothed me earlier, I tried to do the same for Fiona. At last, she calmed enough to speak through her tears.

"I can't get a hold of it. I just can't get a hold of it," she repeated.

"What is it, Fiona? What can't you get a hold of?" I asked her.

"No matter how many times I... I try to envision it... I can't... it won't stay put! It... it can't stay put! But I don't know what it means... I don't know how to... I just want to erase it!"

"We all have things we want to erase, Fiona. We all have things we want to control, and it's not always possible. We don't always have control," I said, trying to sound sensible even as I felt so overwhelmed and bewildered by the awful sight of a vulnerable, sobbing Fiona. Fiona, whose very soul seemed made of grit and claws and the burn of a good whiskey.

"I can't understand it and I can't unsee it, and now I'm afraid I won't be able to... to stop it..."

I ventured a guess based on the fact that we were lying in a fresh pile of plaster dust. "Is this about your sculpture, Fiona? Is this about the sculpture behind the curtain?

I expected denials and anger and even a shove away, but she only nodded, fresh tears spilling onto her cheeks. "Yes."

"Can I... can I see it?" I asked. "Or... are we sitting in it?"

She wiped her face and waved a trembling hand at the curtain behind her, as though to say, "Go ahead, if you must."

Heart pounding, I did as she bid me, reached past her shoulder, and yanked the curtain open.

The statue in front of me was almost identical to the one I had seen the last time I'd looked behind the curtain, except it was larger. Again, every detail was exquisitely crafted, except for the face. Except where before the face had been hacked to pieces, the place where the facial features ought to be was completely smooth—an absence of identity. I just stared at it, trying to comprehend what I was seeing.

"Well? Say something! You can't just sit there in silence when a bloody blind woman shows you something!" Fiona snapped, sounding just a tiny bit more like herself. The familiar fiery note helped me to find my voice.

"I'm sorry, uh... it's... I mean it's... disturbing, I'll give you that," I said. "But I don't... I'm not really sure what I'm looking at."

"This is my vision," Fiona said, flinging her hand violently in the direction of the sculpture in acknowledgment. "This... monstrosity. I can't think. I can't sleep. All I can do is create this damn thing over and over again!"

"When you say vision..." I prompted.

"It's... a Seer vision. It has to be. No spirit-induced vision has ever produced this level of obsession. I can't get away from it, Jess. I can't stop trying to create it, and yet I can never finish it, because it won't hold still!"

"The... the sculpture won't hold still?" I asked, starting to wonder if Fiona had simply gone crazy at this point. But her reply assured me quickly of her sanity.

"No! What in the blazes... no, not the sculpture, you daft girl, the vision! It won't stop shifting and changing! It's as though it's in flux and it's trying to show me something it doesn't know yet!"

I did my utmost to understand this, but everything was still shrouded in a fog of confusion. "I... okay, so... sorry, I'm just trying to catch up here, so don't bite my head off, but...you're saying that this statue represents your depiction of a Seer vision?"

"Yes."

"And it isn't finished because the vision itself keeps changing?"

"Yes!"

I looked at the sculpture again, wheels turning so fast my brain felt like it might catch fire. "You've Seen that someone is going to be stabbed?"

She didn't say anything this time, but her expression twisted with a violent emotion.

"But the statue has no face. So does that mean you… don't know who it will be?"

Again, she said nothing, but pressed her lips together.

"Fiona… what did you mean when you said that the vision won't hold still?" I pressed.

Fiona looked like she might crumple in on herself again, but she managed to keep herself upright. "The face. The face keeps changing. It won't… won't settle on a victim."

"You've Seen a murder but can't tell who the victim will be."

"Yes." She let out a deep sigh, as though the word had been exorcised from her. "Yes, that's the truth of it."

"Is the vision showing you something blurry? Something constantly shifting so it never settles? Does it just flip through faces, like scrolling through photos?" I asked, determined to understand exactly what we were dealing with before I let Fiona's panic infect me, too.

Fiona ran a shaky hand over her own face. "It's most like the last one. A parade of faces, never for more than a fleeting instant before it's replaced with another."

"Did you recognize any of the faces?"

Fiona's face went instantly the color of milk. She nodded.

"Who?" I whispered. "Whose faces?"

"So many of us," she whispered back. "You. Catriona. Your sister. Karen. Celeste. All Durupinen. Over and over again. Each one so clear that I'm sure it must be true, and then gone, replaced by another just as clear. I've driven myself to the brink of madness, I think, trying to pin it down. But I can't do it, Jess, because it's waiting for something. Or someone."

"So you're saying… that there's going to be a death—maybe even a murder —but you can't tell who it will be because… because the murderer hasn't decided yet who the victim will be?"

"Yes. Yes, that's the long and short of it," Fiona said. "And now you know why I've been… well, a bit of a mess."

I stared into her swollen, tear-stained face with its slightly sheepish expression, and couldn't help cracking a smile.

"Yeah, just a bit, Fiona."

She let out one hysterical bleat of laughter, swallowed almost at once again by a sob bubbling up in her.

"Hey," I said, throwing my arm back around her shoulders again. "It's okay. These visions... they're fleeting, you know this. The fact that it can't even settle on a face... I think that's a good thing. It means the thing you're seeing is dependent on so many factors that it's likely never to come true."

"Christ on a bike, child, you must think I'm a fool," Fiona said, swiping furiously at her face with the sleeve of her smock.

"Well, sure, but not because of this," I teased gently. "Is that why you went to Skye with Catriona and Celeste? Because you thought someone might get hurt?"

"When I'd heard what had nearly happened to you and your sister, I knew that going to Skye was a huge risk, and after what I'd seen, I couldn't stay behind. What if that was where it happened and I wasn't there to recognize the signs?"

"You can't just follow us all around 24/7, Fiona," I said.

"I bloody know that!" she snapped. "Why do you think I've been locking myself in here all the damn time? I can't protect you all, so I need to find out which one to protect. That's why I've been working so obsessively. I'm trying to nail down the vision, so I can know for sure."

"But the vision isn't cooperating."

"All it's done is driven me right to the brink of madness," Fiona grunted. "Turned me insufferable. Well... more unsufferable than usual. I'm sorry I haven't... I didn't want to scare anyone unless... unless I knew for sure..."

I thought about everything that had happened over the past few weeks, about the explosion at Polly's house, about the attack in the old spirit block. There's no doubt we'd been dancing around the edges of something very dangerous for a long time now. Was Fiona's vision related? There was no real way to know, just as there was no way to know what danger we'd face next. Should I be panicking, knowing that death was circling us like a vulture? Maybe, but for some reason, I wasn't. Maybe it was because, on some level, I already knew it. Weren't we always risking something? Weren't we always chasing after the very things that threatened us? I looked at that sculpture and felt, rather than fear, a sort of grim acceptance. Yes, we were all in danger right now. Yes, that could mean something terrible would happen. But I already knew all of this. We all did. We knew the risks and accepted them.

I looked at Fiona. She still looked troubled, but some of the bright hysteria had faded from her eyes, and her whole body drooped. She was exhausted.

"I think you need to lie down," I told her.

She jerked her head up to glare at me, a protest on her lips, no doubt a demand that I don't baby her, and that I mind my own damn business and that she'd sleep when she was good and ready. But we locked eyes, and the fight went out of her. "Suppose you're right," she said.

"If you can give yourself the rest you need, things might become clearer," I told her, helping her to her feet. "Obsessing over visions has sent more than one Seer right off the deep end. Who knows how much clearer things could become if you let yourself rest."

Fiona grunted, shrugging irritably, but she let me lead her over to her living quarters in the far corner of the studio. She slumped down onto the bed, crumpling like a ragdoll. I yanked off her boots and stood them by the end of the bed. By the time I tracked down a half-clean blanket, Fiona was snoring with her mouth wide open. I smoothed the blanket over her, and watched her face twitch for a moment before letting myself out.

As I left the tower, I wondered if I should tell anyone else what Fiona had told me. Was there any point? What would any of us do differently? Would we stop trying to find Polly? Would we stop trying to solve the mystery she left for us? We were already on high alert with security, what with the wedding coming up in just a few days. The truth was, the knowledge wouldn't change a thing. We would press on as we had, and meet any consequences that followed.

When I reached the entrance hall, my phone buzzed in my pocket. I recognized the number, and my heart leapt.

"Cat?"

"Yeah, it's me. Listen, I'm not sure if I'm going to make it back for the wedding."

"What? Why? What's happening?"

"I'm following a lead. That bloke who attacked you in the old spirit block, Gabriel Durand? It turns out he was one of the personal guardians to Simone de Chastenay. And I thought about what you said, about your dream, that you thought the guards might be speaking French, and I suddenly wondered, what if this… this conspiracy wasn't coming from Skye? What if it was coming from somewhere else?"

"Where else… oh!" The realization was like a slap in the face. "Havre des Gardiennes?"

"Right in one," Cat confirmed. "I'm on my way there soon. Simone is locked up, of course, but she has plenty of loyalists who would be more than capable of planning something like this. I'm wrapping some things up here on Skye, and then I'll be arranging a flight."

It felt like there was something large obstructing my throat as I said, "Be careful, Cat. Seriously."

Cat snorted. "What are you, my mum? I'm always careful. But I can't say when I'll be back, so… just in case, apologize to your sister for me?"

"There's no need. She knows how important this is. Just… just take care of yourself."

"Jesus, Ballard, are you going soft on me? Get a grip." Cat drawled, and ended the call.

So Cat was off to France. I was writhing with restlessness that I couldn't just hop on a plane and meet her there, but wedding preparations literally surrounded me. I had to stay where I was and pray that if there were answers to be found at Havre des Gardiennes, then Cat would find them.

On Friday afternoon, we all descended on Fairhaven for the wedding, along with an absolute entourage of garment bags, boxes, and suitcases. Karen's stress had turned her into something of a drill sergeant, and she shot orders at everyone, flipping constantly through her binder of notes and checklists. Vans and trucks lined the gravel drive outside of the front doors, and vendors and workmen were streaming in and out. Apprentices and Novitiates had vacated the castle a week earlier when classes officially ended, but the halls were more crowded than ever. Many of the clan guests had taken advantage of their clan rooms in the castle, and were staying there rather than at the local hotel. You couldn't move without bumping into someone carrying flowers or lighting equipment, or table linens. The doors to the Grand Council Room were closed, and the courtyard was blocked off to guests in an effort to keep the full visual effect of the decor a surprise. Even I got in trouble for trying to poke my head in.

"I'm not even allowed to look?" I asked, thoroughly annoyed as Milo marched me away from the double doors.

"No."

"But I've been staring at sketches and swatches, and reference photos for months. I know what everything is going to look like," I said, in a voice that came dangerously close to a whine.

"That's not the same thing as seeing the final effect. Even Hannah isn't allowed in there. Now scootch!"

There was no rehearsal dinner, due to the last-minute change of venue, but the dining hall remained open so that all the guests and the wedding party could eat at their leisure. And so it was that Hannah and I spent the night before her wedding eating chicken Caesar salad and dining hall cookies off of plates on our laps.

I held up my bottled water. "Happy wedding eve!"

She smiled and held hers up as well for a toast. "Thanks."

"You nervous?"

She just shrugged. I didn't press it.

There was a soft knock, and Karen poked her head through the door. "I just wanted to let the bride know that set-up is done for the night. Everything looks beautiful, and we're on track for a flawless day. Also, that thunderstorm that was predicted to roll through in the afternoon has shifted miles north of us. The sun will be shining all day!"

"Thanks Karen," Hannah said, smiling. "Not just for the update, but... for everything. All of this."

Karen beamed. "It's been my absolute pleasure. Get some sleep, okay? No need to worry. Everything is under control." And she backed out, closing the door behind her.

"We probably should try to turn in early," I said, setting my plate aside. "It might take a while to settle down."

"Yes, I suppose you're right," Hannah said with a sigh.

We changed into our pajamas, brushed our teeth, and climbed up into the same four-poster beds we'd slept in on our very first night at Fairhaven. I stared up into the canopy, wondering if I'd be able to quiet my racing brain; but the next thing I knew, I had drifted off so deeply that I didn't even hear the opening or closing of the door as Hannah slipped out in the middle of the night.

22

VOWS

"Jess?"

"Huh?" My body was trying to rouse me even as the mind was still wrapped in the tendrils of a dream. I tried to remember it as it unwound itself from my consciousness. There had been a beach, and a lighthouse and a woman with—

"Jess!"

The voice was more urgent now, and the dream released me all at once, so that my eyes flew open and I sat bolt upright in my bed, gasping at the sudden connection to reality.

"Are you okay? Sorry, mate, I didn't mean to scare you."

I blinked the sleep out of my eyes, and was finally able to focus my gaze on Savvy. She was standing beside my bed, her red hair haloed in gold from the light of the full moon streaming in from the window.

At once, my head was a chorus of alarm bells. "What's wrong? Did something happen? Do we need to—"

Savvy reached down and cupped my shoulders in her hands. "Everything is fine. I'm supposed to tell you everything is fine."

"What does that mean, you're supposed to tell me? Who—" My gaze landed on Hannah's empty bed. "Where's Hannah?"

"Hannah's fine. Everything's fine. I'm just supposed to come get you and bring you with me," Savvy said.

"Bring me with you where?" I asked, still not moving.

"Down to the edge of the lake."

"But why are we—"

An aggravated voice broke right into my head, making me yelp in alarm. "Jessica Ballard, for fuck's sake, can you please just follow a direction for once in your life without asking five thousand questions?" It was Milo, and he sounded equal parts annoyed and amused.

"No, I can't actually, not unless someone—"

"Jess. It's a surprise. A good surprise. Okay? Just throw some shoes on and go with Savvy."

"But—"

"You're not gonna want to miss this. Trust me." And he yanked his presence right back out of my head, making it spin.

I looked at Savvy, who grinned. "Come on, mate. Better do as we're told."

Bewildered and still half-delirious with sleep, I staggered out of my bed and then fumbled around under it until I found both of my sneakers. I stuffed my feet into them, pulled a sweatshirt off the back of my desk chair, and stifled a yawn.

"Okay, fine. But I might be sleepwalking."

We crept down through the dormant castle, a playground now for flickering shadows and drifting spirits, while all the living inhabitants slumbered. I knew that, in just a few hours, it would be abuzz like a beehive as florists, caterers, musicians, and others transformed the entrance hall and the ballroom into Karen's vision of a wedding fever dream. It was the calm before the storm, and I was suddenly grateful I had a chance to experience it, to bask in the calm and quiet before the impending mayhem.

"Are you sure we're supposed to go out onto the grounds?" I asked, as we approached the huge front doors. The guards there were glaring at us, but Savvy flashed her badge, and they grudgingly stepped aside to let us out.

"Dead sure," Savvy replied, strolling along blithely, as though she liked nothing better than being summoned out of bed for a moonlit stroll in the middle of the night.

"But you have no idea why?"

"Not a blooming clue, mate. Milo just told me to come fetch you."

I ground my teeth together. I really hated surprises. Like, a lot.

At least it was a beautiful night for a surprise. The cloudless sky was sugared with stars, and the round belly of the moon silvered the trees and lit the dewdrops on the grass like fireflies. We followed the path toward the lake, and found that the moon had made a long, shimmering track down its center that looked like a fairy road, like we could trip down it if only we were as insubstantial as moonlight. On the far bank of the lake, larger lights gleamed.

I pointed to them. Savvy shrugged and kept walking.

We skirted the bank and came around the great curve of the water to find a trellis, woven of grapevine and threaded through with little golden lights. Finn, Kiernan, and Milo were standing there. Finn waved at us as we approached, then dragged his hand down his unshaven face, smothering a yawn. We joined the three of them under the trellis.

"What's going on?" I asked again.

Finn shrugged. "I am likewise in the dark as to the purpose of this mysterious outing, although Milo promised me that he'd clue us in once you'd arrived."

With that, we all turned to Milo, who was smirking.

"Milo?" I prompted.

Milo held up a finger, and his eyelids fluttered closed. "Hang on, just let me savor this moment of withholding a delicious piece of gossip," he whispered reverently.

"Milo!" came three aggravated voices. Only Kiernan remained silent.

"I also know the gossip," he explained.

Milo sighed. "Okay, fine. Now that we're all here. This wasn't my idea. It was Hannah's, so I'll have her explain."

We followed his gaze and turned to see Hannah walking toward us from under the trailing shadows of a nearby weeping willow tree. There was a serene smile on her face that calmed my nerves instantly.

"What are you up to?" I asked as she joined us.

"Following your advice," she said, still smiling enigmatically.

"I don't remember advising you to drag me out of bed on the night before your wedding when I'd been specifically ordered to get approximately fifteen hours of beauty sleep," I said, glancing at Milo, who smiled beatifically.

"You didn't," Hannah said. "But you did tell me that I should take more control over my own wedding. That's why we're here."

"I... still don't understand."

"Look, tomorrow is going to be a spectacle. A beautifully designed, flawlessly executed spectacle," she added to Milo, who had opened his mouth to protest, "but a spectacle nonetheless."

"Right..." I said slowly.

"I sort of felt like we'd been removed from our own narrative, and I'd just let it happen, because I was too busy trying to please everyone. Kiernan could tell something wasn't right, so eventually he asked me, and I told him."

"And that wasn't okay with me at all," Kiernan said, taking up the thread. "And so I asked Hannah, what was the most important thing to her about our wedding."

Hannah's smile warmed. "And I said, marrying you, of course. Being together."

"And so then I asked her what would make her the happiest. If we could go back, and begin again, no wedding planning, no decisions made, just the two of us, newly engaged, what would she do, if she could start over?"

"And I thought about it, and the answer came to me. The most important thing to me was for Kiernan and me to have this moment—*our* moment—without the prying eyes of strangers and the distractions of string quartets and high-heeled shoes and hovering photographers."

I looked at Hannah, and then everyone else. "Hannah, look, I totally get it. I've been saying for months that this wedding had spiraled out of control. But it's... it's a little late to cancel everything now. The castle is full of guests already, and the decorators will be here before the sun even comes up."

"I know that," Hannah said, still smiling. "I don't want to cancel the wedding. I just want to have a smaller one first. Tonight. Right here."

"I... oh!" I looked around again. At the trellis. At the perfectly quiet moonlit night. At Hannah and Kiernan's expressions. And finally, I understood. "You're getting married... right now?"

"Yes," Hannah said. "And then tomorrow, we'll get married again. And it won't matter who's there or what goes wrong. Because we'll already have this moment. And I think that, as long as I have that, in here," and she pressed her hand to her heart, "it will carry me through the day."

I blinked, absorbing this.

"What do you think?" Hannah asked, her eyebrows pulling together as she tried to read my reaction.

"I think," I said, "that it's the most 'Hannah' thing I've ever heard, and I love it."

Hannah's face split into a smile once more, a broader one. "Okay, then."

"What do we do?" I asked.

"Milo is our officiant. Savvy and Finn are our witnesses. And Jess, well... I was kind of hoping you could give me away."

My breath caught in my throat. "I... I mean, sure, I can."

There was a huge sniff, and we all turned to Savvy, who was struggling to get a handkerchief out of her pocket. "Ah, bollocks. Sorry, but I just... bloody hell, this is just so... so romantic!" And she blew her nose like a trumpet into the scrap of fabric. "And I don't even like romantic stuff!"

Hannah giggled, then grabbed my hand and led me away from the trellis toward the tree she'd been standing under when we'd arrived on the bank of the lake.

"Hey, so I'll do this whole 'walking you down the aisle' thing, but let's get one thing straight first," I said, taking her other hand so that we were facing each other. "It took us eighteen years to find each other, and while I am perfectly happy to share you, I will not now, nor will I ever be giving you away. Got it?"

Hannah's eyes sparkled with something more than excitement. "Got it," she whispered, and then flung her arms around my neck in the fiercest of hugs. When she let me go, the tears were glimmering on her cheeks. I brushed them away with my fingers.

"Ready?"

"Ready," she whispered.

"Okay. Let's get you married."

We turned back toward the lake. I extended my elbow toward her, offering my arm, and she slipped her cold little hand through it. I glanced at her. Not a stitch of makeup, hair streaming down her back, wearing jeans and an oversized sweater; but my God, the expression on her face. Tomorrow she would be dressed to the nines, a living image from a bridal magazine, photographed from every angle, but I would always think of my sister on her wedding day just like this.

There was no music except for the summer wind in the trees and the crickets singing in the tall marsh grass. There was no red carpet or trailing bouquet of flowers. But nature hummed, and the moonlight lit the way to the trellis. We walked slowly, and when I wasn't sneaking peeks at my sister's glowing face or Kiernan's almost dazed expression, I caught Finn's eye. He winked at me, and my heart seemed to expand in my chest. Maybe Hannah was on to something. Maybe walking down the aisle wouldn't be so bad, if we did it like this.

We arrived beside Kiernan, the lights in the trellis casting a golden glow over our heads. Savvy had the handkerchief pressed over her mouth, and it was barely enough to suppress the blubbering.

"I'm sorry, I don't know what the blazes is wrong with me." The words were muffled by the handkerchief and the continued onslaught of tears.

"Better to get it out of your system now. If you did this tomorrow in full glam, I'd be forced to kill you," Milo hissed.

"Jess," Hannah whispered from beside me. She looked significantly down at her hand on my arm, and then at Kiernan.

"Oh, shit! Right, sorry. Also, sorry for swearing at your secret wedding," I babbled. Then, with a mental slap to pull myself together, I took Hannah's hand and placed it in Kiernan's waiting one. He closed his long, slender fingers around hers and smiled at me, his eyes aglow with happiness.

"Take care of her," I managed to choke out.

"We'll do it together," he replied, and I laughed a little before stepping back to stand beside Finn. He reached over and entwined our fingers just in time, because I suddenly felt that I might possibly faint or burst into noisy sobs. Focusing on the feeling of his hand in mine, I managed to succumb to neither.

We all turned to look at Milo, and a hushed expectation fell over us.

Milo looked suddenly panicked. "I... what should I say?" he gasped. "When you suggested this whole thing, I sort of just thought the words would come to me, but—" He gulped.

Hannah just smiled again. "Milo, you've watched enough reality TV weddings for several lifetimes. Just wing it. Whatever you say will be perfect."

Milo took several deep breaths. "Right," he murmured to himself. "Right. Okay. Here goes nothing." Then he composed his features, and when he lifted his face to look at us again, he looked in control of himself.

"Dearly beloved," he began, and then shook his head. "No. No cliches. Not for the least cliched wedding of all time." He cleared his throat and tried again. "If any of you ask me about this tomorrow, I will deny ever speaking these words, but... a wedding isn't about the spectacle. It's not about the flowers or the lighting or, yes, even the dress(es). It's about two people coming to an understanding that to live without the other is unfathomable. It's about realizing you are stronger together, happier together, better able to face whatever this mad world throws at you. Hannah, I wasn't sure there was a person like that out here for you, not because you don't deserve it, but because you had always faced the world with such bravery and determination. It was hard to imagine you needing anyone in such a way. Jess and I can both attest, you are the bedrock, the absolute foundation of every relationship in your life. We would be lost without you, but you... Hannah, you would still find your way."

It was my turn to stifle a sob this time, and I let a thought drift across the connection. "Jesus, Milo, you actually expect me to believe you didn't script this?"

"I don't know what you're talking about, this is *totally* off the cuff," he said, and I could hear the wink in his voice. Whatever he said about a wedding not needing spectacle, he couldn't simply wing it. It wasn't in his nature.

Savvy blew her nose. Finn squeezed my hand again.

"But then Hannah met Kiernan, and he provided something she never had before—an anchor. A port in the storm. A safe, soft place to land. A home. When Hannah found Kiernan, she found home—her heart's home. And personally, I will always be grateful to Kiernan for that. I used to think there was no one good enough for my best friend. I've never been so happy to be wrong.

"And so, Hannah and Kiernan, I invite you to share your vows with each other," Milo said, and gestured toward them both before expelling a shaky breath. He'd just barely gotten through it.

Hannah reached into her pocket and pulled out an envelope. "I wrote this letter to give you tomorrow morning, before the big wedding," she explained. "But I'll just read it to you now, because it says everything I wanted to tell you." She tore it open with shaking fingers and cleared her throat nervously.

"Kiernan," she began, and for a moment, I almost wished I wasn't there to hear what she had to say. It was so intimate, so private—despite being invited, I suddenly felt like an eavesdropper with my eye shoved up against the keyhole of their happiness. No wonder they hadn't planned on saying much more than "I do" and "I will" in front of a castle full of people. All of this passed through my thoughts in the moment it took Hannah to take a deep breath and keep going.

"Kiernan, for a long time, I hid. All the truest parts of myself, hidden away. Even after I finally understood who I was and why I had my gift, I was still much more comfortable in the shadows. I never had the confidence to seek connections with people—everyone I'd ever let in had pushed me away. A friend like Milo helped me to peek my head out of my shell, and finding Jess helped me to trust in myself more. But I was still never sure, never entirely confident in truly being myself, until I met you."

She unfolded her paper, chancing a glance up into Kiernan's face. He was beaming back at her, and I was watching his smile fill her up as she continued to read.

"You weren't afraid of me, despite everything you had heard. You weren't wary of me. You were kind. Considerate. You didn't prod me with questions or push your own assumptions onto me. You were patient—you gave me space and an ear to listen. Each new facet of myself I revealed, you welcomed with quiet affection. The more I let you in, the more I wanted to let you in, until I realized that I had no need for all the walls I'd put up, and all the doors I'd locked tight. And I've never felt so free. That's been your greatest gift to me, Kiernan. You gave me myself, and helped me to love every part of me. I can never repay you for that, but I will spend the rest of my life trying. I love you, Kiernan."

She looked up and smiled at him, a slow, blooming smile that transformed her face into something shining and pure. My breath shuddered down my throat, and I swallowed a sob.

Kiernan looked like he might explode with happiness. He pulled his paper out of his back pocket and adjusted his glasses. I couldn't imagine anyone being able to speak coherently after hearing a letter like that, but his voice was steady and warm as he spoke.

"Hannah, there are so many things I love about you. I love your strength. I love your quiet grace. I love the way you always want to put the needs of others before your own, even though I try hard not to let you. I love that you chose to confide in me, that you saw me as a friend worthy of your confidence, and that you let me prove that I am just that. I love that you didn't let my own insecurity stand in the way of getting to know each other. I love your bravery and the way you take care of the people you care about. I've always been much better with reading words than writing them, but I know that, even if I don't have the right words to express it, you've always understood exactly what I mean to say—exactly what I feel. From this day forward, I hope that you won't feel like you need to be so brave or so strong. I hope that I can be those things for you. I hope you won't feel that you need to put other people before yourself, because I will always put you first. Most of all, I hope that, for the rest of our lives, you will know, deep in your heart, that you will never be alone again."

A laugh burbled up Hannah's throat, a sound of unadulterated joy, and it echoed off the trees around us, throwing ghosts of laughter toward the stars. And I knew right down to my bones that no cathedral on earth ever witnessed a moment so pure.

They took each other's hands and then looked at Milo, whose entire form was flickering and glowing with the strength of his emotions.

"Hannah and Kiernan, you have pledged your love to each other, and I'm happy to say that the notion of 'until death do you part' will place no limits on your time together. So, by the power vested in me by—well, by you, actually, like five minutes ago—I hereby pronounce you husband and wife. You may seal your vows with a kiss."

They stepped toward each other, closing the last little bit of distance between them, and kissed—a gentle, tender kiss that nonetheless elicited a maniacal whoop of delight from Savvy, who threw her handkerchief into the air in a fit of celebration. Then we were all laughing, and also crying, and also shouting congratulations while we jumped up and down, but also tried to hug each other, so that we very nearly fell over in one big, cheering heap. Then Kiernan pulled a bottle of champagne out of his backpack, and we all whooped and cheered as he popped the cork into the moon-drenched sky and then passed the bottle around, so that each of us could take a celebratory swig right from the bottle.

To this day, it was the best wedding I've ever been to.

23

THE BIG DAY

The day of Hannah's wedding dawned rosy and draped in a gentle fog. When I rolled over, the warmth of the morning nestled gently against my cheek. I found that the space beside me in the bed was already empty. I blinked the sleep out of my eyes and wedged myself up on my elbow, looking around. Hannah was there, tucked into the corner of the window seat, her arms wrapped tightly around her knees, her face turned to absorb the full glory of the early morning over the grounds.

"Hannah?"

She turned, and for a moment I held my breath, afraid her face would be full of something like doubt or fear. Instead, a smile broke gently over her face in the same way the sun was spilling over the horizon.

"Good morning," she said.

"Is it?" I asked. "It's your day, so you get to make the executive decision on that."

Her smile widened, brightening every feature one by one. "Yes," she said. "It is definitely a good morning."

I untangled myself from the covers, shuffled across the room, and folded myself into the opposite corner of the window seat.

"Happy wedding day," I said.

"Thanks," Hannah replied, a joyful flush spreading over her cheeks.

"How are you feeling?"

She considered this for a moment, eyes focused on the watercolor beauty of the morning.

"Ready," she said.

"Well, I'm glad to hear it. It wouldn't be a very fun day for the rest of us if you weren't."

She chuckled lightly, nudging me playfully with her toe.

I followed her gaze, and for a few minutes, we both sat in silence, watching the sun chase the darkness away with its creeping golden fingers.

"How did you sleep?" I finally ventured, when the morning had settled comfortably into every corner of the grounds.

"Surprisingly well," Hannah said. "I thought I'd be up all night, tossing and turning, but I wasn't, which is a relief, because I don't think I could have faced the day if I'd been exhausted."

Personally, I was relieved as well. Sharing a bed with a restless bride would have left both of us groggy and cranky. I didn't function well in the clutches of sleep deprivation, as literally everyone who knew me was well aware.

"Are you hungry?" I asked. "Karen arranged for breakfast to be brought up when we were ready."

"I don't think so. Not yet, anyway," Hannah said. "I'm enjoying the quiet, for the moment."

"Yeah," I said. "Quiet is going to be thin on the ground today. We should enjoy it while we can."

I glanced at the clock—it was only a few minutes after six o'clock. As we sat in companionable silence, we listened to the sounds of the castle waking up around us. Slowly, the silence was punctuated with the opening and closing of doors, the murmur of voices, and the gentle patter of feet along the floors. Little by little, the day was beginning to belong to other people besides us.

I took one of these last, serene moments to look at my sister. She was getting married today. Married. Like some kind of adult. And yet, despite all the chaos and stress in the lead up to this day, she didn't look the slightest bit flustered. In fact, she looked completely unbothered, like she'd woken up two days from now on a beach in Greece instead of in a jam-packed castle full of guests and staff all intent on making her the center of attention whether she wanted to be or not.

I knew the reason why, of course. She was already married, and she would keep the secret talisman of the private moment in her heart all day, an anathema to the stress and bustle and meaningless motions of the day.

"I wasn't convinced I'd ever get married," Hannah said suddenly into the quiet that had settled so comfortably between us.

"Really?" I asked.

"Does that surprise you?"

I shrugged. "A little, but only because you've seemed too sure of Kiernan from day one. I never noticed any hesitation or angst about it, unless you were just hiding it really well."

"There's no way I'd be able to hide that from you," Hannah pointed out.

"True."

She sighed. "I never imagined I'd do so many normal, everyday things. I didn't think I could make friends until I met Milo. I didn't think I would ever have a family of my own until you and Karen found me. Before I understood who and what I was, I thought all of those kinds of relationships were out of my reach. I scared people away too easily, and I had to hide so much of myself just to be around them. How could I ever open up to someone enough to share my life with them? Sometimes I just used to hope to meet someone with similar delusions to mine—then we could happily live outside reality together. Two peas in the same unhinged pod."

"But you weren't unhinged," I reminded her.

"No, I wasn't. But I had to learn that—really learn it—before I could start to find my place with other people. And even that wasn't easy. Even among the people who were supposed to understand us and accept us, there wasn't much understanding or accepting at first."

"Yeah," I said, and I had to brace myself against an onslaught of memories, made all the more vivid by the fact that we were sitting in the very same room where we had endured many of them. This bedroom door was the one they graffitied on our arrival. Those beds were the ones they'd abducted us out of, the night they left us to the mercy of the Elemental.

"But we got there, eventually," Hannah said, her gaze trained outside the window again. "We grew up. We learned about ourselves. We found our people, the ones who didn't shy away or judge us. But even then, I couldn't imagine opening myself up to someone on the level of a husband or wife. I just... wasn't sure if I had it in me. I was still really protective of myself."

"Of course you were. When had this world and the people in it ever done anything but betray your confidence when you gave it?" I asked. "It took a long time for you to open up to me, and I'm your twin."

"Have I ever apologized for that?" Hannah asked with a little grimace.

"You never needed to," I told her. "Believe me, I understood. And we got there, didn't we?"

"Yeah, we did. We got there."

She reached for my hand, and I extended it to her. Our fingers twined together so naturally, and I was reminded of the very first time our hands had touched, when we felt our connection racing through our veins, demonstrating from that first moment how deep and unbreakable our connection was. Our bodies already knew it. It was our minds and our hearts that had to catch up.

"I'm really proud of you," I told her.

She looked up into my face and smiled, a slow-blooming smile that crinkled her nose and lit a fire of happiness in her eyes.

"I'm really proud of us," she said.

I could gratefully have stayed there for hours, the two of us together in the peace and glow of the morning, but finally, reality intruded on our little pocket of contentment. A gentle knock on the door meant Karen had woken and found her way to our room.

"Good morning to the bride and the maid of honor," she said, her voice thick with emotion from the moment her slippered feet crossed the threshold.

"Karen, don't cry already, we haven't even had coffee yet!" I said.

"I know, I know, I'm sorry," Karen said, flapping her hands impatiently. "I barely slept a wink. I hope the two of you managed to get a little rest."

"A little," Hannah confirmed, winking at me.

As if on cue, another knock announced the arrival of a team of caterers wheeling a small tea cart. They bowed and smiled their way into the room, depositing their silver trays wordlessly on the table, and slipping out again. I could smell the coffee in the tall silver pot and felt my senses starting to sharpen at the mere thought of the caffeine.

"I wasn't sure what you'd want, so I just had them bring up a bit of everything," Karen said as we gathered round the table. Besides the coffee, there were stacks of buttered toast, piles of croissants and Danishes, a heap of fluffy scrambled eggs alongside crisp bacon, fat shiny sausages, and a bowl of baked beans. Years living in England, and I still hadn't quite gotten used to beans as a breakfast food.

Hannah and I each loaded up a plate and sat down to dig in. Despite her insistence that we eat enough to keep our strength up, Karen barely managed more than a few nibbles to the corner of a croissant. Her energy had a manic edge to it, and I was relieved that she didn't attempt to have any coffee, or we might have had to sedate her.

Halfway through our breakfast, Milo showed up. We felt him before we saw him—a gentle prodding nudge to the connection.

"Oh, thank God you're both awake. I tried to wait until a reasonable hour, but you have no idea how hard that is when you don't have to sleep anymore!" he gasped, the thought in our heads transforming mid-sentence to words in our ears, as he came sailing through the wall with the same kind of slightly unhinged energy Karen was brimming with. The first thing he did upon arrival was put himself within six inches or so of each of our faces.

"Are you sure you want to do that? I haven't brushed my teeth yet," I grumbled.

"I'm checking for signs of sleeplessness, but you both look positively dewy. Did you take the sleeping pills?" he asked, still hovering offensively close to my face.

"No, we didn't need them," I said. "Seriously, Milo, have you heard of personal space?"

"It is the wedding day, and I am your stylist. There is no such thing as personal space," he insisted. Next, he floated over to the breakfast table and inspected the contents. "Oof. Try not to drink too much coffee, your teeth will—"

"My teeth will tear you limb from ghostly limb if you come between me and my caffeine today," I snapped. "Now, back off and let everyone enjoy their breakfast in peace."

But it seemed we had reached the limit of peace for the moment. Now that Milo was there, flitting around like a ghostly pinball, it was hard not to start feeling the excitement of the day creep in. I suddenly found that I wasn't as hungry as I'd been a few moments before, and only managed a few more bites of my breakfast before I pushed my plate away and gave up, watching Hannah tuck in instead. Wedding jitters weren't getting in the way of her appetite, at least.

The next knock on the door brought Savvy, her mom Alice, and Rana into the room around ten o'clock. Between them, they were wheeling a clothing rack heavily laden with garment bags and a two-tiered cart covered in accessory cases, boxes, hair supplies, and a garment steamer.

"The cavalry is here!" Alice announced. "Happy wedding day, Hannah, my love!"

"Thanks, Alice," Hannah said. There was a slight air of resignation in her voice now—the tedious part of the day was about to begin.

"Ah, brilliant, food!" Savvy said.

"You already had breakfast," Alice snapped.

"That was ages ago! And I probably won't eat again until dinner, once this one gets me strapped into me dress properly," Savvy said, pointing at Milo. "Mind your business, woman. If I want to be a hobbit and have second breakfast, let me bloody well get on with it." And with that, she tore into a pain au chocolat with blithe enthusiasm.

Rana already had her hair rolled up in curlers with a silk scarf tied over the top, looking bright-eyed and excited. "What can I do to help?" she asked the room at large.

We all looked at Milo. We all knew better than to think anyone else was in charge from this moment on, even Karen.

Milo glanced at the clock. "Well, our hair and makeup team should be here momentarily, so let's get everything set up for them, and then Alice and I can check the dresses and steam anything that got wrinkled on the way over."

Sure enough, it was only a few minutes before there was another knock and two more of Milo's team were at the door, a pair of young and bubbly girls named Brie and Yvette. Everyone who worked for Milo was either Durupinen or Durupinen-adjacent, and so there were no worries about breaching the code of secrecy. It was the only way Milo was able to continue to operate under the radar of the fashion industry and the paparazzi. And of course, there was the added bonus of the fact that they could come to Fairhaven to help their ghost boss get us all ready for the wedding without a fuss.

With the arrival of Brie and Yvette, the elaborate getting-ready process began. First, we all changed into the contents of the first garment bag—matching turquoise silk robes with our initials monogrammed onto the chest pocket. Our hair was set in curlers, our makeup applied layer by tedious layer, including false eyelashes that were attached to our eyelids one by one with tweezers. While this happened, Karen buzzed in and out, phone in hand, still coordinating the arrival of all the vendors. She showed in the photographer—a tall, slender woman who said very little, but began snapping candids of our preparations discreetly from various corners of the room, while her assistant set up tableaus of objects to shoot as still life: the bridal shoes perched on the windowsill, the wedding rings stacked on an open book, the veil hanging from a hanger and draped down in the sunlight in front of the window seat. As the resident artist, I found this totally fascinating, and had to stop myself from following the photographer around. Instead, to stop myself from harassing the poor woman—and to keep myself occupied while I waited my turn for the next round of hair and makeup—I pulled out my sketchbook and flipped open to a clean page. I needed to do something to dispel the feeling that I had turned into a life-size Barbie doll.

I amused myself by drawing some sketches of the others as we prepped—a profile of Hannah, her hair coiled and twisted into an elaborate design and pinned to the back of her head; a rendering of Milo, his hands pressed palm to palm in front of his mouth as he contemplated the exact positioning of a rose against the soft cascade of Hannah's veil; a portrait of Karen, eyes shining with unshed tears as she watched Hannah examine her own reflection in a mirror that Brie held up for her.

"That's beautiful," Rana said, bending over my shoulder to take a peek.

"I'm just messing around," I said. "It keeps me from getting nervous about what's waiting for us downstairs."

Rana chuckled. "Well, in my amateur opinion, you should frame those and give them to the bride when she gets back from her honeymoon. Photos are all well and good, but you've really captured something there."

I looked down at the sketch, trying to see it from an unbiased perspective. It really wasn't bad. Maybe I could clean them up, get them matted in the city…

"It's time for the dresses!" Milo announced, his voice vibrating with joy.

The bridesmaids changed into our dresses first. Milo had designed them all in the same fabric, but each with a different silhouette and varied accessories. Mine, for example, had a plunging neckline with braided straps and turquoise and amber beading sewn into the belt. Savvy's dress brought the fabric twisted up in a single strap over one shoulder and then tied in a bow around her neck, making the most of her toned shoulders. Rana's dress was strapless with a sweetheart neckline and intertwined strands of blue and green beads that came up and tied around her neck.

"A trio of mermaid goddesses," I decided, as we stood together in front of the mirrors. "Or maybe sirens?"

"With the queen of karaoke in our midst?" Rana asked. "Sirens for sure. She could definitely lure some men to their deaths with the sultry power of her voice."

"Oi, hold your tongues unless you want me to front the band at the reception," Savvy said, but she grinned nonetheless.

At this point, Karen reappeared in her own dress, a stunning emerald green satin sheath set off perfectly by the heirloom necklace she'd borrowed from the vault. Despite her worries that it was too elaborate or over the top, with its simple silhouette, it was absolutely perfect.

"Karen, you look gorgeous!" I said.

"Thank you, Jess, I feel rather gorgeous," she said, blushing just a little. "But enough about me, how uninteresting. I've brought your jewelry as well." She held up the two wooden display boxes we'd taken from the vault, the ones with Hannah's and my jewelry in them.

"Oh, right!" I said. After all the chaos of the last few weeks, I'd honestly completely forgotten about the necklace. Now, as she took it out and draped it around my neck, I was able to appreciate how well I had chosen—the stones set off the dress beautifully.

"Oh wow!" Rana said when she spotted it. "That's beautiful! It looks like an antique!"

"It is," I told her. "It's been in the family for centuries."

"Well, now that's lovely, isn't it?" Rana replied, smiling warmly. Little did she know it wasn't nearly so simple. Other people wore family jewelry for sentimental reasons. We chose our accessories as a show of power—a shiny little "back off" to anyone who wanted to question our place at the table. Agnes' necklace rested against my chest, warming to my skin, and I felt, somehow, safer.

"Now it's time to get the bride into her dress!" Milo sang.

This was the moment Milo had been waiting for for months, and we all knew it. And as much as it was the bride's day, this tiny sliver belonged to Milo, and no one knew it better than Hannah. She made sure the photographer was ready, showing her exactly where to stand so that she would have the best view to capture the reveal.

"Now, before I show everyone the first dress, I just have something I want to say," Milo fluttered. "I honestly didn't think this was a dream I'd ever get to fulfill. Designing your best friend's wedding dress is already a tall order, but in my situation, well... it's a bit more complicated." His form was flickering with emotion now, and I could tell he was barely holding it together. "But we're here, and I just want to say, Hannah, that you are absolutely stunning today, but not because of the makeup or the hairstyle or yes, even the dress you're about to put on. It's your happiness that makes you almost unbearably gorgeous. The dress is only going to enhance what nature and the promise of a husband like Kiernan have already done. Let's think of it as the cherry on top of the beautiful happiness sundae that is your wedding day. Also, I hope you love your dress even half as much as I love you."

Savvy made a gurgling, sobbing sound, and we all turned to see her diving for the nearest tissue box. "Blimey, mate, you could have warned us you were going to make a speech," she blubbered. "How's a girl supposed to keep her bloody makeup intact, then?"

Milo grinned, and then, with a flourish, used his energy to push an old-fashioned dressing screen to the side, revealing Hannah's ceremony dress behind it. There was a collective gasp around the room, and Milo closed his eyes for a moment, taking in the sound of everyone's astonishment like it was the sweetest music he had ever heard.

The dress was truly a work of art, the full effect, multiplied in its glory by the three-sided mirror it hung in front of. The bodice of the dress was strapless and crafted of ivory satin, embellished with curling vines of gold thread and seed pearls which trailed down onto the skirt, which hugged tight to the waist and hips before flaring out trumpet style and extending out into a stunning twenty-foot train. Over the top of the satin underdress, a second layer was wrapped like gossamer, creating long, nearly transparent sleeves and cinching in at the waist with a pearl-encrusted belt, before shimmering out over the rest of the gown, making it look like the whole sartorial confection had been delicately draped in dew-dropped cobwebs.

We descended on Hannah, following Milo's instructions carefully, ensuring the dress came off the hanger and onto Hannah gently and without incident. We smoothed the skirts and fluffed the petticoats while Milo zoomed around her like a whirling dervish, tucking and fastening and praying under his breath that everything was perfect.

"Milo, we have a problem," Hannah whispered, staring mesmerized at her reflection.

Milo's expression shifted into one of utmost horror. "What?! Where? Is there a bead missing? A trailing thread? I have everything we need, just let me—"

"No. Not that."

"Well, what then?" he asked, almost desperately. "What's the problem?"

"It's so beautiful that it will break my heart to take it off," Hannah replied in a trembling voice.

Milo made a sound like he was choking, and then broke into a slightly hysterical combination of tears and laughter rendered all the more adorable by the fact that he couldn't actually produce tears. Within seconds, everyone was doing some combination of laughing and crying. Savvy blew her nose so loudly she sounded like a foghorn, and Rana shushed her.

Karen handed Milo the circlet and, supremely carefully, using incredible energy precision, Milo placed it perfectly in Hannah's curls so that it glimmered like fallen stars between the tresses. This crowning detail complete at last, we stepped back from her.

And as we gazed on, watching her marvel at her own reflection in the mirror, it was clear that everything was perfect.

Karen glanced at her watch, and her eyes lit up with excitement. "It's just about time!"

24

IN PLAIN SIGHT

Fairhaven had been transformed.

I would never have expected a place I knew so well, a place so full of dark and disturbing memories, could ever become, by some sort of design alchemy, the blueprint for a fairytale happily-ever-after; but damn it, I was wrong. If there was one thing I was sure of as I snuck a glance over the bannisters at the splendor below, it was that I would never dare to underestimate Karen or Milo ever again when it came to event planning.

It seemed impossible that one place could hold so many flowers. They spilled from the chandeliers, wound their way around pillars, and clustered in bowls, vases, and urns in every conceivable corner, nook, and crevice. Candles and webs of fairy lights illuminated every stony surface, until the ghostly castle of nightmares had been transformed into a fantasy dream.

The view from above was dizzying. Below us, hundreds of dresses swirled and milled in a kaleidoscope of colors. The walls fairly vibrated with the buzz of conversation, mingled with the sweeping melodies of the chamber orchestra already playing out in the courtyard. I searched for familiar faces, but everything was too busy, too ever-changing for me to be able to recognize anyone. Among the guests, servers in sleek black suits circulated with their shining silver trays. At first, I was upset—were we actually missing the hors d'oeuvres? But then I realized that the trays only held flutes of champagne, and my growling stomach calmed down.

"Jessica!"

I turned at the sound of the saccharine sweet voice to find Evangeline, the wedding coordinator from The Grand Dutchess Hotel, standing directly behind me, immaculately dressed in a lilac pantsuit, with a clipboard in one hand and an earpiece in one ear.

"Evangeline!" I said. "I didn't... what are you doing here?"

Evangeline raised an eyebrow, like the question was a ridiculous one. "Whatever do you mean? I'm the wedding coordinator, of course." Then understanding dawned on her perfectly contoured features. "Oh, I see. Your aunt didn't tell you. She hired me to continue in my role at this new venue, since... since..." Suddenly, her huge brown eyes were sparkling with unshed tears that she had to blink away and blot with a handkerchief. "...since The Grand Dutchess burned down."

"Of course," I said. I should have realized, as a member of the Durupinen clan, that Evangeline would have been a safe person to poach from the hotel staff to continue the wedding planning. "I'm sorry, I just didn't realize. Um... nice to see you."

Evangeline's face broke into a perfectly polished smile, all trace of tears already gone. "You as well. Don't go too far, the florist is about to pass out the bouquets, so don't disappear on me, please. Do you need anything? Would you like me to send a server up with some champagne? You look stunning, by the way."

"Um, thanks. And no, I'm okay," I replied. I didn't think champagne was a good idea. My stomach was already roiling with nerves. I continued to watch the crowd below, scanning the faces, wondering if anyone among them was planning to make a scene or, worse, pose some sort of real threat to us.

A moment later, Evangeline was flapping her hands and stage whispering for all of us to come away from the railings and line up for our bouquets. I gasped when the elaborate arrangement was placed into my hands. Were flowers supposed to be this heavy? And here I thought I had to drag my ass to the gym to get toned arms when all I needed to do was lug around one of these bouquets, apparently.

"I can't believe this is ol' Fairhaven," Savvy said, goggling at the decorative transformation. "Cleans up nice, doesn't it?"

"Cleans up nice?" Milo repeated weakly, looking like he might actually faint from a surplus of offense. "Nice?!"

"That's the Savvy version of a glowing compliment," I whispered to him.

"Remember, she once described the take-out order with extra chips as 'posh food.'"

Milo smiled weakly. "Still, do you think—"

"It's magic, Milo. Absolute magic. It's all anyone will talk about for at least ten years," I assured him, and finally felt him settle into contentment beside me.

Evangeline talked very quickly into her earpiece, and then clapped her hands to get our attention. I suddenly felt like I was being herded onto a pageant stage by a neurotic stage mother.

"The staff are escorting all the guests to the courtyard now. We just need to wait for the go-ahead when everyone is seated. If anyone needs a last minute touch up, now's the moment!" she gushed.

This was Milo's cue to circle us like an overly-critical vulture. As he made his inspections, I chanced another glance over the railings. Sure enough, the crowd was disappearing through the doors at the back of the entrance hall. Now that the doors were open, I could hear the music from the chamber orchestra more clearly, floating in from the ceremony space outside. They were playing Pachelbel's Canon in D.

I turned to check in on Hannah, to see how the anticipation was affecting her, but she was the picture of composure. Her features were serene, her posture upright but relaxed, her bouquet resting in her hands instead of clamped there, white-knuckled.

"You ready?" I asked her.

"Oh, yes," she said with a beatific half-smile. There was no doubt in her eyes, no spark of anxiety.

"Did Milo drug you?" I whispered.

She elbowed me hard in the ribs. I hid my grunt with a laugh. Of course, she was calm. She was already married. Everything that happened today was superfluous to the commitment she'd already made. What was there to be nervous about, really?

Wolves in sheep's clothing, a voice in the back of my head whispered. I batted the voice away. After all, the place was crawling with security, and there were appearances to be kept up. Worst case scenario, someone accidentally on purpose spills some red wine on someone else. If that someone was the bride, Hannah literally had three dresses, so we had that contingency covered. And if someone decided to make me the target... well, any excuse to change back into sweatpants. I'd probably shake the woman's hand.

"It's time!" Evangeline announced, lifting both her hands to get our attention. "We can proceed down the stairs, single file, like you practiced yesterday. You will stop just inside the doors to the courtyard, and then wait for my signal to walk down the aisle. All right?"

Everyone nodded. Karen was shifting from one foot to the other, her eyes so bright that I knew she was fighting for her life against the urge to cry. I leaned in and whispered in her ear.

"How do my boobs look?"

She blinked at me, then burst into laughter.

"That's better," I said with satisfaction. "You were starting to look morose."

We descended the stairs in the order we'd be walking down the aisle, Rana and Savvy first, then me, then Karen, Milo, and Hannah. We proceeded through the entrance hall, where the air was heavily perfumed with all the flowers, and toward the doors. We hovered there as Evangeline gave each of us a last inspection, smoothing a couple of stray curls and fixing a tiny smudge of makeup near Karen's eye. Then she positioned herself right beside the open door and gave a cue to the musicians, who seamlessly transitioned their music from Pachelbel's Canon to another processional song.

"Rana, go!" Evangeline whispered, and Rana, beaming from ear to ear and clutching her flowers, swept off down the aisle. There was an audible sighing at the sight of her. I felt Milo vibrating with excitement behind me. If people were gasping at the sight of the bridesmaids, we were already off to a great start.

When Rana reached the halfway point of the white, petal-strewn carpet, Savvy got the go-ahead to follow her. Her walk was more of a strut, but her smile was contagious, and she waved enthusiastically at several people, which caused a titter or two of amused laughter. I felt a poke in my arm.

"You're up, Jessica," Evangeline said.

I looked back at Hannah and winked at her. She blew me a kiss. And I was off down the aisle.

Eyes. So many pairs of eyes staring at me. It actually snatched the breath right out of my lungs. I suddenly wanted to crawl out of my skin, leave it behind and flee, like a Walker. My eyes began to search automatically for an exit and then…

I spotted Finn.

He was standing at the end of the impossibly long aisle, looking more handsome than I'd ever seen him look in his flawlessly tailored gray suit, with his hair tied back in a sleek ponytail. His face, when he spotted me, broke into the most disarming of smiles.

"Wow," he mouthed.

Just look at Finn, I told myself. *Just keep your eyes on him and ignore everyone else.* A second later, I found I could propel myself forward, that my numb legs were in fact working, and I even managed to hitch my smile back into place as I concentrated on closing the distance between us. Once I got moving, it was easier to keep going. I was even able to sneak a glance here and there at the guests. Annabelle and Flavia grinned at me from the aisle. Mackie waved frantically with a tissue in her hand. Tia was already full-blown sobbing, but managed a watery smile anyway.

And then I reached the cupola, draped in a riot of roses and peonies, and hydrangeas. Finn was smiling at me, his chest puffed out as proudly as if he was the groom and this was his wedding day—a thought which, for some reason, didn't seem so frightening in the moment. I turned to take my spot and, as I did so, chanced a glance at Kiernan. He wasn't looking at me, though. He wasn't looking anywhere but at the very place where, as the music swelled, my sister appeared.

I'm so glad I caught the look on his face when she stepped into view. I think, of all the happy moments I remembered from that day, that look on his face will stay with me the longest. The smile. The stars in his eyes. The prideful swell of his chest. If I'd harbored a single doubt that Kiernan and my sister would be together forever—and I didn't—it would have vanished in that moment.

Then I got to turn and watch my sister stun the crowd.

Not everyone could see that both Milo and Karen were walking her down the aisle, each of them looking like a parent bursting with pride. Hannah swept between them, radiant from the points of her shoes to the gems winking in her hair. Her veil and train floated along behind her, sweeping the flower petals along like a tide. Like me, she had found the one face she wanted to look at and simply locked eyes with him. For all her worries about the size of the guest list, I was convinced she didn't clock a single person on her way to the cupola. At last, she arrived beside me. She smiled at me as she handed me her bouquet, and then kissed both Milo and Karen on the cheek. Karen placed Hannah's hand in Kiernan's, Milo floated back to the front row, and Kiernan and Hannah turned toward each other. Finn caught my eye, winked, and the ceremony began.

"Congratulations! What a breathtaking wedding."

"Many happy returns! Everything is just gorgeous."

Half an hour later, every tiny detail of the ceremony, from the vows to the music to the cord and candle ceremonies to the precisely timed release of the butterflies, had gone perfectly. Thoroughly enchanted with all of it, the guests were wasting no time accosting the wedding party, pressing in on all sides for a glimpse of the bride and a chance to give their congratulations.

"Seriously, the most beautiful wedding I've ever seen in my entire life!" Tia gasped, pulling Hannah into a hug.

"I'm so glad you liked—" Hannah attempted to answer, but she was already being grabbed and hugged by Annabelle from behind.

"You look like a fairy princess!" she squealed. "Where's Milo? This is his doing, isn't it?"

"Oh, did someone summon me? I thought I heard my name," Milo replied, appearing out of nowhere.

"See? Who needs to be a Caller? Just speak a compliment out loud and summon a ghost instantly!" I said. Milo tried to stick his tongue out at me, but he was grinning too hard to pull it off.

Evangeline appeared beside me just as suddenly, though no one had summoned her.

"I need to steal the bride and groom for portraits on the grand staircase," she said, smiling blindingly. Kiernan and Hannah gave each other a long-suffering look and slipped away to follow her. I chatted with Flavia and Annabelle for a while, catching up on the gossip from the Traveler camp, but made an excuse as I saw the Traveler High Priestess Ileana starting to drift our way. We'd become allies during the Reckoning, but that didn't mean I wanted to get stuck in a corner talking to her.

I wove through the knots of chatting and drinking and eating people, accepting the random congratulations and compliments and ignoring the occasional smirk or judgmental side eye. I recognized a knot of the former Apprentice mean girls in the corner near the fireplace. Their expressions told me they were trying to find things to criticize, but I knew even they would be hard-pressed to find anything to complain about. Peyton was among them, looking impeccably put together, but frailer somehow, like she needed a good vacation. Then I remembered that the last time I'd seen her, she'd been pregnant with twins and reeking of smugness at the thought of carrying a complete Gateway into the world. Now that the Gateways had been restored and there was no genetic prize to claim, I wondered if she regretted her arranged marriage and early motherhood. Not enough to talk to her, though, and so I veered in the other direction.

I began to feel claustrophobic, and slipped through the pressing crowd back toward the bar area that had been set up in the entrance hall. I found Fiona there, stirring an amber liquid in a highball glass with a skinny plastic straw.

"Come here often?" I asked her, sidling up beside her and snatching her drink. I stole a sip that burned all the way down, and coughed a little.

"If you're going to steal a woman's drink, you should at least be able to handle it," she grunted.

"That was smoother in my head," I admitted, sputtering a little bit more. "What is that, battery acid?"

"Single malt."

"Gah." I took a flute of champagne from a tray on the end of the bar instead. "So? Enjoying yourself?"

Fiona's face twitched. "Spiffing," she grumbled.

"Aren't you glad you came?" I said. "Better than sitting up in your tower all alone, isn't it?"

"Debatable."

"Your tower doesn't have scallops wrapped in bacon, though," I said, snatching two from a passing tray and handing one to her.

She popped it into her mouth. "I'll give you that one."

"Look, I hope you're able to relax and enjoy yourself a little. You're worrying about something you can't control and barely understand," I reminded her. "I'm a Seer, Fiona, I get it."

"Do you? Then you should get that the very reason I'm worried is because I can't control it, and I don't understand," she retorted, her mouth twisted into a sour little knot. "And I'm going to keep worrying until that's no longer the case, so sod off and let me wallow, would you?"

"Okay, fine. I give up. Wallow away. Just don't disappear until you've had dinner, at least. The menu is incredible, and you don't want to wallow on an empty stomach," I told her, just as a chorus of bells rang and the doors to the Grand Council Room began to open slowly, inviting everyone into the newly transformed ballroom for dinner and dancing. "Are you coming?"

"Yes, yes, I'll be along, now sod off and let a woman enjoy her drink."

I gave up and walked toward the Grand Council Room, but only got the briefest glimpse of the general splendor before I felt a hand on my arm. I spun to see Finn standing behind me.

"Every time I turn around, you've disappeared," he accused me.

I smiled, lacing our fingers together. "Well, enjoy me while you can find me, because after I stuff myself full of this five-course dinner, I intend to completely vanish before someone tries to make me dance."

He raised one eyebrow. "Even if that someone is me?"

I considered. "Hmm. Probably, yeah."

Finn chuckled and pulled me in for a kiss. "You look utterly bewitching, by the way."

"Thanks," I said. "You're looking very dapper yourself."

His smile transformed into more of a grimace as he tugged at his collar. "It's all a bit… confining. I don't suppose we all get a costume change like the bride? Something with some breathing room?"

"Unfortunately, I think we'll have to stick it out," I told him, leaning in to add, "I have flip-flops in my purse. Don't rat me out."

"Cheater," he muttered, his eyes twinkling. He leaned in for another kiss when there was a staticky sound from the region of his belt.

"Can't someone else do that?" I asked. "You're the best man."

"Yes, but I'm also physically incapable of relinquishing control of security, you know this," he answered, as he struggled to get the radio unclipped from his belt. "Carey here, over," he said, and then mouthed to me, "Sorry! I'll see you in there."

I joined the sweeping tide of guests flowing into the Grand Council Room. The walls had been draped in cream fabrics, and the chandeliers dripped crystals and garlands of flowers. Seriously, were there any flowers left anywhere else in the UK after this wedding? It must have taken a semi truck just to transport them all. The effect was enchanting, of course, and as I skirted the dance floor, watching people mill about to find their tables, I thought Milo and Karen might just be able to go into the event planning business together.

People were being ushered to their seats as servers swept around filling champagne glasses, pushing in chairs, and draping napkins over laps. Savvy and Rana slid into seats on the left of me, leaving a spot for Finn at my other side. The music from the band swelled, and Hannah and Kiernan entered the room to thunderous applause. The first of the dress transformations had taken place—the long train and the sheer overlay on the dress had been removed, along with the veil, revealing a glittering strapless gown with a line of tiny crystal buttons down the back. In her hair, Hannah now wore just the circlet from the vault. She was flushed pink with embarrassment at all the attention, but Kiernan pulled her close and we all watched as they danced together—nothing fancy or choreographed, of course, just two riotously in-love humans, spinning on the spot, staring into each other's eyes, delirious with joy at the gift of each other. When the music ended, they came up to the table, both grinning sheepishly. There was a ringing of bells, and the servers flooded out of the doors with their silver trays. The meal had begun. Finn dropped into the seat beside me.

"Everything okay?" I asked him.

"Seems to be. Bit of confusion with the valets, but it's sorted now. Aw, blast, did I miss the first dance?" he asked, as a salad was placed in front of him.

"Yeah, sorry," I told him. "But the food is here, and I promise you, you would have been sadder to miss that."

Despite my previous worries that I wouldn't fit into my dress after the dinner, I managed to eat everything without busting a seam. Happily, I didn't have to test that by standing up in front of everyone. One request Hannah would not budge on was that she didn't want any long, embarrassing speeches, so Finn stood and gave a simple toast instead.

"I'd like to ask everyone to raise their glass to the bride and groom, Hannah and Kiernan. May your life together be filled with joy, comfort, and adventures great and small."

Everyone said, "Cheers!" Applause broke out as Hannah and Kiernan shared a kiss. Then the music rose from the band and people began to fill the dance floor. Finn looked at me, smiling awkwardly.

"I... I have two left feet, but I could... I mean, if you wanted to—"

"Let's not embarrass ourselves," I told him, grinning. "I was born without rhythm or grace."

He sighed in relief. "Oh, thank God. Of course I'd have done it for you, but..."

I kissed him. "A true martyr. But there's no need."

Hannah and Kiernan shared another dance and then started circulating the room, greeting their guests. Finn's walkie-talkie went off, and he excused himself once again. Savvy and Rana were tearing up the dance floor. I was just debating heading back to the bar for another drink, and wondering how soon was too soon to change into my flip flops, when I felt something nudge my elbow and looked down to see my sketchbook sitting there beside my empty plate. I looked up to see Karen grinning down at me.

"I know you're not much of a dancer or a small talker, so I thought you might need something to do," she whispered.

I grinned. "Thanks. Seriously."

She winked and swept off into the crowd once again, smile in place, the consummate hostess.

I settled back into my chair, the sketchbook laid on the table in front of me. I gazed around with a new set of eyes—eyes eager for inspiration. The room was full of people dressed to the nines, milling about, sipping on champagne while sneaking covert glances at each other over the rims of their glasses. Now that I was considering what to draw, I suddenly realized just how layered the scene in front of me was. It wasn't simply wedding guests having a good time. It was powerful people demonstrating their power. It was less powerful people trying to make connections. It was jealous people attempting to make themselves look better. It was ambitious people trying to make their mark. It was beautiful women trying to outshine each other. It was morbidly curious people trying to suss out a fresh bit of scandal. Everywhere, glasses were being refilled and plates were being emptied as people vied and flattered and clawed and gossiped their way into whatever position they thought the most advantageous to them. It was almost shocking how obvious it was, once I decided to look for it. Was this what every wedding looked like, or was it only weddings where the guest list was the nest of vipers known as the Durupinen elite?

My intention had been to find some small human moment to sketch, but nothing I saw inspired me to capture it—in truth, I wished I'd never started looking to begin with. So instead of scanning the room for random inspiration, I looked for my sister. Finally, I spotted her in the far corner. She and Kiernan had been waylaid in their progress around the room by a pair of particularly elderly women. Hannah was leaning politely forward, tilting her head so that the smaller of the two women could shout directly into her ear over the sound of the musicians. Kiernan stood beside her, holding her hand and looking slightly dazed at his good luck, that of all the people in the room, my sister had chosen him. I felt a smile starting to spread over my face. A sketch of Kiernan. Hannah would like that.

I pulled the pencil out from the sketchbook's spiral binding, careful not to break the tip, and began to flip forward to a blank page. But before I could find one, a sketch caught my eye, and I slowed my hand, staring at it.

It was one of the sketches I had done of Agnes' tapestry, in my attempt to understand what part of the image we were meant to decode. But this time, something caught my eye, something that made my heart begin to pound in my chest, and my breath to come in sharp, rapid bursts.

My hand flew to my own throat. Oh my God. How could I be so stupid?

I'd overlooked it, a mere accessory, interchangeable with a hundred other accessories my ancestor might have worn. I'd been searching for hidden words, obscure symbols, something that would require careful decoding. It hadn't occurred to me that the clue from the tapestry, the very thing Polly meant to point out to us, could be so obvious—so simple. There hanging around Agnes' neck was a necklace—a wrapped chain adorned with gemstones, and a large, amber-colored stone dangling from it, set elaborately with twisted vines of wire, encircled with still more gemstones.

It was the same necklace that currently hung around my own neck.

Things started to fall into place: the break-in at the vault, when nothing was taken. Who breaks into a space like that, full of so many near priceless treasures, and leaves it all behind? The answer, of course, was someone who couldn't find what they were really looking for, because that thing had already been removed. We'd had it all along, the key to the Casting Cage, tucked safely in Karen's possession all those weeks while we ran around aimlessly in every wrong direction looking for it. I wanted to scream, and yet, at the same time, I wanted to cheer. My fingers contracted, closed around the necklace, and I felt the massive amber stone under my trembling fingers, cool to the touch and yet feeling, suddenly, like a hot coal I had to fling away from me. It was dangerous. Someone was willing to lie, to steal, to kill for it; and here I was, traipsing around wearing it like a red carpet accessory around my neck.

I had to tell someone.

My eyes scanned the room. I had no idea who I was looking for, only that I couldn't keep this information to myself. And then I spotted Celeste standing by the corner of the platform, chatting with a small knot of other women. I rose shakily from my seat, hoping my expression wasn't betraying my utter panic, and made my way over to her. I forced myself to walk slowly, casually, even as everything inside me wanted to scream. I descended the three wide steps to the floor, and drifted over until I was standing just behind Celeste's shoulder.

"Excuse me, High Priestess?" I said, nudging her ever so gently with my elbow.

Celeste turned curiously, and her face broke into a slightly confused smile when she saw who had addressed her—probably because I wasn't sure I'd ever called her High Priestess in my life. Nevertheless, she took my hand warmly between her own.

"Jess! Congratul—"

"So sorry to interrupt. Could I have a quick word in private?" I asked, smiling so hard it felt like a grimace.

Celeste's smile faltered a little. Her gaze became searching, boring into my eyes, trying to find some clue before she said, "Of course. Ladies, please do excuse me." She was still holding my hand, and now she tightened her grip on it and led me from the edge of the platform to the back corner of the room, shielded slightly from the rest of the guests by the great velvet drapes that hung down behind the platform.

"What's going on?" she asked, her face falling at once. Clearly, I hadn't done a very good job of masking my anxiety.

"The key. The key to the Casting Cage," I whispered. "I know what it is."

Celeste tensed up, her fingers tightening around mine. "You do? But how did you—"

"I just... realized it. I'd seen it before, but I didn't put two and two together. But just now, I looked through my sketches of the tapestry, and it just clicked."

"What is it? And do you know where we can find it?"

I swallowed hard. "I'm wearing it," I muttered.

The excited flush drained from Celeste's face. "You're wearing..."

I pointed to the necklace, and her gaze followed.

"It was Agnes Isherwood's," I explained in a hiss. "I borrowed it from the Clan Sassanaigh vault because I thought it would match my dress. But she was wearing it in the tapestry! The same damn necklace, and I didn't even look twice at it, because... well, it was just a piece of jewelry, why would it matter? Celeste, is there any way—"

"I'll take you there myself. Let's go."

She turned and walked right out the door behind the curtain, and, with one fleeting look over my shoulder, I followed her.

My mind absolutely spun as we hurried along the corridors and up the staircases to Celeste's tower office. Would anyone notice I was gone? How much time did we have before I had to be back for all the planned formalities of the reception? The dancing had only just begun—surely I had a bit of a window before people started looking for me? If I missed something, I could always just make an excuse—Hannah would understand, when I finally had a chance to explain it. Because one thing was for sure—it wasn't safe for me to wander around that room full of people with a priceless artifact someone wanted to kill for, casually slung around my throat.

We finally reached the top of the spiral staircase—barefoot, in my case, as I was forced to abandon my absurd footwear for my own safety. There were no Caomhnóir patrolling outside the door.

"Don't you usually have guards up here?" I asked. There had been one at the bottom of the steps, but the office door itself was typically under guard.

"Certainly, but we needed all the security downstairs. We couldn't waste the manpower to guard an empty office, not with so many guests and vendors wandering the grounds." She removed a key from the pocket of her dress and jiggled it around in the lock, cursing quietly, until there was a loud, satisfying clink and the handle turned under her hand.

Rosy summer evening sunlight was streaming in through the window behind Celeste's desk, bathing everything in a golden warmth. The sounds of the musicians playing down in the Grand Council Room had spilled out onto the grounds, and were now drifting upward like seeds on the wind. Celeste had apparently stepped away from her desk mid-task; the surface was littered with papers, pens, and books. She hurried to the wall where the fireplace was set, and started probing with her fingers in the space between the mantel and the chimney stones.

"What are you—" I began to ask, but she interrupted me with a triumphant "Ah-ha!" There was a deep clunk and a whirring sound, and then a panel in the side of the chimneypiece slid aside to reveal a safe built into the wall. Celeste turned to look at me.

"I told you I would keep it secure," she said, smiling, and then began to turn the dial.

I held my breath as she carefully input the code, and didn't exhale again until the door hissed with compressed air and swung open. There were several envelopes and scrolls of paper, and there, perched on top of it all, was the Casting Cage. Celeste removed it carefully and set it down with a sense of reverence upon the desktop. We both stood staring at it, almost as though we expected it to react in some obvious way to the presence of the necklace.

Nothing whatsoever happened.

"What should we do?" I asked.

"Pick it up," Celeste murmured.

I hesitated a moment, and then reached out and picked up the Casting Cage. Instantly, I felt a thrumming sort of energy, like something had woken up inside the confines of the box: something sentient, and powerful, and only just realizing it was trapped. At the same time, I felt the necklace against my skin come alive as well, energy coursing through it, warming it like lifeblood.

"I can feel it," I whispered. "This is it. This is the key."

We let this realization wash over us, staring at each other, marveling.

"What should we do now?" I asked.

"I've never opened a Casting Cage before, and we don't know what's in it or what it will do," Celeste said. "And so, I think it would be ill-advised to try it now, especially with everything going on downstairs."

"But what do we *do*?" I repeated. "Because I can't just go back downstairs with this thing hanging around my neck!" The thought was inconceivable. What if something happened to it? I suddenly felt like I was wearing a ticking time bomb as a fashion accessory.

"We'll lock it up—both of them—just until the wedding is over," Celeste said, "and then we'll come back up here as soon as all the guests have gone."

"But I thought it was dangerous to keep the key and the Cage together?" I reminded her.

"Not dangerous, simply bad security," Celeste said. "But this is only for a few hours, and I'll have some of the Caomhnóir come back up to guard the office. They'll be perfectly safe."

"Oh, I think not."

The voice came from the doorway. Celeste and I both spun, startled, to look for who had spoken.

At first, I was confused. All I could see was a pair of hulking Caomhnóir, their broad shoulders and barrel chests filling the doorframe. But then they parted like a brawny, unsmiling curtain to reveal a woman standing behind them, wearing a long, ice blue cloak. She stepped between the men, lifted her hands to her hood, and drew it back from her face.

Simone de Chastenay stared at me, an amused smile playing about her lips.

25

MASTERMIND

For a long moment, all I could do was stare. I had lost the ability to process what I was seeing. Simone de Chastenay could not be here in Fairhaven Castle. She simply couldn't be. It wasn't possible.

Of course, she wasn't the Simone de Chastenay I had first met upon arriving at Havre des Gardiennes more than a year ago. When I first laid eyes on the High Priestess of the International High Council, the most powerful of all Durupinen, it was rather like stepping into Rivendell and meeting an elf. She was gorgeous, glowing—a fantasy vision of ageless perfection with cascading hair and flawless skin, despite the fact that she had been, at the time, more than seventy years old. A lifetime of rampant Leeching had rendered her the possessor of an almost immortal youth and beauty. I remembered being struck speechless in her presence, filled with awe. That awe had quickly turned and soured, first into disgust, and then hatred as I realized why she looked the way she did, and what atrocities she had committed in the name of her own power and vanity.

Now, at least, her appearance reflected her advanced age. Her skin draped loosely from her bones, creased with fine wrinkles. Her hair, though still long, was thin, revealing a mottled scalp beneath. Her eyes, once bright, were cloudy with age, and her mouth, as it broke into a wider smile at my shock, was nearly devoid of teeth.

"Simone?" Celeste's voice came out in a croak of disbelief.

"I imagine it must be rather a shock to see me," Simone said. She was so small, so frail, standing between her two guards, that she looked rather like a child posed between their parents. "I promise you, I am shocked every time I look in a mirror. The ravages of time are merciless."

Even as I reeled in shock at the sight of her standing there, my anger spiked at her words. How dare she expound on the ravages of time when she spent so many decades draining the life force out of spirits, just to fend them off.

"What are you doing here?" Celeste asked. "You're supposed to be under lock and key at Havre des Gardiennes."

"Oh, I was. But then I heard about this wedding, and I simply couldn't miss it. The social event of the decade, and I didn't even rate an invitation. An oversight, I was certain, and so I remedied the situation."

"You broke out of jail just to watch my sister walk down the aisle?" I asked, finally overcoming my shock, and finding my voice. "I didn't take you for the sentimental type, Simone."

"Ah, yes, Miss Ballard." Her milky eyes shifted from Celeste, and rested on me once more. There was a terrible chill in that stare, and something shifted in her expression—something dark and almost feral. I knew, in that instant, that she would have pounced on me and torn me to pieces with her bare hands if she had had the strength. "I really ought to insist that the formalities of rank be preserved. It is disrespectful, no, to address your betters by their given names?"

I laughed, one sharp, humorless bark. "My betters? A bold assessment from a woman who betrayed her sisterhood, and the entire spirit world, for personal gain and vanity. And I'm sorry, what am I meant to call you, if not your name? You aren't the High Priestess of the International High Council anymore."

"And yet, no other Durupinen has stepped up to take my place, so fractured and divided is that sisterhood you mention. Fractured and divided by your actions, I might add. You speak of my betrayal, but deny your own?" She clicked her tongue in admonishment. "Things are shattered because you broke them apart."

"Things are shattered because people like you forgot what we were supposed to stand for," I shot back. "You lost your way, and the spirit world called you on it. That's not my fault."

"Simone, you haven't answered my question," Celeste said, taking a cautious step forward, so that her body was angled ever so slightly between Simone and me. "You have been sentenced to imprisonment for the rest of your natural life, and yet here you are, standing unshackled and free, in Fairhaven Castle. How?"

"Oh, I would have thought you could work that out on your own, Celeste.

You're a clever girl, after all. Did you really think that those who oppose you and your misguided policies were limiting their resistance to speeches on Council Room floors?"

Celeste did not reply to what was obviously meant to be a rhetorical question, though her knuckles had gone white as she balled her hands into fists at her sides.

"The factions that oppose you have long known that further action would need to be taken, that the official channels would never allow for the outcomes we desire. It began in amateur, misguided ways—those young women who tried to employ witchcraft, for example. Sloppy. Desperate. But others have been more careful—more calculated in their resistance. They have successfully prevented, as you know, the election of a new High Priestess of the International High Council for all this time. This has not been a simple matter of disarray, but of coordinated efforts to ensure that no candidate ever has enough support to assume the mantle."

"You say this as though I am not already well aware of it," Celeste said, the words eking their way out through her tightly clenched teeth. "You think I haven't noticed the political scheming and coalition building?"

"It goes far deeper than that, my dear," Simone said. "For well over a year now, my own supporters have been infiltrating the guardians, bribing the persuadable, and blackmailing the unpersuadable. We have kept the top seat vacant, ready for my return, even as we gathered the means to secure it. And in the meantime, we have been searching for the one thing we needed to take power again. How accommodating of you to find it for us."

Celeste and I both looked down at the Casting Cage now sitting on the desk between us.

"So, you're responsible for Polly Keener's disappearance, then," I said.

"It was carried out at my behest, yes," Simone said. "It was almost too easy to set things in motion. Some members of the International High Council asked her to gather all that she could dig up about the historical circumstances that led to the Reckoning. We enticed her with the idea of a presentation at Havre des Gardiennes, the highest honor any mere Scribe could hope for. The foolish woman leaped at the chance, of course. Worked night and day."

Anger bubbled under my skin, but I uncharacteristically kept my mouth shut. From what little I knew about Polly Keener and her obsession with her research, I had absolutely no doubt that Simone's description of her enthusiasm was accurate.

"We had hoped for clues—a tiny lead that might take us in the right direction to find what we needed. Never in our wildest dreams did we imagine the woman would stumble upon it herself. It was more than we could have wished for, too good to be believed, but our sources within the *príosún* confirmed it; she had found something of great importance."

"But she didn't give it to you," I said, unable to keep the satisfaction out of my voice.

"No, she did not," Simone said placidly. "She might be foolish enough to place your disgraced clan on a pedestal, but that foolishness did not extend so far that she was unable to recognize the import of what she had found. She knew what would happen if it fell into the wrong hands. Most unfortunately, she was unable to recognize which hands were the wrong ones."

"Oh, I think she was pretty damn clear on that point," I said.

"She attempted to hide her findings," Simone went on as though I had not spoken. "It was almost endearing, her pathetic attempts to keep from us what was rightfully ours."

"Not that pathetic, if you needed me to find it for you," I said.

"I will admit we underestimated her in one regard. I was convinced an hour or two of torture would be more than sufficient to crack her resolve. She held out far longer than anyone expected before she began to talk."

A wave of nausea washed over me as I remembered the dreams—Polly in a dank cell, begging for them to stop, swearing that she'd told them all she knew. I had to swallow back bile as I stared at Simone's lined and placid face, betraying not a hint of emotion as she spoke of torturing an innocent woman, locked away in a dungeon at…

Oh my God. Catriona.

"The Trackers were suspicious," I said, the words tumbling out. "They are at Havre des Gardiennes even now, no doubt unraveling your whole plot."

Simone shrugged. "They may well be. But if they are, they will meet more than enough resistance to keep them busy, and even if they fight their way out, it will already be too late. We will have regained all that you have taken from us."

"I've taken nothing that you hadn't stolen in the first place," I spat back.

"The Gateways were not stolen. They were protected; and as their protectors, we had every right to them. What a nuisance you still are, Miss Ballard. I never imagined it would be you standing directly in our path again. But of course, all the while we were trying to get information out of Polly

Keener, you were a thorn in my side once again. I still don't know how you knew to come looking."

"Polly wrote to my sister and me before you kidnapped her. We knew that she'd found something to do with our clan, and that she was worried that it would fall into the wrong hands," I said. My voice sounded thick as panic swelled up in my throat, making it hard to swallow. My eyes darted to the two Caomhnóir. They were both massive and armed. There wasn't a chance in hell of getting past them.

"Did she indeed? Clever girl, wasn't she? Well, your arrival complicated an already messy situation. We attempted to neutralize you, of course, but you managed to slip out of that one. You are quite inconveniently difficult to kill."

"Yeah, I actually get that a lot," I ground out.

"Polly, too, showed more resilience than we expected. But she cracked eventually, as they all do. We extracted what information we could from her—that she had found the Casting Cage, and where she had hidden it. And most importantly of all, what was inside it."

My heart thudded out of rhythm. "You... you know what's inside?"

Simone smiled. "Oh, yes. You see, a journal was the first discovery—a journal belonging to Agnes Isherwood. Polly found it, concealed inside a hidden compartment in Agnes' podium, an artifact held in the *príosún*."

I knew exactly the podium she was talking about. I had seen it, touched it, and run my hands over it during our search of the archive. But by then, there had been nothing to find; it had already given up its secret to Polly.

"The journal led her to the Casting Cage, concealed in the cornerstone of a monument in your clan's graveyard. And the journal also described what was inside, and how to open it."

"So what exactly is—" I began, but she raised a hand to silence me.

"Patience, child. All in good time."

I ground my teeth together at being called a child, and waited.

"By the time Ms. Keener gave up this information, and despite our attempts to stop you, you had already retrieved the Casting Cage from the depths of the *príosún*. That left the key—but Ms. Keener did not know where that was to be found, only that it was in your clan's possession. She was no longer useful. She will have been disposed of by now."

I could barely take in her words. Polly was dead. I thought perhaps I'd known it, deep down, but hearing it out loud still felt like a slap to the face, even bringing angry moisture to my eyes.

"So you killed Polly," I said, my voice surprisingly calm given the rage bubbling under my skin. "But you still needed the key and the Casting Cage."

"Yes, I did. We knew you left Skye and came directly here with your discovery, which meant the Casting Cage was at Fairhaven. That meant we would need to come here, too. We needed an excuse to infiltrate the castle, and so we created one. A wedding celebration, right here on the grounds."

"You burned down The Grand Dutchess Hotel," I said, another piece falling into place. "But... hang on, that doesn't make sense. You couldn't possibly have known that the wedding would be at Fairhaven instead. Celeste was the one who suggested that."

"Actually," Celeste said slowly, "I didn't. I was among other Council members when Karen broke the news to me. It was Clarissa MacLeod who suggested we move the wedding to Fairhaven, and I made the offer to Karen on the spot."

I turned back to Simone, horrified. "Clarissa MacLeod? She's involved in this?"

Simone cocked her head to one side like a curious bird. "Naturally. And she's not the only one."

I swallowed hard. I'd called the clans a nest of vipers several times in the last few weeks. I had no idea exactly how apt that description had been.

"So you had a way into the castle, where the Casting Cage was," I said, my voice flat with rage. "But you still needed the key. You broke into our vault, but found the necklace was already gone."

"I assumed that meant you had discovered its significance and removed it for safety. Fairhaven was surely the only place safer than where it had already been stored. Or at least, it had been, before it became the gathering place of every single Durupinen with the power and position to thwart you. Imagine my astonishment when I was told you were wearing it around your neck. We knew then we couldn't let you out of our sight tonight. And when you disappeared from the reception, we followed."

"You speak of Durupinen who will thwart me. Thwart me from doing what?" I asked. "You still haven't told me what this Casting Cage is meant to contain."

Simone's smile widened. "I think it's time we all understand that. The two of you will follow me out to the Geatgrima."

"And why exactly would we do that?" Celeste asked. "You may have loyalists left, but you have no power here, Simone. We do not kneel to you anymore, and we do not follow your orders."

"You have no choice, I fear," Simone said, "unless you'd like me to alert my compatriots down in the Grand Council Room of your defiance. One word from me, and they'll stop dancing and start taking hostages."

I froze. Beside me, I felt Celeste stiffen. I glanced at her, and her mouth was pressed into a flat, angry line. She looked at me, and without a word, I knew what she was thinking. We had no choice.

"Very well," Celeste said. "Lead the way, Simone."

26

THE PRICE PAID

My entire body was buzzing with fear. It echoed in my ears and zipped up and down my limbs. Beside me, I could almost hear Celeste's brain working. What were we going to do? How were we going to get out of this without people getting hurt? Because if we both knew one thing with having to say it out loud, it was that we could not allow whatever Simone's plan was to come to fruition. We had to stop it, at any cost.

The guard who had stood at the bottom of the tower staircase had vanished, though whether he'd been a co-conspirator or simply disposed of by the two gorillas now marching on either side of us, we had no way of knowing. What I did know was that we could walk directly to the Fairhaven Geatgrima without passing anywhere near the Grand Council Room, which meant that the chances of anyone seeing us and intervening was almost non-existent. We had to find another way out of this. As much as I didn't want to endanger anyone else, I had to warn them.

Keeping my face neutral, my stride steady, I opened the connection.
"Milo?"

He was there, buzzing with happy excitement. "Jess! Where did you disappear to? I was just about to open this bad boy up, it's time to—"

"Milo, listen to me, we're running out of time."

Before he could reply, I dumped the entirety of what had just happened in Celeste's office into his head.

"Oh my God. OH MY GOD."

"I know. I need you to find Finn and alert him. Savvy and Rana, too."

"I don't know where—"

"And then I need you to find somewhere safe for Hannah and Kiernan to disappear to."

"How do I—"

"Make up some excuse. Lie your ass off if you have to! Say she needs a touch-up. Tell her the photographer wants to get some special shot. I don't care what you tell her, just get her out of there! And Karen, too!"

My head awash in Milo's mounting panic, my thoughts began to spiral. Tia was down there. And Annabelle. And Flavia... oh my God, how the hell were we going to protect everyone?

"Milo?"

"Yes! Yes, I... okay. I'll figure it out. Don't close this connection! I need to know what's happening!"

"I'll do my best," I said. "Tell me when they're safe! Oh, and Milo—"

"Yeah?"

"I don't know who else is in league with her except for Clarissa MacLeod, so don't trust anyone who isn't in our immediate circle, and for God's sake, don't let Clarissa anywhere near them!"

I felt rather than heard his understanding, and then he was gone. I refocused on where we were going, and found we had already reached the hallway that would open onto the central courtyard. We were nearly out of time, and we hadn't seen a single person who could raise the alarm. It would be entirely up to Milo. I actually smiled to myself, just a little. If Milo was in charge, I liked our odds.

At the end of the long, dark stone corridor, an arched doorway led out to the central courtyard where the Geatgrima stood. Simone stepped aside so that one of her Caomhnóir could heave it open. The sight of the Geatgrima, looming in the gathering darkness, sent a dagger of fear right through my heart. It was finally, after centuries, restored to its rightful state. The idea that that might end in the next few minutes made me want to be sick. My stomach roiled, and my anger also.

Simone seemed to be battling against her own body as she led the way toward the ancient stone archway. Her gait was labored and unsteady, as was her breathing, but when one of her Caomhnóir reached out to offer assistance, she batted his hand away.

"I'm perfectly well! Keep your paws to yourself, insolent boy!" she warbled.

Celeste and I looked at each other, but said nothing. Undoubtedly, she was thinking as hard as I was about a way out of this mess. Watching the strange desperation in Simone's manner, I thought I was starting to understand why she had taken this chance, and gone to such lengths to do all of this. The woman was on death's door. She would rather burn the world down than face mortality, even with all she knew about the existence of the spirit world. Well, I thought darkly, she wasn't the first person to go to such lengths, and she certainly wouldn't be the last. She would have made an exemplary Necromancer.

As we approached the Geatgrima, the Casting Cage clutched in my hands felt like a living thing, pulsating against my palms, even as the necklace thrummed against my neck. They yearned for each other, drawn together by the magic that united them, the magic that was, if Simone had her way, about to be unleashed.

I jumped in alarm as Milo's voice burst into my head, "Jess, something's happening in here. I got Hannah, Kiernan, and Karen out. Savvy and Rana have them all, and I came back looking for Finn, but now they're closing all the doors. There are Caomhnóir stationed at each one. They did it quietly, I don't think people have really noticed, because they're all dancing and drinking. But I don't think they're letting people out. I think they're trying to keep us all corralled in here!"

"They let some people out," I informed him, for I had just spotted a group of people entering the grounds from the other side of the castle, sweeping over the grass. At the head of the group was Clarissa MacLeod, who was evidently recovered enough from her near-fatal stabbing to help plan a coup. The others were Council members as well: I spotted Geraldine Porter, as well as Patricia Lightfoot, who I don't think I'd seen since I'd attended her daughter Roisin's wedding several years earlier. I also saw, with a stab of anger, that my former teachers, Siobhan and Keira, were also among the group, though they hung further back, and kept their eyes averted from us. I glanced at Celeste; her expression was hovering somewhere between fury and devastation as she watched the women approach. They stopped a couple of yards from the Geatgrima, waiting for Simone's orders, no doubt. Several of them looked at us, all smugness and triumph, while others stared at the Geatgrima itself, with undeniably hungry expressions. It took every ounce of my self control not to fly at the lot of them, claws out.

Simone cleared her throat. "It is truly a day of celebration—perhaps just not the celebration some of us expected." She smiled at me, and again, I had to restrain myself from violence. "Tonight we take back what is rightfully ours, what has been stolen from us, and retake our rightful place in the hierarchy of the spirit and living worlds."

"Your rightful place is in prison, for conspiring with our enemies," Celeste said, and though her voice was not loud or even angry, there was steel in it—a quiet strength that Simone could not match with her unhinged warbling. "As for the rest of you, you are traitors. You have betrayed your sisterhood, your legacy, and your calling. You should all be deeply ashamed, and it is not too late to make it right."

The faces staring back at us flashed a range of reactions, from amusement to the shame Celeste had rightly placed upon them. But none looked like they had the courage to stop what was about to happen.

In reply to Celeste's words, Simone approached me and reached for the Casting Cage. I made no movement to relinquish it at first, though I knew I had no choice when I felt the grip of the Caomhnóir tighten threateningly on my upper arm. I released my hold on the box and allowed Simone to take possession of it, though I knew she could do nothing to open it, not yet, not while I still had the key around my neck.

"This is the secret we have fought so hard to unearth," Simone said, and she held the Casting Cage up so that the other women could see it. "Unremarkable in appearance, but astonishing in its power. According to the records of Agnes Isherwood, the woman who created it, it contains the very Casting that will return the Gateways to the bloodlines of the Durupinen."

So there it was, the truth we had suspected but couldn't prove; the Casting that would reverse the Reckoning lay within that simple wooden box. The watching expressions of the other Durupinen shifted at the revelation of that truth. Some softened with reverence, others sharpened by greed, and still others marred with wariness. These women, I realized, were not a united front, single in their intentions.

"If you have summoned us here," Siobhan said, her voice trembling, "then that must mean you have also found the key."

So Siobhan, at least, knew how the Casting Cage worked.

"I have indeed," Simone said. "Young Miss Ballard has been foolish enough to wear it around her neck this evening. I welcome her foolishness, however, as it has made our task tonight so much simpler."

Every pair of those eyes turned to look at me now. I lifted my chin and glared back, defiant.

"You who stand in this courtyard now, you have been loyal to me," she said. "Perhaps not from the very start, but over time, you have been drawn to my cause, and you have proven yourselves committed to it. You all will step into great power when the Gateways have been restored to our blood, and I have been restored to my throne. I will make sure of it. You will each have your reward."

"I see," Celeste interrupted. "So it's bribery, is it? Is that all I needed to do, as your High Priestess, to gain your loyalty? Ought I to have relied on bribery and favors rather than my trust in your honesty and commitment to the spirits who rely on you? Would that have bought your cooperation?"

"Your time is over, Celeste," Patricia Lightfoot said. "Your reign of weakness and capitulations ends now. We have long wished to oust you, but tonight, when our gifts have been restored, we will ensure it."

"And when the Geatgrimas fail, and the Sentinels are called, as they were before," Celeste asked them, "What then? You will sacrifice your sisters for your greed?"

"The Geatgrimas held for centuries upon centuries," Clarissa said dismissively. "And they shall do so again."

"Oh, and you know that for sure, do you?" I asked, breaking my silence at last, and feeling every pair of eyes latch onto me. "You think, because it worked that way once, it will still hold true, even after the Gateways have been so badly meddled with?"

"Why should it not?" Keira asked, though her voice sounded uncertain.

"A hundred reasons, none of which, apparently, any of you have considered. You're so focused on your own gratification, your own power and privilege, that you haven't really even considered what this could mean for your daughters, your granddaughters. They are the ones who will pay the price for what you do tonight; maybe not right away, but certainly sooner than you think. Is that what you want?"

"We do this for our daughters," Geraldine Porter said. "You can't twist this with your rhetoric, insolent girl. You are the one who took it upon yourself to steal their futures from them, not us. We are restoring them."

"Their futures were collapsing before your eyes, and you were going to let it happen if I didn't intervene," I said. "And what about the spirits you're bound to protect? What about them?"

"We will protect the spirit world as we always have," Clarissa said. "Your traitorous clan knows nothing of loyalty or duty. You abandoned your gifts and your calling. You do not have the right to tell us what to do with ours."

"My mother's mistakes are not mine," I said. "It's true, I didn't want this gift, but I've honored it regardless, which is more than I can say for any of you."

"Enough of this," Simone said, her voice more powerful than I would have thought possible, coming from her shriveled little frame. "We are not here to relitigate past events. We are here to set them right, and we will not be dissuaded or delayed any longer. This has been predestined. Agnes Isherwood created this Casting Cage because she knew, one day, we might need it. That day is now. Now we make right what has been broken."

"Jess! What's happening out there? People are starting to realize they can't leave! Hannah and the others are going to—" Milo began, but I shut out his voice. I couldn't lose my focus, no matter what was happening in the castle. The true emergency was here, now, right in front of me. I would have to trust the others to keep each other safe, because Simone was walking toward me now, the Casting Cage in her hands.

"Do you know how this device works, Miss Ballard?" Simone asked, and her voice had a deadly silkiness to it now, as she hobbled toward me.

I did not reply. My body and brain were screaming at me to find a way out of this, and I had nothing, absolutely nothing…

"It requires a key, yes, but it requires something else as well," Simone said, offensively close to me now. Her rotted breath wafted into my face as she cracked a satisfied smile. That satisfaction reminded me of what I already knew but which, in the terror of events, I had forgotten.

A sacrifice. The Casting Cage required a sacrifice.

"To transfer the Gateways between the worlds of the living and the dead, the Casting Cage demands a life," she said. Behind her, I heard a gasp from one of the others. "And I think, given the amount of trouble you've caused us all, that life should be yours."

27

BAIT AND SWITCH

"Wait, you... you never said we had to kill anyone!" Keira said, looking stricken now. "We just had to help you get into the castle, you never said—"

One of the other women silenced her with a look, but Celeste pounced on the dissention in the ranks.

"Is that so?" she said, looking from Simone to the others. "You mean to say she lied to you about what would happen here today? Have you stopped to wonder what else she's been lying to you about?"

No one answered. A few traded anxious looks, but most continued to stare blankly and unconcernedly—a few even eagerly. I repressed a snort. Yeah, I had no doubt some of these women would gladly kill me themselves, just for funsies. It gave me a sense of grim satisfaction, even as sheer animal terror started to course through me.

"I'm sure she's promised you all kinds of things in exchange for your help," Celeste went on, just a hint of desperation in her voice. "But what makes you think she can keep those promises? Why gamble everything on the word of a woman who has betrayed us all?"

"We gamble because we have nothing left to lose," Clarissa said. "We have already lost what is most precious to us. Do you really not understand that?" She didn't sound angry or resentful. She sounded... truly curious.

"No," Celeste replied. "No, I suppose I don't. Because what was most important to me, always, was protecting the spirit world. The rest of it means nothing."

"Oh, so you would cast off that mantle of power you cling to so tightly?" Clarissa asked with a decided sneer in her voice. "You would hand it over, for the sake of some righteous principle? Don't make me laugh."

"You alone find the idea humorous," Celeste calmly replied.

"I grow weary of this back and forth," Simone suddenly snapped. "We have waited long enough. The Gateways await their return to the bloodlines. We cannot delay."

Blood thundered in my ears as she turned back to me, a gleam of something wicked in her otherwise clouded eyes. "It is only fitting, Jessica Ballard. You tore us asunder. And now, with your sacrifice, we will mend what was broken and reclaim our power."

Simone stepped toward me again and, with one withered hand, reached out and unsheathed the dagger from the belt of the Caomhnóir holding me. Fight or flight took over, and I struggled to get away from her, but the hulking Caomhnóir's grip was like iron bands around my arms. Somewhere to the left of me, Celeste was struggling against her captor, too, but I couldn't tear my eyes from the knife. A surety settled over me as the dying sunlight glinted off the blade—this was Fiona's vision. This was what she had seen, one of its fleeting possibilities, and now all the missing pieces had fallen into place. The universe had decided. If Fiona went up to her tower now and finished her sculpture, it would be my face she finally carved upon it.

I was the one who would die.

Simone reached toward me, but not with the knife—instead, she grabbed onto Agnes' necklace and, with one sharp yank, pulled it from my neck. I felt it cut into my skin and gasped as it came away. She held it up, grinning toothlessly at it, and then faced me again.

"Goodbye, Jessica Ballard of Clan Sassanaigh," she whispered. "It's time for you to join the spirit realm."

Out of the corner of my eye, I saw movement. A voice shouted, "No!" I closed my eyes as the dagger rose. Something hit me—hard—and I fell.

Everything went dark.

This was death, I thought. Simone had stabbed me, and I'd fallen. For one wild moment, all I could feel was grateful that being stabbed to death wasn't nearly as painful as I'd expected it to be. Then I opened my eyes and realized I wasn't dead at all. My hands scrambled frantically over my chest, my neck, my abdomen, searching for a wound as my vision adjusted. But slowly, I realized there was no wound.

There was, however, blood. Lots of blood. But where had it come from?

I turned and saw the mountainous Caomhnóir, who'd been restraining me, lying in a heap on the ground, his eyes rolled back into his head, and blood covering his neck. He had fallen and taken me with him right to the grass. Then I turned and saw the second Caomhnóir sprawled in the grass, unmoving. What in the world?

I turned to the sounds of scuffling behind me, and saw Celeste rising from the ground, her shaking hands also covered with blood.

"Celeste! No!"

I got up and staggered toward her. She turned at the sound of my voice. There was blood all down the front of her dress. Oh no. Please, God, no...

"Jess!" she gasped.

I fell into her, but she did not collapse. She pulled me into a strong embrace and held me against her. "Are you all right? Are you hurt?"

"Wh-why are you asking *me* that?" I cried, pulling away from her so that I could look at her, my eyes roving her torso, looking for the source of all the blood, looking for a wound that didn't exist. "You're... you're not bleeding. It's not yours?"

She met my eye and solemnly shook her head. Then she turned, and I followed her gaze.

Simone lay slumped in the grass. The hilt of the dagger stuck out from her barely rising chest. Her eyes, glazed, her mouth open in an "O" of surprise, a trickle of blood at the corner of her lips. I watched as her fingers hovered helplessly over the dagger hilt, like some fading part of her brain was telling her to pull it out, but her hands couldn't respond. Then, with a sound halfway between a gurgle and a sigh, her chest fell, and did not move again.

"I'm sorry," Celeste whispered. "God help me, I'm so sorry. I had no choice."

We stood with our arms around each other, staring in horror at Simone. I'd forgotten entirely about the rest of the Durupinen standing there in the courtyard with us, until a strangled gasp echoed through the emptiness, and I turned to see several of them moving slowly toward the body. Clarissa reached it first, kneeling down to check for a pulse, which, based on her expression, she knew she would not find. Then she paused.

"Clarissa..."

It was Celeste who spoke, and there was a warning note in her voice. It took me a moment to realize why. Clarissa was no longer looking at Simone's lifeless body. She was looking at the Casting Cage lying in the grass beside her.

Clarissa glanced over at us, and in that split second, I saw the decision form behind her eyes. Before we could react, she had bent over and snatched both the Casting Cage and the necklace from the ground. Then, with a grimace and a grunt of effort, she reached over and wrenched the knife from Simone's sunken chest. Celeste swore under her breath. Behind Clarissa, Keira bent over and retched into the grass, and Siobhan sank to her knees, her face paper white.

"Clarissa, don't do this," I murmured, and though she stood several feet away, I knew she could hear me. She certainly met my eye, but the expression there did not waver.

"I'm sorry," she said. "I'm sorry, but we've come too far. It's time to finish it."

Celeste took a step toward her, but Clarissa raised the knife, pointing it at her High Priestess, and Celeste froze.

"Stay away from me, Celeste. No one else needs to get hurt," Clarissa said. "Frankly, I wish there had been another way. But what's done is done, and Simone need not have died in vain. We can still carry out her wishes and her plan. We can still take back what is ours."

Slowly, Clarissa backed toward the other women. A few gathered eagerly around her, while others hovered back, looking wary.

"All we need to do," Clarissa said, taking charge now, "is place our hands upon the box as it opens. Our hands must be smeared with the blood of the sacrifice. Just a drop will suffice."

Keira backed away, shaking her head. "No," she whispered. "No, I'm... I can't."

Geraldine Porter stepped boldly forward and put out her hand. "I nearly sacrificed my daughter to this cause. I will not back down now."

Clarissa nodded her approval and pressed the knife to Geraldine's hand, leaving a smear of blood behind. The others stepped forward one by one, extending their hands. The last to join them was Siobhan. She hesitated, and then, looking at Celeste, she said, "I'm sorry, High Priestess." Then she thrust her hand at Clarissa, who pressed the dagger against it.

"Don't!" I called out, shaking Celeste's grip off of me and starting toward them, but it was too late. They each had their hand placed on the box. Clarissa cast the dagger aside, and placed the central stone of the necklace into the indentation on the top of the box. There was a strange shift in the air, like the tang and charge of static, and then the lid of the box flew open. A blinding light erupted from the inside of the box and expanded like the blast of a bomb. We were all thrown backward with the force of it. I hit the grass flat on my back, knocking all the breath out of me, and for a moment, I saw stars. I lay there, trying to get my lungs to inflate; all the while, dread was pulsing through me. We hadn't stopped it. They'd actually done it.

The Gateways...

We'd failed...

I wrenched myself up from the ground, head spinning from the blow and the temporary lack of oxygen. Beside me, Celeste was also struggling to get back to her feet. My vision was blurry, and I growled with frustration that I couldn't see what was happening. I looked down at the fuzzy outline of my own hands, trying to see if I felt the old power coursing through them. Was it in me? Was the stolen Gateway coursing through my blood once again?

"Jess! Jess, are you all right?"

I opened my mouth to answer, but stopped. That wasn't Celeste calling out to me. Those weren't her hands touching my face, pulling me roughly into a hug, gasping with relief.

It was Hannah.

I blinked the rest of the clouds from my eyes, and saw her face swimming in front of me.

"Hannah, I failed," I whispered. "I failed, I'm... I'm sorry, I was too late, I..."

"Jess, stop it. Stop apologizing. Just tell me you're okay!" she cried.

"I'm not okay!" I cried out, tears filling my voice. "I mean, sure, okay, I'm alive, whatever good that does, but I'm not okay! Nothing is okay! They did it, Hannah! They stole the Gateways again, they..."

"Jess, stop. Listen to me. They didn't. It didn't work."

"Of course it worked! I watched it! The... the Cage, it opened and this... this light came out of it." I swayed, trying to hold on to the details.

"Jess, look at me. Feel this." Hannah said.

And she intertwined her fingers with mine. And I felt... nothing.

Well, not nothing. I felt her skin, warm and soft. I felt the familiarity of her. But that rushing, pulsing power that used to flow between us when we held hands... it wasn't there.

"I don't understand," I muttered.

"I don't either. But it didn't work!"

I tore my gaze from her to look around the courtyard. It was full of people, living and dead, who hadn't been there a minute before. They had poured in from all the doors that led to the courtyard: Savvy and Rana, sweaty and disheveled and still in their bridesmaid dresses; Finn, already sprinting toward me, his expression frantic; Kiernan, his tie askew, glasses fogged; Karen, face glazed with tears, hair coming down out of its elegant twist; about two dozen Caomhnóir now surrounding the group of women still gathered around the remains of the Casting Cage; and ghosts. Ghosts *everywhere.*

"I Called them. When Milo told us what was happening," Hannah said, answering the question in my look. "I thought we might need backup."

And then, from behind a line of Caomhnóir, Catriona appeared, her long hair flying out behind her, her face blazing with anger, looking like an avenging angel.

"Cat! You're alive!" I gasped, my voice so hoarse now that she couldn't hear me from where she stood, halfway across the courtyard, barking orders to the Caomhnóir who were now rounding up the rogue Durupinen.

"I don't... what's happened?" I asked weakly.

But Hannah was no longer crouching beside me. She had stood up, and all the ghosts around the perimeter of the courtyard snapped to attention, awaiting her orders. Finn skidded to a stop beside me, dropping down and gathering me into his arms in a hug so tight it squeezed out what little air I had left in my lungs.

"Jess, I'm sorry. I'm sorry, they created a diversion and by the time we got back—"

"Finn, I don't understand what's happening," I said. "They opened the Casting Cage, but—"

I didn't finish my sentence because Clarissa MacLeod was shouting. I turned to see her struggling against the restraining arms of the Caomhnóir, attempting to take her into custody.

"Let go of me, you fool. I am restored! The Gateways flow through my bloodline once more! We hold the power now, your bloodlines and gifts are secured thanks to us! Arrest her!" She pointed a trembling finger at Celeste, who stood beside me, shaking but upright. "She murdered the International High Priestess!"

"She disarmed and neutralized the greatest traitor this sisterhood has ever seen," Catriona roared. "You, on the other hand, are going to spend the rest of your life in a *priosún*, and may you rot there."

Clarissa laughed; a mad, maniacal sound that for an instant made me think of her sister. "You cling to a power you've already lost. When the rest of our sisterhood understands what we've done for them, the power we've restored, they will crown us all, and those who worked against us will pay dearly."

"No."

The word rang through the courtyard. I turned, as everyone else did, to look at the speaker.

My sister.

Hannah stood so calmly, so sure of herself, her flowing white gown blossoming around her in the gathering darkness, surrounded by a legion of spirits. She ought to have been concerned, frightened, even devastated—but she wasn't. Her expression was almost beatific in its understanding.

"You have restored nothing," she said, looking first at the lifeless form of Simone and then at the other Durupinen. "You have failed."

Clarissa looked like she wanted to laugh again. She opened her mouth and then shut it. Like everyone else, she was riveted by my sister.

"If you had torn the Gateways from their rightful place, I would feel it. But I feel nothing. Nothing at all," Hannah said. "Do you?"

Clarissa hesitated. "My daughter is the Gateway now," she said, after a moment of searching for words. "She is the one who—"

"But you should still feel it," Hannah said. "That connection doesn't go away. You should still be tied to it—bound to it. It should always be a part of you. So tell me, Clarissa. What do you feel?"

Clarissa hesitated again. Around her, Geraldine and the others were stealing glances at each other, or else looking down at their own hands. The question in each of them was clear: *did they feel different? Hadn't it worked?*

"I don't feel anything."

The voice came from an entirely unexpected quarter: Milo. He hovered near Hannah, and his expression was odd—a mixture of confusion and hope.

"What did you say?" Hannah asked, turning to look at him, but it was Clarissa who answered.

"I didn't say anything!" she snapped.

Hannah turned and looked at her again. "I... wasn't talking to you."

Clarissa watched in apparent mystification as Hannah turned to Milo again. "What did you say, Milo?"

"I said I can't feel anything from any of them," he said. "No pull at all. Certainly not a Gateway, and... and not even..." Understanding dawned in his features. Suddenly, without warning, he flew at Clarissa, shrieking at the top of his lungs like a banshee.

She didn't so much as flinch. She continued to stare at Hannah, seething with confusion.

"Who are you talking to?" she demanded once again.

And it clicked. I understood.

"Oh my God."

Now Clarissa rounded on me. Indeed, it felt like every eye in the courtyard was on me now as I pulled myself out of Finn's arms and stepped forward, the truth blooming in me like a flower.

"You can't see him," I said.

"Can't see who?!" Clarissa practically shrieked.

I laughed. After everything that had transpired that evening, I actually laughed out loud. The sound was jarring, and it drew every eye.

"I don't know what's happened. I don't know how you've done it, or... I suppose how Agnes has done it, but... there's a ghost standing six inches from you, Clarissa, and you can't see him, can you?"

Clarissa's eyes went wide. She snapped her head first to the left, and then to the right, her expression growing wilder with each second that passed. "What are you talking about? There's no ghost here! There's nothing!"

"He's there!"

It was Keira who spoke. Keira had, in the end, refused to participate in the blood ritual, refused to place her hand on the Cage. Her eyes were wide with wonder as she pointed a shaking finger directly at Milo.

"He's right there! It's their spirit guide! I recognize him!" she cried.

And that was the moment I realized it wasn't only Clarissa. Every single Durupinen who had agreed to Simone's blood on her skin, who had chosen to assist in the opening of the Casting Cage, searched the seemingly empty air with increasing desperation for a spirit they could no longer see.

Hannah raised her hands and thrust them forward. Every spirit in the courtyard flew toward the group of panicking Durupinen, forming a tight circle around them, hovering just beyond their reach.

"Every spirit in the grounds of this castle is here," she said, her voice ringing with righteous, angry triumph. "And you can't see them. You'll never see them again. That is the price you have paid for what happened here today." She turned to Celeste, who looked as astonished as the rest of them at what had happened. "High Priestess? What is your command?"

Celeste shook her head a little and then drew herself up, assuming her mantle of power once again. "Take them down to the dungeons," she said with ringing finality. "They've done enough damage for one night. Let them wallow in the consequences of their own greed."

And we watched in silence as they were led away.

28

HAPPY ENDINGS

"How is it possible that we thwarted a catastrophic upset of the living and spirit worlds, and yet still managed to pull off the wedding of the century?"

It was Milo who posed the question from the sofa the next afternoon, where he lounged in apparent exhaustion.

No one could blame him. We were all exhausted. The previous night had been one of the most momentous in any of our lives—in more ways than one. And now, as we lay around our room at Fairhaven, we finally had a moment to take in the scope of it all.

"Well, Kiernan said thoughtfully, "I suppose it helped that the bar never closed and the band kept playing through everything."

It was true. Despite the cataclysmic battle taking place out in the courtyard, most of the guests never realized anything was amiss until after the reception ended. And some of them—like Tia—would never know the full extent of what had happened; the code of secrecy would ensure that.

"Look, if I'm being truthful, I still don't bloody understand what happened out there," Savvy said. Rana lay in her lap with her eyes closed, and Savvy stroked her hair as she spoke. "I mean, I understand what was *supposed* to happen—the evil plot, as it were. But what was the cock up? Where did they go wrong?"

It was a question that had haunted all of us for the vast majority of the night —a question I hadn't yet revealed the answer to.

While everyone else had slept, drained from the day's events, I had been unable to do so. The gaps in my understanding were throbbing like wounds. I'd slipped from my bed and made my way to Celeste's office. I knew I would find her there. I didn't expect to find Catriona as well. Celeste ordered us a pot of tea, and the questions just started spilling out.

"I knew something was wrong right from the off," Cat told me when I asked her about her trip to Havre des Gardiennes. "When we arrived, the security was oddly light. When we asked to be brought down to the dungeons, they were completely flustered. Didn't seem to know who to ask or how to arrange it. They left us in one of the reception rooms, waiting for ages, and finally, I just lost patience. I knew my way down there, so I took my team and we just showed ourselves in."

"They didn't want you to figure out that Simone was gone," I guessed. "They thought, if they let you down into the dungeons, that you'd see that her cell was empty."

"Yes, I imagine that's true," Catriona said. "But instead we found exactly what we were looking for."

I blinked. "What do you mean?"

"Polly."

A bolt of anger shot right through me. "You found her body down there? They didn't even bother to—"

"Jess, Jess, slow down. You're getting ahead of me. We found Polly, yes, but she wasn't dead."

After the day I'd had, I didn't think I had any capacity left to be shocked, but I was wrong.

"Polly is alive?!"

"That is what I said, isn't it?" Cat droned.

"But... I don't understand! Simone told us she ordered her to be killed!"

"She may have done, but with her gone from the castle, no one had gotten around to carrying out that particular order," Cat said. "She's in rough shape, though. You can see her tomorrow, if you like. She's down in the hospital ward. Mrs. Mistlemoore is doing what she can for her, but we think she'll recover all right."

A sob tried to creep up my throat, but I swallowed it. I was too tired for a crying jag.

"Thank God," I said instead. "Oh, thank God. So that's how you knew what had happened? Polly told you everything?"

"She was too weak to tell us everything, but she told us enough that we were able to fill in the blanks. Then it was a mad dash back here to try to thwart Simone's plan. Luckily, you'd already managed to do that."

"No, we didn't," I said bitterly. "I mean, we tried to, and I know it worked out in the end, but we were no heroes. Whatever went wrong with that Casting Cage had nothing to do with us."

"But it did have everything to do with Agnes," Celeste said; and to my astonishment, she was laughing.

"Do you know something I don't?" I asked.

"I didn't at the time," Celeste said. "Believe me, Jess, I was just as astonished as you were when the Casting Cage didn't work. But as I have found out in the hours since, the Casting Cage *did* work. It worked exactly as it was meant to."

I rubbed my forehead. "I'm sorry, it's probably the exhaustion and the shock, but I'm not following."

"I retrieved the Casting Cage from the courtyard," Celeste said. "It was important evidence, and I knew it would need to be examined at some point. But when I picked it up, I discovered that there was a message carved into the inside of the box."

"What kind of message?" I asked.

"It was from Agnes," Celeste said. "It was written in a very old version of Britannic, but the gist of it translates to: *What you reap, so shall you sow.*"

"...and should I know what that means?" I asked.

"Unless I'm very much mistaken," Celeste said with a chuckle, "it means that the Casting Cage was a trap."

"A trap for wh—oh!" And despite the brain fog, it fell into place. "Agnes knew. She knew that, someday, someone might try to internalize the Gateways again. She wanted to prevent that from happening."

"That's exactly right," Celeste said. "She wanted not only to thwart the attempt, but to ensure that those misguided enough to try it would never be able to participate in Durupinen life again. She succeeded. As far as we can tell, every one of the Durupinen involved in tonight's attempted coup can no longer make any contact with spirits."

"Oh my God," I whispered. "I never considered that it was possible to strip a Durupinen's gift from her like that. That must have been one powerful, terrible Casting."

"Oh it was," Celeste agreed. "And that's why Agnes protected it the way she did. By concealing it in a Casting Cage, she could not only disguise it as another Casting but also ensure that, once it was used, it would disappear. There is no instruction or record of the real Casting in Agnes' journals. There is no way to replicate it or weaponize it against other Durupinen. It's simply... gone."

And so, in answer to Savvy's question, I filled the others in on what I had learned about the Casting Cage and Agnes' trick. I expected awed silence. I did not expect the roar of laughter from Savvy that caused Rana to jerk out of her lap in alarm.

"What's so funny?" I asked.

"Are you having me on?" Savvy asked, through tears of mirth. "That's the funniest bloody thing I've ever heard! Even Agnes, a thousand years removed, knew she couldn't trust these Council hags."

I had to laugh then. Not only was it true, but it was another thread tying Agnes to me. I felt closer to her—and to our family's legacy—than I ever had before.

"There's one thing I'll never get over, though," Milo said, wiping his eyes.

"What's that, then?" Finn asked.

"The second reception dress," he wailed. "Hannah never even got to wear it!"

As impossible as it seemed, the danger that had loomed over us for weeks like a swollen storm cloud was gone. Suddenly, I was helping my sister close her suitcase as she was getting ready to leave for her honeymoon.

"I can't believe it," I said. "You'll actually be able to relax and enjoy yourself for real."

"I can't believe it myself," she said, looking down at the rings sparkling on her left hand. "I'm married. Is it crazy that, after everything that happened yesterday, that's still the most astonishing thing to me?"

I laughed. "No. Okay, well, maybe a little, but I get it. It's weird. You're a Worthington now."

"Actually, I'm not," she said, and smiled a little slyly.

"What do you mean?" I asked. "You just said—"

"No, I mean, I am, but that's not my name. I decided not to change it."

"Really?"

"Yes. I spent a long time not feeling like I belonged anywhere, because I didn't even know where that name came from. Now that I truly understand, I'm not ready to give it up. I'm a Ballard girl, and I always will be." She sighed, but it was a sigh of contentment. "Shall we go down and see Polly before the car comes?"

Polly Keener looked much the worse for wear, but the smile on her face when she saw us was like a ray of sunlight bursting across her bruised and battered face.

"I'm so sorry, Polly," Hannah was saying, taking the woman's hand in hers. "I'm so sorry that proximity to our clan put you in so much danger."

"Stuff and nonsense," Polly said, squeezing Hannah's hand. "It was proximity to Simone de Chastenay that put me in danger. My work for your clan has only ever brought me joy."

"What will you do when you're feeling better?" I asked. "Go back to Scotland?"

"For a spell, yes," Polly said, "But not to Skye. I'm going to have a nice long holiday with my brother and my niece. But then, I..." she flushed with embarrassment. "Well, I think I might... might run for a Council seat. Is that... is that foolish, do you suppose?"

Hannah sat up, looking surprised but pleased. "Not at all. I think it's brilliant!"

"Yeah, I actually heard a few seats had opened up," I said dryly.

Polly shook her head. "I'm still flabbergasted about the Casting Cage, but I shouldn't have been."

"Why's that?" Hannah asked.

Polly shrugged. "I think it's safe to say that I know more about Agnes Isherwood than any other Durupinen living. I thought it strange from the beginning that she would preserve the Casting that stripped the Gateways from the Geatgrimas. It seemed like such a reckless and dangerous thing to do, and Agnes, for all her controversial decisions, was anything but reckless. She would have done all she could to protect the Gateways. In a way, I should have known it was a trap right from the beginning."

"Well, I for one am glad you didn't," I said. "Because otherwise, our sisterhood would still be riddled with traitors and snakes in the grass waiting to strike. I think you should run for that Council seat. It's time to shake things up. These rich and powerful clans have been in power for too long. That's how we got into this mess. We need some new blood—a fresh start."

That was easier said than done, but hey, a girl could dream.

We all gathered around Hannah and Kiernan to say goodbye as the driver heaved all the matching luggage into the trunk of the sleek black car.

"What are you going to do with yourself for two weeks?" Hannah asked.

"Oh, I'm sure I can find some apocalyptic mischief to get into," I said.

Hannah laughed. "Don't have too much fun without me."

I rolled my eyes, "Says the girl who is about to spend two weeks lounging on a sailboat in the Mediterranean."

"Don't forget to take lots of pictures!" Milo said. "And I left the list of which beach ensemble to wear on which day, it's color coded with the—"

"I'm sure I'll figure it out, Milo," Hannah said, and flung her arms around him. "Thank you for the most beautiful wedding ever, bestie."

"Oh, sweetness, the pleasure was all mine," he replied.

"You, too, Karen," Hannah said, hugging our aunt. "Thank you. Everything was absolutely perfect."

"Well, except for the bloody struggle for domination that took place out in the courtyard," Karen said a little weakly.

Hannah shrugged. "Every wedding has a hiccup or two."

They got in the car and we all waved and waved until they vanished down the winding country road. Even after I couldn't see them anymore, I still stood, looking at the place where they had disappeared.

A happy ending, against all odds. I wanted to savor it.

Finn stood beside me. He reached down and intertwined his fingers with mine.

"Well, I guess you were right."

"I usually am," I said. "But about what in particular this time?"

"Weddings. What a nightmare. Definitely more trouble than they're worth."

I laughed. "I suppose."

Finn raised an eyebrow. "You suppose? Aren't you the one who's sworn off marriage?"

I hopped up onto my tiptoes to kiss him.

"Never say never," I whispered.

EPILOGUE

The beach. I kept dreaming of the beach.

On some level, this made sense. My sister was on her honeymoon in Greece, regularly texting me sun-drenched selfies from a number of stunningly beautiful sandy beaches. Surely this was just my subconscious jealousy manifesting in my sleep?

But then I realized this beach I kept dreaming of was the wrong type of beach. This wasn't the pristine white sand and jewel-bright turquoise waters of the Mediterranean. This beach was rocky, faced by jagged cliffs topped with waving dune grasses. This beach looked out over darker waters, stormy waters. There was a lighthouse off in the distance. I'd seen beaches like it, back on the Northeast coast of the US, but I didn't think I'd ever seen this particular beach.

I was always alone for the first few nights. Then the dream changed.

Now, a woman stood on the beach. Wind-whipped silver-threaded curls around her face, which was lined with both age and worry. Her narrow shoulders were draped in a shawl, its tassels dancing like excited fingers reaching back toward the cliffs behind her.

At first, I just watched her. Studied her. I wasn't at all sure she knew I was there. I approached closer, my feet sinking deeply into the soft sand. To my surprise, she turned to look at me, meeting my eye before turning back to gaze at the waves again.

I came to a stop beside her, but she didn't turn again. Something inside me told me to honor the silence, to wait for her to speak, and so I stood in that silence, training my gaze out over the water as well. Was there an answer out there? Some sort of message or sign? All I could see was storm-tossed water and salty spray, and gulls wheeling in the battering hands of the wind. Still, I waited, hoping my patience would be rewarded.

And finally, it was.

"I'm still not sure this is safe." Though she stood right beside me, her voice seemed to come from very far away. I had to strain to hear it.

"Not sure what is safe?" I asked.

"You."

That pulled me up short. In all the years I'd been connecting with spirits, I'd grown accustomed to the fact that they were drawn to me. The presence of the Gateway had always acted as a sort of signal that I was, by definition, safe. But then, I reminded myself, it wasn't there anymore. The Gateway was like a light in a storm. I was nothing but a blown bulb now—an abandoned lighthouse.

"You can trust me," I ventured.

"I hope that's true. I don't seem able to reach anyone else as clearly as I can reach you. This new form... it's disorientating."

"Lots of people feel that way, at first. It does get easier."

But she shakes her head. "I'm not supposed to be here anymore."

"I know. You're meant to Cross. Do you... need help with that?"

"Perhaps, but that's not why I've come to you. It's my family."

I could feel my body relaxing into the dream now. Okay, now we were on familiar ground. This was an unfinished business situation. Nothing I couldn't handle.

"What about your family? Do you have a message for them? Do you want me to find them for you?"

"No, I know where they are. I've even made contact."

I blinked. "With your family? So you've been... haunting them?"

The woman looked at me. "I came back to warn them. There's something they need."

"Well, can you tell me what it is? I promise, I've helped lots of spirits in situations like this."

"It's something only you can give them. Something that has already been in your possession."

I frowned. "Your family needs something of mine? What is it?"

"It is not yours, but it has been entrusted to your care in the past. It is a book, an ancient grimoire that belonged to my family."

My heart sped up. "A grimoire... isn't that... a spell book?"

"Yes. It was lost generations ago. We have gone to the ends of the earth trying to track it down."

My heart sped up. I'd only ever known of one spell book—the one Gemma and the other girls had used in their misguided attempts to internalize the Gateways last year.

"How did it come into your hands? What do you intend to do with it?" The woman's voice had become sharp, accusatory. I raised both hands in surrender.

"I don't intend to do anything with it! I don't know how to use it, and I don't want to learn. That book has already caused a shitload of trouble."

The woman narrowed her eyes. "You are not a witch?"

"Nope."

"But then how did I connect with you? Only witches can—"

"I promise you, I'm not a witch. Are you saying you are?"

But the woman was backing away from me. "What are you, if not a witch?"

I recognized the fear flaring in her eyes and could feel her pulling back from the connection. "Hey, hey, it's okay," I intoned, keeping my hands up. It's a bit complicated. And if you're a witch—a real one—then you'll understand that sometimes we have gifts that others don't understand—gifts that can put us in danger."

The woman nodded once, sharply, but still kept her distance.

"I'm a Durupinen. We help spirits when they have trouble Crossing from the world of the living to the spirit realm. We keep our existence a secret from the rest of the world, for our own safety, much like witches have done over the centuries. That's probably why you're still here, why you didn't Cross at once when you died. You wanted to remain behind for some reason. I know it's confusing, but I promise, I can help you."

"The grimoire. Explain why you have my family's grimoire."

"I don't have it anymore. It was only in my possession briefly."

The woman's face went slack with terror. "You've lost it?! What happened to it?! Where is it?!"

"It's okay! I gave it to a professor. A professor who seemed to understand the significance of it. She still has it now, as far as I know."

"Who is this professor? How do you know you can trust her?"

"She's a colleague of a friend of mine, another Durupinen. I think we can trust her, she really knows her stuff, she—"

"What is this professor's name?"

I hesitated. "Vesper."

The woman's face crumpled with relief. "Thank the goddess. Thank the goddess it's back in our hands at last."

"Do you know Professor Vesper?" I asked.

"No. But I am a Vesper. And that book belongs with my family. I need you to get it back. Get it back and bring it to my family."

The waves were crashing so hard now that the spray was hitting us. The woman faded, flickering like a flame about to go out.

"Hang on! Where is your family? How do I find them?"

The woman was barely visible now, her grip on the vision slipping. As the beach crumbled away, as darkness swallowed the sand and the water, as I felt myself drifting towards consciousness, the woman's last words echoed quietly in my ears.

"Bring the book to Wren Vesper. Wren Vesper of Sedgwick Cove."

ABOUT THE AUTHOR

E.E. Holmes is a writer, teacher, and actor living in Massachusetts with her husband and two children. When not writing, she enjoys performing, watching unhealthy amounts of British television, and reading with her children.

To learn more about E.E. Holmes and *The World of the Gateway*, please visit eeholmes.com